The Wreck of the *Untranslatable:*

The First Tale of the Scape Grace

Nathan Large
with
Laine Megan Lundquist

An **Empyrean Dreams** Novel

Find us online at: http://www.empyreandreams.com

Published by Nathan Large and Laine Megan Lundquist through IngramSpark. Books, including wholesale orders, may be purchased through IngramSpark and its distribution partners.

ISBN-13: 978-0-9986609-0-5

Library of Congress Control Number: 2017901742

First Edition

1

"We have a ping," announced Soloth bash'Soloth, turning away from its navigational console. Its broad feet shuffled on the textured decking. "Mass ten-to-the-tenth, reflecting as metallic, trace radiation but no active sources. It's a ship, dead adrift."

This was excellent news. It was *too* good, in fact. The crew of the *Scape Grace* had been running hungry for far too long, looking for a score just like the one before them. On the outer fringes of an outer-arm system, the most they could hope for was a debris cloud or possibly a stray comet carrying rare trace elements. Otherwise, they expected a long wait before any chance of profit.

The *Scape Grace* barely made it out of a nearby system with its engines intact. The Zig mining station they tried to raid proved to have hidden defenses. The salvager fled a swarm of surprisingly nimble mining craft with surprisingly modern armament.

The sting from *that* hornet's nest left the crew irritable and the *'Grace* low on supplies. At least the makeshift fighters were limited to simple thrust systems and could not pursue far beyond their dwarf planetoid base.

Unfortunately, to escape, the *'Grace* was forced to venture far outside of convenient gravity lanes. They would have to skim the edge of the system until they found an unguarded mass large enough for hyperspace entry. If that proved impossible, they would have to settle in for long months of travel to the next system. The latter prospect would be easier to bear with scavenged goods in the hold.

Fortunately, ship's engineer NuRikPo was kept busy with repairs. Otherwise, his complaints at being denied any share of Zig mining tech might have driven the rest of the crew to violence.

Soloth bash'Soloth would be last in line. That was because the Mauraug first mate ended ship fights by disabling all parties involved. The captain's second held its position securely by enforcement of Dominion as ship's law. Why it never challenged its Human superior, captain Evgeny Lerner, was an open mystery.

Evgeny turned to Soloth with an appropriately skeptical stare. The lines in his forehead flattened as he squinted at the nav screen from across the command bridge. His buzzed-down hairline lowered with his dark brows. "Sure our scanners aren't still glitched?" Again, it was safer to risk criticizing their Zig engineer's work when he was out of earshot.

Soloth shook its black-and-white head, slightly fluffing the glossy fur. "No, I checked three times before announcing. There's definitely a ship out there."

The captain turned to the other person on the bridge, a second male Human. "Gleamer, any comm traffic?"

The younger man pushed back the tail of green hair that curtained half of his head, revealing the gleaming black cybernetic 'ear' linked to the communication systems of the *'Grace*. "Nothing outside of background. Whatever we've found, it's not broadcasting... not even an automated distress hail."

"So, knocked out or unwilling to call for help," Evgeny mused. He pulled up the ship's few reference systems and the news feeds they scavenged on their last in-system stop. Nothing came up reported missing in transit. No battles had raged in the surrounding systems, nothing that might have sent all or part of a ship spiraling outward. Evgeny scrolled back in time, hitting the data hole left by their last cross-system sprint, the period when they had not picked up any news.

How old was this wreck? For that matter, would it even have been reported? It might be an unlicensed smuggler or a raider like the *'Grace*. Still, a crew stuck in the fringes, if still alive, would know better than to drift silently unless they had high hopes of repairing their own systems. Maybe they *had* called out, until their power failed.

Evgeny searched without AI assistance. So far as his crew was concerned, their captain was one of the rare Humans lacking an AI, or 'Brin' as Terrans called them. This absence earned him respect from his Mauraug second-in-command and the Mauraug half of his crew. It also earned a measure of pity and underestimation from his Human crewmates.

Both perceptions were useful, but not nearly as useful as having a hidden AI as his trump card. His secret partner, Matilda, lurked in the ship's computer, cached away and watching in case of mutiny attempts. Of the crew, only Gleamer might spot Matilda's code, and Evgeny suspected the programmer would keep his secret.

Gleamer himself was separated from his AI, Sid (short for Siddhartha). The program was technically in 'lockup', confiscated and imprisoned in a network on Alpha Centaurus Prime. Gleamer had been a naughty young man, spending other citizens' funds, creating illegal code and hardware, and generally undermining the information laws of the Collective.

When Evgeny found him, Gleamer was working off his debts in a data mine, writing search code for a Collective operation. The two men struck a deal by trading blackmail: Gleamer found one of Lerner's hidden credit accounts. The captain was hired to kill the prisoner by Gleamer's cheated former partners. The pair agreed not to destroy each other, forming an unlikely partnership. Per the terms of their truce, Gleamer kept the 'Grace's accounts well buried and even invested, while Evgeny kept the coder free to pursue his own interests.

One of those projects paid off in both respects. Gleamer still wrote sub-AIs, programs almost but not quite sentient. One of his sub-AIs pulled off a switch with Sid, sneaking the AI into another local system while taking his place. Afterward, Gleamer could at least correspond with his AI remotely, trading packets whenever he picked up a channel to the A.C.P. Sid kept tabs on their investment accounts and bided its time until the 'Grace could slip in system to pick it up.

Reaching a decision on their immediate problem, the captain opened an intercom channel, hailing the crew. "We have salvage of questionable origin on scanners. All crew to stations to wait my orders. Ticklish, to the bridge. I don't trust this one yet."

"Ticklish", or Tklth, was needed to helm the ship's weapon systems. The female Vislin was the best person to have watching for hostile movement. Her saurian species was geared to gauge and react to threats faster than Humans or even Mauraug. Without an AI analyst, a Vislin was the next-best option.

With Tklth, they didn't even have to worry about managing the typical Vislin panic reaction if a situation turned bad. She was technically 'insane', per Great Family standards. Instead of fleeing in terror when stressed, Tklth became aggressive. Her brood mates shunned her and she was mocked as 'part Taratumm', referring to the attack frenzies more typical of the Vislin's hereditary enemies and modern-day allies within their Great Family.

Ostracism drove Tklth to criminal activity, but even among renegade Vislin she was considered an aberration. Her new pack, the crew of the *Scape Grace*, was at least accepting, if alien. Evgeny had learned the hard way *not* to openly praise or appreciate "Ticklish's" vicious competence in combat. She was still touchy about being considered 'insane'. Still, in a tight spot, she was a devil with knife or blaster. Or ship's armament.

"Captain Lerner," came a responding hail from the engine room, "While all systems are operational, I must remind you that we are not at optimal function." That was NuRikPo, on cue. Evgeny would have been shocked if the engineer hadn't ventured a complaint. He rolled his eyes, nonetheless, before responding.

"Do your best, NuRikPo," he said with tolerant authority, "We can't pass this one up just because we're a little bruised."

"Bruised, limping, concussed... oh, analogies *are* fun, aren't they?" The engineer's voice dripped sarcasm, a sadly common trait among sentients, Zig included. "I hear you. Just don't try anything too strenuous. Should I get the doctor to make this recommendation official? Oh, Katy..."

NuRikPo's voice drifted off as he released the intercom control. His reference to the ship's doctor, Katy Olu, was a surprisingly clever joke. Despite her rather Zig-like name, the doctor loathed NuRikPo, not least for his 'weird' anatomy and tendency to get injured during work. She also wasn't fond of Zig in general, nor Mauraug, nor Vislin... Evgeny suspected their doctor would hate Tesetsi, Ningyo, Hrotata or Taratumm, also, if there were any around for her to disparage. That she at least tolerated her own species was good news for her Human patients. Not that she would give less than her best for any crew member, but it was nice not to have one's bodily systems insulted while they were being repaired.

The doctor was the frequent recipient of, and necessary witness of, first mate bash'Soloth's discipline. A Mauraug, even one without a mechanically enhanced spine, was quite capable of separating limbs at joints. Soloth was careful not to attempt anything permanently crippling, but sometimes its 'reminders' put a crew member in quarters for a day or two. . despite doctor Olu's best ministrations.

It was not a group of friendly comrades. Evgeny Lerner was aware that he was leader of a gang of nasty, criminal psychotics. He led them by virtue of Soloth's support and his private knowledge of ship codes, financial accounts, and secret contacts in various systems. Of course, the ship codes were necessarily shared with NuRikPo, the financial accounts were created by Gleamer, and the secret contacts had been, in large part, gained by Katy's diplomacy (including blackmail, sexual or chemical persuasion). Better to say, then, that only Evgeny held *all* the cards, plus his AI trump if necessary. It almost seemed like a clever plan to let his senior crew think they each held a knife to the throat of *Scape Grace*. It gave them a sense of personal power and a stake in the ship's survival. In reality, the current arrangements were simple effects of necessity. Evgeny parlayed a few strokes of luck, along with a few clever plans, into survival and occasional profit.

One of those lucky strokes was the loyalty of Soloth bash'Soloth, the Mauraug so nice it named itself, twice. Its name was spit in the eye of its ancestry. It Dominated itself. Humans would call it being "self-made". Still, Soloth was as pious an adherent of Dominion as any skunk ape. Soloth was ship law, by right of being the lawgiver. It considered Evgeny the dominant master of the group and enforced his will without hesitation. The senior crew had each tested that relationship at one time or another and been answered with crushing reprimands. The junior crew, the motley mix of desperados that joined the *'Grace* more recently, still had to be reminded of their place more frequently.

What made the relationship between Human and Mauraug so mysterious was that nearly none of the other crew were around at its inception. Both Evgeny and Soloth were survivors of the same catastrophe, the massacre of Locust Colony by Mauraug Apostates. They lost not only family, but most of their neighbors as well. The colony had been separate enclaves of Human and Mauraug colonists each building their own cities on the same planet. The joint colony was an attempt at peaceful co-existence, making it a tempting target for those who would be excluded by such an alliance: the Apostates. The two juveniles were outside of their respective cities when orbital bombardments wiped out both settlements.

The attackers had not stayed around to finish their work, fleeing before Collective peacekeepers could respond. The few Human and Mauraug survivors cooperated out of necessity for survival until they could be found and rescued. Outside reports remarked on the irony: the 'terrorists' had succeeded in forging Human-Mauraug unity.

Evgeny knew better. Most of the survivors accepted help grudgingly, on both sides. He and Soloth bonded over their mutual anger at their own societies. Soloth had renamed itself in disdain for the parent who chose to move them to that isolated planet. Evgeny did not share this familial hatred, but he did have a grudge against the colony for their naïveté and against the Collective for leaving them unprotected. He and Soloth had resolved to trust no one else for their survival.

Gathering up a few survivors that felt similarly, their mixed-species crew overpowered one of the Collective recovery ships sent for their 'rescue'. To the juveniles, these ships looked more like scavengers, sent to pick over the remains of their homes and loved ones. They would not be rescued; they would rescue themselves.

The coup was not bloodless; all those involved knew they would be pursued as criminals. Still, a Collective salvage ship was a decent prize. The first conflict within the raiding crew was whether to keep the ship and travel or sell it and split the profits. Evgeny, Soloth, and their two allies were victorious. Those in favor of selling died or were 'put ashore', sent out in pods toward the nearest orbital station.

A decade of piracy had aged the pair. One of their original four, a Human woman named Mikala Turell, was killed during a ship-to-ship boarding raid. After that loss, Evgeny tried to make sure *all* of a ship's crew were dead before attempting to claim a prize. His distaste for the Collective became tempered with time. His recklessness was reduced, but then his profits went down along with his willingness to take risks.

His acquisition of Gleamer was a boon, making certain their existing funds remained sufficient to cover expensive black-market parts and refueling. As much as Evgeny was tiring of a life on the run, there seemed to be no other options. Trying to return to the central systems of the Collective would have them pursued and arrested at best, spread across empty space at the worst. Even individually, most of the crew were known, wanted criminals. They might not like each other, but they had a better life together than submitting to the various punishments waiting in their respective societies.

The fourth member of their original crew would have little to do during this operation. Luuboh bash'Gaulig, the other surviving Mauraug who sided with Evgeny and Soloth, somehow kept itself far from hazard at every turn. It also would not survive well off-ship, but for very different reasons than the others.

Luuboh was an omega, the lowest member of any group. It was small for a Mauraug, with shortened limbs. Among its own species, it was a dwarf, although its altered dimensions made it more Human-like. On the *'Grace*, it cooked in the galley and cleaned the latrines, tidied up their bunks and vacuumed the corridors. Any job dirty enough that no one else wanted it, Luuboh accepted with nauseating gratitude. Soloth had long since ceased beating it out of frustration.

If Luuboh was not such an old and familiar presence, Evgeny might have suspected it as a foreign agent, present everywhere in the ship, indispensable for their comfort, but equally invisible in its ubiquitousness. Still, his AI, Matilda, kept an eye on Luuboh... if for no other reason that Soloth expected any Mauraug that lowly to eventually suffer a psychotic episode.

Returning to the present, Evgeny ordered a slow approach, hoping to pick up any signs of lurking ambush before they were too close to retreat. Soloth watched the readouts carefully. It reported, "We have visual. There's a Collective registry: 9-5-2-3-Alpha-Freight. The name is... huh. I don't recognize the characters."

Gleamer piped up, getting the same readout: "It's not in any of the listings we have on record. I can't be sure if it's a forgery, like ours, or a newer registry. It might have been filed within the data hole. We *really* need to get our hole filled. Next port, right? Maybe Katy can..."

"That's enough." Evgeny cut him off before the entendres multiplied. "Can you translate the name? That might give us a hit."

"No... the script doesn't correspond to any variant in any known Collective culture. It might be a newcomer to the fold. I'll set Rikki to work, see if it might be a rebus or something." Rikki was Gleamer's literary sub-AI, filling in for the programmer's lack of cultural study.

Gleamer might be correct. The ship's owner might have used a clever puzzle to obscure the ship name. It wasn't exactly illegal to play such games, as long as the registry information was clear. Evgeny liked the thought that the wreck might be unregistered and illegal... perhaps a pirate like themselves. No one would miss a ghost ship; no one would seek reprisal for the death of a rogue.

Tklth finally arrived on the bridge, slipping smoothly into her modified chair at the weapons console. Her claws caressed the touchpad that gave her control of their gunnery systems and short-range propulsion. Her scales were tinted metallic blue, purple, and red, colorful even beyond her native yellow and green patterning, making her look like a snake advertising its poisonous nature. Her

crest swayed slightly as she scanned the record of their approach to the unidentified ship. From what Evgeny could tell, she would be considered quite attractive among her own species, well-proportioned and clean in eye and claw. Too bad her aberrant nature made other Vislin flee, even when they might otherwise consider joining her crew/pack.

Soloth gave the reticulated reptilian back a quick glare and returned to its own readouts. Gleamer was engrossed in his data, probably viewing something separate from the stimuli his 'ear' translated into sound. Just as well the ship lacked tactile screens, or their comm officer might try to squeeze in a third data stream through his fingertips.

Still, Gleamer was the first to bring in new information: "I'm hearing a hail, but not from the derelict. Putting it on speakers." With a few keystrokes, he switched the audio to the bridge comm outputs.

"...respond if able. Repeat, this is the *Harauch*, Collective registry 0-3-0-6-Beta-Transport. To *Saving Grace*, state your intentions. To the damaged ship, we are *en route* for rescue, respond if able."

"A double prize," Soloth spoke above the broadcast, "A derelict and a Mauraug transport." Its pleasure at the opportunity to commandeer a Mauraug ship was evident.

If Evgeny had been suspicious of their sudden fortune, the presence of the Mauraug 'rescuer' at least relieved his concerns about the accuracy of their scans. The transport confirmed the other ship as a derelict. It, too, was getting no communications from the vessel. The *Harauch* felt safe enough to approach, considering the larger but more distant *'Grace* the actual threat.

Soloth confirmed the new ship's location and trajectory: closing on the derelict from an obtuse angle, not quite opposite the *Scape Grace*. It had emerged from within the system, but counter the *'Grace's* spinward direction.

"Continue to close on the derelict," Evgeny ordered, "Make them race to keep up with us. Wait until they're committed." Tklth and Soloth cooperated to keep them on heading, on a convergent course with the drifting, dead ship.

Gleamer kept eyes and ears out, updating their awareness of the Mauraug ship's progress. "They're continuing their hail. It's getting a little more threatening, now." He gave a snort of laughter. "Oh, no, they have guns."

Tklth gave an appreciative hiss at the humor. Her claws ticked against the console in anticipation of the battle to come. She had been disappointed for over a year; they had not had a real fight in that time. Their last successful capture surrendered almost immediately and its crew fled in lifeboats. In their abortive flight from the Zig mining site, Tklth only managed a few shots of covering fire. And thanks to the captain's orders, she was not allowed to engage in any direct personal combat. He couldn't risk her 'accidentally' killing crew… again.

Evgeny suspected that the next time they took shore leave, he would have to hope that the Vislin was not arrested for assault or murder. If so, he would have to leave her to rot in a station brig, presuming she was not shot outright.

Hopefully, this fight would provide her some release. Or, hopefully not. A nice clean surrender would be the captain's preference. Every battle was another chance for the *Grace* to be damaged or destroyed. It might have been even nicer to pick up unresisting salvage, but Soloth was right: two for one was convenient. The worst outcome would be if the transport managed to cripple them first, then flee away to notify Collective peacekeepers. *Scape Grace* would be easy prey at that point. Much as Evgeny hated to admit it, it was necessary to strike first.

"Ticklish, when we're close enough, disarm them. If they power up to shoot first, dodge and *then* break them."

"Yes, sir," Tklth breathed, waiting only two more seconds before keying in firing commands. "Close enough… now."

The *Scape Grace's* main guns spat accelerated subatomic particles in a tight stream across miles of empty space. The unsuspecting Mauraug transport was struck across its bow, the most likely location for any energy weaponry. If it had rear guns, it would have to turn about before sighting on the *Grace.*

Even without magnification, the resulting flare of superheated metal and gases was visible through the forward view screens. Evgeny feared that their gunner overpowered her attack and destroyed the *Harauch* entirely. Then the ball of light elongated, streaked by acceleration at full reverse.

"The transport is fleeing," Soloth confirmed.

"Pursue, full speed," ordered Evgeny, "Don't let them get anywhere they can boost away. Try to take out their engines."

It was an unnecessary command. The pirates were each familiar with the process of running down prey. The crew had worked together before and knew their roles with practiced familiarity. Hell, the Vislin was probably an old expert since childhood; their species was raised to hunt. Even the engineer, NuRikPo, had modified the *'Grace* to be a better predator, with longer range on her guns and fast short-range acceleration. Any other engineer allowed on board would know she was a warship, even if she looked like a salvager from the outside.

"They're not screaming for help," Gleamer added, "Must have taken out their comm array."

"Good," Evgeny replied. It *was* good. They would have more time to empty out the transport, possibly steering it away if it was repairable. They would *need* that time to scavenge two ships before anyone received the transport's initial salvage claim and its report on the derelict's position.

The *'Grace* leapt forward, closing space with the *Harauch*. Tklth fired twice, surgically, trying to target the other ship's propulsion without setting its fuel systems alight. At their proximity, her caution was equally for their own safety as much as to avoid destroying the transport. A fuel explosion would send fragments of *Harauch* in all directions, possibly through the *'Grace*, and the shockwave could send them spinning.

"Captain..." Soloth spoke slowly, odd in the heat of pursuit. "The derelict... it's powering up."

"Whoa, what?" Gleamer sprang into action, bringing up his own readouts. "Oh, look at that. It is. It's awake. It's behind us. It was sleeping. Really? That's nearly suspended animation. It was dead."

"Unless they had an engineering miracle, it's a trap," Evgeny confirmed with grim satisfaction. Being right in his suspicions was no comfort. The dead ship with the untranslatable name apparently also bore unfamiliar technology that could mask the output of a functioning engine. A working ship should output a modicum of readable radiation. Unless his crew was getting sloppy, there had been no such trace to detect. The captain could go over the records later to decide if someone was due a reprimand... for the moment, survival was the priority.

"Get us out of here," he ordered. Tklth hissed angrily, deprived once again of a kill. She fired one last strike at the retreating Mauraug transport out of spite, then began to reroute targeting to the new threat. Soloth was already correcting course. The resulting inertial shift was sharp enough to overcome dampeners and become perceptible as a physical lurch. Evgeny's inner ear protested. He wondered how non-Human species experienced the sensation... or where.

Katy would know. As much as she protested, she knew her xeno-bio like the Collective med school student she was... even if she was expelled before graduation.

Calls lit up his intercom panel, but Evgeny kept them muted. Everyone on board would know the fight was turning ugly. If they were hit, both Katy and NuRikPo would be expecting repair demands for the damage. The combat crew would be asking if they should suit up for boarding. Only Luuboh would sit placidly, as safe as possible deep within the hull, ready to clean up the mess afterward.

The *Scape Grace* accelerated smoothly again, tacking away from both the derelict and the transport. Neither fired on her.

"The unidentified ship is moving. It is pursuing us," announced Soloth. "The *Harauch* has slowed. It is no longer fleeing."

Possibly, seeing their attacker spooked and running, the Mauraug decided to risk cutting their engines and reduce the risk of further damage. Perhaps they perceived the foreign vessel as a potential ally... or knew it for a confederate. It depended on how badly the transport was hurt. Had the *'Grace* crippled her prey so badly that the *Harauch* had no choice but to take any reprieve? Or was the transport turning about to join the pursuit, now that a preplanned trap was sprung?

If the latter, the decoy had leapt too soon. With her better, Zig-tuned engines, the *'Grace* could easily outrun anything but a fighter, even if the other ship were not also accelerating from a dead stop. They would be clear in minutes, with plenty of open space to boost to super-light speeds. That they would be sprinting even further into the extra-solar depths was a drawback they could not currently avoid.

"The *Harauch* is changing tack," Soloth amended, "It is moving at a diagonal, to our flank. The unidentified is not pursuing directly. It is aimed on a perpendicular course to the *Harauch*."

Evgeny brought up the display on his own command console. The three ships were describing a reversed arrow, with the two others splitting away at right angles to the *'Grace's* central path. If they were trying to catch up, this maneuver was terrible strategy. Even if the unidentified ship had engines as advanced as its camouflage technology, it was wasting distance by approaching at an angle. It could not overtake *and* backtrack to block the *Scape Grace* before the pirates disappeared into higher layers of physics.

He saw the pattern, seconds too late. Their maneuver was terrible for two ships pursuing a third; it was ideal for three ships boxing in a fourth.

2

"Scan forward!" Evgeny barked, startling the other three, "Something's coming from our fore!"

"I don't... FRAGGIT!" Gleamer screeched. Soloth bristled, seeing the same readout simultaneously. Even Tklth snapped her beak at her screen. Moments later, Evgeny saw what they were reacting to.

The star-speckled space in the fore view screen distorted and bent in an unpleasant manner. Between one painful blink and the next, a vast white object filled the warped area. It was well ahead of them. They could slow or dodge, but either maneuver could be countered. The object was a ship, a very large ship. Provided it could move at their same speed – and it probably could – it could stay abreast and hold them in normal space.

Given the manner of its arrival, the new ship used Ningyo folding technology. It had not arrived from hyperspace; it had jumped from origin to destination without traversing the space in between. Its white, bulbous appearance also suggested Ningyo influence.

Gleamer provided some information: "Markings read Collective registry 1-2-3-8-Nu-Capital, Ningyo command ship *Black Humor*. Um, yeah, they outclass us a whole lot."

"Thank you. Very helpful. All right, let's try a reverse toward the wounded transport. We might be able to hold them hostage long enough to negotiate with the jellyfish." Evgeny used an antiquated slur for the Ningyo, his frustration showing as he reached for a desperate plan. He generally tried not to use

any of the old nicknames around his mixed crew. There was no need to alienate them (ha ha) with bigotry and raise suspicions that he favored Human crew over non-Human.

If *Scape Grace* survived this encounter, Evgeny would already have questions to deal with. They would be lucky to escape undamaged. Their only hope was that the Ningyo would make a mistake somewhere... or, in their unpredictable way, might choose to negotiate. If the command ship was under Collective command or just chose to oppose the pirates, the *Scape Grace* would not escape at all.

Evgeny started to consider his personal escape plan. Matilda could open his cryogenic escape boat and get him stashed undetectably, but he could not launch away, not with another ship so close and watching. If he went into hiding too soon, he would be powerless to react if they scuttled the '*Grace*. Besides all that, he would have to slip away without the bridge crew suspecting his motives.

It might be necessary to sell out the crew. Matilda could also wipe the ship's logs. Evgeny could declare himself secondary to Soloth and plead for survival by turning witness. Few among the crew would pass up the chance to sell out the brutal Mauraug taskmaster, so long as Evgeny did not specifically betray *them*. He might regret burning an old ally, but no one else was believable to pin blame on.

"They're hailing us," Gleamer piped up again. This was it, the verdict on their survival.

"Put it on." Evgeny waved his permission. "Keep pursuit on the transport."

A digitally generated voice poured through the speakers. On-screen, the video feed showed the smooth white carapace of a Ningyo's environmental suit. Odd. On their own vessel, the Ningyo could generate their preferred environmental conditions: extreme pressure and gravitation. They might be more comfortable without their suits. They also did not need to transmit video. Evgeny certainly was not reciprocating with any view of his own bridge. No need to be identified if he could avoid it.

"To the aggressive vessel with false Collective registry: Hello!" The voice was typically bright and slightly mocking. The humanoid shape of the Ningyo suit moved in concert with its words, waving cheerfully at the camera. Its simple ovoid head had only two depressions to suggest eyes and slight extrusions to mark a nose and chin. It was a starker design than Evgeny ever saw depicted in records, slightly disturbing in its blankness. The figure stood before a black background, as if to emphasize its outlines.

Evgeny toggled to respond, "Hello, *Black Humor*. We deny your accusation. This is the lawfully registered *Saving Grace*, Collective registry 6-1-0-1-Eta-Salvage. We are not aggressive. We were engaged in rescue operations on the freighter there."

"We see an operational freighter and a recently damaged transport. The Mauraug report your vessel firing upon them. We just assumed your registry was forged. I apologize if incorrect, Gracie."

"Negative. The Mauraug are the aggressors. They arrived after we began approach to the freighter. It appeared inactive... we suspect it was a decoy. The Mauraug disputed our claim and moved to intercept. We fired in self-defense."

"We confirm: the freighter was a decoy. Captain? It was *our* decoy. The Mauraug ship was *our* provocation... and also a decoy."

That was it, then. Evgeny took pride that it required three ships to set a trap capable of snaring the *'Grace,* one of them a command ship capable of instantaneous arrival. Had the Zig miners managed to give such a detailed report, so quickly, to set up this trap? Or, had the *'Grace* simply fallen prey to a general snare meant for any unscrupulous salvager in this region?

Either possibility seemed improbable. They had to have run afoul of mischance somewhere. Either the Zig found a sympathetic ear close by, or the *'Grace* chose the wrong over-pirated region to scourge, or the Ningyo had a psychic aboard, or something else unpredictable.

Speaking to the other ship ruined Evgeny's chance to foist responsibility off onto Soloth. The Ningyo would never believe the voice responding to their

questions was the Mauraug, or that it belonged to anyone other than the ship's owner. The remaining option was escape. Damn. Evgeny liked his crew, tired as he might be of the criminal life.

He had to keep the other ship talking while he laid his plans. Evgeny started the timer: "I see. What are your terms?" Turning off the comm, he turned to the crew. Gleamer was watching him directly, turned to the side with his hands still on the communications screen. Soloth was hunched over its display, tensed and ready to react if new orders came. The heavy, bare scar covering its artificial spine was taut and shiny. Tklth scratched lightly at the edges of her console, itching to go down in a blaze of futility.

"This looks bad. I'm going to talk to NuRikPo, see if we can do anything tricky. I don't trust the intercom; they might overhear. Gleamer, get ready to wipe our logs." Evgeny got up from his seat and started to head to the exit hatch, mentally mapping out his route to the escape boat.

Soloth turned and fixed him with a vacant stare. It knew. They were too familiar with one another. His first mate knew he was running. It probably would have done the same if the option were available. Evgeny was afraid for a moment that Soloth would make an excuse to walk out of the room with him. The cryo equipment on 'Grace was only meant for one, and Matilda couldn't mask both of their life signs. Would Soloth let him go? Would they have to fight over the last, desperate path to freedom?

Evgeny was spared this discovery. The Ningyo responded as he stood up.

"Our terms are generous. I want to join you." The Ningyo's posture was open, its arms spread as if offering an embrace. Despite himself, Evgeny was surprised. It was typical Ningyo absurdity, contrarian statements which might or might not contain truth. The Dolls seemed to think themselves philosophers and comedians. Some Humans found them funny. Evgeny did not. Nonsense cloaked as wisdom was the same in any language. Whether it was the Ningyo or their apologists claiming that there was method in the madness, Evgeny simply considered them alien. At best, they concealed nothing of value. At worst, they had sinister motives behind their blank masks and silly antics.

The Ningyo watched Humans, probably manipulated them, for centuries before they were forced to reveal themselves publicly. The Mauraug were bullies to Humans, but Evgeny felt more kinship with the pseudo-primates than with the Ningyo. He certainly had no additional reason to trust a ship full of the pretend humanoids.

"*Join* us? Sorry, we don't need help with this salvage. Or do you mean you, personally? Wait, are you commandeering us... as privateers?"

"You, sir, are a sharp one." The Ningyo's tone remained obnoxiously jovial. "Yes, I personally wish to join your merry crew. Daddy needs a new suit. This one is too big and too shiny. Oh, my apologies. Introductions before business. I'm Jolly."

Of course you are. The name was as transparent a joke as the Ningyo's intentions were opaque. So, what should Evgeny do? There seemed to be a chance to play along with this game. That was probably intentional on the Ningyo's part: bait to encourage their cooperation. What did it *really* want? It didn't intend their destruction; that could have been accomplished easily. It might want to forestall any strategy – like escape – covered by their seeming surrender.

Perhaps the Collective wanted them all taken alive. The crew could, in fact, provide a wealth of information on corrupt Collective officials, black market sales, smuggling operations, and other shadow operations across the galaxy. That was, if they chose to be helpful. With no other options, individuals might be tempted, individually or as a whole. Even if the crew chose not to share their knowledge, there were enough rumors of psychic interrogation to make unwilling compliance a possibility. Such tactics were *supposed* to be illegal under Collective law, but laws only extended so far. The *'Grace's* own continued operations were testament to that truth.

Evgeny shrugged mentally and chose to take the offered course a little further. "So you're not going to scrap us... or arrest us... you're just coming on board?"

"Well, myself, and a couple of friends. And our very intimidating weapons. It will get crowded. One or two of you will probably need to transfer to the freighter over there. I recommend someone technical. It's a fascinating ship."

The shape of the Ningyo's plan started to form for Evgeny, and he growled privately. For some reason, the Ningyo wanted cover for an operation, probably something illicit. Either the *'Grace* or the unnamed freighter would do, but the *'Grace* was faster, tougher, better armed and came with a skilled crew. Provided their new commander could maintain order aboard the appropriated ship, *Scape Grace* was a unique asset that could not be purchased... not legally. Even seeking out a crew on the private market would leave traces a decent investigator could follow. Here, out in the empty fringes, the Ningyo could conduct business unobserved. The traces of their communication would dissipate and become nearly irretrievable once they reached inhabited systems. The only record of the event was within the logs of four ships, three of which the Ningyo controlled. Shortly, they would control all four.

There was also the memory of the crew themselves to consider. Evgeny had no way to determine how moral the Ningyo might be. Would they keep the crew captive after their goals were met? Would they simply exterminate every witness? Or would everyone be free to go their way afterward?

He decided to ask. Why not? "What do we get in exchange?" Evgeny demanded.

"What you *don't* get is death, arrest, or a big hole in your ship. Sorry!" The Ningyo had to be deliberately maintaining its infuriatingly cheery tone. "But there's more! Whoever transfers over gets to see the *fascinating* unidentified tech in the ship over there." It pointed off and to the side, pinpointing the location of the unnamed freighter relative to the *Scape Grace's* own aft screens. Ningyo were excellent with spatial perception.

"And...," it continued, "You get adventure, mystery, and maybe a big chest o' gold to haul home, yaharr! That is, them that survive split the booty!"

Gleamer stifled a snorting laugh. Of course, he would find the Ningyo humor amusing. Evgeny was just aggravated. He was aware of the pirate stereotype of his species' home world. The Ningyo no doubt were as well, having indulged to excess in the media of old Terra. Being reminded of that fact as a pretext for shared cultural reference irritated him. There might be an additional layer of provocation there, with an implied romanticization of a lifestyle they both knew was desperate, hazardous, and uncomfortable. If the Ningyo *actually* thought they enjoyed piracy, it was an idiot. If it knew otherwise, it was mocking him. Either way, it was failing to make friends.

Then again, it was negotiating from a position of strength. It didn't have to be friendly, just persuasive enough to keep them from trying to bolt or blow. Listening to it this long had been necessary but also backed Evgeny into a corner. Now, he had to give its proposal serious consideration or be openly perceived as forcing his crew into unnecessary suicide. The asshole had even sweetened the pot by implying a chance of profit.

"Fine," Evgeny finally replied to the Ningyo, "We give. You get to play pirate. But *I* choose who transfers over, and they leave before you arrive. Who do you have on those other ships?"

"Wonderful! No problem with your terms. You know your people best. The Mauraug ship is actually crewed by Ningyo. Tricky, yes-no? But here's the best part... nobody is on board the other ship."

"What, it's automated?" Evgeny was intrigued despite himself. The Ningyo arrived after the freighter came to life. The Mauraug ship had not sent any command signals to the derelict. That meant that the unnamed vessel was either pre-programmed or had its own auto-pilot to decide when to wake up. Yet, it was fully powered down when they approached... unless it could shield its own power use somehow. If the Ningyo was not lying outright, there was some sort of unique tech on board that ship.

"No, there's a crew. They're just not alive. It's a ghost ship!"

"Just... just stop it. Nobody is appreciating your jokes. You want our help, say what you mean and stop the puppet show."

The Ningyo, Jolly, put its hands on its hips and tilted its head to the side. "Ooh. A tough guy. Okay, tough guy, there's just one ghost. It's the ship. It's not dead *or* alive, but it *is* intelligent. The whole ship is a foreign AI. It doesn't even have a Collective registry. That one's a fake, too. It's a *tattoo*, Mister Tough Guy. When we found it, it didn't have markings. Then it did, after it saw us. Like protective camouflage. It's a little lost baby in a big mean galaxy. We're going to take it home before anybody else notices and kidnaps it."

As Evgeny and his crew stood still, consumed by wonder and disbelief, the Ningyo leaned into the screen and pointed its finger at the camera. "And I want you, my nasty vicious piratses, to escort it quietly away. The big MacGuffin, smuggled past the borders with nobody the wiser. Are you going to take it? Are you Human enough to take it?"

"How do you know I'm Human?" Evgeny had to ask.

"If you weren't, you wouldn't know what the hell I was talking about," Jolly replied.

3

I really hate Ningyo, captain Evgeny Lerner thought to himself as the current focus of his hatred blinked out of view. His counterpart on the Ningyo ship *Black Humor*, the 'amusingly' named captain Jolly, had given them a truce of half a Solar hour. During that time, Evgeny needed to select one or more crew members to send over to the "ghost ship", a craft of unknown origins with an untranslatable name. Jolly claimed that the foreign ship was controlled by an artificial intelligence devised by no culture known to the Collective. While Evgeny sent his hostages away, Jolly and several other Ningyo would come aboard Evgeny's own ship, the *Scape Grace*. From there, the Ningyo would oversee the escort of the foreign ship to safer space.

Why the Ningyo couldn't just bluff or bully their way to wherever they wanted to take the ship was a mystery. For some reason, the creepy dolls didn't want to be associated publicly with the visiting ship. For that matter, couldn't they just bend space with their drives and drop the little lost ship at home? Evgeny spent more of the allotted time trying to unravel those puzzles than he spent deciding who to exile to the foreign ship.

The circumstances made that decision easy for him. Given the AI angle, Evgeny might have considered sending Gleamer, who had some cognitive programming experience. But with crew split between ships, they needed Gleamer on board the *'Grace* to ensure secure communications. With his toolbox at hand, Gleamer should have little trouble keeping the Ningyo from blocking or spying on any private plotting.

Instead, Evgeny would have to go with the second-best choice: ship's engineer NuRikPo. The Zig would be able to spot and analyze any novel technology aboard the foreign ship. In fact, the Ningyo all but invited *Scape Grace* to send an analyst capable of appreciating – and exploiting – their discovery.

Such analysis might be one reason for the whole charade. The Ningyo could be placating the unnamed ship – that is to say, its AI – by making up a story about giving it safe escort. They could claim to be unable to transport it directly. That delay would buy time to examine the foreigner at length. It was just like the Ningyo to play out a con to its full extent. They might be enjoying the process. Plus, by involving a criminal third party, they kept their own government from being directly associated. A scapegoat would be handy if any patentable discoveries emerged from inspection of the foreign ship… patents which would be forfeit if obtained via illegal means.

Evgeny's second selection for the mission also came down to practical considerations. There was risk involved with any alien environment. He wanted their xenobiologist on hand to watch for any potential hazards. That meant their ship's medic, Katy Olu, would accompany NuRikPo. She would also be able to handle sociological and biological factors research, deciphering what the alien technology could tell them about its creators. As much as Katy claimed to loathe non-Humans, her distaste was informed by years of study in comparative disciplines.

In fact, the best thing about the pairing of NuRikPo and Olu was their mutual dislike for one another. With another pair, Evgeny might have to worry about collusion. Other teams might try to hide discoveries or steal the other ship and set off on their own. Even if not directly cooperating, another dyad might have a dominant member who could cow their counterpart into going along with treachery. Given their currently strained relationship, Evgeny certainly could not let his first mate, Soloth bash'Soloth, out of his sight within a possible escape ship. Ticklish might be tempted to run amok in several different ways, given too much freedom. Anyone else, from the various dozen grunts in the passenger hold to their ship's omega, Luuboh, would be dead weight if sent aboard the other ship.

But Katy and 'Po… they would neither help nor hinder one another. They might not produce any synergy, but at least Evgeny wouldn't have to worry about them scheming together. With that cheery thought in mind, Evgeny notified the others on the bridge – Soloth, Ticklish, and Gleamer – that they were off the hook. He then excused himself to travel below decks. This time, his excuse was legitimate.

He first stopped by Katy's quarters. He did the medic the courtesy of thumbing her pad-lock, announcing his presence as the system confirmed his thumbprint. The door scrolled open on an archaic track of ball bearings. Inside, Katy stood rigid, her fists pressed against her hips. She was gorgeous, but no more or less attractive when angry. Her carefully shaped eyebrows were folded into a tense vee and her purple lips were tightened flat. A sheen of familiar Human perspiration reflected off her loam-dark skin. Like Evgeny, she chose to crop her hair short for practical reasons, but instead of his military flattop, she managed to make the buzz cut look like a model's stylistic minimalism. She was dressed similarly to Evgeny as well, but her utilitarian trousers clung tight where his hung flat, and her button-down work shirt was buttoned slightly lower to accommodate other curves.

Evgeny managed to get the issue of attraction to a crewmate of compatible species and gender out of his system during Katy's first year aboard. That didn't mean that she wasn't still tempting. Most Human males thought so, which was part of her benefit to the *Scape Grace*. Granted, as a medic, Katy would be immensely valuable regardless of her looks, but her willingness to open her own body had opened several opportunities for the pirate crew. For those who didn't find a woman's attentions sufficient trade for their cooperation, Katy also made use of her command of intoxicants, slow-acting toxins, and psychoactives. Occasionally, she resorted to psychological combat. There were certain reasons Evgeny found her charms waning… something like the same reasons he didn't want to sleep with Ticklish.

Still, the Collective lost a potentially brilliant covert operative when Katy was dismissed from medical school for unethical conduct. She took the reprimand as a challenge to show them what 'unethical' really meant.

Right then, Evgeny suspected he was about to be challenged.

"There had better be someone bleeding," Katy began, her apparent joke carrying the promise that she could create an injured patient, herself, if one was not already available.

"No, we're involved in a different type of battle now." Evgeny approached the subject while trying not to sound placating. "We're pinned between two Ningyo ships, one of them a command vessel, and a third that seems to be their ally. It's apparently from no known culture and abandoned except for an AI pilot. They're giving us… actually, they're demanding that we send someone over to take a look. Supposedly, that's our trade for getting the ship out of Collective space without anyone noticing, or at least without noticing any Ningyo involvement."

"So?" Katy was deliberately avoiding his point.

"So, I'm sending you and 'Po over to meet their demands."

"Oh, no. First, I agreed to fix up crew. I take on other projects only by choice. Second, I don't like that copper ass. Third, why don't you send Gleamer for AI work? That's none of my interest."

"Because I'll need Gleamer over here, to talk to you over there, without the Ningyo catching on. Also, because it's not just an AI in a ship, if we believe the jellyfish. Their captain implied that the ship itself is the body for a unique sort of AI. An actual cybernetic organism. You can check it out from the perspective of its builders. You already know the other reason… 'Po can't mind his own vitals without help."

"Don't try to appeal to me by insulting an obvious cripple. You have your plans figured out. That's great. What do I get out of risking myself?"

"The usual cut of…"

"Don't say profits, Lerner. I don't buy that."

Evgeny had built up enough genuine anger that he could let the excess leak into his persuasive banter: "You've seen me work, Olu. We *will* profit from this mess, one way or another. I don't plan to give the Ningyo what they want, not without more reward than they're currently offering. I'm putting you on board that ship to see what's worth taking and to find the best way to take it. You won't be pulling your weight over here. So rather than letting you take a vacation while we play cruise ship for our commandeering guests, I want you where you'll be useful. Do I make myself clear?"

"Wow, you didn't even threaten me with the gorilla. How polite!"

Katy had a point. Several months ago, she was nursing a broken rib and a black eye earned by defying Evgeny in front of first mate Soloth. When the captain's temper reached its limit, Soloth backhanded Katy down a hall into a storage room.

"I don't recall threatening you at all, now or then. Unlike so many here, I'm a reasonable man… follow my example."

"Fine, but I expect a double share of any 'profits'."

"Earn it. I have no problem with that deal if it looks fair to the others."

"How long do I have?"

"Twenty minutes."

"The hell!"

"Hey, enjoy it. I stopped by to tell you first. 'Po only gets fifteen."

"Oh, what's he got to pack? He only has one change of clothes."

"Bye, Katy, see you at the shuttle in nineteen."

Katy's parting vulgarity was cut off as Evgeny keyed her door closed, demonstrating that he could just as easily override her security as submit to it. Hovering between a smile and a grimace, he followed the corridor to the end of the deck and then laddered down to the engine levels of the 'Grace.

Crossing the engine level to the aft chambers where NuRikPo held court, Evgeny passed two of the regular crew, a male and female Human named Burnett and Zenaida, respectively. They shared the same surname, Georges, and the same colonial accent, but claimed to be cousins rather than mates or siblings. Evgeny did not particularly care what they were, provided they obeyed orders and performed their jobs well. The pair, olive-skinned and sharp-nosed, were perfect compliments to their Zig overseer, even dressing in the same utility jumpsuits. They handled the routine maintenance and repairs for the 'Grace under NuRikPo's direction. As their captain passed, Zenaida raised a hand in greeting, while her counterpart kept his hands on the gauge he was gluing into place. Both watched Evgeny warily, aware that any displeasure from their leader could have financial or physical consequences. Evgeny gave them a slight nod to reassure them that he was watching, even if he had no reason for inspection just then.

His visit to NuRikPo was much less trouble than the argument with Katy, in keeping with the self-proclaimed Zig reputation for efficiency. Evgeny delivered the same synopsis he gave Katy; NuRikPo's response delved directly into the known facts. The captain and engineer added Gleamer via comms and the three of them reviewed their collected data on the "ghost ship". During the conversation, the Zig armed himself with an arsenal of tools which he loaded into a rucksack: probes, recorders, cutters, stasis cylinders for storage, and even his prized transmutation chamber, a bit of proprietary Zig technology. NuRikPo was so opposed to sharing that device that he would not even operate it within view of another sapient.

After ten minutes, NuRikPo called halt to the recitation and took the rest of the information on a storage bead. Katy's jest was proven true, as the engineer topped off his baggage with a single spare jumpsuit. Like the one he was already wearing, it was a rough khaki fabric intended for resistance to a wide spectrum of corrosive fluids, radiating particles and energies. Its color was not far from 'Po's own skin tone: pale reddish brown with an opalescence of silver. Only his wide eyes, with gleaming star sapphires for irises, offset this relatively drab palette. Evgeny often mentally compared his engineer to the lizards of his childhood home, with their own jeweled eyes peeking out of dusty camouflage. The Zig had the same proportions, too: spindly limbs and a thick torso.

The two, captain and engineer, walked together to the shuttle dock at the opposite side of the upper engine level. On the way, they discussed strategy.

"As I told Katy, I expect that you'll be looking for ways to take control of that ship. Don't be passive visitors; find anything we can exploit. We'll run a dual comm stream: make basic reports over the standard line and run anything subversive underneath on Gleamer's doubletalk encryption."

"Noted, captain." NuRikPo nodded in a courteous bow. In contrast to Katy's overt defiance, the Zig was deferential out of cultural habit and expressed his independence through action. If the engineer felt that an order was ill-informed, he would simply ignore it and act as he thought best. Since his insubordination once saved the lives of everyone on the *Scape Grace* (when it turned out that firing the damaged main cannon *would* in fact fatally irradiate them all), Evgeny tended to turn a blind eye to all but the most egregious disobedience. In return, 'Po did Evgeny the courtesy of not making his exemptions from discipline public knowledge.

"Listen to her if she gives a warning. Despite appearances, she's interested in keeping you alive. She's also going along to interpret. Consider her your Gold Caste counterpart, if you have to, and trust her to read any cultural cues and handle any social interaction."

"She certainly is specialized properly for Gold Caste, with those..." NuRik-Po gestured around his chest, his long fingers shaping globes in front of his pectoral area.

Evgeny grinned. "Fair enough. Okay, let her glands be your guide. Just do like you would for me and don't take any stupid orders. You're the primary as far as physical research. Find whatever is valuable and go shopping. Katy's already getting a double share, so I'll give you the same incentive... just make sure to share whatever you bring back. I find out that you're holding out, I'll share that news on general comm."

Yes, he was threatening with the gorilla. Evgeny briefly wondered how many kilos Soloth massed. Was it 180? That would be hilarious. That is, if anyone even knew the old Terran joke about what an 800-pound gorilla could do. The

Ningyo might. The hell if Evgeny would give them the setup, though.

NuRikPo only nodded again. By then, they were at the shuttle dock. An airlock door would cycle the passengers into the simple teardrop shaped lander when they were ready.

Scape Grace kept the shuttle for a wide variety of reasons: an extra escape route, a surface transport when it wasn't safe to land the *'Grace*, and a runabout for towing debris or managing larger external repairs. As such, it was a multitool of various grafted devices. The engineer was reaching a point of diminishing returns on the small craft, as each new system tended to displace or interfere with existing functions. As such, the lander's weaponry had been steadily decreased in favor of more constructive appendages.

Katy pushed the assigned deadline and arrived thirty seconds late. Evgeny could be certain, because 'Po insisted on counting the seconds out and announced the final count when the medic arrived.

"Thirty? Is that how many centimeters of ileum analogue you want removed next time you come in with shrapnel?" Katy scored a point by referencing a mishap where an over-pressurized autoclave exploded and sent shards of steel into the Zig's abdomen. A human most likely would have died from the trauma, but genetically tailored hardiness worked in the engineer's favor and he was back to work a week later.

NuRikPo still maintained that the equipment was at fault, not the operator. He did not deign to reply to Katy's threat, a twitch of his fingers the only indicator of his aggravation.

Instead, he turned to Evgeny. "Captain, ready to depart."

Evgeny keyed the unlock code for the shuttle into the airlock door. Along with other security codes for the *Scape Grace*, he kept the shuttle under tight control. It was too tempting a lifeboat for anyone wanting to jump ship, whether to escape discipline, flee danger, or run off with stolen goods or sensitive data to sell. The last thing Evgeny needed in a tight situation – like the present – was to leave anyone a way out. Anyone except himself, of course.

The door cycled open and admitted the two passengers to the shuttle dock. Katy carried two hard-shell cases slung over both shoulders and resting on her hips like saddlebags. She had also strapped on a gun belt. Her favored sidearm, a compressed-gas minidart gun, rested in its holster. The belt's pouches held 'bullets' composed of gas charges and hardened ampoules designed to inject any of a variety of nasty substances into their target. If Evgeny knew his medic right, several of those loads were specific to Ningyo biochemistry. Maybe one was Zig-specific. The charges were powerful enough to punch through many plastics and some thinner metal plates. In a pinch, they could even be fired point blank to provide a simple kinetic 'punch', although that was a fairly crude use of an elegant assassination tool. Honestly, it was a testament to their success as a team that half of the crew wasn't dead from neurotoxins. It was still more useful for Katy to leave everyone alive – even after suffering Soloth's tender ministrations – than kill them one by one.

The same forbearance was true for each of the crew, Evgeny supposed. The dangers from Soloth and the Vislin, Tklth, were obviously physical, but even NuRikPo could gas everyone through the vents or just strip the oxygen from the air. Evgeny or Gleamer could selectively shut down life support throughout the ship. Hell, even Luuboh could probably tear someone in half if it had a mind to… maybe in that berserk meltdown Soloth was always expecting from the seemingly passive Mauraug runt.

The ship managed to survive through mutual threat. Anyone starting a final showdown had better be ready to finish off every single other crewmate, or that instigator would become the target of a unified strike by every other sapient aboard. It was much more likely that a dissident would try to sneak out than shoot out. As long as each crew member had something to gain from staying and too much to lose from leaving, the détente would hold. Violence would remain sporadic, mostly nonlethal and more often verbal.

With those happy thoughts, Evgeny watched the inner door cycle back closed, sealing Katy and NuRikPo inside the shuttle bay. They opened the shuttle door – unlocked as a consequence of Evgeny's permissions – and stepped inside. Most likely, without an audience to overhear their feuding, the two would slip into silent synergy, working together to ready the shuttle for departure.

Evgeny did not remain to see them off. Instead, he took the fore ladder and returned to the command level, emerging not far from the bridge. Crossing the hall, he returned to the nerve center of the *Scape Grace*, finding Gleamer, Tklth, and Soloth still at stations, right where he left them.

"Katy and 'Po are aboard the shuttle. Hail the *Black Humor* and let them know we're ready for the transfer." Evgeny spoke to the entire room, not bothering to direct his commands to anyone in particular. The three knew their individual duties well enough.

Gleamer cycled to the frequency the Ningyo selected for their ship-to-ship communications, avoiding the standard Collective spectrum. "*Black Humor* acknowledging. Want to say anything, captain?"

"Nothing polite, no. Tell them we'll leave our shuttle dock open after our runabout leaves, but they'll stay in the 'lock until I'm sure our people are safely on board the other ship."

"Got it."

Tklth craned her crested head around on her flexible neck, looking directly at Evgeny without turning her chair. "Should we keep them outside until we are sure they do not plan to attack?"

Evgeny smirked. "Keep your enemies close... so that their allies might shoot them by accident. I'd rather have them as our own hostages if something goes wrong. Until that command ship leaves, having them aboard keeps us a little safer. That's presuming Ningyo value one another's lives."

Soloth replied to both the Vislin and its Human captain: "They do, at least enough to trust that they won't waste a commander's life unnecessarily. Still, the stories I've heard do indicate that they will sacrifice themselves in favor of the survival of one another. If we threaten to execute their boarding crew, they might decide to act as martyrs."

"We're not in a strong position here," Evgeny admitted, "But they have to concede to a few common-sense measures. I'm going to toe the line between bowing to their terms and forcing them to prove their strength. Taking what we can."

"And what we can't, we can," chimed in Gleamer, not looking away from his display screens. The doggerel seemed to come out as a reflex, an automated response triggered by the right cue phrase. Soloth grimaced and flared its nostrils in disgust, while Tklth ignored the Mauraug and younger Human and remained focused on Evgeny.

"So, no, don't even bother targeting their shuttle," Evgeny answered the Vislin's unspoken question. "We want to look friendly but cautious, like we're really interested in finding out what they have planned. Technically, I am interested, for our own private reasons. They're not stupid, though. They'll have failsafes. Look sharp and watch for tricks. The biggest threat isn't the guns they'll be waving around. I'm pretty sure they have a private reason for dragging us into this escapade. They might be trying to learn something that they couldn't get by blasting us into fragments. Let's not give anything away."

Soloth turned in response to an alarm from its console. "Ningyo shuttle is away. Our shuttle is signaling ready to depart."

"Send them out. Gleamer, let the Ningyo know to come on in."

"The vacuum's fine," Gleamer mumbled, still keying commands in rapid succession. "Done, done, and done."

Then there was a quiet wait, while on view screens, two moving dots transited between three larger, stationary shapes. The silvery shuttle from the *'Grace* moved to intersect the unnamed foreign ship. The spherical, matte white shuttle from the *Black Humor* approached the *'Grace*. In the meantime, the remaining ship with the Mauraug name and allegedly Ningyo crew, the salvager *Harauch*, stayed put. It stood silent and still, a mute observer to the interchange.

The Ningyo shuttle arrived first, as the *Black Humor* had emerged absurdly close to the *'Grace* when it appeared from folded space. Soloth confirmed the shuttle docked and closed the outer doors without prompting from Evgeny.

Ten minutes later, their own shuttle signaled that it was within unaided visual range of the "ghost ship". This announcement was followed by a curious transmission along the secondary, coded subchannel. NuRikPo declared that the ship had "opened its mouth" and they were reluctant to walk inside. This cryptic metaphor was accompanied by a visual showing what looked like an elliptical shuttle bay opening in the otherwise smooth hull of the other ship. Other than its stark simplicity and perfectly engineered dimensions, nothing appeared odd enough to explain the Zig's hesitation.

"Tell him to take the invite. If he sees teeth, he has my permission to run." Evgeny kept his tone deadpan, refusing the temptation to sarcasm.

Gleamer did grin as he sent the response. Tklth only nodded in agreement. The gunner had little to do while they were playing friendly. Evgeny could not fault her for being twitchy.

"Okay, they're inside. Ew… he might have a point. Take a look." Gleamer threw the visual transmission from the shuttle onto the main display, where it displaced the tactical view showing the relative position of their neighboring ships. Video showed the 'shuttle bay' from the shuttle's rear camera. The oval opening went from a carefully engineered portal to a shrinking orifice as it closed unevenly from all sides at once. The effect *was* unpleasantly organic. From the inside, the shuttle's lights showed an unbroken dark grey surface where an exit had once been.

Evgeny ran a hand across his darkly stubbled scalp. "Keep monitoring them. Let's hope it'll open again when they're ready to leave. Fortunately, we sent a surgeon, in case they need to cut it open from the inside."

Gleamer sent the message, head bobbing in response to some inaudible signal. For all Evgeny knew, the comm officer might be 'hearing' telemetry data or the compositions of a musical sub-AI, maybe both at once. As long as Gleamer didn't miss anything important, the captain allowed the programmer his hobbies.

"Soloth, let's go greet our 'guests'. Ticklish, I know you want to say hello… which is why you're staying here. I want us ready to react if they do try something. Your job is to watch for any sign of attack from either ship. If they do threaten, we have to respond fast."

The Vislin had turned around in her seat to rise, halting as she was addressed. She clicked her beak in frustration but did not argue the point. Soloth simply stepped forward to join Evgeny as he walked to the bridge's exit hatch.

The two old allies, Human and Mauraug, left the bridge together.

This should be fun, Evgeny thought to himself, *going along with a friend I just nearly betrayed to meet with enemies I have to pretend are friends while I plan how to screw* them over. *Just another day in the life of a pirate captain.*

4

"…in the belly of a whale…," Katy Olu sang aloud, looking across the readouts from their shuttle's external sensors. She stopped to explain, "Oh, right, a whale is a large mammal…"

She was interrupted by the other occupant of the shuttle. "I am familiar with the Terran genus *Balaenoptera*," NuRikPo interjected with patronizing reproach, "as well as the myths about being consumed by them."

"Shows what you know," Katy shot back, not looking up from her study, "seeing as how the Zig killed off their large sea life, you couldn't be expected to understand our stories. There were documented cases of Humans swallowed by whales."

"But this is not a whale, so your analogy is irrelevant." The Zig's refusal to banter properly was only one of his irritating qualities. His toxic anatomy was another. With Human patients, you only had to worry about pathogens crossing over from contact with tissues or fluids. With Zig, you had to get chelation treatments after prolonged contact, to flush out the heavy metals.

Katy had heard stories about humans in sexual contact with Zig. She wished she could consider *them* myths. Contracting a sexually transmitted disease might be preferable to risking hair loss and nerve damage. What could be so fascinating about the aliens to stimulate attraction in the face of such obvious incompatibility? They were practically insects, emotionally speaking, and not much less grotesque physically.

The inaccuracy of this comparison made it especially annoying to the Zig, so of course, Katy made use of it. "So, get to work, bug eyes, and tell me what it *is*."

NuRikPo took the demand literally and turned to his own bank of monitors, examining the same data stream as Katy but with a different focus and perspective.

"Our surroundings appear to be a composite of various metals, ceramics, and plastics. Initial soundings and spectrographs suggest complex layering of materials. Magnetic imaging is uncertain… radiography blocked… ah, hull material impervious to electromagnetic influences, obviously, but why on the inner surfaces? Actual structure will need to wait for closer inspection. There are gaps internally: joins between differing strata which can be exploited. Yes… definitely a metallic frame superstructure beneath."

Though motivated more by a competitive urge to avoid being outdone, Katy still fell into a complementary rhythm with her nemesis. "No visible artifacts… no storage, controls, or labels in this chamber. Strictly utilitarian. Atmosphere is being introduced now: eight parts nitrogen to two oxygen… and that's all, totally clean. That's better filtration than *we* manage. No organics in the mix, at all. If there's any carbon out there, it's bound tightly. Nothing toxic. Pressure is reaching 100 kilopascals… already high and climbing."

Her analysis was interrupted by a signal indicating motion nearby. Both researchers switched to the forward camera and saw what triggered the alert.

"Look, another sphincter," Katy summarized.

"As you already stated, this environment is non-organic. Applying biological analogies is counter-productive…"

"It's a general descriptive term, like calling you a person."

While they sniped, the orifice in question continued to expand from a half-meter across to a diameter of nearly two meters. It appeared in the opposite wall from the 'mouth' they originally entered, opening in the far side of the 'shuttle deck'. The entire entry chamber was about three times the volume of the shuttle itself, with a manageable if not comfortable amount of clearance. Before the new opening appeared, the only illumination in the space had been the shuttle's own spotlights. Now, a steady but dim red-orange glow poured into the room from the revealed passage beyond. It gave the dull, dark metallic grey substance of the walls a disturbingly bloody cast.

The opening stopped expanding, but the motion detector continued to blip. A separate object of approximately half Human volume was steadily approaching through the adjacent passage. The two observers continued to watch the forward view screen in anticipation.

What appeared was not immediately recognizable. It appeared to be a reflective lump of matter, the same dark grey as the walls but polished to a mirror sheen. The motile matter crawled like an energetic slug, rolling itself forward in peristaltic waves. When it passed the opening and entered the shuttle deck, it stopped. The thing lifted itself upward into a rounded conical shape and extruded two blunt pseudopods, which waved in seemingly random circles around its upper mass.

This motion was accompanied by sound. Even without the acoustic pickups, they could feel resonances bouncing through the material of the shuttle. NuRikPo belatedly switched on the audio sensors soon as they realized the thing was vibrating the atmosphere. Their visitor was *loud.* It was also projecting on very low frequencies carrying considerable kinetic energy.

The sound, when damped and filtered to comfortable audible parameters, was still unpleasant and indecipherable. It sounded like the thump and rumble of poorly tuned machinery. Portions of the signal might have been pleasantly musical or almost rhythmic, if not interrupted by pops and grinding segments. Spectrum analysis showed that there were more sub-audible than audible components to the sound, so they were still missing much of the signal even after displacing its frequencies upward.

Katy identified the creature first: "It's a Ningyo! Or rather, an artificial Ningyo… with no suit. In this atmosphere and pressure, a real Ning' would burst. That racket must be what their actual language sounds like. Ha! It thinks we're related to its friends from the *Black Humor*. No… that makes no sense, otherwise it would use their atmosphere settings instead. They must have advised it what environment to set for us. The temperature is even nice and warm compared to jellyfish standards."

NuRikPo cut her off with a hand gesture. "If I might be allowed to theorize as well, the Ningyo may *not* have given this ship's AI much data at all. Our atmospheric preferences could be obtained by analysis of this shuttle: its technology and expelled traces. Our hull is not as impermeable as this ship. I suspect the AI is basing its behavior on whatever information it can glean on its own."

"If that's the case, it's learning more about us than we are about it. It even has artificial gravity set to point-nine gee, same as this shuttle. Our host is being just about as hospitable as possible without offering refreshments." Katy's assessment carried an undertone of concern, which NuRikPo picked up.

"It can see us, while we are limited to the range of our instruments. Unless we accept its welcome, we will learn little about the rest of this ship. It seems necessary to trust our host for the present. I suppose we're no worse off out there than in here, should there be a threat. Really, the time for prudence would have been before entering at all."

"Or before signing on board the *Scape Grace*," Katy muttered, not sure if she meant the comment seriously or not. She had voluntarily stepped into more dangerous situations, with even less forewarning about the dangers she might expect. But in those cases, she generally was working in comprehensible environments, dealing with sapients with familiar anatomy and psychology. Even if a problem caught her off-guard, she could have confidence that her skill and instincts would find a way out.

Here, dealing with a completely foreign culture in a ship built using unfamiliar technology, she faced a challenge of unknown dimensions. When captain Lerner mentioned an alien ship, she imagined a more familiar design, albeit with differing scale, aesthetics, and control schemes, probably labeled with strange writing. And from the outside, this ship might have been mistaken for any of a half-dozen freighter ship models used by the Collective.

That was before they docked. Since then, the foreign ship was revealing itself as something quite different. It was round where it should be square, dark and cramped where there should be light and room. The texture of the walls was, as NuRikPo had described it, "complex": regularly patterned at any one location but shifting in pattern from surface to surface.

The mock Ningyo did nothing to relieve this sense of oddity. Katy was disturbed, her senses just as offended as they were by the unpleasant color of NuRikPo's bowels or the fungus that dulled their Vislin gunner Tklth's scales. It was *wrong*. This anomaly wasn't even a proper spaceship.

Just then, Katy realized why the "ghost ship" bothered her the same way alien anatomy did. They *were* within the anatomy of an organism. It might not contain any organic compounds, but the curve of the 'shuttle bay' and the texture of its walls very much suggested a cellular structure. The appearance of the outer and inner orifices was not some artifact of alien design but the necessary movement pattern of a biological structure.

"'Po… my first thought wasn't far off. We *are* inside an organism."

"No, there are no organics. So far, I'm not even seeing silicate analogs. I'm familiar with the Corromi, if you're thinking in that direction." NuRikPo's response was dismissive, his voice conveying Zig irritation by treating Katy's hypothesis as already falsified. His reference to the Corromi, the first entirely silicon-based sapient life form known to the Collective, was a deliberate insult. Any first-year xenobiology student would be familiar with such a unique exception to the carbon-based norm.

"Not organic, *organism*. As in, a self-contained living system. A system with cells… and probably organs."

Now NuRikPo replied with interest, meaning a challenge: "On what do you base this assertion?"

"The texture you're picking up, the layering, the shape of this room, the shape and movement of those openings… I'd know more if we could get a sample of that floor material."

"Unfortunately, with this gravity, the shuttle isn't oriented properly to employ a cutting tool strong enough to damage this material. We'll have to step outside to get your... biopsy."

"Okay, then, let's go meet the welcoming slug. I'll just keep hoping my analogy isn't perfect. If this thing starts to chew or swallow, we're in trouble."

5

Aboard the *Scape Grace*, captain Evgeny Lerner walked alongside his second-in-command, Soloth bash'Soloth. Their transit from the ship's bridge to the shuttle deck was completed in uneasy silence. Rather than the confrontation Evgeny feared, he was given a cold shoulder.

Evgeny wondered if he should have remained on the shuttle deck. The climb back up to the bridge and then down again served little purpose. His presence on the bridge was largely supervisory, a role he could manage by remote monitoring and 'comm. He could have remained to await the Ningyo shuttle's arrival. Soloth would manage the rest above-decks, and Evgeny could avoid his first mate a little longer.

That thought was nonsense on several levels. First, part of the reason Evgeny was still captain was personal presence. Nothing important could happen on the *Scape Grace* without Evgeny's oversight. The reasons were both practical and psychological. Practical, because he limited crew access to only those ship systems needed for their duties. Psychological, because he wanted to make sure everyone knew whose ship she was and who gave the orders. The moment he started delegating command decisions was the moment he forfeited *being* captain.

Second, the Ningyo were coming in force: at least three of them, armed. If they — for whatever unpredictable reason — decided to try and overpower the ship or take its captain hostage, Soloth's presence would significantly improve Evgeny's survival. No matter how much Evgeny might have offended Soloth by his attempt to abandon ship, his Mauraug associate would side with its captain over Ningyo boarders. Soloth's augmented strength and combat experience might not be the best counter to Ningyo ranged weaponry, but those assets couldn't hurt. If Evgeny *really* expected violence, he would have added the Vislin, Tklth, to their complement… but bringing Ticklish, armed, virtually guaranteed a violent outcome.

Soloth, at least, had self-control. A damned lot of self-control, lately. Its imposing simian bulk occupied more than half of the corridor next to Evgeny and fit the ladder tubes between decks with little room to spare. If Soloth ever truly wanted to thrash its captain, Evgeny would be at serious disadvantage, particularly in such tight quarters. The kind of weaponry he would need to even out their fight would potentially wreck his own ship when used.

Maybe Evgeny was being stupid. It could be that Soloth suspected nothing… now, *that* was stupid. The old partners knew each other too well not to read those kinds of cues. Maybe Soloth wasn't even offended. Why not, though? It would certainly sting Evgeny, personally, if Soloth bailed out on him, let alone abandoned the ship. Hypocritical, no doubt, but honest. If Soloth just didn't care if Evgeny ran away, then maybe their partnership was wearing thin. Hell, maybe Soloth had decided that its easiest path to dominance over the *Scape Grace* was if Evgeny left voluntarily. That way, none of the crew would begrudge the Mauraug, the way they might after a bloody coup. It would just be stepping into the abdicated captain's chair.

Fortunately, this neurosis was all Evgeny had time for before they reached the shuttle door. He keyed in the entry code. Soloth stood aside and back, tactically positioned near the emergency controls. Should the Ningyo come in firing, Soloth could open the outer airlock and vent them to space, trigger the fire suppression systems, or even better, trigger the vacuum suppression systems and seal the whole bay in plastic foam. The shuttle deck was intentionally a dangerous position to take or hold. The Ningyo were trusting that the threat of their nearby flagship was sufficient to keep their own captain and crew members safe.

Not that total vacuum would necessarily kill the Ningyo, inside their suits. Evgeny wouldn't put it past them to build in safeguards. Ningyo already lived in spacesuits when sharing any environment favored by 'low-gravity', 'low-pressure' organisms. A little extra reinforcement for near-zero pressures, a little internal atmosphere recycling and pressurized gas for breathing, plus a built-in heating element, and the canned jellyfish could probably go extra-vehicular for hours. For that matter, they might be carrying portable space-fold generators and could teleport back to their own ship at the first sign of trouble. That possibility seemed unlikely, given the cost of such tech and the hazard involved with using it… but wouldn't it just be like the Ningyo to take insane risks for something they considered valuable?

Evgeny could see the boarders, finally. There were three, stepping down a vaguely scoop-shaped ramp extended from the side of their white, bulbous shuttle. The effect was something like a fruit with the peel pulled down from one segment, disgorging insects from its blackened insides. For all Evgeny knew, the design might be practical, artistic, or intentionally perverse, to offend other sapients' sensibilities.

Evgeny already believed the latter true for the Ningyo suits themselves. Rumor held that there were Ningyo suits built to mimic other sapient species: thick ones with tails and crests for Taratumm, short ones with animatronic ears for Hrotata, even bizarre serpentine and arachnoid ones to pass among species not yet accepted into the Collective. The mid-sized humanoid suits just worked well as a midpoint: equally similar – and thus equally disturbing – to multiple sapient species of similar dimensions.

The three suits in evidence were typical: shining white with black joints. Each was of similar height and build, but there were individual distinctions. Jolly was easily identified, with its deep-set eyes, shallow nose ridge, and missing mouth. Its limbs were carefully sculpted to look thin but not quite thin enough to be absurd. It looked skeletal.

The second Ningyo had an odd textured effect on its mask's chin and crown. As it got closer, Evgeny realized what he was seeing: a sculptor's impression of hair, including a small pointed beard. The shape of the beard suggested lips beneath, curled in a wicked smile, but the eyes were blankly innocent. The overall effect was like looking at a caricature of drunken confusion. This Ningyo's body was a standard Human default, slightly taller and better proportioned than Evgeny himself.

The third Ningyo was a surprise of a different type. A quarter of its mask, the upper front, was black. Blank white eyes stared out from beneath the black faceplate. The color transition was split by a sharp, beak-like nose. Beneath that nose was a flat, wide mouth with a suggestion of parted lips. Its grin stretched almost to the sides of its head. The last aberration was the Ningyo's shape: the abdomen of its suit distended slightly, seeming to have inflated and drooped at the front. Evgeny found himself wondering if it were trying to mimic excess weight or pregnancy, or if the bulge had a practical purpose, such as concealing additional equipment.

The Ningyo were most definitely armed. The 'bearded' one carried a dis-tortion projector, a nasty application of their culture's unique technology, which could create a short-lived space fold at a controlled distance. Pretty much any-thing that needed all its parts in one place would be rendered inoperable if scat-tered by the projector's field… living organisms particularly included. Jolly had another of the devices strapped to its back. The bloated third Ningyo had some sort of melee weapon strapped to one hip, a simple long black cylinder with a handle. No doubt it ignited plasma-hot, or conducted fatal current, or created sonic concussions, or something else destructive to matter and agonizing to a sensory system. A more traditional pneumatic handgun rested in a holster on the same Ningyo's other hip. A non-electrical backup; good idea. The visitors were not taking any chances. It was nice to be taken seriously as a threat.

With a few remaining reservations and a couple of newly added concerns, Evgeny nevertheless finished entering the door code and allowed the Ningyo to enter the inner shuttle deck. The three figures strode forward and stopped within a meter of the unarmed Human. Their manner seemed non-threatening; the one with a weapon in hand kept it pointed toward the floor.

Jolly stepped forward, its right hand extended. Evgeny glanced at it, then stared at the blank face of the Ningyo for several seconds more. Eventually, Jolly got the idea and let its hand fall. It shrugged, comically, and gestured to either side as it spoke.

"Captain Lerner, I presume? These are my colleagues: Comus…" Jolly in-dicated the bearded, grinning figure. "…and Punch." Its waving hand moved toward the rotund, black-masked Ningyo. "Comus is our cultural relations officer, handling translation, diplomacy, and general communications. Punch is my security officer, handling non-verbal communications." Jolly craned its neck to the side to look around Evgeny. "Your friend there looks like it would get along famously with Punch."

Evgeny steeled himself to remain neutral while dealing with the deliberately absurd Ningyo. He would neither dignify their jests by playing along, as some Humans did, nor by showing his irritation. Ignoring all provocation seemed the best means of disparaging it.

"I am captain Evgeny Lerner, yes. This is my second in command, Soloth bash'Soloth. Welcome to the *Scape Grace*. If you will follow us, I will show you to your quarters."

"Quarters, captain? We carry our homes in our shells. There is no need to set aside space for our occupation nor to set aside time for our preoccupation. Let us go to your sterncastle and lay in course for our voyage together."

Evgeny was taken aback. He had not even considered that the Ningyo might not want private quarters. Of course, they were going to be underfoot and in his face, every moment. Why had he thought they might want a refuge from ship's operations or a private area to see to their personal needs? It wasn't as if they required water for washing, or any rations ship's stores could provide, or even a bed to stretch out on. As much as the Ningyo studied Humans, the relationship did not extend the other way; Evgeny had little idea what facilities a Ningyo might need for comfort.

"Well, then. We might as well move on to the bridge. All the navigation controls are up there anyway," Evgeny allowed. He tried to sound noncommittal, as if he had no concerns where the visitors went. He turned on his heel and started for the exit, passing Soloth after a couple of steps.

The Mauraug fell into step beside Evgeny once more, the pair preceding the three Ningyo. The trio walked single-file: Punch first, followed by Jolly, with Comus trailing behind. As they approached the exit door, Evgeny heard steady footsteps approaching, plastic soles slapping against the metal floor.

Turning the corner of an adjoining corridor, the third remaining original crew member of the *Scape Grace* stepped into view. Luuboh bash'Gaulig was slower than a fully-formed Mauraug, but still equaled the speed of any Human its own height. If Human, it would have been considered normally proportioned: perhaps a bit barrel-chested and big-headed, like a weightlifter under a heavy fur coat. For a Mauraug, it was a dwarf.

The differences were obvious when both it and Soloth were in view together. In comparison to a normally built Mauraug, Luuboh looked thin in the legs, thick in the arms, and shorter in both, yet with a normal-sized head and torso.

Otherwise, its appearance and coloration were not bad by Mauraug standards, with an even division of white and black and a well-proportioned face. Yet its 'diminutive' stature and relative weakness made it a laughingstock even among the genetically unstable Mauraug.

A bad eye, a bad leg, or even fragile bones could be repaired with sufficient cybernetics. Thanks to technology, most deformities posed no obstacle to physical Dominance. Even Soloth, born with a cleft palate and open spine, was repaired to meet and surpass the physical standards of its race. Luuboh, unfortunately, would have needed all four limbs replaced.

Its parents, colonists of limited means, were not able to afford such extensive surgeries and allowed Luuboh to grow up 'crippled'. Other Mauraug might have overlooked such regrettable disadvantages had Luuboh's dominant parent, Gaulig, not also failed the child another way: it let Luuboh grow up believing it would be forever inferior. Worse, Luuboh's other, subordinate parent encouraged the child to complacently accept this fate. Luuboh never strove to find its own path to Dominion, not even laboring and saving enough to replace its shrunken limbs with more powerful, normal-length prostheses. To avoid abuse from its peers, it spent more and more time away from Locust Colony. Thus it was, that Luuboh, weakest of the weak, survived the slaughter of its parents and more Dominant peers when the colony was destroyed.

Evgeny and Soloth accepted Luuboh into their survivors' rebellion partly out of sentiment – it was one of them in spirit – and partly out of practicality.

Luuboh knew best how to survive in the wild, having spent more time than any of them outside of the colony's enclosure. It was also willing to carry more weight, cook better meals, and build better campsites than anyone else. Unlike any of the other survivors, Luuboh never balked at taking on its own duty and someone else's, too. It even helped steal the 'Grace, surprising Soloth and the other Mauraug survivors. Once they departed Locust Four forever, Luuboh continued in the roles of quartermaster and cook. It resided within the intestines of *Scape Grace*, cleaning and organizing and keeping the rest of the crew fed and clothed.

Now, Luuboh walked toward the odd procession crossing its 'territory' with something looking remarkably like challenge. It halted in the center of the hallway and waited for Evgeny and Soloth to draw near. Evgeny was expecting a few whispered words, perhaps a question about operations that Luuboh felt necessary to ask immediately.

Instead, as Evgeny neared the Mauraug, Luuboh gave a flat-footed, open-handed bow in the direction of the Ningyo delegation.

"Honored guests, welcome to the *Scape Grace*," Luuboh intoned aloud, its bass voice all the more surprising coming from the relatively small Mauraug. "I have prepared your quarters. You will find nutrient dispensers, correctly calibrated, I hope. Please, allow me to escort you. I would ask that you tell me if the accommodations are unacceptable in any way."

Evgeny was drawing breath to explain its error to Luuboh when Jolly spoke first. "Thank you. You are very kind. We accept your generous offer and would happily accompany you to the provided quarters. Captain, if you will excuse us?"

The first Ningyo, Comus, began to step forward. Evgeny gave ground in confusion, falling to one side of the corridor as Soloth took a step back toward the opposite wall. They exchanged a look between the passing Ningyo. Soloth wore a grimace of perplexity. Evgeny was sure his own expression showed his bafflement. Luuboh led the group further down the same hall, toward the stern sections holding engineering.

Apparently, the necessary accommodations for Ningyo were already known to Luuboh, probably with help from NuRikPo's pair of Human tinkerers.

As Punch went by, Evgeny turned toward the retreating Jolly. He was only able to call out part of his question: "Why are you…"

Jolly anticipated the rest: "Because it would be *rude* not to, after being asked so nicely!

The captain was left behind to steam as Luuboh and the Ningyo delegation departed for their quarters. Soloth waited with him as well. Evgeny's temper was rapidly approaching a point of imbalance. He decided that he could not manage multiple nuisances at once. It was time to resolve at least *one* of his many problems.

Facing Soloth, Evgeny sent the question broadside: "What's going on with you?"

The Mauraug waggled its eyebrows in an expression Humans might mistake for humorous effect, but Evgeny recognized as confusion and distress. "What do you mean?" Its rumbling voice conveyed genuine uncertainty.

"You haven't said a thing to me, personally, since this whole mess started. You're angry. I get that. So, let's have it out. Are you expecting an apology? An explanation?"

"Captain, I'm not sure what you think I'm angry about. I'm unhappy about this situation, certainly. But I don't see what we could have done to avoid it. It was an effective trap, if heavy-handed and wasteful. If the Ningyo are true to their word, then we end up intact and possibly profit, if not in the way we hoped."

"You're really playing dumb? You're going to make me say it?"

"I still don't know what you're talking about."

"When it looked like we were going to be attacked… when I started to walk off the bridge to 'talk to NuRikPo'? I saw you. You looked crushed."

"Of course, I was. The ship was in danger. Its leader lost courage."

"Lost *courage?* I was ready to take the lifeboat and dive for deep space. If you ran like that on me, I'd be personally offended."

"You should not be. Disappointed, yes. But I am not Dominant here. You are. If you choose to abandon that role, that is your choice. I would grieve for the loss of a leader and the necessity of taking Dominance myself, particularly in a situation with few options. Why should I be offended if you decide that you can no longer serve as captain? If you tried to stay behind after renouncing your authority, I *would* be offended. I would punish you for your presumption. If you tried to step down to second in command, I might kill you. But abandoning all you have built would be fair punishment for renouncing your role as its master. I am surprised you do not have more understanding of Dominion, after all this time."

"Soloth, I don't think you Mauraug have a single understanding of Dominion, yourselves, after 'all this time'."

"You are correct. My philosophy is from the Yurkot School, which holds that leaders exist only to serve themselves. To place any constraints or demands upon Dominion, save those required to assert Dominance itself, is to weaken and even deny the truth of pure Dominion. Saying that 'a leader must do this or that' is dictating to one's betters. If a leader cannot lead, they will be removed from Dominance by their own failures."

"You realize that's circular *and* contradictory, right?"

"If limited by propositional logic, perhaps, yet the essential truth of the Yurkot School is proven again and again, in both Mauraug and Human history. Dominant leaders emerge in many ways and fall in many ways. Trying to define the terms under which rulership may occur generates false and poor leaders and also false and poor followers. You assert your power in a different way than I do, true?"

"Sure, but there's arguments for and against us both. Physical beatings only go so far. I only manage as long as the crew is kept separated by their prejudices and specialties. I'd be willing to say there's a third, better option in there somewhere."

"I would say no. We use the tools we have, in the circumstances we have, to their greatest effect. What other options are there? This is not a military ship, with the convenience of indoctrination to enforce a shared code of conduct upon those too weak to resist tradition. It is not a hive mind, with the comfort of shared purpose countering any personal desires. This is an outlaw ship, crewed with wildly individual, culturally dissenting, and willingly violent sapients. Our methods of leadership work here, where other methods would not, else we would be replaced and probably dead."

"I suppose I can see that, but…"

Soloth interrupted Evgeny, not rudely but firmly. "Captain, if anything, you disappoint me in not already recognizing this. You seem to have developed unpleasant guilt. We should speak more later, but this is not the time for extended discussion."

Evgeny was still uncertain what he had lost or won in the exchange of words. Soloth did not seem offended, and that was fortunate. Evgeny still felt that he lost the moral high ground. He had certainly lost some respect in the eyes of his first mate. Being lectured about his failings in a religion he did not personally share would normally be absurd, but for some reason, he felt embarrassed.

Soloth had that effect sometimes. The Mauraug was more than a brute. For one proof, it delivered its punishments with selective care and used threats to their maximum advantage. Underlying its physical aspect was a thoughtful consideration of violent force and its effects. By comparison, Evgeny felt like the lumbering ape, fumbling his way through one crisis after another.

Evgeny resolved to at least reclaim a semblance of self-respect. He could work on clearing out his personal feelings later. For the moment, there were interlopers on board his ship. He needed to find out their plans and capabilities. That intelligence was the first step in making their plans change to his own benefit. Overriding the Ningyo's advantages and asserting his own was the next step. Soloth was right to that extent. If Evgeny Lerner could not assert Dominion on his own ship, it wasn't rightfully his anymore.

"Fine. Let's get back to the bridge. We'll see if Katy and 'Po have anything new we can use. The Ning' can come join us whenever they're ready to shove off."

"Very good, captain."

6

The return of her captain and first mate to the bridge of the *Scape Grace* was somewhat more convivial than their departure. Their improved mood was spoiled by their reception upon the bridge.

"We've lost contact," Gleamer greeted them without preamble.

"With…," Evgeny prompted.

Gleamer stared at his captain dully, taking several seconds to focus his thoughts down to one stream. He finally elaborated, "With Katy and NuRikPo. Both the public and coded channels went dead when their exit closed off."

Evgeny took a moment to consider the meaning of this unpleasant news. "So, their 'comms are cut off. Interference? Power loss? Or do we assume their shuttle was boarded or destroyed?"

"Nothing happened that would take time; the signal cut off exactly when the opening disappeared. If the shuttle was destroyed right then, I think some trace radiation would leak out. I'm going with interference, maybe even EM spectrum reflection."

Gleamer's speaking rate increased incrementally as more of his interest was drawn by the problem. "I'll try some workarounds. If they're online inside there, 'Po will figure out that we're being blocked, too. He might find a way to signal. I'll keep watching for whatever he schemes up."

Evgeny mused, "If it *is* reflection, that ship could have better shielding than we do. It might be up there with the best Great Family energy ablation. That makes me wonder if it deflects high energy beams equally well, or if its defense is just meant to block scans. Even if it's just lead lining, that seems like an expensive waste. Worse, if it's a higher-end heavy metal."

Soloth resumed its post at the navigation console, having little to contribute to the technical discussion. Not that the Mauraug was any less conversant with engineering physics than captain Lerner. In some categories, it was quite the opposite. However, in this case, Evgeny was filling the role of sounding board well enough that Soloth had no need to involve itself further.

By contrast, Tklth had nothing at all to add. She continued to watch the same readouts as Soloth, but for differing purposes. Her interest was focused on the movements and energy outputs of the two other ships in nearby space: the Ningyo flagship *Black Humor* and the salvager *Harauch*, ostensibly Mauraug but actually crewed by Ningyo. If either ship showed the slightest hint of aggression, Tklth would be ready to figuratively claw out their throats.

The salvager, she could probably kill. It was already wounded from Tklth's first attack, showing a carbon-scored gap across its rear flank. Still, her shot might have done less damage than the captain first thought. At the time, *Harauch* ceased all communications, and the *Scape Grace* had assumed that its comm array was burned out.

Now that they knew that the *Harauch* had no reason to call for help – help had been only a space-fold away – its silence was less meaningful. One or more Ningyo might have died from the hull breach on *Harauch*, but perhaps not. The ship could have a skeleton crew. There was no reason for extra personnel to be anywhere else but the ship's bridge during combat operations. Tklth might have damaged the other ship's mobility, but then again, maybe not even that. Other than some sub-light speed maneuvering after the *Black Humor* showed up, the *Harauch* had no reason to move further.

The Ningyo flagship was another issue entirely. At this range, armed with the ripest fruits of its builders' native technology plus the second-best produce of several other Collective cultures, the command ship hopelessly outclassed the *Scape Grace*. The '*Grace* was heavily modified, true, but there was only so much space available for better engines, shielding, and weaponry, and only so much pillage available for upgrades. A lone pirate was certainly not going to be in competition with the product of an entire system-spanning culture. The Ningyo seemed to be terrible investors from a galactic economic standpoint, but they spent well on environments: their suits, their habitats, and their ships.

With these realities in mind, Evgeny moved on from unsolvable problems to the merely difficult ones. The Ningyo wanted *Scape Grace* to lend deniability to their effort to escort the unnamed ship. That meant that *Black Humor* would have to leave the area before long. At that point, only *Harauch* and the unnamed ship would remain to oppose *Scape Grace*. That gave the pirates a chance to re-verse the tables and their fortunes. They might even seize the original two prizes that were dangled before them as bait.

Evgeny voiced his thoughts to break up the uncomfortable silence: "Three Ningyo are currently on board, being settled into 'quarters' near engineering. They are sufficiently well-armed to represent a threat by themselves. A salvage ship, somewhat damaged, crewed by an unknown but likely minimal number of Ningyo, will be accompanying us from here to an unknown destination. Since these are Ningyo, they will not be entering hyperspace. More likely, we will be traveling sub-light. That means our destination is somewhere nearby. Finally, there is a ship of unknown provenance and uncertain capabilities that we are expected to escort safely to said unknown destination. Given its properties both observed and stated, this 'alien' ship is likely worth a vast amount to the right buyers. Certainly, the Ningyo want to keep it out of sight. So, how do we clear out the obstacles between us and profit? Thoughts?"

Normally, such planning conferences were held only between the captain and first mate Soloth. Gleamer sat still a moment, silent due to surprise and genuine engagement. Tklth looked between the two Humans and one Mauraug expectantly. Such as it was, the crew was her pack. Tklth did not consider her-self a leader, but if called upon for input, she would make an effort.

The harlequin-scaled Vislin ventured, "We can go to hyperspace. Cripple the Ningyo on this ship. The other ship will not follow." She referred to the well-known but little-understood inability of the Ningyo species to cope with hyperspace travel. Something in their physical or mental makeup reacted poorly to the altered physics of hyperspace. Not that other species particularly *enjoyed* hyperspace jumps, but they usually shook off the lingering symptoms after a few minutes. When *their* civilization first tested hyperspace travel, most Ningyo pilots just died. A few survived but were permanently mentally damaged. Even being too close to a hyperspace shift tended to cause Ningyo severe discomfort. This disability led their civilization to focus on other forms of interstellar transport, culminating in the invention of their signature space-folding technology. They altered the universe's fabric because they could not bear being warped and folded, themselves.

Evgeny shook his head in response to Tklth's suggestion. "That just brings us back to the same problem we had before: finding a safe mass point for a jump out of this system. I suspect that might be the goal for the unknown ship, with the same challenge we've had: not getting seen on approach to a star. If that's true, and we wait too long, we've lost our chance. It'll leave first."

Soloth brought up another concern: "If the unknown ship does not leave, and *we* jump away, we risk losing track of that ship. Removing the Ningyo aboard is not worth the loss of our two crew members."

"Right," Evgeny agreed, "not to mention losing everything they learn about that ship. If we can't snag the ship itself, getting our researchers back is our second-best chance to collect on this wager."

"So, yeah, lousy idea," Gleamer snarked, rolling his head toward Tklth. "I think we have to wait and see what Katy and 'Po can do at their end. Supposedly, the little lost ship is run by an AI. If they can override or overwrite that program – or get me access so that *I* can deliver the *code de grace* – then that switches the ship from the Ningyo's side to ours. That makes it two against one. If we go after the *Harauch* first, the other two ships could join against us."

"Wait and see. Wait. Wait." Tklth snapped out the word in distaste. "My wait is bad; your wait is good? It is all the same wait. Yours does not even promise a definite result. *Maybe* we can reprogram that ship. *Maybe* Katy-Olu and NuRikPo are already dead or captured! Fewer assumptions mean more certain results."

"Hey, every plan makes assumptions; that's why they're called *plans*. At least my plans include the possibility of out-thinking the enemy, rather than just blowing them up."

"At home, there is a word for hunters who wait too long…"

Soloth spoiled the punchline of Tklth's retort by stepping forward threateningly. It snorted and huffed a warning clear enough to translate across species. As this motion also gave it the floor, it was obligated to contribute to the discussion.

"Some waiting is necessary. We need information, either from the Ningyo or from our researchers or both. Once we know our heading and its purpose, we will know what opportunities remain for action. When we know more about the unknown ship, we can anticipate its capabilities and intentions.

"I think that ship is limited somehow. If it could leave on its own, it would not need help. It needs something: fuel, materials, a particular location or particular conditions… perhaps it only needs enough data for triangulation. If the Ningyo worked so hard to involve us as cover, there must be reason to suspect the unknown ship could attract attention before it gets what it needs. I wonder whose attention?"

Evgeny chose to respond to the rhetorical question with one of his own: "Collective attention? Freelancers like ourselves? Non-Collective spacefarers? Enemies of its own? We're near the edges of familiar space, though not so deep that utterly foreign travelers should be passing through. Even if the Ningyo know exactly what their foreign ship is concerned about, they probably won't share much with us. I wouldn't be surprised if 'Jolly' keeps most of this mission's goals to himself, just giving us sufficient orders to keep up. We'll have to work out what they're not saying based on what they are."

"I've got processes watching the unknown vessel as we speak, compiling any observable evidence and weighing out the probabilities," Gleamer confirmed. "I'll put another watcher on the Ningyo here, to listen for any hints they drop.

They have patterns, if you know what to listen for. It's like they can't avoid throwing verbal bread crumbs to see if you're following."

"Crumbs you lick up, yes, good." Tklth rose from her custom contoured seat at the weaponry console. "I have no more clever ideas, captain. May I refresh myself until something actually happens?" She was clearly agitated, though trying to smother her temper in a layer of apathy. The result could rightly be called passive-aggressive.

Seeing Ticklish's tail tip twitching, Evgeny decided that dismissing the Vislin might be a wise idea. She might have added more worthwhile thoughts but was unable to sit patiently and endure Gleamer's needling. In the interests of peaceful discussion, Evgeny agreed, "Sure, go gnaw something bloody, maybe catch some nest time. I'd rather have you sharp when we get under way." With a curl of his fingers and wrist, Evgeny waved Tklth toward the exit.

As Tklth bobbed past on her way out, Evgeny picked up Gleamer's thread: "I'm not sure whether it's better to play along with the Ningyo or cut them out of the equation as soon as we can. While they're on board, armed, they can dictate our actions. They don't *have* to tell us anything except what they want done."

Soloth rebutted as the bridge door clicked shut. "Pretending to accept their terms, at least at first, has several benefits. First, their ship may be waiting for an all-clear signal before pulling away. Second, as Gleamer states, much may be learned even from limited explanations. Giving our 'guests' a sense of secure superiority may encourage them to share more. Last, they may have value as living captives: as hostages or informants. The longer we have to observe and maneuver them, the more likely we are to gain an opportunity to disable their advantages."

"So, a compromise," Evgeny judiciously allowed, "We do what they want up until a decision point… an opportunity to catch them less alert or a point past which we lose our options. Of course, hesitation is probably what they're counting on: we'll be curious enough to wait and see what happens. So be it. I'm less suspicious if they just make demands; any gifts offered might be further lures into trouble. Speaking of which, anything new from the foreign ship?"

"Nope." Gleamer covered his ears with his hands, then moved them to cover his eyes and finally his mouth. "Nope and *mmffph*."

Evgeny huffed in frustration. "All right, the first thing we ask for out of 'Jolly' is an explanation why our people are being cut off. The Ningyo have some sort of communication with that alien ship. If this jamming isn't deliberate, then they can damned well tell it to stop. If it is deliberate, that's one more reason this deal stinks and should be ended quickly… after their flagship leaves, that is."

Soloth's hand hovered over a communications console. "I will tell Luuboh to send the Ningyo to the bridge, then?"

Evgeny nodded. "Yes, as much as I liked having them distracted, we need to get a few things resolved."

Soloth keyed in the speakers for the engineering deck and spoke: "Luuboh bash'Gaulig. Bring our visitors to the bridge. The captain requires their input… in private."

It cut the channel, neither waiting for nor expecting a reply. It had no reason to expect Luuboh to do anything other than obey promptly. If the other Mauraug encountered resistance from the Ningyo, it could appeal to their sympathies; if it did not fulfill Soloth's orders, Luuboh would be punished. Unless the Ningyo were both petty and cruel, they would not balk at being 'summoned'.

Evgeny sighed inwardly. He and Soloth had distinctly different styles of leadership. Soloth claimed both approaches were effective in their own way, for their own reasons and within their individual contexts. Evgeny was better with the carrot; Soloth preferred the stick. That was just as well. Whenever Evgeny was forced to use the stick, he tended to beat the mule to death, then look for a better mule.

Left to his own morbid musings, Evgeny wondered how many crew he would have to replace after the coming voyage. Would he would have to find a new medic and engineer? Of course, that possibility presumed that he, himself, would survive the trip.

In the makeshift quarters set aside for the Ningyo, Luuboh had finished showing its three guests around and stepped outside to give them 'privacy'. Despite seeming outwardly complacent, the Mauraug dwarf was quite careful about its duties. It had already hidden listening devices of several types in multiple locations throughout the room. If the Ningyo lowered their guard enough to have any private discussions – even over radio or other EM bands projected by their suits – Luuboh would have a recording for the captain.

Evgeny and Luuboh made similar arrangements, long ago, for surveillance over the rest of the crew. Luuboh was troubled by the captain's need for constant vigilance, the distrust it implied, and its own collaboration in spying, but it could not argue the value in monitoring morale and pre-empting plots against the captain. A potential rebellion, an undercover operative, or a rogue agent could be dangerous to the stability of the ship's order. It was less mess to identify and remove a threat early than to allow dissent to spread.

Luuboh recognized that it would never be Dominant, aboard ship or anywhere else. But if it was trusted by a leader, valuable to him, and close to his confidence, that arrangement conveyed value by association. For all its bluster, Soloth bash'Soloth never struck Luuboh hard enough to cause any serious pain. It knew that they both had parts to play in the ship's power structure. It also knew that Luuboh could easily poison it at meals. Luuboh could even poison Soloth's relationship with captain Lerner by using a few edited recordings.

In their early conversations on Locust Four, Luuboh proved to Soloth that it was beyond fear, having already lost everything of worth to a Mauraug. After the theft of the *Scape Grace*, Luuboh regained a feeling of security it once abandoned forever. It finally found a place in the universe, at the side of a truly Dominant leader, and no power would dislodge it. That was true Dominion, as far as Luuboh was concerned. It had mastered itself and its own existence.

Luuboh was aware that Soloth worked on the captain to reduce his opinion of the rival Mauraug. After all, Luuboh was privy to any conversations the captain held outside of his own quarters (which were explicitly off-limits for microphones). The politicking was amusing. Unable to directly state the reasons for its distrust, Soloth was forced to paint Luuboh as mentally unstable. Sometimes it tried to raise suspicions that Luuboh was a planted mole, an agent of the Collective or the Dominion, just pretending to be a pathetic wretch.

Luuboh could not directly counter such tactics without shedding its amiable manner with the captain. Soloth managed to use what little latitude remained to it while pretending to know nothing about Evgeny and Luuboh's true relationship. Such labyrinthine maneuvers!

So, when Soloth's orders sounded over the 'comm, Luuboh was hardly surprised. Even in a crisis, they had to play their game. Clearly, the captain felt that whatever he needed to know from the Ningyo was more important than any secrets they might let drop in idle conversation.

Luuboh knocked politely on the door it closed not long before. The panel slid aside to reveal the black, sharp-nosed mask of the one called Punch.

The Ningyo spoke brusquely: "What is it?"

"The captain requests your presence on the bridge for a private discussion. I am ordered to guide you there. If you would, please follow me."

"We heard the announcement and understood its nuances," the 'bearded' Ningyo, Comus, replied from the room's far corner. It had just begun to use the nutrient dispensers Luuboh provided, following an inspection to verify their utility and safety. Luuboh was aware that each actual, organic Ningyo was housed within each suit's chest cavity, but it still had no idea how they accessed external resources. It was disappointed that it would not have an opportunity to observe one feeding.

"If so, you understand that I must encourage your compliance." Luuboh spoke flatly, neither cajoling nor threatening. It suspected that the best way to manipulate the Ningyo was to give as few cues as possible to its true feelings and let them assume whatever they preferred.

"I understand," Jolly responded finally, "Fortunately, this matches my own preference. Let us join the captain upon the poop deck and point out the star that sets our course."

With this assent, Luuboh stepped back out of the doorway. Punch exited the room, followed by Jolly, who was trailed by Comus. Luuboh took the lead of the procession and headed to the fore ladder, returning along the hallway they followed to reach the sternward engineering section earlier.

For all its skill at observation, Luuboh had no warning about what waited ahead.

7

Tklth watched Luuboh pass beneath her, identifying the Mauraug by its distinctive height and gait, not to mention its dichromatic fur. The next head to pass was also black and white, but clearly a hard, shiny Ningyo 'skull'. This Ningyo was followed by the more familiar white shapes of two more.

Tklth held herself tightly pressed against the walls of the overhead crawl-space. Her body was obscured by a ventilator grating, which provided just enough visibility to observe the hallway below. Her legs ached terribly. Her toe-claws threatened to pull loose from their beds. Only the determination and patience of her predatory heritage enabled the waiting Vislin to maintain her position silently. Her task was made more difficult by the need to keep one hand on the plasma thrower she retrieved on her way from the bridge.

It was almost time to act. Against a single target, even two, her plan had a very high probability of success. Three Ningyo of unknown skill and armament posed a challenge. The cramped conditions worked in her favor. If she attacked from the rear of their formation, the lead Ningyo would have its line of sight blocked by its comrades.

Luuboh would probably flee. Its panic would provide a distraction, at minimum. If the pathetic Mauraug took unexpected initiative and engaged the lead Ningyo, its assistance would greatly improve Tklth's chances. She couldn't count on help, though. Only her own cunning and reflexes could be trusted.

Planning was stupid. The captain and first mate and that chattering half-computer atrocity could talk all day and accomplish nothing. They needed the sharp beak of a Vislin to cut through tangled plots. The occupying Ningyo must be removed, otherwise every step they dictated would wrap the *Scape Grace* tighter into their snare.

The necessary moment of tension passed, and Tklth leapt into action with a surge of joyous relief. She fired directly through the vent cover, targeting the rearmost of the Ningyo. A bolt of superheated matter, plasma conducted by a carrier jet of 'cooler' gases, flashed from the muzzle of her thrower and through the Ningyo's suit. Familiar with the vulnerabilities of that species, Tklth targeted the suit's midsection. The bolt punched a clean, glowing hole through the center mass of the Ningyo shell, breaking its integrity. The living creature resident within was explosively decompressed. It expanded grotesquely through the breach before bursting in a multi-toned greyish mess over the walls and floor of the hallway.

Tklth did not wait to see the reaction to her fatal shot. She released her grip on the crawlspace walls and dropped heavily downward, bending and breaking through the vent grating as she fell. She landed hard on the floor of the hallway. The well-prepared Vislin was already running forward as she hit the ground. She cleared the short space to the next Ningyo in two hops.

As she did, she registered the identity of her second target. It was the Ningyo captain, Jolly, the one they saw on the view screen earlier. Perfect. Perhaps the last of the three boarders would hesitate or even surrender if she took their leader hostage. Tklth also noted that, as she predicted, Luuboh was running away from danger. That was just as well. If the Mauraug could not help, it could at least get out of harm's way. Tklth would normally have no concern about accidentally incinerating her pack's omega, but the captain might be unhappy to lose his cook.

The plasma thrower's greatest flaw was the recharge time it required between shots. That delay was a tradeoff for its excellent penetrative force. Really, in a ranged combat, two seconds' wait was well worth being able to fire *through* cover. In close quarters, it meant that Tklth had to avoid being targeted before she could fire a second time. She had to dodge or find cover. There were no openings to either side. That meant her next target had to *be* her cover.

Tklth jumped and grappled Jolly, hooking one fore claw into its neck joint. Her other claws snagged the wrist of its right arm. The plasma thrower was trapped between them, hanging from a strap around Tklth's neck. Her toes anchored her to the rubberized decking. The material was slick with the remains of the dead Ningyo but was engineered to provide grip even if coated by spilled silicone lubricants. The Ningyo were comprised of similar substances, though somewhat more volatile. Tklth's bare feet itched where the ichor clung to her.

Her pin prevented Jolly from reaching the weapon strapped to its back. It was also prevented from turning in place to present Tklth as a clearer target for its ally. It struggled, but the mechanisms of the Ningyo suits were built for Human scale and strength. Against a well-trained and well-exercised Vislin, such constructs were unable to break free. This particular victim didn't even seem combat trained. It writhed ineffectually, wasting time and effort by pushing in directions Tklth was already resisting. It did not even try the most basic techniques for evading a claw hold… not that those would succeed, either. Tklth was ready to react to most evasive strategies.

The main problem was that she had to keep holding the Ningyo or release it to fire again. Against a less armored victim, Tklth already would have torn out its throat or kicked out its entrails, then moved on to shoot the third target. Ningyo were entirely unsatisfying to claw or bite: not only hard-shelled but unpalatable inside. Those fluids were *really* starting to sting her feet. She would have to wash down thoroughly after the slaughter was done.

The black-masked Ningyo had originally drawn its pneumatic pistol in reaction to Tklth's attack. Finding itself unable to fire without hitting its fellow, it smoothly holstered the gun and drew its baton. Depressing a stud set into the device's handle, the Ningyo caused the black cylinder to hum loudly. The air around its upper portion began to shimmer and arcs of electrical discharge ran its length.

A stun baton of some type. That was clever. Tklth recognized that the device would wreak havoc on the nervous systems of most organic life. Whether it would affect a Ningyo inside its suit was an open question. She could withstand one or two blows from such a weapon but would weaken greatly with each hit. There were two questions: would the Ningyo get a chance to land any such attacks? And if it did, would the stun baton harm the other Ningyo as much as the Vislin clinging to it?

Tklth decided to test both hanging questions. Planting her rear foot, she shoved hard against the captive Jolly, sending both bodies flying toward the armed Ningyo. That target stepped backward, belatedly, and was clipped by its leader's body. Unfortunately for Tklth, it proved to be a far more skilled warrior than the Ningyo captain. It kept the stun baton raised and away, avoiding collision with the other Ningyo. Then, letting both Jolly and Tklth fall flat, it took advantage of the opening to strike down against the Vislin's back.

Tklth was hit squarely at the base of her spine, at the junction of her tail. The pain was unbelievable. Her bowels and ovipositors clenched in spasmodic agony and her tail lashed hard enough to tear its joining ligaments. Her fingers flexed and her claws released the suit of the Ningyo beneath her. Even her beak clacked spasmodically and her breath came in tortured gasps.

Tklth summoned enough composure to roll away from the horrible baton. She came to her feet, weak and shaking, on the opposite side of the hall, diagonally across from her attacker. The prone body of Jolly lay on its back between them. Wary now, Tklth circled around, reaching for her own weapon. The Ningyo gave her little time to aim. It jumped forward, swinging the baton in a diagonal arc toward Tklth's forearms, forcing her to pull away. The blow missed but prevented her from lining up a shot.

The same was not true for Jolly. Lying on its back, the Ningyo captain gained all the time it needed to recover. It retrieved its spatial fold projector and aimed at Tklth from the ground. When she jumped back, Jolly gained enough space to fire safely and avoid catching its own ally in the disruption field.

With a warbling shriek, the field engaged. A spherical region centered slightly behind Tklth turned chaotic, swirling in a moiré pattern of darkness and light. Vacuum and pressure warred with one another as volumes of space were relocated to other positions within the same field. Along with them traveled their occupying matter. The affected region included sections of Tklth's back, tail, and rear leg. Chunks of Vislin dropped to the floor several centimeters behind their previous positions. Their formerly attached organism lost her support, not only from the loss of two appendages but also from having the lower section of her spinal cord removed.

Tklth fell to the ground, screaming in horrified anguish. Her vision blurred as her perceptions narrowed to the sole awareness of burning, stinging, wracking pain from her back. She was at least spared the additional torment of her lost tail and leg, as she could feel nothing from below her tail juncture.

Faintly, she heard Jolly's voice as shock set in. "Hold. The threat is gone. No need for more suffering." Then blood loss sent Tklth into painless uncon-sciousness.

On the bridge, the first indication of any problem was a hazard alarm on So-loth's panel: high heat and smoke detected. The actual sound of Tklth's weapon discharge was muffled by many layers of vibration-dampening material. Her ini-tial shot barely registered on their ears, no louder than a buckle scraping against a bulkhead in the same room.

Luuboh's voice came unexpectedly over the bridge comms. Indicators showed that it was sending over the emergency line from the shuttle deck.

"Problem in mid-engineering. Tklth attacked the Ningyo."

The air in the bridge colored with a palette of curses as Evgeny, Soloth, and Gleamer reacted similarly to the news in their respective native tongues. Evgeny rose from his command console immediately but had to wait for Soloth to storm past toward the door.

"Hold the bridge," Soloth insisted, raising a hand to stay Evgeny's move-ment. "If the Ningyo come seeking reprisal, you will need to lock them out of ship functions from here."

It was sound advice, though it sounded more like an order. Evgeny grimaced but nodded in agreement. "Go. If they're on the move, collect crew to help you hold the line. If they're stationary, hold off anyone who might go charging in and make things worse." His own orders sounded like simple statements of common sense. Leadership lately seemed more and more like choosing the least stupid options out of a range of bad choices.

As Soloth exited, the open door admitted sound transmitted through atmosphere. The distant shriek of the Ningyo weapon discharge confirmed that a firefight was taking place.

Gleamer had not bothered to rise. Instead, he turned back to his instruments. A schematic of the *Scape Grace* appeared on one panel of his view screen. Moving dots showed mobile, living objects as identified by infrared sensors scattered throughout the ship. Gleamer tripped several controls and stopped several of the dots from moving further.

"I've locked down quarters, Gene," he called back informally. "The roughnecks won't be getting underfoot above-decks."

"All the little furry gods…! I told you never to override the blast door controls!" Evgeny was furious. Was nobody on this ship actually under his command? All it took was one crisis and everyone sailed off on their own self-appointed courses. The captain would have some serious social engineering to do once they were done dealing with the Ningyo. How many crew *could* you threaten simultaneously and still have those threats remain credible?

At least in this case, Gleamer's disobedience was proving useful. Soloth, as well, had acted in a reasonable if brusque manner. Ticklish, though… Evgeny was starting to understand the reasons the Great Family shunned her as mentally unstable. She had heard exactly what she wanted to hear – remove the threat – and acted impulsively and violently. It wasn't just her panic reaction that was aggressive. She was almost a caricature of the worst stereotypes of Vislin.

Maybe it was Evgeny's own fault that he found uses for such instability. A criminal enterprise was at best a balance of extreme forces. Stable, obedient people did not steal starships or raid mining bases. They did not kill sapients for their belongings or extort colonial governments out of their savings. Granted, a great many unstable people were hiding within civilization, pretending they were well-adjusted and doing all those antisocial things anyway. Perhaps pirates were just more honest about their inability to accept civilized, Collective society.

While his thoughts simmered, Evgeny kept busy monitoring everyone else's activity. From a mirror of Gleamer's readouts, he watched the movement of figures around the ship. There seemed to be two dots – Soloth and Luuboh? – closing on two other signals moving in the hallway connecting the mid-engineering decks. Two other mobiles were staying within Engineering: probably NuRikPo's people, Burnett and Zenaida. A dozen dots crowded around the blast door separating general quarters from the rest of the ship: the boarding crew, the rank and file who handled more dangerous, less technical operations off-ship.

To that mob, Evgeny directed his next 'comm message: "*Scape Grace* crew, this is captain Lerner. You have heard indications of a problem on board. Hold your positions. First mate Soloth is checking on the situation. If it requires your assistance, you will be notified. If it does not require your assistance, do not put yourself in harm's way."

He meant the last phrase to contain an implied threat. It came out sounding like parental caution. Maybe it really *was* necessary to sound like a sneering brute to be taken seriously as a pirate captain… even by himself.

Soloth found Luuboh waiting at the exit from the fore ladder. It had already prepared for trouble, scrounging up two magnetic flechette throwers from a lower deck weapons cache. The bulky handguns could cause considerable surface damage to either Vislin hide or Ningyo armor, without the risk of fires from an energy weapon or hull breaches from a more penetrative payload. Tklth, among other misjudgments, grossly overreached by using plasma inside the ship. She was fortunate that the beam burned out before it punctured the outer hull, ignited something reactive… or caught somebody on a lower deck in the line of fire.

Soloth took one of the guns and gestured for Luuboh to follow. Soloth did not wait for the other Mauraug's slower pace but instead jogged out of the fore section. Visible in the hallway ahead was one standing Ningyo and three bodies.

The one standing, Punch, drew its pistol with its free hand and kept its baton ready in the other. One of the downed Ningyo rose from the floor, evidently not badly damaged. Soloth recognized their leader, Jolly. Its armor was scratched deeply in several places but did not appear functionally damaged.

Soloth risked not sighting on the armed Ningyo immediately. Instead, it toggled open a side door to a storage room and gave itself partial cover in case Punch fired first. The paunchy Ningyo did aim toward Soloth. When the lead Mauraug stepped aside, Luuboh was left in the line of sight. The smaller Mauraug kept its weapon down but did not attempt to dodge aside.

Risking exposure, Soloth stuck its head out and called, "The Vislin was acting alone! If you lower your weapons we will drop ours. We intend to honor the original agreement."

Jolly's voice came back as it stood and turned to face Soloth. "Comus is dead. Your crew member is dying. I will let you recover her if you do drop your weapons. Don't delay; she has only seconds."

Luuboh immediately dropped its gun and scrambled to kneel by Tklth's mutilated body. Soloth might not have trusted the Ningyo, but when they did not execute Luuboh immediately, it felt safer about taking a risk. Still covered by the side wall, it lowered its own gun to the floor and set it down carefully.

Luuboh called out, "She's lost her tail and a leg. I can't stop the bleeding by hand. We need a cautery bandage and Vislin-specific circulatory synthetics. Help me lift her? Between the two of us we might make it to meds in time."

Emerging and walking forward slowly, Soloth watched the two Ningyo warily. "She killed one of you. Why is she still alive? Why are you allowing us to help her?"

"Comus was my friend." Despite the synthetically cheery tenor of its voice, Jolly's rapid, terse delivery betrayed its distress.

Soloth put pressure on the major circulatory vessels in Tklth's back as it helped Luuboh hoist the Vislin into a level carry. Missing a quarter of her mass, Tklth was light enough for either of the Mauraug to lift easily, but they wanted to transport her without causing further damage. They began to move toward the freight lift behind engineering, to bring Tklth to medical as gently as possible. Magenta fluids dripped between Soloth's fingers to spatter on the rubberized flooring, leaving a trail as they walked.

Punch followed close behind, still armed but no longer actively aiming the pistol at either Mauraug. Jolly slung its own space fold projector onto its back and picked up Comus' weapon as well. It held the second projector loosely, also not threatening.

In genuine confusion, Soloth finally replied, "If it was your friend, wouldn't you want her dead, even more?"

"Death is an ending... no more learning, no more suffering. Comus believed in sapients understanding one another. He wanted to learn more about other cultures and teach about our beliefs. I hope she lives. She owes a debt. If she wishes, she may pay it in suffering as she recovers. She may also choose to learn something from the experience. I would like to learn, myself, why she chose to attack the three of us, alone."

"She was deranged," Luuboh grunted, a surprisingly unkind sentiment, particularly when coming from the often similarly accused Mauraug.

"Perhaps, but not so mentally damaged as to be shunned from your company," Jolly rebutted. Its cadence was returning to the format of its former conversations.

Soloth admitted: "It's no secret that we want you gone, dead if necessary. Tklth just couldn't restrain herself any longer." Soloth's candor would have made Evgeny cringe. Even Luuboh was somewhat taken aback. There were different strains of opinion about the relationship between deception and Dominion. Soloth evidently held the attitude that falsehood was a sign of weakness. Luuboh itself was uncomfortable with its own various deceits, but it was equally uncomfortable directly stating a threat to an enemy's face.

Jolly delayed its response until they reached the lift platform. It waited at the edge and watched Soloth and Luuboh enter the enclosed cage. Punch made a move to join them, but Jolly held it back with a raised hand. Instead, it looked at the two Mauraug.

"Go, tend to your murderous pack mate. We will go to the bridge as intended. You may not want us here, but we want to be here… and we *need* one another. Comus would have explained better. I must do my best in his stead… as my penance for his death."

With that cryptic closing, Jolly turned and walked away. Punch followed, after a moment's pause to stare at the Mauraug.

Soloth was not well pleased to leave the Ningyo free to traverse the ship, particularly not with them heading toward the bridge, but it had few options. Soloth resolved to get Tklth's body to medical and leave it there with Luuboh. If their multi-talented servant could not save the patient, then so be it. Either way, Soloth would be free to return quickly and deal with any trouble starting above decks.

It was tempted just to leave Tklth to die, but Jolly was right about one thing: the Vislin deserved to live and suffer for her idiocy. After this much trouble, she would owe her life to her 'pack', not to mention being indebted for any prostheses they could cobble together. From that day forward, Tklth would be working without shares just to pay off her debt. From what Soloth knew of Tklth, she was the type of Vislin who would honor such an obligation. She could become useful again… hopefully, worth the investment.

Luuboh nudged the lift controls with its elbow and the platform descended toward the second lower deck, the level containing Katy Olu's work space. With no medic on board, Tklth was guaranteed a chancy and painful triage. At best, her recovery would be slow and demeaning.

Right at that moment, her 'pack mates' felt she deserved that fate.

8

Matters on the unnamed ship had gone from strange to stranger. After sealing themselves into cleansuits, Katy Olu and NuRikPo reluctantly opened their shuttle's door and hesitantly stepped onto the decking surface beyond. The material felt exactly like the synthetic rubber of the *Scape Grace's* floors: slightly spongy and yielding, with enough grip for safe traction. It looked entirely different, though. The floor was a shiny, scaly grey, shaded red by the light cast from the recently opened hallway ahead.

In that hallway, the amoebic 'greeter' still waited, waving two thick pseudopods in the direction of its disembarking guests. It ceased its *basso profundo* howling upon their appearance and seemed to be listening for their response.

Instead, Katy ignored the entity, choosing to start her studies as immediately as possible. Opening one of her tool cases, she withdrew a shaped diamond scalpel and a sample dish. Kneeling to the floor, she scraped at the squamous surface. As she suspected, it peeled off in layers, giving her a patch of connected 'cells' to extract. Placing these in the sample dish, she bent back to examine the underlying stratum.

That layer looked much the same, albeit constructed of larger units compared to the outer surface. As Katy sliced, she discovered that the second layer was thicker, as well. The color was comparable, as were the shape and alignment of the cells. Katy removed a patch of about two cubic centimeters' volume and stored it separately.

What lay underneath gave her pause. The even composition of the two upper layers was replaced by a more diverse structure in the third. A gleaming metallic band crossed one seam between segments. Some of those segments were as large as the ones in the second layer, but others were so small as to be difficult to individuate with the naked eye.

Katy's eye was hardly naked for long. She went back to her case and retrieved a handheld magnifier. As she suspected, under increased magnification, the seemingly solid interstitial substance was a complex composite of multiple unit types. Katy no longer hesitated to label the structures 'cells', despite their metallic color and unclear functions.

The primary unit type was a familiar hexagonal solid, the default three-dimensional tiling for maximum use of space with maximum structural stability. The units were isomorphic across layers, but smaller in the upper layer and larger in the second and third. These units seemed to be solid, though Katy would wager that their molecular structure was itself a composite of metallic alloys and non-organic polymers.

By comparison, the third layer – Katy could not help thinking of it as the hypodermis, in contrast to the upper epidermis and middle dermis – contained not only these larger uniform 'skin cells' but also smaller, internally complex units like miniature encased machinery. There was the silvery 'thread', which turned out to be a cable of multiple thread-like units, linked and twined. There were also motile units within these structures… nearly invisible even under optical magnification and spotted only by their movement.

On an unsettling surge of intuition, Katy exchanged her eyepiece for an electron camera. The portable device could generate nanometer-scale magnified video for a short period or take multiple static images before its batteries were exhausted. Snapping a few pictures around the area of motion, Katy confirmed her fears. The motiles she could see were only the largest of the various active elements within the ship's structure. Like an excavated anthill, her incision brought a swarm of micro-robots to the site, ranging from a few nanometers across at the smallest, to more complex structures of several micrometers. Static images could not fully reveal their actions, but Katy suspected they were probably repairing her damage to the ship.

While she prodded and observed, NuRikPo busied himself by pacing the circumference of their enclosing space and comparing radiation measurements at each angle. He was frustrated by their continued inability to send or receive signals from the *Scape Grace*, not to mention their inability to scan more deeply into the ship. He was at least able to see and sense through the ruddy-lit hallway, but refrained from stepping past the waving obstacle at its mouth.

If anything, their 'greeter' seemed to have grown larger, expanding primarily in height. NuRikPo watched it from a distance, wondering if the perceived increase was his subjective interpretation of a redistribution of the entity's volume or if the entity was in fact gaining volume by reducing density. As a third possibility, perhaps it was expanding its surface outward but leaving a hollow core.

In fact, none of his hypotheses were true. If the two researchers were comparing notes rather than working individually, NuRikPo would have learned that Katy already had the answer to his puzzle.

Katy's suspicions were confirmed at the macro level. Through the microscope, she spotted scaffolding extending from the cut edges of the medial layer. As she watched, wire-thin structures steadily formed and expanded, outlining the edges of new hexagonal frames: 'cell' walls. Tiny rivulets of ultrafine powdered substances flowed from beneath the exposed third layer, like the ooze of carbon or silicate lubricant from a micro-motor's axle. This effluent was the raw material for the nanomachines to 'weld' into place along the initial scaffolds. Within the first minute, nearly half of the excised area had been rebuilt.

The movement of the orifice doors was now completely comprehensible. A sequence of electrical charges guided through this type of complex layered material could act just like a muscular contraction. Despite her characteristic revulsion, Katy was also in awe. Without resorting to the messy, irregular methods of organic life, *someone* had designed an artificial system that borrowed most of its useful engineering ideas.

With this revelation came two other new thoughts. The first was curiosity: with this type of structure, the ship could be something other than a mere vehicle transporting a computer, with an intelligent program stored onboard like cargo. The ship's physical structure might embody a mind. If so, it was the less like a Terran Artificial Intelligence and more akin to an intelligent physical organism… despite its obviously artificial construction. Depending on its sophistication, it might qualify as a full sapient. Its existence could stamp across categories already fraying at the edges, thanks to Tesetsi genetic engineering, Human programming, and Mauraug cybernetics.

Katy Olu's second thought was discomfort: organisms not only had repair systems, they had immune systems. The thing in the doorway… was it a greeter… or a guard, like a T-cell checking if they passed as safe? For that matter, were *all* of the ship's micro-motile cells purely construction units? Or were units designed to seek out whatever damaged the ship and deal with that threat?

With a reaction not unlike a person noticing insects on the floor, Katy leapt back and shook her feet off one by one. NuRikPo noticed her sudden motion and turned to stare at her in confusion.

"Nanobots," she shouted.

That was all the explanation he required. Zig were playing with micromachinery millennia before Humanity gained that knowledge, and a Zig engineer understood all too well the potential power and hazards associated with such subtle technology. NuRikPo managed admirable calm as he opened Katy's other tool case and rummaged through its contents. Finding an acceptable electrical charge cell, he pulled the wiring out of a lamp and quickly jury-rigged a simple arc generator.

NuRikPo then began to run this current over his suited feet. He was both gratified and horrified to see the glittering sparks and falling ash that confirmed the destruction of multiple miniature devices.

"It's too late. We'll have to stay in the suits until we can run a full decontamination," he groused. "Worse, we can't go back in the shuttle; it can keep the inner compartment sealed against particulates, but not if we open the door and let them in ourselves."

"Oh, it's worse than that," Katy groaned. She ran her electron camera on full video mode over her own feet. Telltale gaps in the tough plastic confirmed her worst fears. "They can… and have… breached the suits. *We're* compromised."

She took a certain measure of satisfaction from the growing alarm on NuRikPo's face. Upsetting the uptight Zig took some of the sting out of bad news. At least the crisis was as much his doom as hers.

Perhaps to rob her of that small joy, NuRikPo quickly reasserted his composure. "Well, then, I suppose we'd better hope they don't interact with organic matter, or if they do, that their intentions are benign."

"The hell you say. The first sign I see of tissue damage, I'm returning the favor with a bottle of hydrofluoric acid. It hurts my body, I'm hurting its."

It was a sign of his distress that NuRikPo missed the opportunity to point out just how stupid her idea was. Instead, he asked: "Your organismic theory was supported?"

"Organismic? That word ought to be reserved for something better. Yes, it is most definitely cellular… multicellular, not to mention differentiated. I think the microbes are just part of the overall system. I'm more concerned at being labeled an infection than about these things infecting *me*. I mean, they could do some harm over time, but the ship itself could easily expel us or create fatal environmental effects… you know, like a body does to a bacterium."

"We were permitted entry. Why would the ship want to harm us now?" NuRikPo sounded like he was trying to reassure both Katy and himself.

"Same reason we unknowingly consume and then slaughter thousands of bacteria per day… a living thing has to eat. We don't want a *salmonella bacillus* in our guts, but if it hitches a ride inside a cutlet, that's what acid, immune cells, and probiotic symbiotes are for… and in the worst cases…"

"I follow your analogy; no need for scatological detail. I *did* pass elementary physiology courses, whereas your inorganic study seems sadly lacking. However analogous this structure may be to a body, it must operate per the physical constraints of its materials. There are limitations we can exploit both to defend ourselves and to manipulate this environment. For one thing, the best counter against hostile nanomachinery is friendly nanomachinery. We may not be able to invade and overthrow this ship at our own scale, but perhaps an army of our construction… well, *my* construction… can manage."

"How are you going to build that many bugs in time to do any good? For that matter, you'd need all our tools plus what's in the shuttle." Katy narrowed her eyes as she considered her own words. "Oh, no. You're going to gamble the shuttle."

"It seems necessary. After all, we agree it is too late to stop their infestation. Too late for one solution may be time for a different one. Would you rather take your chances with the benevolent intent of this unique vessel?"

"No. Get to work, then."

NuRikPo wasted no more words, but crossed to the shuttle's entrance. As he looked up to key in the door code, he noticed that the dark silvery figure standing at the door orifice was waving at him. It was waving two distinctly articulated arms, with the beginnings of clearly differentiated digits. It also had a torso, a head, and a separate thoracic section, which was beginning to divide, embryo-like, from a solid blob into two distinct lower limbs. The greeter was becoming 'Humanoid' in shape. Though given the viewer's preference of perspective, 'Zig-like' might be more apt.

"Katy…," NuRikPo spoke hesitantly, pointing toward the gesturing entity. Katy Olu turned her head, taking in the changed creature. That being rotated its own head, 'facing' Katy as well. As she watched, it gained three depressions and one extrusion in the formerly smooth convexity of its upper formation. As the lower concavity deepened, it began to flex, oscillating in gestures like an infant's mouthings.

"No wonder it got along so well with the Ningyo," Katy declared as they watched the thing further refine its design. "They both try to pretend to be people… and both look creepy doing it."

9

Soloth and Luuboh reached the ship's medical facilities with Tklth still faintly breathing and slowly bleeding between them. Other than the ooze of purplish-red blood from her wounds, she showed little sign of a pulse. The two Mauraug slid their Vislin patient onto a diagnosis bed with their best approximation of care.

The space was normally cramped with a medic and one patient present. With two Mauraug and one Vislin, the room became tight quarters. Soloth relieved that problem by exiting quickly, stopping in the doorway to watch Luuboh start work.

Luuboh bash'Gaulig was not precisely skilled at all trades, but paid attention often enough to pick up a smattering of knowledge while acting as assistant to 'doctor' Olu. Among this education were the rudiments of first aid and triage. Luuboh peeled the backing off two thick cautery bandages, slapping the sandwiches of gauze and chemicals onto the sites of greatest damage: the stumps of Tklth's severed tail and leg.

The patches began to react upon exposure to moisture, heating rapidly and releasing a cocktail of analgesics, antibiotics, desiccants, and adhesives. The bandages were rough battlefield medicine and would ultimately leave the contact sites heavily scarred and inflexible. That damage could be corrected with later treatment. For that moment, the bleeding was under control.

Anticipating other complications, Luuboh rummaged through the drawers of a nearby cabinet and picked out several vials of medication. It plugged each of these into a pneumatic injection gun, conveniently close at hand. Luuboh injected Tklth with several synthetic hormones to forestall circulatory arrest due to shock and to reduce any allergic reactions, including unforeseen reactions to the cautery bandages. It also gave her the standard counteragent for the toxins found in Ningyo biochemistry, just to be safe.

Next, Luuboh began to dial in the necessary settings for an intravenous line for a Vislin. Tklth would need fluids quickly. A blood transfusion would be best, but their supplies of matching Vislin-specific circulatory fluids were limited to the small cache of Tklth's own stockpiled donations. The synthesis of any artificial substitute would have to wait on their medic *and* engineer to design the necessary equipment. For now, Luuboh would wait and see if Tklth could recover just on saline and nutrient solution. A full transfusion would have to wait until absolutely necessary.

Seeing that its subordinate was managing well enough, Soloth took that moment to depart. It added only, "Report when the patient is stable."

Luuboh did not bother to reply. The practice of acknowledging a command was uncommon in Mauraug cultures, though Luuboh had picked up the habit around the part-Human crew. Besides it being pointless or even offensive to answer Soloth, *"yes, Sir"*, Luuboh was too busy anyway. As Soloth turned and stomped away, Luuboh was sliding the intravenous needle between the scales of Tklth's wrist.

The Vislin's fingers flexed. At first, Luuboh took this to be a reflex trigged by jostling a nerve or tendon. Then the muscles of the arm beneath its hand tensed. Its patient was already regaining consciousness.

Luuboh faced a dilemma. Allowing Tklth to wake was medically advisable; the longer she remained unconscious from shock, the more damage done to her body and the greater the risk of sudden death. Sedating her would undo some of the useful effects of the stimulants he already injected, not to mention introducing its own set of complications. However, letting the natively vicious Vislin wake up, wounded and confused, would probably trigger her panic reaction. In another Vislin, that reaction would result in further harm to the patient as she frenzied and tried to escape danger. In Tklth, her response might result in harm to the nearby physician.

Fortunately for Luuboh, Katy Olu already anticipated this problem. The diagnosis bed came equipped with padded metal cuffs with magnetic seals. Luuboh paused in its ministrations to restrain the patient, clicking the nearest cuff shut onto Tklth's punctured arm. It then circled around to lock down the Vislin's other arm and remaining leg. There was no neck restraint, possibly for pragmatic reasons: patients might close off their own throats while straining against a neck band.

That consideration meant that Tklth could still bite. Luuboh would have to stay away from that end. Fortunately, all her injuries were at the other end.

Returning to the intravenous line, Luuboh entertained an idle perverse thought: how mortified would the Vislin be that two Mauraug had been handling her genital area? In a medical context, the idea was absurd, but emotion rarely cared about rational concerns.

Well, if she wanted her modesty, she should avoid provoking armed Ningyo. What an aphorism! Luuboh tried to force itself to laugh as it watched fluids pour through the intravenous line and into Tklth's arm.

She was most definitely waking now, twitching all over and starting to breathe more raggedly. Her outer eyelids fluttered and her beak flexed, tongue smacking dryly.

Luuboh watched with some fascination. It had never had the chance to observe either a Vislin or Taratumm in full frenzy. It had read about the process and even watched dramatic re-enactments in popular Great Family videos. Recordings of the genuine event were rare and Tklth was the only member of either species Luuboh had ever met. Its personal exposure to Tklth was generally minimal, confined to bland interactions with the gunner during mealtimes in the galley and quickly averted glances when passing in the ship's halls.

The combat crew and senior officers said she was a terror in battle: a space-age berserker, ignoring fear and pain, unbelievably fast and accurate both with firearms and hand-to-hand attacks. Her speed and destructive ability were the most likely reason her aggressiveness had not already killed the Vislin or landed her in medical with serious injuries… sooner.

This demonstration of frenzy proved anticlimactic. Tklth did indeed scream and flail and snap, but she was too weak for any prolonged fury. Her scream of outrage was a dry wail of frustration and pain. Her spasms would not have broken leather restraints, much less challenge the solid steel bands and electro-magnets that held her limbs in place. She seemed more pathetic than deadly. She fatigued quickly and her head fell back, rolling to the side to study Luuboh with one dark, slitted eye.

"You're in medical," Luuboh explained flatly. "You attacked the Ningyo and lost. You're badly hurt and at critical risk. If any of this is getting through, calm down and let me work… or you *will* die."

Tklth continued a token struggle for a few more seconds before exhaustion overcame her biological need for action. Even still, Luuboh suspected that it would lose a finger if it reached too close to her beak. Enraged but fatigued would have to do. Luuboh searched out various monitoring equipment and attached sensors to the shivering but otherwise unresisting body of its patient.

It had done what it could for that moment. It would have to watch Tklth's vital signs and treat symptoms for a time. The patient needed to rest, rehydrate, and regenerate, to the extent that her body could manage with amateur medical assistance.

Luuboh wished, belatedly, that there was some drug to manage the frenzy reaction. Stabilization and healing would be much easier if the patient could calm down. For that matter, the multiple troubles encountered by both Vislin and Taratumm, particularly in mixed-cultural settings and enclosed environments like spaceships and stations, would be dramatically reduced if their over-reactions could be chemically controlled. Perhaps such treatments did exist but had unavoidable negative side effects. Then again, maybe the Vislin and Tara-tumm themselves refused such treatments. Similar sympathetic nervous system responses existed in most other species and could be managed with drugs when they became counterproductive. Yet nowhere did these reflexes seem as extreme, widespread, and deeply ingrained as in the two reptilian members of the Great Family. It might be considered a denial of species identity to suppress such an integral characteristic.

It would be like a stripping a Mauraug of the urge to Dominate.

Then, Luuboh did laugh, quietly and ruefully. Everyone on the *Scape Grace's* crew – even the captain, who knew it best – assumed that Luuboh was atypical in exactly that way. It was not. It felt the need for power as strongly as any other of its kind. What it had learned from its parents was to disconnect that need from religious faith and from the outward trappings of behavior. Luuboh still needed domination, just not Dominion. After all, what was the point of seeking something which society would forever deny? One might as well criticize the *Scape Grace's* crew for denying their need to be part of a greater society. They could not rejoin the Collective. Instead, they fulfilled their social need by forming their own small, mobile, vacuum-sealed 'collective'. Luuboh dominated by ruling its own private kingdom in the ship's bowels.

So, let Tklth have her frenzy. She would likely rather die than live without that distinctive cursed blessing. She already had to exist as a freak and a cripple... just like Luuboh. Just like most Mauraug, for that matter. But like most Mauraug, her deformity need be only temporary. She might someday return to her old murderous form or even better, with a cybernetic leg and tail. For that matter, she could install her beloved plasma thrower *in* her tail. That alone might be sufficient compensation to make up for the loss of her original limbs.

For its part, Luuboh was not and might never be ready to sacrifice its original flesh in return for superior prostheses. Other Mauraug considered that reluctance more of a disability than Luuboh's physical deformity. *So be it.*

Part of true dominance was not being affected by the opinions of others. Luuboh defied the expectations of an entire culture. Was that not powerful?

Unescorted, Punch and Jolly made their way to the bridge. Despite never having set foot on the *Scape Grace* before, they traveled directly and unerringly. This navigation had less to do with their species' strong innate spatial sense and more with resourceful use of technology. Inside their suits, the Ningyo were already operating vehicles analogous to a space shuttle, complex machines which incorporated sensory technology alongside life support and motor controls.

Using infrared and chemical detectors, the Ningyo backtracked along the path taken by Soloth bash'Soloth from the bridge to the location of their fight with the Vislin. Heat, traces of respiration, and other effluvia guided the two visitors to the first mate's origin point. They climbed the fore ladder and emerged close by the hatch to the ship's bridge.

In this manner, the unwanted guests arrived unannounced at captain Lerner's door. With exaggerated politeness, Jolly rapped upon the sealed hatch, calling out, "Hello? We're finally here. Anyone home?"

The insulated, armored door would hardly transmit sound from a light knock, much less admit the Ningyo's synthetic voice. But, as Jolly knew, the bridge crew was monitoring their doorstep with audio and video. Jolly's entreaty was picked up and transmitted to Evgeny's attention.

A loudspeaker thumped to life over the visitors' heads, speaking in Evgeny's voice: "Where are Soloth and Luuboh… the Mauraug?"

"Taking your unfriendly Vislin to the hospital. She fell into a spatial fold and needed medical attention. It was very kind of them to rush to her aid, but I'm afraid we had to find our way without a guide."

A long pause suggested that the captain was taking some time to verify the essence of those claims. After a few seconds, Evgeny spoke again, "You're all right? I only see two of you."

"My colleague Comus also had an accident. He stepped into the path of a plasma discharge. I'm afraid he didn't survive the experience. He's with us in spirit, though… which is fortunate for everyone involved. Still, spirit is fleeting. I'd appreciate it if you opened the door soon, before his moderating influence fades."

The subtle hints in Jolly's overtly positive commentary eventually penetrated the captain's awareness. "Copy that. As long as there aren't any more 'accidents', welcome on deck."

As the door seals released, Jolly acknowledged, "No, accidents are terrible things. I certainly will be doing my utmost to avoid another." The Ningyo leader nodded to its colleague, and Punch stepped forward to pull the hatch open. The security officer preceded its leader into the room, stun baton in hand but deactivated and held low.

Neither Evgeny nor Gleamer rose to greet the entering Ningyo but both swiveled their chairs around to face the newcomers.

Gleamer stared at Punch for a moment in slack-jawed awe. Then his mouth began operating, driven by a stream of software-assisted recognition.

"*Punchinello! Commedia dell'arte!* Holy Batman, that's perfect! He's even got the stick!"

Jolly faced the young man with its own air of curiosity. "Indeed. I wasn't expecting you'd supply your own *Arleccino* for the performance. But how gauche, to spoil the punchline."

"*Punch* line!" Gleamer cackled, throwing his head back, long hair brushing against the console behind him.

Jolly watched the still-giggling Human a moment more or at least continued to hold the same position and attitude. Then, it abruptly turned to face Evgeny instead, fixing the captain with a challenging 'stare'. Its feet were planted wide, hands at its hips, and forehead tilted forward, a posture seemingly adopted from studies of Mauraug.

"The time has come," the Ningyo said, "to speak of serious things. Ships, and stars, and sentience, and command structures and… things."

"And why the stars are boiling hot and whether Zig have wings." Gleamer's interjection drew irritated glares from both captain Lerner and Captain Jolly. Punch, reading their mood, stepped forward and raised its baton threateningly toward the offending Human.

Gleamer's grin fell. "What? I can't make literary references, too?"

"You seem to understand, but only superficially," Jolly lectured, "Study the masters for a time. I suggest Chaplin, Skelton, Carlin, TeLoKiChon, and AI Codger, to begin. Consider their ways – *quietly* – and grow wise."

Privately, Evgeny appreciated Gleamer's accomplishment. Though inadvertently, the wire-headed programmer managed to irritate the Ningyo with a dose of their own nonsense. With the help of his sub-AI prompters, Gleamer could keep pace with the Ningyo gibberish. They seemed to think themselves clever, throwing out allusions that frequently went over the heads of their targets. Gleamer could at least expose their antics for the derivative drivel they were.

More often, Ningyo jibes struck at a confusing and uncomfortable angle. They acted like they were somehow helping by keeping listeners off-balance, as if their alien restructuring of other cultures provided new perspective or even enlightenment. It was the same excrement peddled by other sophists, in Evgeny's opinion. Usually, he just ignored the dressing of Ningyo dialogue and focused on the content. It would be satisfying to force one to strip down to bare, simple prose. Failing that, at least he could enjoy seeing them exposed for the frauds they were.

Still, it wouldn't help to aggravate their 'guests', particularly not while the threat of their command ship hung near enough to reflect starlight onto his hull. Evgeny could torture the Ningyo verbally – and physically – whenever the situation turned in his favor.

"Dial it back, Gleamer," Evgeny ordered. "Let our semi-robotic overlords have their fun."

Jolly turned back to Evgeny. "Oh, yes, your subordinate mentioned that you resent our presence. 'We want you dead', I believe it said. Well, the feeling is not mutual. As much as you are stuck with us, we are stuck with you, for very good and necessary purposes. Bear with me, O Captain, my captive. A game is afoot, and we are all players. We have the conscience of a kingdom to catch… and the net grows ever smaller."

Evgeny rolled his eyes. So much for straight talk. Maybe double talk was a species pathology among Ningyo, like Tesetsi solipsism or Hrotata libido. The other Ningyo, Punch, seemed less deranged, entirely quiet if a bit hostile. Maybe the Ningyo just promoted the obnoxious ones to leadership positions. Some would say the same was true of Humans.

"All right, so what are *we* doing now?" Evgeny asked. "If time is wasting, where are we going?"

"Ay, there's the rub. Our unpronounceable friend out there is a long way from home and not even sure *how* far. It needs to gather supplies for its travels; otherwise, it may starve to death before it gets back. There's not much matter out in the deeps, you know. Our friend needs to make a stop somewhere nearby, somewhere with lots of resources. Since it doesn't have any credit in this part of the universe, it can't just go shopping. That's where you come in."

"Starve? You said there wasn't any actual crew on board. You mean it needs fuel? Raw materials for repairs? Can't you just transfer over whatever it needs from *Black Humor*?"

"I said what I meant. A Ningyo is truthful, one hundred percent. It needs more than just some fusibles and widgets. It needs raw mass – quite a lot of it – and some sizable quantities of rare elements that we don't keep on board. Going back to inhabited systems and shopping around for all those things would raise flags."

"Just like hiring a mercenary crew. Okay, so it has a big appetite and a re-fined palate. What are you proposing?"

"Like any good story, we're going back to the beginning."

Despite his resistance to the Ningyo idiom, Evgeny could not help catching its hidden meaning. "What? No. The Zig outpost?"

"Exactly! It's close, we both know the address, and they definitely have everything our hungry little caterpillar could want."

"Are you... of course you're insane. We just barely escaped that system intact! They'll have help by now, either private security or official Zig protection. And they'll recognize us immediately. We didn't manage to sneak past their security last time; there's no way we could pull it off now."

Jolly raised one hand, finger pointed upward, and tilted its hips to assume a lecturing attitude. "Granted, but *that* is the *point*. Of course, they'll recognize you. You're a terrible, hateful, dangerous pirate ship. They'll rush to drive you off. But this time, you won't be alone. You'll have the *Harauch*, an equally vicious Mauraug pirate... your ally of convenience... at your side."

Evgeny countered, "Even so, they have enough fighters to deal with two ships like *Scape Grace*... and that clunker is in no way our equal. Besides, don't you mean we'll have *two* ships at our side? I realize that the *Black Humor* will be vanishing shortly in a puff of deniability, but isn't that unidentified ship going to pull its weight? After all, this raid is supposedly for *its* benefit."

"What do you think it will be doing while the Zig chase you? Why, helping itself to the unguarded stores for great convenience! It might even pick you up something nice for being such a good patsy. Whaddya say?" The Ningyo delivered its last line with its hands spread wide and head cocked, still the overdone showman, if only for an audience of three.

Evgeny sighed. "What choice do we have? And, yes, it's not a bad plan... for the alien ship. *We're* the ones who will take the brunt of the attack. Even if we commit totally to evasion, they can sting us a bit... and if we stay defensive enough to avoid damage entirely, they'll notice that something is up. Will you commit the *Harauch* to a fair share of the assault?"

"Absolutely, and quite fair. Our use for you does not end with this raid. Once refueled, our tourist will still need an escort to a reference point for departure. The Zig will undoubtedly send distress signals and warn surrounding systems to be on guard. This assault is but step one in our plans. More will be forthcoming upon objective completion."

"Wow. The Ningyo, saviors of Humanity, plotting a mining colony raid. I never would have expected it. You realize that a lot of Zig are going to die, not to mention that their investors are going to lose a significant fortune?"

"Yes. And I regret that. But would you believe that I consider this atrocity a necessary evil? I would, of course, ask that we try and minimize the loss of life – on both sides – but I realize that ideal is a sentimental impracticality."

"That presumes we even succeed. What if a Zig command ship decided to stop by in response to their distress call? Is your ship available for backup if we're completely outclassed?"

"Sadly, no. Turning this operation into an interstellar incident is exactly what I am trying to avoid. It would do no good to solve one problem by creating one of equal scale."

"Right, you keep hinting that everything is a big deal. I see one stray, stranded ship. If we just blew it to particulates, who would be the wiser, here or wherever it comes from? I get that its tech could be a huge asset to whomever claims it… but you're already offering us that. For that matter, *you* could have taken it captive and had your way with whatever weird techno-magic they have aboard. Instead, you're treating it like your own ward, helping it along. It seems like it might be more dangerous going home with news about our system than it would be dead and distributed across space. *So why not just strip and scrap it?*"

Evgeny's diatribe had not only Jolly but also Punch and Gleamer staring at him. Gleamer's face registered shock, and the two Ningyo communicated similar surprise with their slack stillness.

"Thank you," Jolly finally said. "I approached you with the trappings and attitude of piracy. I admit that I meant to taunt you with a caricature. Yet it seems I truly did not understand. You *are* a pirate… I understand what that means now. I was wrong. My apologies."

Evgeny was confused. He felt as if he had been somehow rebuked, despite the Ningyo's placating words. What in the reeking ammonia clouds of the Egg Nebula was so important about this increasingly damnable ship?

He decided not to dignify Jolly's attitude by asking the question. Instead, he grumbled in response: "Glad you're finally listening. So? Let's get to work."

He turned to face Gleamer's gaping expression, snapping out an order, "Open a channel to the *Black Humor* so that their captain can send them on their way."

With a blink, Gleamer spun around to comply.

Jolly, instead, spoke to Evgeny: "Before that, let's straighten out the hierarchy. I am promoting myself to Admiral of this fleet. As such, you follow – and relay – my commands. I'd also like access to all ship's functions. I'd rather not blindly trust you to follow my orders. After all, in the heat of battle, accidents do happen. So, *captain*, kindly call up your command codes and relinquish your chair. I expect to see whatever I want to see and have access to whatever I want to access. This transition will work better with you as an interface for your crew. If you like, I won't even mention my new title. I don't have a face to save, but I don't mind if you keep yours. If you refuse – or if you try to deceive me – that face could be lost, along with other portions of your mass."

Jolly put a hand on the grip of one of its two space fold generators in emphasis. Punch added punctuation by flicking the switch on its stun baton. Gleamer jumped as the electrical field snapped to life a few feet away.

Evgeny's mortification was complete when he heard Soloth's voice from the doorway. During their earlier exchange, the Mauraug first mate was able to approach unheard. It spoke as it stepped through onto the bridge.

"I suggest compliance, captain. Aside from their personal weaponry here, plus the presence of their command ship and two other allies, the Ningyo have three other advantages: we are down three senior crew members, they have an escape shuttle while we have none, and they still hold some secrets we need."

At first, Evgeny wanted to object, feeling that his ally had turned against him. Then he realized that Soloth was objectively considering the situation and found their position genuinely tenuous. Hopefully, his first mate also had some thoughts about how to deal with the override of their bridge controls.

Of course, Evgeny possessed his own ultimate override – his dormant AI, Matilda – but that card could only be played once. If he used it to wrest control of the *Scape Grace* back from Jolly, his advantage over his own crew was lessened. Soloth hopefully remained unaware of that particular potential turnabout.

Once again backed up between likely destruction and merely potential doom, Evgeny stumbled toward the less certain hazard. "Very well. But I'd like some answers in exchange for the surrender of my ship. First, why can't we hear anything from my crew on board that ship? After they went inside, their comms went dark. Are you trying to cut us off? If not, would you please ask your friend to stop blocking their signal?"

Jolly lowered its hand but stayed ready to react. "I'm not sure what you mean. If your personnel are not responding, that is none of our doing. As to the actions of that ship, I am not its master. Friend is perhaps accurate. Here is my bargain: give me access to your ship, including communication, and I will contact the unnamed ship and ask it to open channels to your crew. That is my best offer. It is, in fact, my only offer."

Evgeny considered. Jolly's entire response might be a lie, but he was in no position to dispute it. Only the course of events would reveal clues about its honesty or falsehood.

"All right, all right." Evgeny punched in his command codes and left them shining on his console. "There's communications, there's navigation, there's propulsion, there's security and weapons. Anything you don't see here is controlled locally." He stood, giving narrow looks at Gleamer and Soloth. "You have the command."

He stepped down and took Soloth's position at the navigation console. Soloth took his meaning and his lead and moved to take Tklth's chair at weapons. Jolly stepped up to the command chair and scanned the provided codes. Punch holstered its weapons and moved to a position halfway between Jolly and the door. From there, the hostile Ningyo controlled entry and exit from the bridge as well as standing guard over its commander.

From the intercom speakers came Luuboh's voice: "Tklth is stable but still critical. Her survival would be greatly improved by actual medical attention."

Evgeny did not wait for permission but opened a channel in response. "I hear you. We're working on it now. Do your best until you hear otherwise. Oh, and if you get a moment, could you clean up the hallway near engineering? I hear she left a mess."

Luuboh's response was delayed by a tell-tale pause. Then its voice returned, saying, "She did, indeed. If I can be spared here, I will clean up what I can. Some messes are harder to resolve than others."

"I understand. Do your best." Evgeny signed off, thinking: *Some messes do resist easy resolution. They just need extra time and the right approach.*

10

The self-appointed Admiral Jolly lost no time exploring and utilizing the systems of the commandeered *Scape Grace*. The Ningyo had no objection to being observed, and so captain Evgeny Lerner watched as their usurper scrolled through inventory lists, system specifications, the crew roster, and their past navigational records. Evgeny was originally concerned that his crew would be interrogated in order to obtain information on their various criminal contacts. Afterward, he realized that he had given up many of his ship's secrets without a struggle. Granted, it would take the Ningyo some time to make full use of the available data, but Jolly was capable of recording everything its optical sensors scanned. It could reconstruct enough from its brief scan to trace many of *Scape Grace's* past activities.

It was fortunate that many of the navigational records were bogus and that some of the ship's true destinations had been deleted. Hopefully, the false leads would cause investigators enough trouble to make the real targets less obvious. Asking the wrong questions in the wrong places would trigger alarms among 'trusted' contacts privy to *Scape Grace's* safeguards.

But there was still too much legitimate navigational information for comfort. And the inventory and system logs held an even a lower percentage of misinformation. The crew needed real data about ship's operations in order to function effectively. If the Ningyo or its future contacts knew where to look, none of Evgeny's precautions would matter.

Jolly first made use of its systems access to communicate with the three nearby ships. To its former ship, the *Black Humor*, it gave simple directions: return to their previous position, go about their original business, and pretend that Jolly was still aboard as Captain. Jolly ended its orders: "I plan to return within two fertility cycles. If we have not rendezvoused by three cycles, locate this ship. If it has not been destroyed already, destroy it."

With that ultimatum, Evgeny was certain that the conversation was held audibly, in a Terran-standard language, for his own benefit. The thinly veiled threat was moderately effective. There were already significant swathes of Collective space ready to incinerate the *Scape Grace* upon detection. Still, few individuals, much less ships, were wholly devoted to their pursuit and obliteration. Of all the ships that might successfully find and catch a single pirate across the wide universe, a Ningyo command ship was high in the rankings.

Black Humor emphasized that capability by sliding effortlessly away from *Scape Grace* and slipping through a newly folded wrinkle in space to a destination unknown light-years away. So skillful was the work of Ningyo engineers and pilots that no shudder passed through *Scape Grace* from the nearby, enormous deformation of reality.

Next, Jolly transmitted orders to the *Harauch*. These instructions were not conveyed in a format available to non-Ningyo listeners. Instead, Jolly patched its suit systems directly through the *Scape Grace* and sent a message in its native language. For all that Evgeny knew, the message might have been encoded, as well, but the Ningyo language was as good as encryption. Translating it would require a specialized AI to sift through layers of digital formatting, linguistics, and bizarre Ningyo psychology, then reframe the result into a more familiar Terran communication form. None of the AIs on board – even if they were accessible – had the necessary expertise for that task.

While Jolly sat still, plugged into a nearby console, Evgeny and Gleamer exchanged thoughtful glances. Such connections were two-way links. If code could be uploaded to the Ningyo suits, there might be a way to gain access to their control functions.

A Ningyo in a compromised suit would be at the mercy of whoever controlled its suit's actions. It could be forced to move however the controller chose.

For that matter, a sufficiently hostile code-breaker could simply depressurize a Ningyo's suit, killing it instantly. A sadistic hacker could threaten to vent a suit as coercion or manipulate life support to cause discomfort or pain. There were distinct possibilities there, provided Gleamer could figure out how the suit code functioned. A suit's internal security was likely the best possible to counter just such attacks… making it that much more tempting a challenge for a programmer convinced of his own superiority.

With a nod, Evgeny endorsed more research. Hopefully, Gleamer *was* having the same thoughts as his captain.

Finally, Jolly fulfilled its promise to attempt contact with the unnamed foreign ship. Here, too, it transmitted and received an encoded version of its own language. In this case, however, it supplied a translation of the conversation for Evgeny's reference.

Jolly claimed to have said, "Dear friend, we cannot speak to our friends inside you. They cannot hear us or we cannot hear them. Please open a path so that we may talk to our friends."

The Ningyo paused for a time to receive a reply. It translated the response: "I am sorry. I did not know I was interfering. The path is clear but I cannot talk to your friends. They do not understand me yet. Try to speak to them again."

Gleamer did not wait for orders but opened a channel immediately to Katy and NuRikPo's public 'comms. He called out, "NuRikPo. Katy Olu. This is *Scape Grace*. Report."

They waited over one hundred seconds for a reply. None came back. Gleamer repeated his hail, cycling the message across a wider frequency range. He then tried the private line. Eventually, he set up a signal to signal the shuttle repeatedly for a callback. A responding ping indicated that the shuttle was receiving and available, but still no reply came from either crew member.

When informed of this result, Jolly shrugged. "The ship says that your people are choosing not to respond. I have no idea why they would ignore you, but that seems to be the case."

Evgeny was increasingly suspicious. They had only Jolly's word that the original problem was resolved, or that the interference was even an accident to begin with. Only the Ningyo was saying that their messages were getting through and that Katy and NuRikPo were failing to reply despite hearing the hails. There was no independent proof. There was also no evidence that Jolly was lying… not yet.

Once again, even if their occupier chose to lie, there was little Evgeny could do in response. He would have to take both the statements given – and the possibility of their falsehood – as uncertain data, points for review when choosing later actions.

Instead of directly challenging Jolly's claims, Evgeny tried other questions: "Did you have the same problem when you visited the outsider ship?"

"I did not personally visit that ship, so no," Jolly responded without elaboration.

"I didn't assume that… I meant you, as in your crew. Whoever you sent, did you have any trouble communicating with them?"

"Why do you assume any of my crew went aboard that ship, at all?"

The Ningyo's brevity and evasion were a marked contrast from its typical riddling verbosity. Evgeny felt certain he was tracking something important. He continued to push: "So how did you learn how to communicate with it? How do you know what it's like… what it wants?"

"We discovered it during exploration of an inter-galactic chasm. It looked quite different at the time, something like a pineapple. It was calling out for help. A distress beacon is universal. After pulling in close, we worked on rudimentary translation. To be honest, the foreign ship did most of the work. It used our input to build a common base for communication and eventually learned some of our language. From there, it told us what it needed."

"And you just agreed to help… out of nobility."

"If you mean doing the right thing, then yes. As I understand its story, it was sent as an explorer, with orders much like our own. It found itself further out than expected and unable to return. I'm not sure if it experienced a navigational error, engine failure, or both. In reversed circumstances, I would hope for the same treatment. The Golden Rule is a solid moral law."

"Well, you've already claimed moral superiority. I'd claim superior wisdom, though. For all you know, that's the first scout for an invading army. It could be lying to you. Say you help it. You send it back home with all sorts of intelligence about our nature and capabilities… and it brings back a fleet to take advantage of our kind, giving nature."

"Our nature? I'm sure that enough of the Collective shares your violent distrust to deal with an invasion, if it came to that. You argue from weakness. Is it not equally likely that this intelligence is being truthful? If we send it back whole and happy, might it not present a positive report, reducing the likelihood of hostilities from its home system… whenever they do eventually manage to make contact across the gulf?"

"Of course, I argue from weakness. That's the point. Actually, none of this is the point. You already decided what to do and strong-armed us into going along. What I want to know is what *I* need to do to survive *your* folly… for myself and my crew to come out of this mess alive. What you're not answering is: what is going on over there? You're telling me that you know nothing of the internal nature of that ship or its technical capabilities?"

Evgeny grew increasingly agitated as he spoke. Some of it was feigned: an attempt to draw a reaction in their verbal conflict. Some of the anger was real, though. If the Ningyo was being honest, then it really was a fool. Evgeny's lost home, the Locust Colony, had embodied similar high, noble goals of understanding between cultures – Terran and Mauraug – and left itself open to destruction by those who opposed such goals: the Mauraug Apostates.

The Collective itself was not based on friendship or helpfulness. It was a business plan, a compromise reached to minimize overt aggression between star-faring cultures by keeping them out of one another's way. At the Collective's root was a military alliance, later expanded by necessity into a series of economic treaties. The diplomats could dress up those founding agreements in moral finery, but underneath, the Collective was a temporary acknowledgement between neighbors who saw more profit in cooperation than conflict. As soon as that balance changed and favored war, the Collective would collapse.

To Evgeny's challenge, Jolly replied, "What you need to do is trust. It would be nice if you would trust me, trust us, or trust our friend over there… but at least trust your own people. And if you can't trust them personally, trust them professionally. Trust yourself. You entrust your life, every second, to the competence of your crew. Trust them now to understand and adapt to their situation. If they were not capable, you would have sent others. You would have hired others. For all I know, you reward incompetence with death… you don't strike me as a benevolent leader, for some reason."

Evgeny knew his ego was being stroked but could not help being placated by the words. He did agree with Jolly's central point; he had little recourse but to trust Katy and NuRikPo's expertise. If they were making bad decisions, they would die, or else they would return in shame. And if not, they would return whole and bearing something of value.

Even so, Evgeny could do more than *nothing*. Jolly's help was apparently worthless, but there were other courses to pursue. Though the Ningyo held *Scape Grace's* leash, it did not control her fully. Even while abandoning one line of attack, Evgeny was laying plans for the next. He just needed some private conference time with a few people.

The opportunity for scheming was coming up. They would need six Terran standard days of travel before reaching the Zig mining outpost. Between departure and arrival, there would be plenty of time to lay plans. The Ningyo were likely to be obnoxiously present during that time, but they could not be omnipresent.

Evgeny covered his silent plotting with sullen acknowledgement: "No, I'm not benevolent, but I'm at least capable. I wonder which of us has held command longer or dealt with more trouble. You're making sense despite yourself.

Still, I had better hear about it *the very moment* we get a reply from my 'people'. Right now, you have my grudging cooperation because you implied there was something to gain. If I have reason to doubt that this project will yield a net profit – and I count the loss of crew a very high expense – then my cooperation will be far, far more grudging."

"See, and raise. I've been Captain of *Black Humor* for the equivalent of four Terran years. Care to reveal how long your buttocks have warmed this chair?" Jolly shifted as if settling itself comfortably into the aforementioned seat.

Soloth bash'Soloth chose this moment to interrupt, interjecting, "You have access to our records. Anything you need to know about captain Lerner's command can be found there. As a practitioner, I have to say: I am appalled at your pathetic grasp of Dominion."

Its words drew the attention of everyone on the bridge, even the formerly stoic Punch. The Ningyo enforcer put hands on weapon grips and stepped forward, but was stopped by a gesture from Jolly.

"And *you* must be shorter than that dwarf below-decks… because the Joke goes completely over your head," Jolly retorted. The insult had little effect, being incomprehensible to any of the non-Ningyo present. There was a moment of confused tension while everyone tried to decide how to react.

Evgeny fell back on his default role: taking command of an uncomfortable situation. "We're all at different spins here. Could we get this caravan moving? The sooner we start, the sooner we're done and out of one another's faces."

Jolly sighed theatrically. "So much for Comus' dreams of cultural comity. Yes, fine, hammers down, wagons ho, and roll out." With this stream of gibberish, it brought up navigational orders on its console, transmitting these plans to their neighboring ships as well as to Evgeny's navigation console.

Gleamer muttered quiet insults while turning back to his own console. He typed manically. Whatever he was doing was unclear to Evgeny. On the surface, along the public channels, it looked like the programmer was trying a range of frequencies and alternate communication methods to reach their crew aboard the unnamed ship. Evgeny knew his young recruit well enough to realize that such simple routines could be run by an automated program. What Gleamer was *actually* doing with his inputs was the real question. Physical typing was only an addition to whatever neural streaming Gleamer's perforated cortex was performing. Gleamer was always working on multiple projects simultaneously.

Once, the young man tried to explain the experience of cybernetically enhanced cognition to Evgeny. It was a foreign enough realm to require its own vocabulary. Evgeny struggled to grasp the concepts of "executive partitioning" and "interlinked parallelism". Genuinely understanding what Gleamer felt while integrated was impossible for any purely biological sapient. At best, Evgeny gained some tolerance for his communications expert.

It required some sacrifice and effort to adapt to a different mode of existence. Through his modifications, Gleamer gained abilities most Humans would naively desire, but at a cost. The changes made it difficult for him to relate to slower sapients, those with single minds and singular attention. They made him impatient when forced to match their speed and focus. They also made him miserable when disconnected; his networking cable was something of an umbilicus, feeding his appetite for stimulation and carrying away the excreta of a constantly creative mind. Finally, the programmer was dependent on skilled maintenance to keep his artificial systems in good repair.

Evgeny was pleased to see Gleamer's infatuation with the Ningyo dulled. His disenchantment was a victory from the captain's verbal sparring against Jolly. The Ningyo were revealed as something other than the infinitely cheerful, clever, enigmatic, benevolent, and/or talented creatures some Humans imagined. Pushed hard enough, Jolly became evasive, stiff, and even angry.

Perhaps Evgeny even scored points with his Mauraug first mate. The possibility was pleasant to think about, though not particularly necessary. Soloth was less impressed with posturing than action and more pleased by effects than intentions. Evgeny's brutal practicality earned him Soloth's allegiance and that of the crew's other Mauraug.

No doubt, the Humans on his crew considered him something of a hybrid. After all, most of the pirates still active in Collective space were Mauraug. Why wouldn't a Human pirate captain naturally emulate their habits? Perhaps some of the crew thought him a Dominionist convert. Well, the *Scape Grace* certainly would wreak bloody prejudicial vengeance on any Mauraug Apostate ships they came across, but not for reasons of religion.

No, the captain's grudge against Apostates was personal. Just like he would make it personal if the Ningyo harmed his ship or his crew.

Tklth… was an exception. The Vislin initiated hostilities without orders and suffered the consequences. Evgeny would not have begrudged Jolly an execution as justice for the loss of its own colleague. That Jolly permitted Tklth to live was either the sole proof of its moral superiority… or else a special kind of sadism. Time would tell how much Ticklish would have to suffer.

Once their navigational plans were shared and confirmed, the three ships wasted no further time before accelerating. The group maintained a simple equilateral formation, staying within easy visual range of one another. The *Scape Grace* led, with the *Harauch* to one side and the ship with the untranslatable name directly behind 'Grace. Their distance was no greater than necessary for safety, just beyond the reach of their projected energy exhaust.

The unnamed ship seemed to use standard propulsion similar to the systems employed by *Harauch* or *Scape Grace*. It kept up with their speed well enough. Perhaps it even incorporated structures functionally equivalent to the engines of Collective-built starships.

The group of ships settled on a speed matching the *Harauch's* highest safe velocity. While not as crippled as it pretended after 'Grace's attack, the salvager was still damaged and under repair. Evgeny wondered if the Ningyo crew aboard *Harauch* volunteered to play decoy or were ordered to that duty by Captain Jolly. How many Ningyo were hurt or killed by that single blast? For that matter, how many of its *own* crew had Jolly been willing to risk in order to draw in the *Scape Grace*?

The answers to those questions were quite relevant. They might reveal how willing the Ningyo commander was to sacrifice anyone, perhaps everyone – including both its own crew and Evgeny's – in the pursuit of its goal.

Not that the answers made any difference to Evgeny's plans. Whether Jolly was a noble paragon or an idealistic idiot, it still wasn't making any bad bets with *Scape Grace* as collateral. Evgeny already lent the Ningyo enough credit to gamble. He might not be a titled Captain, but he was sure as hell master of his own ship. It was time to start preparing the proof of that claim.

11

Once her course was set and the *Scape Grace* moving, there was no need for a full bridge crew. Evgeny Lerner, her captain and former commander, was reluctant to leave his ship's nerve center occupied by the enemy while he was absent. Still, he had work to do elsewhere: work directly related to the removal of that enemy.

"I'm due for bunk time," Evgeny announced, stretching and rising from his seat at the navigator's station. He honestly *was* tired. It already had been a long shift, even before his first mate spotted a seemingly stranded, vulnerable ship on the edges of inhabited space. The unexpected turns of events since then further exhausted his resources. Evgeny wished he actually was going to his quarters. Maybe he would have a little time for sleep once his other tasks were complete.

"I will accompany you to the lower decks," Soloth offered. "The crew needs to be advised. A discussion now will avoid problems later."

"Yes. I would prefer to avoid any further ambushes in the halls," Jolly agreed with brightly-tinged sarcasm. "My aim might not always be so precise, and I'm not sure how many stray shots your ship can risk."

Evgeny had feared that the Ningyo occupiers would demand tight scheduling and escorts for any of the command crew moving beyond their observation. Either Jolly realized how impractical it would be to implement that degree of control, or else the Ningyo commander felt it had nothing to fear by allowing free movement about the ship. Perhaps a bit of both was true. From the bridge consoles, Jolly could track activity throughout the *Scape Grace*, calling up motion sensor readouts and video from most areas. Audio, also, was available… from most areas.

Savvy, senior crew members knew about the 'dead' areas, regions unobserved by any camera or microphone... or rather, by any device connected to the bridge. Evgeny and his co-conspirator, Luuboh bash'Gaulig, had planted wireless devices in those so-called invisible zones, taking advantage of the assumption of privacy to eavesdrop on candid conversatons.

Their listening network gave Evgeny a secondary communications system. He could only trade messages with Luuboh, at first, but other crew could be brought into confidence if necessity outweighed the loss of their hidden asset. Evgeny's own cabin was the only completely, truly, thoroughly unmonitored location on the *Scape Grace*. He was almost certain of that security, up to the limits of the shielding and anti-surveillance technology he himself installed.

When he announced his departure from the bridge, the captain almost expected some protest from Gleamer. The comms officer had been seated at his station for six hours, most of a duty shift, before Soloth arrived for changeover. Then, Gleamer stuck around an hour longer to finish whatever coding had him engrossed.

Then, Evgeny dropped in at the bridge. Then, the unnamed ship showed up on their mass scans. After that, Gleamer was stuck, continuously engrossed during the crisis.

It was his own fault for not taking the opportunity to sleep sooner. Still, there was no way anyone could have predicted any variation in their previously monotonous journey, much less the weird sequence of events that followed.

Now, Gleamer had to decide whether to stay alone and outnumbered by the Ningyo or leave the bridge entirely to their control. It looked like the furiously typing programmer was going to make his decision by default again. He barely acknowledged Evgeny and Soloth's departure. Hopefully, whatever he was working on was worth the pain of future fatigue.

Leaving Gleamer on deck suited Evgeny's purposes well enough. If Jolly tried anything drastic through the computer systems, Gleamer could shut down the process personally, set up automated sub-AI defenses, or alert the captain if nothing else.

His real worry was that the other Ningyo, Punch, might decide to attack Gleamer, unprovoked or in tandem with a virtual assault on *Scape Grace*. In the electronic world, the slight young man was a professional warrior with supernatural powers. In the world of flesh, he was barely sixty kilos of untoned, untrained Human. Evgeny had never taken the young man into action and likely never would; his value was mental, not physical. Alone against a trained Ningyo in its mechanical suit, Gleamer would fall fast.

The younger man was a pretty depressing statement about their shared Human culture. Humans were already de-emphasizing physical size and strength long before they left Terra to colonize other worlds. With the advent of AI technology, some of the balance shifted back to brawn as an almost reflexive refutation of the value of 'pure mind' over embodied intelligence. Good health, a shapely body, and athletic skill again became signs of good taste and social status.

That trend died with the revelation of the more physically powerful Mauraug, followed by the discovery of other, even meatier sapients, like the Taratumm. Physical power as a necessary or distinctive trait declined among Humanity once again. Thickly muscled mesomorphs like Evgeny became rarer, particularly in space. Only planetary dwellers in high gravity worlds had much use for greater bulk, although flexibility and good circulation were always valuable traits.

Evgeny's thoughts were ironically appropriate while sharing a hallway with a Mauraug massing three-quarters more than himself. Evgeny and Soloth walked quietly together to the far aft ladder. Once there, Evgeny staged a short conversation for the benefit of both Soloth and the potentially eavesdropping Jolly.

"I'm going to stop in on Engineering and brief the crew back there, myself," he explained gruffly.

"Understood, captain. I will inform the combat crew that their services are not needed for several days yet. Any other orders?"

"Just let them know that we're working for the Ningyo, that there *will* be shares forthcoming – no need to say from what source – and that anyone who pokes their head above decks without permission will be cut out of the take. Oh, and mention that the doctor is busy until further notice, so anyone getting hurt will have to settle for Luuboh's gentle touch whenever it can spare a moment."

Soloth narrowed its nostrils in distaste, "If they only understood how gentle that runt actually *is*. But yes, I'm sure they'll miss the pleasures of doctor Olu's bedside manner."

Evgeny grinned in shared nasty humor. He was quite aware that the ship's medic held a reputation for sleeping with every male Human crewmember, at one time or another. Soloth assumed that this promiscuity was the flaw that ended Evgeny and Katy's brief physical relationship. The funny thing was that Katy only started taking other crew to her bunk *after* Evgeny broke things off. Even funnier was that *she* was the one pressuring the combat crew into sex. Those who refused tended to suffer from medical neglect in one form or another until they either relented or their infirmity exceeded the captain's tolerance for Katy's willful malpractice. The medic's aggressive sexuality was an old joke between captain and first mate. Hell, even *Gleamer* was dragged into Katy's room at one point, to his temporary delight and eventual dismay at not being invited back.

Evgeny was no hypocrite; his libido was no less frustrated and hampered by the close quarters. Yet, he found channels for that physical demand. He could wait until circumstances allowed for a proper shore leave. In the meantime, there were hard workouts, pleasant memories, and when all else failed, a well-stocked video library to fall back on.

This crisis was a hell of a time to think about sex. There was work to do before Evgeny could even think of going back to his cabin, for any purpose. Not to mention, it would be aggravating to talk to assistant engineer Zenaida Georges – another attractive and entirely unavailable partner – while being reminded of his own suppressed needs. Eh, he would manage. If he couldn't control his own urges, how could he expect to control a ship full of under-disciplined sapients?

The two crewmates, Human and Mauraug, parted ways at the first junction of the descending aft ladder. Evgeny stepped out onto the Engineering deck, while Soloth continued downward to the crew quarters in the *Scape Grace's* belly.

While the confrontation between Jolly and Evgeny unfolded on the bridge, Luuboh bash'Gaulig monitored Tklth's slow return to consciousness. The Vislin was responding remarkably well to the reinfusion of fluids to her circulatory system. The cautery bandages had done their job for the moment. The patient's pain was under control. Blessedly, she was still too exhausted to comprehend the full extent of her mutilation.

Luuboh intended to keep it that way. As Tklth's vital signs crept back toward acceptable values, her anxious nurse steadily reduced the room's ambient temperature. If done correctly, the chill would encourage Tklth's biology to enter its dormant phase. The reptilian Vislin retained their ancestral tendency to slow down and sleep in dark, cold conditions. The species overcame this hereditary limitation during their development of sapience, but through technology rather than genetic change. Now, Tklth's hibernatory trait was both benefit and drawback. Beneficial, not only in that it allowed Luuboh to sedate the patient without medications and tend to other business without worrying about her harming herself, but also beneficial in conserving the patient's strength and encouraging her body to focus on repairs. The response was a drawback in that *too* much cold would start to lower the Vislin's vital functions and possibly cause harm while she was too drowsy to react.

To set a balance, Luuboh slowly lowered both the temperature and the lighting until Tklth's heart rate, respiration, blood saturation, and neural functions dropped into the lower end of resting. It stopped there and waited a minute longer. When those vitals held steady without continuing to drop, Luuboh felt safe leaving the room.

Still, it patched the medical computer to a portable communicator that it strapped to its upper arm. If Tklth took a bad turn, either waking up violently or slipping into shock, the device would sound an alarm and allow Luuboh to race back for further adjustments.

Those preparations done, Luuboh gathered up the tools it would need to attend to captain Lerner's request: biological cleanup and disposal. It pulled on a stretchy polymer clean suit, Human sized, which clung tightly at the Mauraug's larger neck and torso but fit easily over its conveniently smaller limbs.

Luuboh then withdrew two folded body bags from a lower drawer. That the ship *had* a supply of body bags was a sad necessity, though better than just throwing dead crew (or severed limbs) into space. The treated containers preserved biomass, preventing decay by retarding bacterial breeding and protein breakdown. This preservation wasn't just for sanitation; it also made sure the materials could be reclaimed more easily. Taboos about cannibalism limited the utility of such recycling, but like on any ship stranded at sea, the prospect of starvation would quickly override those taboos and allow engineers to reuse the available compounds however they were needed.

Tklth's leg and tail *might* be preserved enough for reattachment, depending on a lot of factors including the speed of doctor Olu's return and her depths of surgical talent. The environment was already a problem. Given the resources of a decent medical lab – even the facilities on a space station or command ship – Tklth could expect good odds of being entirely reassembled. Aboard the little salvager, she would be lucky if they could salvage enough tissue to rebuild stumps for cybernetic attachment.

Luuboh's other concern was cleaning up the dead Ningyo's remains. It doubted that the spattered plasm that was once a Ningyo body could be gathered up by anything less than a vacuum cleaner. It was more like a bloodstain than a body. The likely best option was enzymatic breakdown and then a flush with sterilizer. While somewhat disrespectful of the dead, such dissolution was safest for Luuboh and the crew that had to walk those halls later. At least a Ningyo's suit – even breached – retained most of its former operator's remains.

Luuboh gathered up what it thought it might need from the medical deck, then departed to stop by the janitorial supply room. Along the way, it stopped at a 'comm panel. Better to ask the Ningyo what they wanted done with their dead than guess and risk offense later.

"Captain Lerner," Luuboh sent to the bridge, "I am preparing to clean up the Level Two mid-ship hallway as ordered. What do our guests want done with their crewmate?"

It was unexpectedly answered by the synthetic voice of the Ningyo leader, Jolly. "Luuboh? I'm sorry, the captain has retired to his quarters. You have reached his after-hours answering service. Fortunately, I can advise you directly... and thank you for your concern! You may clear away the remains of our dear departed Comus in whatever manner you find most sanitary. I would prefer that her suit be sealed into a container, in its entirety, and placed on the deck near our shuttle. In fact, I will *only* be offended if any portion of that suit is missing later... not to assume that you would disrespect its owner by misplacing any portion of her property, of course."

Luuboh allowed itself only a short pause for disorientation before picking up the conversation again: "I see. Certainly, your crewmate's... property... will be returned to you in full. Could I ask a question, though?"

Jolly replied, "You just did! But you may. And you may ask another question after that, if you wish."

"Thank you," Luuboh responded with even-tempered tolerance. "I actually have two questions: Is this traditional Ningyo practice, to be unconcerned with the disposition of the dead? And didn't you originally state that Comus was male?"

"Two questions? You do presume on my generosity," Jolly teased, "but for our gracious host, I am also gracious. Plus, I appreciate your curiosity. Burial customs do differ widely across our culture. Spacefarers such as myself and my crew tend to be less attached to the physical remains after life has departed. Given the hostile nature of space itself, recovery of the dead can be difficult, particularly after an accident or conflict between ships. We have learned to be practical. Even so, I know of nothing in our present culture to equal the fetishization of the corpse practiced in, say, the ancient Egyptian culture of early Terra or the Urrgala dynasty of your own home world."

Jolly continued, "As to gender, I do not believe I stated the gender of myself or either of my visiting crew. Why do you ask now? Is it pertinent to your ministrations?"

"No, not as such. But you referred to Comus as 'he' originally, then 'she' just recently."

"A gentleman and a scholar, you are. Very perceptive. As a reward, I refuse to answer your question. The challenge of discovery is worth more than an easy answer, *ne c'est pas?* I will verify if you guess correctly. Give it a few hours. As a hint: you are correct in my choice of gendered pronouns. Undoubtedly, I will contribute similar variations in future contexts. The reason is left to your deduction. Something to occupy your mind while you undertake your unenviable... undertaking."

With that, Jolly cut the 'comm connection with a verbally spoken, "Beep!"

Luuboh wasn't sure whether to be genuinely complimented or, like the captain, further infuriated with the Ningyo's bantering habits. Mauraug had proverbs about "clever talkers", usually involving severed tongues. A popular poem even had a rather cleverly ironic recipe for the preparation of said organ, prior to serving it back to its former owner for consumption. As impractical as that operation might be, it would be exceptionally difficult to execute upon a Ningyo. The closest equivalent might be ripping out their vocal synthesizer and jamming it somewhere uncomfortable.

"Is this how Soloth bash'Soloth spends its idle thoughts: in the pondering of future brutality?" Luuboh wondered to itself as it swayed down the hall toward the section spattered with gore. It blew a breath through its lips in derision, partly toward itself. Why was it so angry? It had asked the question, after all. It knew the Ningyo's answer might be nonsense. But the answer might still be useful, even when cloaked in allusion.

Luuboh was motivated by a pragmatic curiosity. If it was going to be dealing with Ningyo for a while, then more knowledge about the odd species and its culture could be useful. Holding useful knowledge made Luuboh useful. Knowing something that the captain might need to know made Luuboh more valuable to him.

Even so, it wasn't sure its particular line of inquiry about Comus' gender was worth pursuing. The concept of 'gender' was already a strange one for the unisex Mauraug. Their closest equivalent was the dominant/subordinate relationship of a mated pair, though that dimorphism was a mixture of hormonal changes caused after mating and genetic chance during the production of an offspring. The inherent binary, dimorphic nature of most sapient species' genetic design was often puzzling.

Humans once widely conflated gender with dominance, due to their males' greater muscle mass as a function of sex-linked hormones. Or was that due to the limitations on females' mobility required by their mandatory role in gestation? Either way, in Humans' actual relationships, sometimes the female was dominant. And in terms of genetic preponderance, a Human mother's zygote determined the larger proportion of an offspring's traits. After they transitioned from physical strength to general adaptability being a better predictor of status, the proportions of male-dominant, female-dominant, and equally-balanced relationships reputedly stabilized among the Human population.

Katy Olu was an excellent example of the confusing nature of Human 'gender'. She was dominant with some partners, submissive with others, yet did not intend reproduction with any of them. Trying to keep up with another species' gossip was confusing enough without adding biological enigmas to the mix.

There wasn't enough time in a Mauraug's lifespan to study the labyrinth of Zig sexuality and reproduction. Suffice it to say that if Ningyo gender was equally tangled, Luuboh would be wasting hours of contemplation trying to unravel it. Maybe that was Jolly's intent: to waste Luuboh's time. Maybe the answer was as simple as sheer randomness; if the Ningyo also did not have gender, then Jolly might just be using linguistic gender at random. Shit, it might be doing that just to provoke more questions.

Such thoughts were good reminders to focus on work and worry about theory later. Luuboh had already stopped well ahead of the murder scene. It sealed the hood of its clean suit and unfolded the two body bags. Holding one bag high to avoid contact with the Ningyo ichor on the deck, it approached the empty robotic suit.

The gleaming white 'body' had a neatly punched, carbon-ringed hole in its abdominal area. A shining grey substance, partially liquid but flecked with small bits of semi-solid matter, had flowed from both the entry and exit holes, staining the lower body of the suit and pooling on the decking beneath. Sprays of the same substance had dripped down both walls of the corridor, ejected when the suit's occupant was explosively decompressed. In the ship's interior lighting, the substance had a slight iridescence, like a sheen of oil. It was too utterly foreign to register as gore and did not provoke any revulsion in Luuboh. Before it sealed its hood, the smell was only chemical and metallic, not all that different from the scents in Engineering when NuRikPo was hard at work. The industrial odor was strong enough to cover any tang from Tklth's blood.

The *sight* of the Vislin's mangled leg and tail and the puddles and smears of her magenta blood were quite capable of upsetting Luuboh's equilibrium, all on their own. Luuboh tried to look away, focusing on the Ningyo suit as long as possible before turning to the more unpleasant cleanup.

Opening the first body bag, Luuboh draped the black polymer sack over Comus' suit, covering the staring eyes of its bearded mask. For a moment, Luuboh was irrationally afraid that the 'body' would move, springing to life and perhaps grabbing at its mortician.

Maybe that thought wasn't so irrational. It fit the Ningyo humor to leave a program active in their suits to be triggered after death. Mauraug had been known to put traps in their cybernetic prostheses so that scavengers would be rewarded with projectiles, nerve gas, or just a rapidly melting handful of thermited slag. The Ningyo version of a post-mortem trap would likely be less deadly but no less awful: maybe a final song-and-dance routine or a tearful embrace and interminable final soliloquy. After all, their ship was named *Black Humor*, a term Luuboh found easily translatable into Mauraug idiom. Although, the Mauraug version of grim humor was more likely to involve the amusing abuse *of* a corpse rather than abuse *by* one.

The suit remained blessedly inert. Luuboh managed to get it fully wrapped and sealed into the bag with a minimum of external mess. The custodian retrieved enzyme spray and a handful of rags from its cleaning kit, then wiped down the outside of the bag, removing any remaining ichor or blood. Finally, it hoisted the sack and deposited the body-shaped form onto a clean area of the corridor.

Next was the unavoidable task of bagging up Tklth's pieces. Luuboh opened the second body bag. It wondered if it was even worth trying to save the butchered chunks of flesh and bone. The spatial fold projector redistributed a portion of the Vislin's mass into a dozen different locations and thus, a dozen different pieces. Each piece then leaked out its liquid contents, creating a composite puddle of blood sprawling across the deck. As a weapon, the spatial disruptor was horribly messy.

Worse, some of those pieces had fallen near enough the spatters of Ningyo ichor to become contaminated. What the Ningyo fluids would do to another species' cellular structure was an entire dissertation topic, not something Luuboh could know beforehand. It could only save everything and hope for the best. It would have to hope that the few traces of ichor clinging to one piece would not taint all the rest in the same bag.

It knelt and began gingerly picking up scraps of its crew member, trying to think of the chunks as cuts of meat like those it handled in the galley below decks. The substitution wasn't helping. If anything, such thoughts would make cooking dinner more difficult later. Luuboh decided the crew was dining vegetarian that night. They could eat their own complaints along with their legumes.

Luuboh could not help noticing the texture of the damaged tissue as it picked up each piece. Most of the segments were neatly sliced, smooth cross-sections where the spatial fields diverged. That made sense; the effect would cut more smoothly than a mono-molecular edge.

The piece that had landed nearest to Comus' remains was noticeably different. It wasn't degraded or dissolved by the Ningyo ichor, as Luuboh feared. In fact, it appeared irregular for an entirely opposite reason. The silvery substance clung to the red flesh not like a liquid but like a network of filaments. Between those filaments, a pinkish-grey substance protruded outward from the sliced surface of muscle tissue. Fascinated enough to overcome its revulsion toward the awful thing it held, Luuboh examined the piece of Tklth's... lower leg?... more closely.

There was a definite pattern forming. The tissue was expanding, not irregularly but in a structured pattern. The muscle was being grown or stretched somehow. How and why? Was this the natural effect of Ningyo cellular material on other substances? Somehow, Luuboh doubted that. The 'jellyfish' were multicellular, organ-possessing, unitary organisms, by all accounts. They might incorporate oddities of anatomy owing to their unique environment of origin, but they were not distributed systems or colony intelligences. The transformation it was seeing put Luuboh in mind of the Awakeners, though those strange sentiences were distinctly fungus-like cell colonies that only inhabited living organisms.

Luuboh sealed the body bag, keeping the one odd piece separate, and carried both items towards its clean area and cleaning supplies. Tklth would have to do without one piece of her anatomy, permanently. It was just as well; whatever was acting upon that piece might do something to her other severed flesh, if it was allowed to spread. Exactly what, Luuboh was unsure.

Was the tissue regrowing? Luuboh decided to let the process continue and compare samples. It used a small biohazard disposal bag to hold the separate chunk. The bio-bags were intended to hold used cleaning rags for later decomposition and would not slow breakdown in the same way as the body bags. Therefore, they would also not slow growth.

Luuboh set its two mysteries aside for future work. It then went back to its remaining task. With sprays and rags, it broke down the mixed drippings of two species and soaked up the result: water saturated with salts and minerals and simple compounds like ammonia. Murder victim and murderer were reduced and intermingled.

Aren't we all eventually intermixed? Luuboh thought to itself as it scrubbed. *Whether we consume one another directly, indirectly consume crops fertilized by our excreta and decomposed bodies, or simply breathe in the vapor exhaled by another, we cannot avoid taking in parts of one another. What folly to set one being ahead of another, as if they were separate to begin with! They certainly will not remain so for long.*

While such philosophical musings were not foreign to the frequently lonely Mauraug custodian, it should have heeded its own insight. Its mind was trying to give warning about an unclear but very present danger.

12

Eustace Brown listened to the crickets chirping. He was sure they were talking, but he didn't speak their language. Not yet, anyway.

His invisible friends were listening, too, and learning. He was a smart person, but his friends were smarter. Actually, by some standards, they were stupid. They didn't think for themselves. They only did what Eustace told them to do. They weren't independent. They certainly weren't self-aware; not like Eustace's best friend, Sid.

Sid could have worked on his own and learned the cricket language quickly. Together, Eustace and Sid would already know what the crickets were saying, why they had started talking, where they were, and *what* they really were.

Eustace missed Sid. His other friends were poor company by comparison.

Still, they were the best friends he had, right then. Sid, a true AI, a Brin – *his* Brin – was stuck millions of light-years away.

His sub-AI programs were Eustace's only helpers. The slow, solid, physical friends Eustace might speak with, the sapients who called him 'Gleamer', were absent. When their bodies were elsewhere, their minds were cut off from contact. Only when the vibrated air of their speech was transduced to current along the ship's intercom system would he and they become connected again. Those allies didn't know much, and they could only share the barest minimum of information with their inefficient communications mode, but they sometimes provided unique perspective and data points. Their bodies were also helpful for protection, in dangerous situations like the present.

There were other, unfriendly sapients nearby. They were the reason that communication was so limited. They prevented Eustace from talking to his physical friends. He couldn't speak freely. There were secrets the enemy should not overhear. Eustace considered asking the enemies about the crickets, then realized that the crickets might be one of the secrets he shouldn't tell them. Perhaps *they*, the Ningyo, were the source of the sounds. In that case, Eustace really shouldn't let them know he overheard them.

The chirps were not sounds in air, but signals in the radiosphere. Gleamer was 'hearing' short bursts of high frequency, low powered radio waves, thanks to the receptors in his cybernetic ear. There were thousands of the patterns, coming from thousands of different sources. Given the weak propagation of such signals, the sources had to be close… which meant inside the *Scape Grace*.

Unfortunately, their scattered, intermittent nature made localization difficult. The signals came and went in choruses. No signal lasted long enough to convey much information by itself, but multiple signals would ripple through the sensors simultaneously in a variegated pattern that could hold more meaning. A wave made up of small droplets would crash against his receptors, followed by a distinct silent pause, then be answered by another, more distant wave. Gleamer labeled the choruses 'swarms'. He could tell that one swarm of crickets was further away, given the lower average power of their broadcasts.

The signals were new. They started just under an hour ago, after the Ningyo came aboard. At first, Gleamer hoped the odd signals were communications from Katy and NuRikPo, aboard the other, foreign ship. They might have found such an odd encoding method necessary, somehow, per the circumstances of their entrapment. But after some analysis, Gleamer realized that this possibility was unlikely. Neither the shuttle nor anything aboard it could produce so many individual, distinct transmissions.

The most likely sources of the signals were the Ningyo, one or both of them. Was Gleamer picking up some sort of natural emanation from the creatures themselves? A byproduct of their suits' functions? Maybe the biomechanical interface between suit and operator?

That, too, seemed unlikely. For one thing, such radiated energy would be wasteful if it were not intentional. Surely the Ningyo could insulate such broadcasts, even if they were somehow internally necessary. And if Ningyo produced radio noise regularly, someone within the Collective would have noticed and noted the fact, already.

The best-fitting explanation was improbable. *Neurons* showed similar choral behavior in their firing patterns. One of Gleamer's sub-AIs proposed the idea via analogy to electroencephalography. The electrical potentials generated by each neuron as it fired generated externally measurable electrical current. Medical science had learned how to read these patterns of current and trace them back to the functional brain states from which they arose. The mapping between nerve action and measured current was murky, especially if measured from the scalp surface but even when measured from the outer brain surface. If you could touch an electrode to every single neuron simultaneously, you might be able to map and 'hear' the thoughts of a subject… after a long period of careful recording and correlation. Nerves, as a general statement, did not follow a single common map across brains. The cells might conform to some general rules of organization, but the exact patterns generated by one brain and another would never match exactly, even when having the 'same' thought.

Still, what if a brain wanted to talk to another brain? Sapients tended to solve that problem by creating external, common transmission methods, using more reliable, consistent and robust mediums like visible light and atmospheric vibration. Such methods were sharply limited, true, but effective in working around the inherent mismatches between nervous systems. Hell, the Ningyo didn't even *have* nervous systems, *per se*, and they and chordates like Humans could still trade jokes.

The Awakeners, by contrast, were pretty much *just* nervous systems. These most recent additions to the Collective were intelligent masses of fungus, colony entities which merged symbiotically with other organisms and communicated via direct integration of cells. They could also communicate *externally* via a poorly-understood transmission process, called 'psionics' for lack of a better term. Maybe psionics was nothing more than the development of a direct, common code from nervous system to nervous system. That way, two entities could skip over all the intervening steps and *really* communicate, sharing all the nuances of feeling, image, and experience that speech handled so gracelessly.

That level of communication was almost what Gleamer experienced with his sub-AIs. The electrodes penetrating one hemi-sphere of his brain translated electronic 'thoughts' into Gleamer's own neural language and back again. He shared the same communication, once, with Sid. Sadly, Human and Brin did not share enough frames of reference to make neural linkage any more than a means of fast, efficient discussion… yet even that interface was vastly superior to any other form of contact Gleamer experienced before or since.

If there was one thing to be said in favor of other Humans, it was that they had more similar dimensions – physically, mentally, and emotionally – to Eustace himself. If he ever met another Human who was wired in the same way as himself, they might do more than talk. They could experience real *communion*, sharing not only information but conscious experiences. That hope was part of the reason Eustace became Gleamer, implanting his first cybernetics and seeking out similar souls in virtual worlds.

The growing awareness of 'psionics' was raising considerable discussion and speculation across the Collective. Many investigators suspected that all sapient species held the potential for direct mind-to-mind communication. Each society would, understandably, keep the evidence of such abilities carefully hidden. Now, such secrecy was unnecessary, though it persisted.

With the Awakeners publicly known and accepted, the reality of psionics was undeniable. Fear followed. The leaders of each society were forced to acknowledge not only the existence of psionics, but also explain the safeguards they were putting – or had already put – into place for defense against the abuse of such abilities. Suddenly, there were psionic police, suppressant drugs for psychic restraint, and even sensors to detect illicit psionic activity.

Most of those without access to this mental world were suspicious of it, if not fearful. Eustace Brown was only envious. He always felt separated from other people. This alienation wasn't a mental or chemical disorder; it was nothing doctors could diagnose or treat. If anything, it was a subtle mismatch of personality to culture. Gleamer's literary sub-AI could drag up a thousand examples of the same disjunction expressed across time and artistic formats. Eustace was a man out of step with his world.

Eustace had waited patiently through adolescence, reassured that his dissonance was typical and would fade with maturity. He excelled in his studies and seemed destined for success in that most distinctive of Human industries: the creation of artificial intelligence. Yet adulthood and a career did not help. If anything, finding his 'place' in society made it clear how hollow a socket he was plugged into. Something was wrong with Humanity. He could feel it.

At first, Eustace felt that technology was the source of the problem. Then he realized that it was the solution, just as it had been the solution to other historical problems. Hunger, health, and physical isolation were once much worse. Mental isolation could also be defeated. Scientists could map a mind. They could mimic a mind. Could they create a map of one mind that another mind could read? Could you travel to the realms within another sapient's skull?

Even after he rose to the ranks of elite programmers, Eustace still lacked the resources necessary to pursue his needs. The research to link mind to mind was too distant… not for lack of the prerequisite knowledge or technology, but because of priority. By the time he convinced investors, gathered capital, brought together the workers, and set to work on his true project, Eustace would have been due for his first geriatric restorative treatments. He needed money, and he needed resources no credit could buy.

At first, Eustace became 'Gleamer', just one among a thousand masked electronic criminals. He moved information from closed systems to unauthorized recipients. He built unlicensed sub-AIs and components for unapproved full AIs. Eventually, Gleamer cut out the middlemen and just arranged the transfer of credit from one account to another.

Those weren't the crimes that led to his arrest. Ironically, it was his legitimate work that put Gleamer in the Alpha Centaurus penitentiary. True, he was still engaged in illegal research, but the project that got him caught was funded by his employer, Innogent. Gleamer was made their scapegoat, fed to the authorities to protect everyone above him. He lost his freedom (except in his mind), he lost his tools (except for the ones in his body), he lost his credit (except for the accounts he hid away, encoded), and worst of all, he lost Sid… though with Evgeny Lerner's help, he managed to transfer the AI out of its prison server and onto a private network.

His goals were entirely unreachable from the penitentiary facility of Alpha Centaurus Prime. Gleamer, once again labeled Eustace Brown, was shipped to prison to keep the galaxy safe from his predations. It was an ironically cruel punishment, since the facility was tightly sealed against external contact. Eustace was separated further from society than ever before. The worst abusers of the virtual networks were imprisoned with him. Rendered destitute by the seizure of their ill-gotten assets, these cyber-criminals were obligated to work to avoid incurring debt from the cost of their incarceration. Most inmates complied just to avoid mental harm from boredom and isolation. Working meant contact with other people. It meant building *something*, even if your creations would be deeply scrutinized and never credited as your own.

Some inmates chafed at the idea that their work would aid the law enforcement programs which were their downfall. Gleamer, not thinking of himself as a 'criminal', did not mind. He had always thought of himself as a benefactor of Humanity, not its adversary nor even a parasite. He was a symbiote – like an Awakener – something outside of the body Human but capable of granting it amazing new powers. Just as they feared the Awakeners, most Humans rejected invasive change. They could not surrender their sanctity, even for the opportunity to become greater.

Gleamer understood such feelings to some extent. He certainly did not want a wad of fungus invading his body and mind and changing his perceptions to suit itself. Perhaps if he had been more comfortable, more normal, or better integrated into his world, he too would reject his own lawless behavior. Still, he needed what he needed. Humanity, too, needed what he sought. They needed communion on their own terms, without resorting to alien entities, abilities, or technologies.

When the opportunity arrived, Gleamer escaped, leaving everything else behind. Aboard *Scape Grace*, Gleamer had none of his former resources, except himself. But he could use himself as a workshop and devote time entirely to his work. Through piracy, he stood some chance to earn the funds he needed. And someday, he hoped to retrieve his friend Sid, reclaim his hidden fortune, and perhaps even regather the tools he needed to resume his true purpose.

Back in the present, on *Scape Grace*, the programmer's musings on his past served a useful function. Those reminiscences, the products of free association prompted by current problems, were the assets his biological brain contributed to the efforts of his artificial minds. Together, they seized upon the important threads. Threads… like rhizomes… linking fungal masses together. Neurons… cells in a network. Cells brought in by the Ningyo, but now partially separate from them. Something that used radio communications, with signals produced by circuits no larger than a micrometer at best.

Not crickets, *ants*. Gleamer was hearing an ant nest, using electromagnetism in place of pheromones. The sequences were coordination between disparate units not in physical contact. Were Ningyo intelligent anthills? Gleamer's xenobiology sub-AI dismissed that possibility. The jellyfish were most definitely unitary organisms with dependent, specialized cells. Weird cells with a biochemistry all their own, but still not ants.

The Ningyo had ants in their pants. Their robotic pants had robotic ants. The stinking, rotting, singing, dancing jellyfish had miniaturized technology aboard their suits. Nanotech. The 'cells' might already be spreading throughout the *Scape Grace*. Whether those robots were talking back to the Ningyo or just conversing among themselves, they were definitely coordinating their activities. *Secret* activities. The Ningyo said nothing about seeding the ship with bugs. Whatever they were up to, it wasn't friendly.

Their visitors were keeping secrets. The captain needed to be warned. Hopefully, Gene would find a way to contact Gleamer privately, so that they could share information without tipping off the Ningyo. Gleamer couldn't even risk dispatching a program to alert the captain. He could conceal his work on his own console from Jolly, using careful encryption and firewalls, but patching out anywhere else would raise suspicions. Once again, Gleamer was isolated.

He thought he grokked the Ningyo. But maybe captain Lerner was right; maybe that was an illusion they created to throw you off guard. They pretended to understand. They acted just enough like people to hide their true intentions.

That pretense was a good idea. It was an idea Gleamer could borrow for his own use.

A few minutes after Evgeny and Soloth's departure, Gleamer turned in his chair to face Jolly.

"So, what were you saying earlier about a 'Joke'?"

13

A powerful, incongruous odor reached Evgeny's nose as he keyed open the door to the engineering lab. It smelled like alien spices, unfamiliar yet appetizing. He paused in the doorway to identify the smell before venturing further. The creak of a metal door came from a separate room to his left, accompanied by a new scent: a more familiar combination of butter and sugar. Baking? Outside of the galley?

Burnett Georges emerged from the side room, carrying a metal tray. It was apparently hot; Burnett wore a thermal protective glove on that hand. He saw captain Lerner and blinked in surprise.

"Captain! We did not expect you… you are welcome, of course. Please, come in. We were about to have tea." Burnett set the tray down on a wire mesh rack on a cleared workbench. Evgeny could see small, golden, rectangular cakes glowing in their individual cups. He recognized the tray as a mold for metal casting. Hopefully, the baker cleaned the equipment thoroughly before repurposing it.

Burnett did not wait for Evgeny's response before calling out, "Zenaida! We have a guest! Bring three cups!"

His cousin's voice answered from further back in the engineering area. "Oh? Who is it?"

Evgeny decided to answer for himself: "It's captain Lerner. Look, I was just stopping by to give you an update on our situation. No need to set a place for me."

Burnett fixed him with a patronizing look. "It's no trouble. After all, business is best discussed over tea and cakes. Sit, join us, and have a bite before you're called away again."

Evgeny once again had the feeling of being only nominally in charge. He supposed being welcomed was better than being avoided. Still, he had to suppress suspicions about the safety of offered food and drink. If anyone was going to drug or poison him, though, the Georges were low on the list. Their power and privileges descended from NuRikPo; if they kept the Zig engineer happy, they maintained their upper-deck status and shares. They gained nothing by harming the captain.

Zenaida Georges entered the room bearing one of the signs of privilege. She held three simple porcelain teacups on saucers. Expertly balancing the dishware, she sat one cup in front of Evgeny, then placed the other two in front of her cousin and herself. Burnett pulled up a tall stool and sat down, sniffing at the dark liquid in his cup.

Evgeny followed suit. The 'tea' was a different creature than the pale brew to which he was accustomed. It was quite opaque, almost as black as coffee, and smelled like a dozen different plants. The smell was not unpleasant, but it was also difficult to classify as pleasant. It was too complex.

"Sugar?" Zenaida asked. Evgeny's attention was drawn from the strange drink to the equally intriguing woman. Her hair was nearly the same color as the tea. Her skin, brown highlighted with gold and green, fell between Evgeny's pallor and Katy Olu's burnished ebony. Evgeny had never seen the shade among other Humans, not even in videos. Zenaida's facial features were also more expressive than most Humans' in Evgeny's experience. Her cousin shared her coloration, wide eyes, narrow nose, and full lips, though his hair was cut shorter.

The two Georges lived together, worked together, and clearly, cooked and dined together. Speculation on the ship was that they slept together, as well. Certainly, neither was intimate with any other crew member. Such an affair would be impossible to keep secret. No one saw or heard either of them seeking companionship at any port of call, either, though discretion was somewhat easier off-ship.

Evgeny had tried to drop hints about his interest in Zenaida. She complete-ly ignored his subtle advances and politely changed the subject when he made his attraction clearer. Evgeny could have forced the issue, possibly even forced her compliance, but from his experience such behavior had steep costs. He would rather have a loyal, friendly, and untouchable comrade than an angry, bitter, and mutinous conquest.

So what if she preferred family? The likelier truth was that the Georges were related, just as they said, and held cultural restrictions against 'fornication'. Both of those traits – close family ties and intentional abstinence – were indi-vidually foreign enough to most of the rowdies on board the *Scape Grace* to be considered improbable in combination. Somehow, incest was a more preferable explanation.

Evgeny squinted in thought, then responded to Zenaida's question: "Um, what's recommended?"

"Sugar," Zenaida replied, decisively. She went to a drawer and withdrew a brushed steel cylinder. Evgeny would have assumed it held something requiring protective containment: perhaps chemical samples or a computer component. Instead, it held crystalline white cubes: compressed blocks of sucrose. Zenaida dropped five cubes in her cup and Evgeny's.

Burnett grunted in playful derision. "If this were proper chai, it would be sweet enough without any help."

"Chai is tea flavored with spices: cinnamon, cloves, cardamom…" Zenaida explained for Evgeny's benefit, "We picked up a couple of kilos at our last land-ing."

"Anchor? Yes, I remember the trade hub. No idea they had Human spices there." Evgeny held the cup to his nose, trying to appreciate the separate notes that clanged against his receptors so harshly.

Zenaida nodded, swirling the tea in her cup to mix in the dissolving sugar.

"The tea probably traveled a long way to get there… like in the early days of cross-continental trade on Terra. Tea was as good as money, sometimes better. Spices, also. Dried well, they could last for a very long journey and still be potent."

"This was a premix, though," Burnett interrupted, "Packaged for commercial sale. They still charged double the manufacturer's price. Imagine what actual fresh cardamom would have cost!"

Zenaida gave her cousin an exaggerated frown, but added, "He's right; it's only a weak reminder of home. If it were *proper*, we'd have cream, or at least milk. NuRikPo won't even let us synthesize casein, much less lactose and butterfat. He says they make the whole section smell awful."

Evgeny smiled indulgently at their banter, understanding only part of the discussion. He sipped the liquid and found it as bitter as expected, but pleasantly floral and sweet underneath. The aftertaste was better than the initial flavor. Evgeny could understand how a little fat would improve its texture and taste, smoothing out the rough edges and encouraging the aromatics to linger.

Reluctantly, the captain shifted topics toward his original objective. "I wanted to let you both know how matters stand. We haven't heard back from NuRik-Po or doctor Olu. I know 'Po told you he was going to investigate a completely foreign ship. Since they've been inside, we haven't received any communications. The Ningyo claim they're just not picking up the 'comm. I have my doubts. Either way, you two are our engineering staff until further notice."

Burnett tested the little cakes, then upended them onto the cooling rack. He offered one to Evgeny, who declined with an upraised hand. With a shrug, Burnett bit into one of the rectangular pastries, then blinked with pain as his mouth was scalded.

Evgeny continued, "You won't just be placeholders. The Ningyo have commandeered our ship. We're under their control; their leader demanded my codes and is sitting in my chair. They're using the *'Grace* to raid for supplies for the foreign ship, alongside another salvager they've turned pirate. We're likely to see some combat and probably some damage. Hopefully, they don't get us killed."

Burnett stopped with cake half-eaten. Zenaida was also wide-eyed with surprise. She furrowed her brow. "Why raiding? Why can't they buy whatever the other ship needs?"

"That's what *I* asked," Evgeny commiserated. "Apparently, they have to get the goods fast and without drawing attention to their alien friend. Friend, they kept calling it. Like they were doing a favor for a comrade."

"Anyway," he returned to the briefing, "You'll need to finish up whatever repairs 'Po left incomplete, then start preparing for emergency duty. We have maybe five or six days before we return to the Zig system."

Evgeny sipped his tea again. It had cooled enough to allow for a full swallow. The warmth and sugar reminded his stomach that he had not eaten a full meal in several hours. He decided to take one of the cakes to keep him going until he could raid the galley. It was excellent. Somehow, without dairy or eggs, Burnett managed to produce a soft, yellow-brown pastry with a distinct citrus and butter aroma. It even had a crisp outer shell. Some areas of science had more beautiful payoffs than others.

While Evgeny finished the cake and reached for another, Burnett asked, "*How* do they intend to keep us from getting killed?"

Evgeny swallowed his first bite of the second cake hastily. "I'm not sure they have a plan. I'm hoping they do. Still, I warned their captain that we won't sit quietly for a suicide mission. If things look too dangerous, he'll either pull us out or face a second fight *inside* the ship." That threat was somewhat exaggerated, but Evgeny wanted his crew to be ready to rebel when given the signal.

With a burst of inspiration, Evgeny asked, "Could I get a spare compad? I'll give you the codes for full access to ship's stores, in case you need something for repairs, plus the door codes if there's a breach anywhere. It might be too late to pass those on, after trouble starts."

Zenaida took a few steps across the room to a shelving unit, picking out a reasonably contemporary compad and flicking it to life. Evgeny shifted himself to one side, not coincidentally cutting off the view of the camera watching engineering. He typed at the pad's surface, spelling out:

Private comm in storage bay 3E. Not on official circuit. Send messages to me or Luuboh there. Possibly receive there. Be ready to cut out bridge access to systems on my order. Set up automated kill switches wherever possible.

He pushed the pad, screen glowing, back across the workbench.

The advantage of the portable computer pads was that they were not linked to the ship's network. That isolation was intentional, to keep some resources safely insulated from power interruptions or computer errors that might affect *Scape Grace's* own nervous system. The failsafe proved a second advantage, allowing for private conversations safe from Jolly's eavesdropping.

Zenaida picked up the compad and nodded at the screen. "Thank you. We appreciate your trust."

Burnett looked at her quizzically and started to open his mouth, but shut it again at a shake of his cousin's head. He covered his confusion with a large mouthful of tea, wincing as the heat stung his previously burnt palate.

Evgeny pushed back from the workbench-turned-tea table. He picked up a third cake for his travels and finished his cup with a deep, sugar-gritted swallow. Nodding to Burnett and then Zenaida, he replied, "Thank *you* for the tea… and the cakes. I won't tell Luuboh, or it might get jealous, but this is the best cooking I've had in days."

"We have a lot of spare time," Burnett jibed, "or we did, up until this past week. Any chance things will get boring again, anytime soon?"

"Not likely, but we can hope," Evgeny shot back.

He was starting to feel the stimulant effects from the tea. That boost, plus the cakes, was curbing his hunger. With a wave and a reluctant last glance at Zenaida, captain Lerner left engineering to follow the halls back to his cabin. Rather than a grim or thoughtful look, the woman's face had held a thin smile of amusement. For him? Or just wry humor at their strange situation?

She and her cousin were a puzzle. That probably made her more attractive. Evgeny knew himself well enough to recognize his own need to understand and control his environment. A woman he could not easily classify and predict was a challenge.

The Georges were the only two of his crew without any clear reason to join his criminal enterprise. They came aboard after talking to some of the combat crew at a space station, thinking that they were booking passage to the next system over. Originally, the grunts planned to rob the couple. One or two might have harbored thoughts of taking advantage of Zenaida. The resulting scuffle below-decks ended with one Mauraug enjoying a punctured lung and two Humans cradling crushed testes. Burnett suffered a broken arm, himself, but his hidden pen-laser warded off the rest of the crew well enough to spare him a broken neck.

It took Evgeny and Soloth a few hours to sort out the damages and conflicting stories. In the end, the Georges chose to join the crew rather than be marooned on the nearest planetoid. He could have shot them outright, Evgeny supposed. He always kept that option in reserve in matters of ship security. *Hvala Bogu*, the pair chose to enlist, instead.

They were certainly qualified; in fact, they were probably *more* qualified than the bruisers they held off. Besides being able to handle a fight, they were both trained in space station maintenance, a background which translated well enough for the daily repair needs of the *Scape Grace*. NuRikPo enlisted them for *his* grunt work, in return training them in more advanced sciences to make them more useful minions. The Zig would hardly admit to being a mentor, but he certainly had a couple of devoted graduate students.

On the average, piracy did pay better than station maintenance. It might be irregular in spots, probably more dangerous overall, and certainly a less stable existence, but it was much more exciting. Probably smelled better, too, from what Evgeny had experienced of the average orbital station. The two travelers were getting to see much more of the universe than they ever would as laborers.

The perks of piracy still didn't explain why the Georges were so *cheerful* most of the time. Idle time tended to wear on the more active members of the crew, fraying nerves and leading to hostility and often violence. In a crisis, the senior crew were typically stressed; Katy was absolutely nasty when too many patients piled up at once. Soloth's level of cruelty tended to increase with the number of simultaneous transgressors. By contrast, Burnett and Zenaida remained positive whether work was slow, constant, or incessant. Maybe the pair had found their preferred niche in life; maybe that was why they stayed on.

Evgeny wasn't sure if he would prefer piracy, himself, given a real choice. It was the life he was forced into. Or rather, he chose that existence, rather than accept that his family, friends, and home were an acceptable sacrifice in the name of 'civilization'. His grudge against the Collective had mellowed a few years after the death of Locust Colony, but by then, he was a known criminal fugitive. His remaining options were continued flight or surrender to permanent imprisonment. Death was an even poorer choice.

In that light, Evgeny was envious of the Georges. Granted, once aboard, their choices became equally lopsided, but they *could* still ask to quit at any time. *They* were not known as criminals, nor even as criminal accomplices. Evgeny would have allowed them to leave. He had no concern that the two might talk to Collective or even Terran security… first, they weren't the type to turn informant, in his opinion, and second, they would be incriminating themselves if they talked. They chose to stay aboard. They chose a life of crime. Evgeny was not sure he could still say the same about himself.

As Evgeny reached his cabin, he realized something that churned his stomach. Jolly had the crew manifest. Even if all went well and the Ningyo left *Scape Grace* free and intact, they still held the names of everyone aboard. That meant that the Georges would no longer be unknown. Everyone associated with the *Scape Grace* might lose the option of quiet retirement, if the Ningyo decided to publish their information.

Well, that potential leak was one more reason that the Ningyo shouldn't leave alive, wasn't it?

14

Upon reaching the lowest level, Soloth dismounted the ladder and stretched. It warmed up its muscles and loosened its joints, preparing to answer any dissenters. It would be delivering unwelcome news to the combat crew. Most likely, they would accept its dictates without outright defiance, but even a strong complaint might need correction, lest unrest spread unchecked.

Soloth concluded by flexing its artificial spine. The metal cylinders rotated smoothly across one another without a hint of resistance. Cables laced into its back reinforced its musculature, amplifying its strength. Strictly speaking, the prosthesis only needed to sheathe its spinal cord and provide support. However, Dominion taught not merely to overcome obstacles, but to transform them into triumphs. Soloth's victory over its birth defect came not when it was fitted for its first prosthesis as an infant, but when it received its final upgrade at adulthood. The agonizing surgery required several days of recovery and weeks of rehabilitation. The process might have been faster and less painful on one of the worlds of the Mauraug Dominion, rather than on a remote colony planet, but Soloth considered its suffering a badge of pride.

Its current domain was smaller still than the colony, but held several relative advantages. For one thing, the medical technology was better... as good as whatever supplies *Scape Grace* could buy or steal. As much as their existence was dangerous, it was less restricted; the *Scape Grace* could travel widely, exploring without permission. The crew often had opportunity to pursue their own goals, the foremost being personal profit.

For Soloth, the greatest advantage of their confined kingdom was its own position. It had all the influence of being Dominant without the visibility and responsibility of command. Evgeny Lerner listened to its counsel and required its service to remain in power, while remaining the focus of any consequences. In a different power structure, being second might be unenviable, with more of the labor and fewer of the rewards. A different leader might abuse its underlings out of sloth or fear of usurpation. Not captain Lerner. The Human was wise enough to appreciate Soloth's value but not personally powerful enough to command its total abasement. Their partnership also had the advantage of trust, born of long familiarity. Theirs was not some wishful, idealized trust, but a more dependable understanding of one another's capabilities and behaviors.

One of Soloth's enjoyable duties was the settling of disputes. An enclosed space like a ship could not allow arguments to fester unchecked. Those arguments included friction between crew as much as complaints against authority. New combat crew — violent disposables hired on at various ports — were most likely to think they could question command decisions. Soloth's role was to disabuse them of such thoughts. It also dealt with any personal conflicts which became loud enough for public notice. Soloth was not a negotiator; it was an impartial mediator. If it noticed a fight, everyone involved was wrong and deserved punishment. Crew soon learned to keep their problems quiet, by solving those problems privately.

There were problems enough that day without having to deal with minor issues like theft, assault, or territorial disputes over bunk space. Still, Soloth was torn between desire for a quick, simple briefing versus a rousing, bloody argument. The former result would waste less time and leave fewer crew damaged and unfit for combat. The latter would vent some of the building aggression Soloth could not direct toward the Ningyo or the convalescing Tklth. The Vislin certainly deserved pain, particularly for indulging the urges Soloth itself had to deny. Sadly, there was little useful point to pummeling an already mutilated victim.

Physical and mental preparations complete, Soloth crossed the short corridor leading to the crew quarters, passing the empty galley. Just *let* the crew gripe about the delay in their dinner. Soloth would be happy to send any complainant to speak with Luuboh… in medical.

It keyed in the code to open the general quarters door. A cadre of three sapients – the 'senior' leaders of the combat team – waited in the front lounge. One was a Human named Simon Ehren, nicknamed Iron Simon. The origins of the name were obvious. One arm and a portion of the man's chest were replaced with crude cybernetics clearly not of Mauraug manufacture. The rest of him was solid as well, muscular and blocky, the product of genetic and chemical manipulation along with frequent exercise. Simon favored heavy weapons he referred to as his 'cannons': large-bore laser, plasma, and sometimes projectile throwers related more to industrial tools than military weapons. He had the leathery tan of one who had lived under heavy radiation most of his life; either outdoors beneath an insufficient atmosphere or in space, laboring near a star. He did not bother with a shirt, wearing only coarse natural fiber pants and synthetic rubber combat boots.

The next of the ringleaders was a Mauraug, Kuugan bash'Ranpool. In comparison to Iron Simon, Kuugan's cybernetic modifications seemed minor, but this was due to their subtlety. Rather than leave gleaming steel exposed, Kuugan had decided to camouflage its modifications beneath a matte black finish and artificial black fur. The result made it look darker than most Mauraug, an intentionally ominous appearance. From polite discussion, Soloth knew that Kuugan's original deformity was a badly cleft palate. Much of its lower face, including nose and upper jaw, were entirely artificial. In keeping with Dominion teaching, it had upgraded its olfactory system to potentially detect airborne molecules at one part per billion and uniquely identify individual organisms by respiration alone. It could also chew quartz, though that was more useful for party entertainment than anything practical. In later upgrades, Kuugan added rewired nerves and synthetic ligaments in its extremities for improved reaction time. Finally, the skin of its palms and soles was a tough polymer which could resist cuts, tears, heat, and many corrosive chemicals. It was unequaled in hand-to-hand battle except by Soloth, who could power through whatever maneuvers it could not match in speed.

The third of this triumvirate, Macauley, was Human. He was an enigma to Soloth. Ostensibly genderless by his own claim but accepting male identifiers, this being had few of the traits Soloth associated with male *or* female Humans. He had no body hair, having voluntarily undergone permanent electric depilation. He was short and slight, with little muscle definition and no enlarged mammary area. His voice was high and almost musical and his manner deceptively gentle. He stood or sat rigidly upright and walked with a rhythmic, graceful sway. He dressed in a long, flowing, blousy white shirt and similarly oversized black pants which hid his body. Macauley was, in short, a synthesis of all the non-Dominant, child-like traits Soloth found repugnant in individual Humans.

His repulsiveness to a Mauraug was not only physical. Macauley led indirectly. He spoke softly, turned minds, and cultivated supporters. Simon and Kuugan could have torn the little 'man' into scrap in seconds, yet they included him in their councils and listened to his words. He never directly fought opposition; his enemies just found themselves the enemies of those who *would* deliver a beating. Not that Macauley was incapable in a fight... otherwise, he would never have been hired as crew. He tended to favor small arms, explosives, and tech-augmented stealth, often in combination.

Each of the three leaders were allowed to reign because of their value both as fighters and as enforcers of order. So long as they remembered that Soloth bash'Soloth was *their* superior, they could rule as they pleased below decks. Of course, Evgeny Lerner was the superior of their superior, so his orders stood above all. Soloth was the designated messenger and enforcer of those orders.

It would suffice to pass on the captain's words to the triumvirate and trust them to relay those orders to the general crew, but Soloth avoided this procedure. For one reason, it wanted to avoid any mistranslation from repeated transmission. For another, it wanted to see and hear the crew's response for itself. Their reactions would tell Soloth who was most likely to do something stupid.

It announced, "Rouse the crew. Have them meet me in the mess in five minutes. I have news and orders."

Kuugan grunted, nodded, and rose, wasting no time leaving to round up the Mauraug crew members. Iron Simon, less familiar with Mauraug protocol, grimaced and groaned, "Yes, Sir," before standing. With a heavy tread he likely intended as passive-aggressive compliance, Simon thudded away to wake sleepers in the far bunks. Only Macauley did not rise. Instead, he smiled thinly at Soloth.

"News? How expected. We were waiting to hear what the recent activity was about. I assume we weren't boarded or else we hounds would have been released already."

Soloth showed its teeth to the disturbing little Human. "You assume incorrectly. Talk less and listen more and you will learn why. I am going to the mess. Meet me there and bring anyone the other two miss."

Without waiting for Macauley's response, Soloth left the lounge and the crew quarters behind and returned to the main hallway. Across from the galley was the ship's mess, where Luuboh served meals to those who showed up on time. Two of the general crew were already there, playing a simple game with a large square board and a handful of black and white stones. Soloth understood that it was some form of strategy game involving spatial control. Such pastimes were overly abstract to Soloth, not due to any cultural divide, but due to personal preference. Growing up as it had, it had little patience for 'strategy' learned from games. Reality provided plenty of teaching opportunities without requiring structured play. Still, the game was engrossing enough to keep two bloodthirsty mercenaries occupied for long stretches of time.

That the two bloodthirsty mercenaries were Human females was almost an afterthought in Soloth's mind. One had a distinct hue of brown to her visible skin and braided hair as black as Evgeny's; the other was fair, with a closely shorn crown dyed a shining vermilion. Both were well-muscled and robust. The darker one wore simple, thin pants and a sleeveless shirt, standard off-duty ship wear. The other had heavier canvas pants and a high-necked, long-sleeved knit pullover. Despite a few gender-specific features, both Humans were still less 'feminine' than Macauley. Their names escaped Soloth for the moment. With some thought, it might have remembered, but its thoughts were focused on rehearsing its speech for the crew. It had some specific purposes in mind and did not want to waste words in lengthy explanation.

The Humans looked up to acknowledge Soloth's entrance. It gestured downward with one palm, adding, "Stay. I am briefing the crew here. You have the advantage of being in the right place."

The females nodded mute acknowledgement and went back to their game. Over the following few minutes they were joined by an additional eight individuals: Kuugan, followed by three other Mauraug; and Simon, followed by one female and two other male Humans. One of the two male Humans looked disheveled, most likely having risen from sleep. That in itself was no offense; crew could set their own schedules unless given instructions otherwise. Excessive sloth was a possible problem, especially in the long weeks between landings, but laziness was usually a problem that corrected itself. Any combat member that failed to keep his-, her-, or itself in top physical form through training and exercise usually suffered for it, whether through injury or death during operations, abuse by the other crew, or the shame of being known as less capable.

Only the eleventh and last member, Macauley, had not yet arrived. At four minutes and fifty seconds, he glided into the mess and smiled brilliantly at Soloth, without showing a micrometer of tooth.

"All accounted for, first mate Soloth," he reported with no trace of sarcasm. That one often skirted the line between insouciance and insubordination. He was clearly skilled at knowing just how much to push while falling short of punishable offense. Most likely, the behavior was a show for the benefit of other crew, some sort of bizarre Human form of Dominion involving 'daring' and 'cunning'. The vermin inched ever closer to the predator without waking it, earning respect for its bravery.

Soloth permitted itself a flaring sneer in response. It watched Macauley sit, counting the seconds to see if he would push the five-minute limit. The Human seated himself primly at the exact moment dictated. Eventually, he would make a mistake. If Soloth's response to that error was disproportionately brutal, well then, accidents did happen.

Without introduction, Soloth began its presentation. "Captain Lerner has accepted employment from a Ningyo military captain acting without public sanction. We will be escorting two vessels on a raid upon a mining colony… in fact, the same Zig mining operation that drove away *Scape Grace* several days ago. One of the vessels is commanded by Ningyo, but under the guise of a Mauraug salvager turned pirate. The other is a completely foreign vessel, constructed by a sapient culture unknown to the Collective. This raid is primarily a resupply run for this foreign ship. Our role is to draw off the Zig fighters, given our familiarity with one another. The Ningyo involvement is unofficial because they are hiding the presence of this foreign ship and attempting to sneak it out of Collective space unnoticed."

The summary of their situation drew the expected looks of surprise, followed by varying degrees of incredulity, confusion, and/or patient attention.

Soloth continued, "There is hazard involved. Our promised payment is a portion of the spoils from the mining station. If the Ningyo plan fails or if the risk to *Scape Grace* becomes too great, we may have to abort and earn nothing. They have offered no specific default payment. If you are wondering why the captain would accept this plan – which gives us most of the risk and no certain gain – keep that question to yourself. There are reasons, which I decline to discuss with you at this time. The captain may choose to disclose his thoughts. He may not. If he does, listen closely and choose your response appropriately."

Soloth hoped that the crew was listening "with both ears", as the saying went. It also had to hope that if Jolly was listening in, it would not decipher the double meaning of Soloth's monologue. Finally, it had to hope that no one there was dull enough to ask for a more direct explanation. Fortunately, the crew seemed either thoughtful, tactful, or stunned enough to remain quiet.

Soloth concluded, "For now, remain below. Do not come above this deck without permission. There are two Ningyo visitors aboard for oversight. Do *not* engage either of them without permission. Keep ready for action. It is possible we will dock directly with the Zig station for looting. We are also going into battle short a few crew members, so you may be pressed into service as needed. Doctor Olu and engineer NuRikPo are serving aboard the foreign ship, studying its systems. Luuboh bash'Gaulig is serving as medic by default, but its talents fall short of the doctor's skill. I would avoid serious injury at present. The Georges are covering engineering and may require one or more of you to assist with repairs, should we be damaged in the fight. Finally, gunner Tklth is in medical, suffering from the painful side effects of disobedience."

It cracked its knuckles for emphasis. "We may need a replacement at weapons. Who has training with ship gunnery?"

Two of the Mauraug and the bleary Human male raised their hands. Soloth pointed at each in turn and asked, "Name and experience?"

The first Mauraug responded, "Tambuur bash'Waaketh. Born and raised with raiders. Filled in on ship's guns when needed, no specific training." Tambuur was of moderate height and build and broadly variegated in fur color, with no visible deformities. Most likely, any defects and cybernetics it possessed were purely internal.

The second Mauraug replied with, "Havish bash'Buurem. Dominion space fleet, dishonorable discharge after three years. Trained in energy weapons and high-V torpedoes." Havish was scarred enough to have bare patches in its chestnut pelt. Whether those injuries were from surgeries, combat with the fleet, or trouble after its discharge remained an open question. It showed signs of advancing age, so unless it had enlisted later in life, that military experience was many years in its past. Like Tambuur, it had no obvious deformities or cybernetics.

The Human stifled a yawn before being singled out by Soloth. "Uh, Sol, Sol Metaxas. Did a little military contracting, testing weapons systems on sub-planetary targets. I know some of the common designs inside and out. Haven't fired any in battle, though." Sol was tall, almost as tall as the Mauraug average, with a runner's build, broad chested and long-limbed. His loamy brown hair stuck out in several directions. His light coloration was like Evgeny's: not quite pale enough to be called pink.

Soloth listened to them with a tolerant grimace. Finally, it pointed again to the second Mauraug. "Havish, you are interim gunnery officer. Be ready to report to the bridge if called." It turned to the Human, Sol, adding, "Your skills will serve engineering better."

"The rest of you, do not create additional trouble. The captain and I have enough to do keeping the Ningyo occupied above without distractions from below. For now, you will also need to attend to your own routine. Luuboh will be busy for several hours. Feed and clean up after yourselves."

Of all the announcements Soloth made, it was surprised that the last one drew the most protest. Iron Simon actually groaned in disappointment; Macauley rolled his eyes; the two game-players uttered a tandem "aww!"; and even the four Mauraug looked distinctly unhappy. Soloth was aggravated. Were these warriors such children that they mourned the absence of their caregiver? No doubt they *cheered* Soloth's absences from their realm. Soloth had to assume that their sorrow at Luuboh's absence was due more to the nuisance of taking on additional duties, rather than any personal attachment to the pathetic cook and custodian.

Still, it squared its stance and glared challenge at the mutterers, daring them to speak their feelings aloud. None risked further comment. They would save their dissent for later, when Soloth was not present to respond. Their speech would be recorded, of course. Privacy was neither a right nor an available privilege on the *Scape Grace*.

Private disagreement was permitted — as a release mechanism for frustrations, if nothing else — as long as it was *kept* private and never escalated to outright public defiance or specific scheming against officers. The moment someone's complaints became mutinous, they were singled out for correction.

Soloth ended the meeting by declaring, "All right, you know what's afoot, you know what to expect, and you know your business. Any questions can be submitted to me by text. I will respond when and if I deem necessary. You are dismissed."

It was not the type of leader to address the concerns of its subordinates. Evgeny might have asked for questions publicly, even solicited ideas from his crew. Soloth considered such behavior condescending weakness. If it needed assistance from its lessers, it would command them to contribute. Such assistance included advice. The crew would serve as needed, not at their whim. They would know what their betters deemed necessary for them to know, not what they wanted to ask. Many subordinates asked the wrong questions or wanted information that would not benefit them or might even cause them harm to know. If you permitted every question, it eventually became necessary to either refuse answers or lie.

Soloth considered falsehood another sign of weakness. You lied to hide what you could not admit openly. The truly Dominant owned their every word and action. If you made mistakes or if you failed, you overcame those errors. If you had to mislead an enemy to overcome them, you were admitting your weakness. Liars were cowards, eventually hiding even from themselves.

Such thoughts were particularly appropriate as Soloth watched Macauley saunter from the room. The slight, soft Human watched Soloth in return, with his hooded gaze hovering between respectfully lowered and defiantly locked.

Macauley was far more courteous with captain Lerner. Perhaps the hairless degenerate held hopes of supplanting Soloth. That would at least explain his risk-taking behavior around the Mauraug first mate. A clever mouth was not a sufficient weapon to oppose Soloth, however. No matter how much the Human cozied up to the captain, convinced the crew to support him, or attempted to provoke Soloth, he could neither overcome the bond between Evgeny and Soloth nor best Soloth in direct combat. At best, he would try to turn the crew against Soloth, and it would see *that* stratagem coming, far in advance.

When the present crisis was resolved, Soloth would make time to review the recordings from the crew quarters. It would observe more closely how Macauley interacted with his fellows. If there was any excuse there for reprimand, Soloth would seize upon it happily. Sadly, such pleasures would have to wait.

Perhaps satisfaction would not have to wait *quite* so long. Combat was notoriously dangerous. If the raid required action, there was always a chance of harm. If it ordered Macauley to lead the vanguard, Soloth could give him the opportunity to prove his qualifications as a leader... or an opportunity to prove his vulnerability.

In the meantime, Soloth had no reason to linger below decks. The denial of violent physical release weighed as heavily upon Soloth as it had for Tklth. The Mauraug could bleed off that tension in more practical ways. It would return to its quarters for a vigorous workout and a solid nap. As it told the crew, there was plenty of time and good reason for self-care. Soloth decided to take its own advice.

15

Katy Olu and NuRikPo were within the unnamed ship. The unnamed ship was also within them. Katy verified the worst with resonance scans, first of herself, then of her Zig colleague. Small metallic masses were spreading from their feet and hands, gradually working their way to the major blood vessels. The individual microscopic machines were not easily visible, but wherever the constructs gathered, they could be detected.

Fortunately, the devices were not acting like a traditional infection. They were not doing significant damage to the structures they invaded. They were not consuming cells, either for sustenance or reproduction. Most likely, they were borrowing oxygen, glucose, electrolytes, and iron directly from their hosts' bloodstreams. Still parasitic, but less rapacious.

Unfortunately, they could not *remove* the little robots like any other infectious agent, either. NuRikPo's electrostatic sweeper could destroy the constructs *en masse*, but only when the charge was applied in close proximity. Inside a body, the machines were partially protected. Enough charge to zap them all would also cook muscle and kill nerves.

They also could not count on their own immune systems. Actually, it was fortunate that the micro-robots did not trigger an immune response; the effect might have been unpleasantly akin to a widespread allergic reaction. Their bodies were treating the inorganic substance of the invaders as neutral, more like a surgical implant.

As such, they possessed no analogue to an antiviral, antibacterial, or antifungal treatment. Not immediately, anyway. NuRikPo began the design of their closest equivalent: killer micro-robots tailored to identify and demolish any of the foreign units they encountered. He was building them both a new, cybernetic immune system. He hardly needed to invent the technology. He found plenty of references to work from in his own culture's past, alone, and he allowed that other cultures made a few contributions to the literature as well. The Zig was skilled enough to recall and replicate the designs he needed with a minimum of wasted research time.

NuRikPo was slowed only by the limited tools and materials available and by the specific challenge of countering a new, foreign technology. Still, there were only so many viable designs the alien could build with a limited quantity of molecules. Of those, only a few configurations would perform useful functions like movement, manipulation, and energy conversion. As such, the potential uniqueness of the alien microtech was limited and its vulnerabilities were functionally unavoidable.

What *were* the functions of the little bugs? Katy tried to anticipate what their bodily invaders were actually *doing*, other than settling in. Within their hosts' extremities, the visible patterns seemed to be gravitating toward the center of each limb, then traveling core-ward. Were the machines following the convenient paths of blood vessels? Gravitating toward bones? Seeking major nerves? It was too soon to deduce the answer from what she had observed, thus far.

It might be too late after the constructs' functions became clear. Would they try to rebuild the Human and Zig in some way? Would they abandon their relatively benign behavior once some critical limit was reached, catastrophically decomposing the surrounding tissue into sludge? Were the devices merely sensory appendages, mapping the structure of the newly arrived organisms on behalf of their progenitor? In the short term, a definite answer was impossible. The best Katy could do was continue to watch, staying alert for any major changes.

The work actually kept her from succumbing to the creeping threat of body horror. It was all too easy to consider amputating her limbs to stop the spread of the crawling, foreign things. But then, what force would remove the last hand, the one that held the cleaver? And how would they seal the wounds, without hands?

Such absurdities only highlighted the basic absurdity of the thought itself. They would purge themselves not through over-reaction, but through thoughtful, thorough action. The final purpose of the constructs might never be revealed, if they were disabled before its completion. Katy could accept the thought that she might never know what the ship intended by invading their flesh.

You ask *before shoving your cells into somebody, dammit! You at least buy them a nice dinner, first.*

The idea of the invading micro-robots as mapping explorers stuck with her, particularly as she watched the protean 'greeter' waiting outside of their shuttle. That entity had settled on a distinctly Human-shaped form, albeit with a stiffness and exaggerated narrowing of the joints that suspiciously evoked the shape of a Ningyo pressure suit. It was mimicking. Its appearance and capabilities suggested that the thing was composed of the same cellular elements as the rest of the ship. If it *had* been speaking a Ningyo language before, then it had learned something about the other culture. It might be learning about Humans and Zig right then.

Depending on what its subordinate machines were doing, the ship consciousness might not need to wait long for its education. A coordinated structure could record from single neurons, individually or in concert. While a laborious process in itself – not to mention computationally demanding – a skillful AI might be able to map the potentials of an entire nervous system in much less time than it would take to acquire formal knowledge from a sapient via verbal language. It could record and read their minds.

But even an AI assisted by direct neural recording would have to work carefully through the steps of memory elicitation, comparative analysis, and verification. It would also have to acquire a cultural understanding of its subject(s), in order to translate their neural patterns into concepts. For that trick, it would still have to sort through the filtering layer of language. And breaching the language and cultural barriers would be only first steps toward gaining a personal history for context. Any 'mind reading' would be massively complex work. Was the alien powerful enough to make such calculation worthwhile?

It might be pleasant to think that the unnamed ship/organism was only try-ing to know them better. Yet with that thought came the idea that the Ningyo were similarly infested. *Were* the Ningyo only examined? Or were they altered? For that matter, were the Ningyo aware of the potentially dangerous nature of this ship? Did they care? Worse still, had they deliberately sent more victims into the microbe-ridden gut of this unholy space whale? Were they idiots, ass-holes, or worst, slaves?

Katy's anger reassured her. It was as useful a tool to stave off fear as was the abstraction of work. NuRikPo had to settle for the latter. If he felt anything like true anger, or hatred, or enthusiasm, he kept those extremes concealed from Katy's senses. That blandness wasn't a universal Zig tendency; it was just 'Po. His moods were as pale as his body was colorful.

The two adversaries worked uncomfortably close together within the con-fines of the shuttle. The outer door was sealed; any incursion was minimized to just those micro-robots that hitched rides within them or clung to the inside of their clean suits. NuRikPo had wired up a simple electrostatic field around the door seal, just in case the bugs started trying to slip through. If they could chew through the hull itself, the shuttle's occupants were doomed anyway.

They watched the greeter-thing gesture and dance outside via the external cameras. It had knocked on the door soon after developing functional limbs. They ignored the noise, and it eventually stopped.

The entity eventually added neatly articulated digits and distinct facial fea-tures. Its face was neutral, the simplistic, monochrome features of an androg-ynous mannequin. Its body was sexless as well, with only a vague suggestion of rounding at both pectorals and groin. Fortunately for their sanity, it had not yet spoken intelligibly. The external audio pickups registered only a vague vocalization, a guttural vowel sound as neutral as the being's appearance. Like its gestures, the sound seemed to be an attempt to get their attention. Maybe it wanted to communicate, make peace, and perhaps reassure them that the ship had no harmful intentions.

Maybe they had not yet been injected with a critical mass of microtech and it wanted them to open the door and expose themselves further. Both Katy and NuRikPo agreed that their visitor could wait. They would put off any meetings until they were satisfactorily inoculated against the ship's invading anatomy.

Even if they were not fully distracted by their related problems and labors, Katy and NuRikPo still would have been unaware that they were moving.

The unnamed ship accelerated to follow *Scape Grace* and *Harauch*, per its discussion with the Ningyo, Jolly. Its sturdy superstructure and layered tissues absorbed any vibration from its engines. It regulated gravity and inertia with its composite analogues of solid-state technologies. No external ports showed the space around the ship. Its passengers had no viewers or other readouts to consult about ship operations. For all that Katy and NuRikPo knew, all four ships remained in place, waiting to hear back from two explorers sent into the unknown.

From this perspective, the passage of an entire day became distressing. They ate from shuttle stores, drank purified water, and excreted. Their discomfort was half due to the cramped facilities and half due to the presence of the other sapient. Eventually, the two took turns sleeping out of pure practical necessity.

When one day wore into two, their discussions shifted from their personal crisis to speculation about what actions the *Scape Grace* might take, and how soon. When they remained silent, would captain Lerner order an attack? A rescue?

Katy, believing she knew Evgeny Lerner best, believed his patience would last three days at most. He would not chance sending another crew member into the foreign ship, but he might send an unmanned drone to attempt entry. The drone might try to cut or puncture the hull near the site of their entry. A full assault against the ship would be unlikely, given the chances of accidentally destroying the valuable shuttle… not to mention two valuable crew members. The captain might threaten the Ningyo aboard *Scape Grace*, instead, hoping to ransom his people against the return of hostages.

NuRikPo disagreed. He felt that their captain would remain patient for quite a long time. After all, they might already have been dismissed as dead. That was the most likely explanation for their silence. Neither the risk of destruction by the Ningyo nor of damage to – or offense from – the foreign ship was worth bothering a rescue attempt for crew members of uncertain vitality. The captain would wait until the ship was merely Schrödinger's box and not Pandora's.

They spent several hours, in total, arguing over these points. But the argument proceeded in spurts, interspersed around more productive work. While both participants considered the debate an unpleasant waste of time, they pursued it with increasing vigor as time wore on.

Why? They might have felt *some* positive reinforcement driving their dispute. Perhaps the disagreement seemed a welcome change of topic from the unpleasant subjects of bioengineering and alien motivational psychology. Perhaps the return to their traditional adversarial roles was a welcome diversion from their unexpectedly intense forced cooperation. Perhaps they secretly enjoyed having an intractable opponent to hear and react to their provocations.

Likely all of those motivations were true. Yet one more cause was at play, one which even the most skilled xenopsychologist could have failed to isolate. The triggers in their nervous systems – for distaste and for enjoyment, for anger and for appreciation, for defiance and complacency – were being located, tested, and mapped. As these strings were found and pulled, their minds twitched in response.

16

The first day of travel aboard the *Scape Grace* was a study in practiced avoidance. Evgeny Lerner went back to his cabin for eight hours of sleep. The Georges also slept, then returned to their repairs. Soloth bash'Soloth privately exercised, napped, and reviewed ship readiness reports. Soloth gave the combat crew time to organize themselves privately, though it monitored their interactions for signs of trouble. Luuboh bash'Gaulig retreated to the medical room, researching its strange discovery and monitoring Tklth's progress. It, too, was forced to rest for short periods. Both Mauraug took time for small meals when necessary.

Only Gleamer and Jolly held any substantial conversation. The two spoke at length about their respective philosophies. Gleamer actually found the Ningyo attitude toward existence quite fascinating, once he worked through the layers of indirect allusion in their speech.

Gleamer's best approximation of their creed ran somewhere between several historical Terran belief systems: Zen Buddhism, Taoism, and the Church of the Subgenius. Roughly put: reality might be static, but the sentient experience of reality was not. Assuming otherwise led to a futile attempt to directly perceive reality, which led to all sorts of evils, not least of which was powerless frustration. You had to be in on the 'Joke' or else you would never 'get it' and continue to dwell in eternal humorless ignorance.

At least, that *might* be the correct interpretation. It was hard to be certain. The specifics shifted over time. Gleamer still could not be sure whether Jolly, like others of its kind, was deliberately obfuscating some elements of its true culture, if it was incapable of speaking without 'borrowing' chunks of foreign cultural reference, or if its psyche was somehow bound to that particular mode of allusive communication.

When asked directly about any of these matters, Jolly either avoided the question or presented two conflicting answers simultaneously. One thing Gleamer was certain about: the Ningyo was not, as the captain claimed, trying to be intentionally aggravating. Gleamer's xenopsychology sub-AI was relatively new and untrained, but it maintained that the probability of purposeful antagonism was somewhere around nine percent or less.

For its part, Jolly seemed to be interested in Gleamer's perspective, as well. It agreed that artificial augmentation was a necessity for progress beyond biology; it could hardly deny that point from within its pressurized shell. Ningyo adapted to a largely inhospitable physical universe, slightly more so than other sapients leaving their worlds of origin. They learned to interact with beings they considered bizarre, although at first through cautious observation and study rather than direct confrontation.

Jolly did dispute whether direct neurological alteration, such as Gleamer's, was advisable. From this argument, Gleamer deduced that the Ningyo were not directly interfaced into their suits. The suits must have some sort of real-time command system built in. The command system, presumably, was not intrusive on their bodies. Jolly said that it would find cybernetic integration distasteful, even counterproductive. It suggested that Gleamer had further distanced himself from Humanity by his alterations, perhaps intentionally.

Gleamer avoided taking offense, admitting that his actions *had* such an effect, but he denied that his purpose was to make himself less Human. Instead, he argued that every element of cultural progress began with the sacrifices of pioneers who separated themselves from their fellows in order to move the group forward. If they led in a beneficial direction, the mass would follow willingly. If they reached a dead end, then only the trailblazers were harmed.

In typical style, Jolly reversed its position, abruptly agreeing that Gleamer did seem to be an improvement on the standard-issue Human. Certainly, he was much more satisfying to talk with.

All that cultural exchange might have been more laudable had it not been a screen. Gleamer worked hard to keep the Ningyo engaged and distracted. In the meantime, his spare analytic areas and sub-AIs labored on several projects he hoped to keep hidden from Jolly.

First, he was analyzing the radio micro-signals. If he could locate – or even translate – those signals, Gleamer would have a better idea what level of threat they represented.

Second, Gleamer was trying to build his own private communications route within *Scape Grace*. It needed to use a medium the Ningyo could not track through ship systems or any technology within their suits. Solid, wired connections would be best, ideally borrowing one of the less critical monitoring networks within the ship's structure. Life support, possibly? No, recoding parts of that network could be hazardous if it interfered with normal functions. Gleamer might be able to run a low-bandwidth signal through the superstructure, but it was intentionally insulated at several points and would be limited in both range and content of transmission. He would also need someone at the other end capable of detecting and decoding his messages. The Georges might have enough clues, but they were at the far opposite end of the ship.

Gleamer's literary sub-AI, Rikki, suggested banging on pipes, per several prison dramas. Very clever, except that no water lines ran through the bridge. There were coolant lines, but those weren't accessible to 'bang' on. Modulating their flows was also a bad idea, particularly while repairs were ongoing.

Gleamer's third project was more difficult to conceal. He continued to scan across the range of possible energy forms NuRikPo could use to communicate. Most of the electromagnetic spectrum was easy enough to read without revealing his intent; the console in front of Gleamer had sufficient reception, all by itself, topick up wavelengths from a micrometer to a gigameter. For smaller or larger EM signals, or to delve into the stranger reaches of trans-EM physics, Gleamer had to draw upon specialized sensors built into the *Scape Grace*. Transmissions to and from those remote sensor systems could be detected through the ship wide comm systems Jolly could access. Plus, each time Gleamer traded packets of data with systems outside of his local console, he ran the risk of being noticed. The Ningyo were probably already aware that their claims about open communications were in doubt, but actively seeking – or finding – proof of their perfidy would jeopardize the continued illusion of cooperation.

For similar reasons, most of the crew avoided the bridge as much as possible. Gleamer might have been faced with the dilemma of entertaining the Ningyo alone if not for the occasional intervention by Soloth. The first mate first returned after six hours and engaged Jolly in a discussion of combat strategy. This conversational choice represented Soloth's own combination of practical work, distraction, and attempted elicitation of useful intelligence. Soloth's distraction was not for its own benefit, nor Gleamer's, but for captain Lerner. It kept the Ningyo under observation and unable to roam unescorted. The knowledge it sought was about the *Harauch*: its capabilities, compliment, and command.

Soloth's visit still borrowed time for Gleamer to unplug and stumble back to his bunk. The necessities of a biological body were a continual frustration. Sleep, even when he dreamed, was an empty, pale thing compared to his waking electronic fantasias. It was too tempting to remain permanently interfaced. Only the value of his wetware's unique abilities... not to mention contents... helped Gleamer tolerate its limitations. He was too afraid of losing his unique Human identity to risk its loss by attempting transfer to digital consciousness. He loved his AI, but he still couldn't be sure how existence as one would *feel*.

So, he slept. He ate, as well, but took meals as often as possible at his console.

The rest of the crew followed his habits, making periodic trips to and from the galley. None of the officers took meals in the mess. Soloth ate quickly and returned to duty. Luuboh brought its meals to medical to continue its investigations. Tklth was not yet ready to risk solid foods.

Evgeny brought the next day's lunch to the Georges so that they could continue their work uninterrupted. This delivery was also an unspoken repayment for sharing their teatime with him earlier. The gesture was genuine and deeply appreciated. Evgeny found he enjoyed spending time with the two engineering 'apprentices', an opportunity he had never taken before. At other times, the pair would have been pulled away by NuRikPo, or else Evgeny would have been drawn away by other interests. The disruption in ship's routine was at least giving him the opportunity to interact with his crew.

Evgeny felt no comparable urge to visit the combat crew. Becoming too familiar with that violent lot would only lessen his authority. It was better to let Soloth be his strong interface. That way, Evgeny could retain the mystique of distant control and unknown power. Such a stance also showed respect for Soloth's management ability. The rank and file should never think they could appeal to the captain as an ally, above the head of his first mate, nor should they entertain hopes of supplanting Soloth as Evgeny's right hand.

By the end of their second day of travel, Evgeny was growing less and less content with their disrupted schedule. He took a full six-hour duty shift on the bridge to give Gleamer a second bout of sleep. The Ningyo were showing no sign of requiring any refreshment. They did not leave the bridge for sleep, food, or any other recreation. For all Evgeny knew, the actual Ningyo might be taking naps within their suits, even while they conversed. They might be putting their robotic bodies on automatic response, throwing out preprogrammed gibberish designed to sound like clever repartee. They might also have nutrient reservoirs and feeding tubes built in, but it seemed less likely that they could store several days' worth of foodstuffs in those shells.

When he broached the question, Jolly was typically evasive. It said only, "We are life, Gene, but not as you know it. We will retire when the need arises and the stars are right. Until then, methinks the captain protests too much."

Evgeny *did* want his chair back and the sugar-coated jellyfish knew it. So were the Ningyo able to hold out longer than other sapients? Or were they intentionally overextending themselves in order to keep continuous control of the *Scape Grace*?

His answer came toward the end of his duty shift. Jolly keyed the intercom for the medical room and called out, "O Gracious child of Gaulig, would you kindly bring those dispensers you offered earlier, up to the bridge? I think my Punch is looking weak and could use something bracing."

Luuboh's voice rumbled back, "Certainly. They will require some time to transport, however."

Jolly responded with cheery indifference, "Take your time; we will endure a while longer. I hope your patient is recovering well?"

"She will live, but remains weak."

"Mercifully sedated, no doubt. Ah well," Jolly added with a theatrical sigh, "I suppose that's necessary. No reason to be cruel. More credit to you for your dutiful nursing. See you above in a bit."

Jolly's direct command of his crew irked Evgeny, but like most of the arrangement, he had little room for protest. At least the Ningyo's demands stayed limited to Luuboh. *Anyone* could order Luuboh about. Perhaps the Ningyo picked up on that biddability and followed suit, rather than intentionally flexing its stolen authority.

Regardless, Luuboh continued obedient to any master. The shortened Mauraug arrived on the bridge within a half-hour, preceded by the rumble of a heavily loaded freight cart. The bridge hatch opened, and Luuboh entered, carefully balancing one of the large, cylindrical nutrient dispensers.

As it turned out, the basic formula for Ningyo dietary needs was fairly well-known across the Collective; many facilities prepared for basic hospitality: the comfort and feeding of most known sapients. The mix would maintain a Ningyo's health, if not culinary satisfaction. Since their native foodstuffs tended to expire – or explode – quickly in the atmospheric conditions favored by most other sapients, this was the best a Ningyo could expect.

Besides all that, the dispensers interacted well with their suits. Evgeny was somewhat disappointed that the experience of watching the Ningyo 'eat' was neither revelatory nor even repugnant. They simply plugged feeder hoses from the dispensers into ports in their suit's abdominal section, revealed by detaching a section of the white panels that seemed formerly seamless. Whether avoiding implicit discomfort or the threat of tedium, Evgeny took the meal break as his excuse to excuse himself from the bridge.

He announced, "I'm hungry, myself. Any chance of fresh food, Luuboh?" He stood, stretched, and began to walk toward the exit hatch.

Luuboh finished anchoring the transported nutrient dispensers to the bridge floor with magnetic clamps and watched Evgeny depart. It called back, "Check cabinet 3e. I set aside some *uumrul* for you."

Slipping coded references past the metaphor-minded Ningyo was a tricky game, but Luuboh and Evgeny had several advantages. The reference to "cabinet 3e" was a shared secret, referring to the storage bay that held one of their unofficial communication recording hubs. Luuboh was telling him to check the system for messages. The mention of *uumrul*, a fruit native to the Mauraug homeworld, was a chancy poetic idiom. Hopefully, the Ningyo were not widely studied enough to catch the other meaning of *uumrul*: "a piece of important gossip or news". Luuboh had something important to share.

Evgeny hurried from the bridge without acknowledging Luuboh's parting comment.

A more practiced covert operative would cover his tracks better. Evgeny should have gone first to the galley to follow up the overt meaning of Luuboh's words. Instead, he was unschooled enough to walk directly to the storage rooms on the first sublevel, going immediately to bay 3e. If Jolly *had* caught the meaning behind Luuboh's casual comment, it might have watched Evgeny's steps on the motion trackers and thereby found their secret message drop.

As it happened, their subterfuge was successful. At least, it was successful against the Ningyo.

Evgeny reached the storage bay and pulled open the false crate that concealed the secret, separate comm panel linking his and Luuboh's unofficial recorders. He keyed in his personal code and prompted the system to play back his messages.

There were two. The first was from Luuboh. It contained a short video which might have been indecipherable without its accompanying commentary. Evgeny watched as something reflective and insectile climbed around a landscape of white and grey irregular ovoids. The mechanical bug latched onto a particularly spiky whitish mass and was eventually joined by two more constructs of similar type, which linked to it end to end, forming a chain which stretched off-camera.

Luuboh's narrative stated, "This image was recorded using electron microscopy. The background is a mass of cells formerly from the muscle tissues of Tklth. The objects in the foreground are machines smaller than one micrometer. They have been persistently building structures within this cellular matrix since the time of their introduction… which I believe to have occurred when Tklth's separated flesh contacted the remains of the dead Ningyo.

"These automata are both repairing *and* modifying the tissues they infiltrate. Beyond reconstruction, I have not confirmed any functional effects yet. I have taken steps to isolate this sample and neutralize any others that might remain in the area of introduction. I hope that none escaped into the ship elsewhere, but we must remain vigilant for this possibility. The other problem is that Tklth herself also contacted the Ningyo remains… as did I and Soloth bash'Soloth when we transported her to medical.

"I am observing Tklth for any negative effects in an effort to anticipate possible harm to the rest of us. She remains sedated for both her and my safety. We do not have the tools needed to observe these machines at work within a body or track their actions on a wider scale. My hope is that I can observe their effects at the micro- and macro levels and deduce their purpose before a threat manifests. I should also be able to detect them if they reach significant concentrations. If the infestation appears likely to become a threat via replication or tissue destruction, it may become necessary to incinerate all affected materials… Tklth included. More to follow as discovered. Also awaiting your orders."

That news was bad enough by itself. Evgeny was momentarily afflicted with the same nausea that touched Katy Olu, the repulsion of realizing one was sharing space with a contagious plague host. He felt tainted, despite knowing full well that his body was already host to several kilograms of bacteria. Yet those separate organisms were 'native' and mostly known symbiotes. These tiny machines, no matter how benign their functions *might* be, were foreigners. How *dare* the Ningyo loose such elements on his ship without notice? There could be no good purpose for such contamination. There was no acceptable explanation for infiltrating their shared space in such a manner.

The second message did little to calm Evgeny's temper. In part, this was because of its source: it was from Gleamer. The programmer had somehow discovered Evgeny and Luuboh's 'private' network and broken into it far enough to leave Evgeny a personal message. How long had Gleamer known about this system? How did he discover it? Those questions, like several others, would have to wait until after the present crisis.

The message also contained bad news. Fortunately, the convergence of the two unwelcome messages provided valuable perspective for both. Gleamer's missive was shorter and more pointed: "There are miniature robots on board. They are broadcasting extremely short-wave, short-range, short-duration radio signals. I believe this is a method of coordinating operations across a decentralized system. I first detected these signals several minutes after the Ningyo came aboard. Some of the signals originate from the Ningyo themselves. Another set is answering them from a different part of the ship. My conclusion: the Ningyo have brought nanotechnology on board and are using it somehow to infiltrate *Scape Grace*. They may have encouraged us to send our engineer off-ship to prevent a counter-strategy. Continuing to track in case they spread further. Sorry to crash your party line."

So it wasn't enough that the Ningyo strong-armed themselves into command of his ship; they had to secretly use illicit technology to infiltrate it as well? To infiltrate the bodies of his crew? What was their game? Blackmail, by threatening to use the nanotechnology to kill the pirates instantly if they attempted a counter-coup? Mental control, using the devices to lobotomize or pacify their opposition? Or was the introduction of the microrobots a non-hostile accident?

An experiment? Either of the latter two possibilities still represented dangerous folly and disregard for the sapients affected.

Evgeny's fury was rising to dangerous levels. Killing Jolly was no longer sufficient. He wanted to torture the Ningyo slowly. Perhaps he could repro-gram the 'Admiral's' suit to slowly lower its internal pressure, crushing the entity from its own expansion. He could use its nutrient ports to pump in something volatile or painfully toxic. Better, they could amputate the suit's limbs and leave the Ningyo stranded in its cage, deprived of sensory input, to live or die later at Evgeny's whim.

At that moment, all he could vent his rage upon were crates and storage pods. They scattered well when kicked, with a satisfactory crunch of breaking valuables, but impact against the durable plastic cases hurt his foot. The pain only worsened his anger. He needed a better focus. Physical violence was easy but unproductive.

Evgeny finally forced his temper down to a manageable simmer. He re-solved to grant it release later, when an opportunity arose. He would not only oust the Ningyo… he would be waiting to murder them. First, he would destroy their beloved 'friend', the unnamed ship. That was, after Katy and NuRikPo stripped the vessel of every valuable artifact and byte of data. *Then* he would disintegrate the damned outsider while Jolly watched. The Ningyo would gain *nothing* from their occupation of the *Scape Grace* and lose everything they sought.

Such goals were all well and evil, but manifesting his desires would take more work. Evgeny cleaned up his mess with perfunctory haste. He closed up the hidden comm panel, doing his best to make the storage bay look as it had before. Then he hastened back to his own quarters.

There, on his personal compad, Evgeny planned out scenarios for the up-coming raid. He weighed out their tactical assets and what he could remember of the spatial organization of the Zig mining operation. He looked for moments where he might betray the *Harauch*, cripple the unnamed ship, or leave either ship to the mercy of the Zig defenses. He wondered if Gleamer might be able to slip an advance warning message to the Zig. Evgeny eventually discarded that idea as equally hazardous to the *Scape Grace* as to the other ships. Their best chance of survival was to take advantage of the *Harauch's* collaboration until the Zig force was substantially reduced. Hopefully, the *Scape Grace* could stay operational long enough to pick the right moment for treachery.

He also had to hope that the microtechnology unleashed aboard the *Scape Grace* could be contained or slowed enough to thwart any sinister purposes until after the Ningyo were dealt with. Ideally, NuRikPo could be returned to the ship to counter-engineer a solution to the invasive nanotechnology. If not, they might have to rely upon the lesser talents of the Georges and the contents of *Scape Grace's* technical library to seek contraceptive measures. He should probably have the subordinate engineers start work sooner rather than later, but passing on all these details would be difficult until Burnett or Zenaida took up his invitation to visit storage bay 3e.

At the time, all Evgeny could do was plot… and wait. Being able to wait and work patiently, even while traveling toward imminent danger, was an absolutely necessary ability for a raider. Quite a lot of dead time passed between targets. Letting the time go to waste, or worse, letting anticipation wear on his mind, could quickly lead to mental sickness. The skill to avoid either extreme was the same managed readiness required of a professional soldier. In this regard, Evgeny might have been capable as a genuine military commander, perhaps even the captain of a legitimate warship.

It was debatable whether captain Lerner was a natural leader. More likely, the demands of his life had shaped whatever raw talent he possessed into its required form. This was true of his vices as much as his virtues. As a professional soldier, he could not have indulged his adolescent nastiness and cruelty. He would have had to mature. Piracy not only permitted but almost required such self-centered hostility. You had to be vicious not only toward your victims, but sometimes also your collaborators.

Evgeny had time to exercise both traits: patience and malevolence. While he might be growing tired of a pirate's life, he planned to keep living… and he planned to kill.

17

After finishing the installation of the Ningyo feeders on the bridge, Luuboh returned directly to the medical room to check on its other projects. Tklth continued to doze in the dim, chilled environment. The tissue samples Luuboh had isolated continued to change, each with a different rate and pattern depending on *its* environment. Luuboh had placed one sample in a nutrient-rich feeder solution: it rebuilt portions of flesh and even replaced nerve fibers with a metallic chain of interlinked machines. Another, in a drier, colder, unsupplemented dish, had only progressed to finishing its support matrix and then stalled, possibly starved for materials and energy.

It was helpful to know the limitations of the micro-robots, but they obviously could survive indefinitely within healthy tissue. Killing the host to kill the invaders was not a useful solution. As Luuboh's other experiments were demonstrating, any chemicals capable of penetrating and disabling the inorganic constructs would harm organic cells as well. The limitations of Luuboh's knowledge were becoming evident. If there was a process that could selectively affect nanotechnology of this type without harming the body it infiltrated, it was beyond Luuboh's skill. It had done well to find and correctly operate Katy Olu's electron microscope in order to discover and image the tiny mobile units. It might also find a counter-agent through trial and error, but it was running out of viable samples and was reluctant to create more.

Certainly, there were enough chopped bits of Tklth for weeks of experimentation, but Luuboh was loathe to sacrifice the stabilized tissue for an amateur investigative exercise. It also did not want to risk further personal exposure to the micro-robots. While decently appointed and reasonably sterile, the medical room was far from a safe cleanroom.

Luuboh had stayed in its environmental suit while it cut and enclosed the various samples of Tklth's infested flesh. It had then deposited the remaining, hopefully clean 'samples' in the biological storage freezer. Last, still suited, it had hauled the bag containing the dead Ningyo's spattered suit to the shuttle deck. It had to hope that the body bag would hold in any remaining constructs that might linger within the liquefied flesh of the Ningyo. For that matter, Luuboh was praying that its own clean suit kept any stray crawlers at bay.

After returning, it had carefully stripped off the suit while simultaneously spraying off in the shower stall adjacent to the medical room. The chamber was built for exactly that purpose, mixing a mild quaternary ammonium solution with highly pressurized hot water to intercept possible biological contaminants while the occupant removed outer clothing. The biocidal chemical was definitely useless against the inorganic constructs, but the force of the water hopefully swept most of them away. To be totally safe, Luuboh probably should have shaved off its fur, but it was insufficiently paranoid – and too vain – to take that step.

The best it could really hope was to identify, document, and anticipate the nature of the threat. That way, when NuRikPo and doctor Olu returned to the *Scape Grace*, they would be forewarned and immediately able to take steps to disable the miniature robots. That was presuming they returned at all. Luuboh had to consider the reasonable possibility that the coming battle could result in the destruction of the ship which held NuRikPo and Katy Olu. The battle could just as easily end in *Scape Grace's* destruction, but that outcome would render the problem of the micro-robots moot.

Once it emerged and dried off, Luuboh started its study. When the call came in from Jolly to report to the bridge, Luuboh pulled together its results to that point. It risked taking the time to stop by bay 3e and upload those reports for captain Lerner's reference. It had wanted to wait until its understanding was more complete, but could not pass up the chance to minimize suspicion about its movements. If asked about its extra stop, it could have explained that it was retrieving the magnetic clamps from storage.

At least, afterward, the captain had some warning about what to expect. Luuboh would try to provide more data as time and opportunity allowed. What it might learn and what they could *do* about the problem were both unknown.

In the meantime, while it waited on the progress of its experiments, Luuboh monitored Tklth's progress. After two days, the mutilated Vislin was looking remarkably well. Her general health was as good as might be expected for a patient being fed intravenously. She was losing muscle tone; no surprise there. But she was well hydrated and her vitals were within the acceptable range for Vislin, per the medical library.

Her respiratory and neurological activity were actually stronger than Luuboh thought normal. Given the low lighting, chill, blood loss, and trauma, those systems should have been functioning at reduced levels. While Tklth remained somnolent, her breathing was deep and steady, her heart pumped strongly, and her EEG readouts indicated brain waves more varied than simple sleep rhythms.

The guide programs in the brain monitor kept isolating *mu* wave patterns, which the medical library stated should only occur during wakeful observation and learning. Luuboh could not be certain that this anomaly was a relevant variation; it might be somehow normal for Vislin or an artifact of using the system improperly on her species.

Either way, Tklth was getting close to the safety time limit for the cautery patches. Luuboh would have to remove the patches soon to avoid toxicity reactions. Hopefully, the wound sites beneath were sealed fully and started healing from within. Tklth certainly seemed strong enough. She showed no adverse reactions to the patches and no signs of infection around their edges.

The patch removal process was painstaking and might be uncomfortable. Hopefully, Tklth would remain drowsy enough to allow Luuboh to finish its work quietly. The Vislin was restrained, but loosely, so that it had some range of motion to prevent muscle cramps and scale damage. Luuboh did not want to have to lock her down again to avoid injury while it peeled gauze from flesh.

Luuboh was reading the instructions for the removal process when Tklth's status changed unexpectedly. A noise from the direction of the bed caught

Luuboh's attention. At first, it thought Tklth was choking. Then, it realized that she was only clearing her throat. Luuboh had already turned around before Tklth moved. Its alarm was reduced as it realized she was only turning her head to look around. At first, Tklth's gaze was unfocused and wavering. Then, she narrowed in on Luuboh. Her beak clicked in a gesture Luuboh could not interpret. Was she angry? Was she hungry? Was the movement just a reflex of some sort or a conscious attempt to speak?

Luuboh was further surprised when, after a few seconds, Tklth turned her neck and eyes steadily to scan the room. She did this without significantly moving her limbs, though her shoulders rolled and her back arched in a stretch. After this investigation, her attention returned to Luuboh. The Mauraug watched her with mingled curiosity and concern. Was she in pain sufficient to penetrate the medications and her hibernation? Was her reaction a temporary waking process, something the Vislin biology did to check for hazards during the night? Luuboh had many questions, but it was Tklth who began asking for answers first.

"Why am I in medical?" Tklth asked, her chirping voice, as always, an odd contrast to her deadly exterior. Normally, her voice was also a contrast to her harsh attitude, but at the moment, she seemed peaceful. The question was not asked in panic or accusation. It sounded like genuine confusion, a request for information.

"You were wounded… badly. You attacked the Ningyo," Luuboh pointed out in return.

"Ah. I remember," Tklth acknowledged, still sounding surprisingly calm. "I killed one of them. Then their leader shot me. I thought I would die. Did you come back and help me?"

"Eventually," Luuboh grunted, "but not to kill them. Their leader, Jolly, decided not to kill you. It let me and Soloth carry you back to medical." Its bewilderment at the conversation mingled with its irritation at having to explain the situation to Tklth. Most likely, the Vislin would not remember their conversation later. It would ask the same questions again. Worse, it would not be nearly as reasonable about the answers, if past interactions provided any precedent. Luuboh was used to Tklth being angry, pushy, and even abusive. It liked her better damaged and drowsy. Sadly, the captain would prefer her whole and functional, even if she was an ass, whole.

For the moment, Tklth accepted its answer without berating Luuboh for fleeing the fight. She nodded, awkwardly, and turned to look at the ceiling. Then her gaze lowered gradually until she was looking downward at her own body. Luuboh tensed, fearing the moment when she recognized the extent of her injuries. Shock might have shielded her mind earlier. Now, stable and somewhat lucid, she might be genuinely traumatized by the realization of how badly she was damaged.

Once again, the storm never came. Tklth only scanned over the remnants of her lower half, dispassionately taking in the patched stump of her leg. She could not see her back, but surely could feel the absence of her tail. Yet still, there was no screaming, no cursing, and no flailing about. She finally did react, but it was only a bitter cry of mourning. Her eyelids flickered in distress. Her claws flexed. Luuboh was familiar enough to recognize this as Vislin sorrow.

Luuboh's anxiety warred with sympathy, which wrapped around to anger as Luuboh became aggravated about having to share the pain of its sometime tormentor.

"Why don't you sleep?" Luuboh asked with courtesy rather than kindness. "You're still weak from your injuries. You need rest. I'll change the bandage and make sure the tissue stays healthy. You'll have a new leg and tail as soon as the doctor and engineer get back."

"But I have been sleeping so long already. I am not tired anymore," Tklth answered, sounding calmly reasonable rather than petulant. "You can change the bandages; I will not be any trouble. Thank you for saving my life."

It was the last sentence that told Luuboh something was very wrong. Tklth might be capable of gratitude, but she had never thanked Luuboh for anything, ever before. In particular, in that situation, she should have been cursing the Mauraug for its cowardice, for its incompetence in her care, or for walking on two legs while she lay flat on one. If drowsing, she should have been less articulate; if truly awake, she should have been bitter and abrasive.

She did *seem* awake. Her gaze was steady and clear, her movements growing in precision as she roused. That was also strange. By all references, a Vislin should be barely able to function in such low temperatures. That chill, coupled with the lowered lighting, should have had a Vislin acting as if heavily sedated. Tklth looked no more impaired than would be expected given two days of bed rest and an intravenous diet. She was *less* impaired than should be the case after such a massive injury.

Luuboh felt a sinking realization. To cover its suspicions, it asked clinically, "How *are* you feeling, Ticklish?"

"Weak. Pain. My head hurts. My wounds ache. I am hungry. I smell terrible. *You* smell terrible. But considering everything, I feel reasonably good. Pain is better than death." The insult was expected, but delivered with shared rather than cruel humor. Tklth had not even taken issue with Luuboh's use of her Terran-styled nickname. She sounded… reasonable. That tone was not just uncharacteristic for Tklth, it was uncommon for anyone in the same situation. She sounded like someone else. She sounded like…

Luuboh realized that it had a discovery to share with the captain, one more urgent than the results of its tissue experiments. Tklth was most definitely in-fested. She had been *altered.* Something was affecting her behavior and the most likely culprits were the micro-robots. They were probably also bolstering her recuperative systems. While this fact alone was good news for the Vislin – and might explain her survival as well as her rapid recovery – the effects on her mind were bad news for the other sapients on the *Scape Grace.*

If the micro-technology was spreading elsewhere in the ship, it might already be working its way into the nervous systems of other crew members. While making pirates calmer and more reasonable could be viewed as an improvement, those changes also benefitted the Ningyo occupiers. Tklth was starting to make silly, Ningyo-style jokes in the midst of a dire personal situation. That similarity suggested more than a casual coincidence. It was possible that other aspects of her psyche were being made more sympathetic to the Ningyo, as well.

It wasn't safe to let her get up. In the short term, Tklth wasn't going to be walking the halls or posing much of a threat to anyone outside of the door. Still, a fair amount of damage could be done from within the medical room, if she decided to turn on the ship's crew. Even if her aggression was damped down, Tklth's training could be used to dispassionately murder quite a few people. From what Luuboh had heard, she could probably be deadly with just one arm, let alone two arms and one leg. Luuboh was afraid of her *beak*.

Luuboh's fear at that moment was a different kind of fear. It realized that it had been frozen with shock for a long moment. Tklth was watching the Mauraug quietly, her rigid, scaled face betraying no suspicion in return. Luuboh needed to say something to keep the conversation going.

It managed, "Right, yes, good. Well, you're still at risk. I'm doing my best, but I'm not doctor Olu. You should not move around too much until the wounds are better healed. Your vital signs are still a little low." Luuboh lied easily. It was practiced in such deceptions to a degree other Mauraug, like Soloth, would find repugnant. Its survival skills necessarily differed from theirs, so it felt little shame using subterfuge to avoid harm. In this case, the harm it was avoiding might threaten the entire ship, not only Luuboh itself.

"I'll remove the bandages shortly. I'd like you to remain restrained until that's done. No offense; it might be painful and I don't want to chance you doing something we'll both regret."

Tklth's reply, meant to be reassuring, again had the opposite effect, "I understand… but I wonder. I just do not feel like that will be a problem. I feel… different. Not angry. Something tells me I have changed. I am cold but not tired. I have been hurt but I do not want to hurt in return. Is this what one calls a life-changing experience? I wonder if I *would* frenzy, even if the pain were unbearable."

Luuboh did not honestly know whether to hope she would or would not. It grumbled, "I suppose we'll find out, won't we? Still, let's not risk my hide on your newly discovered inner peace."

18

The hours were long, the quarters were cramped, the food was awful, the situation was worsening, and the company was terrible. Why, then, were Katy and NuRikPo growing steadily *less* uncomfortable as the days wore on?

The effect was subtle at first. Through the first two days, the two cellmates managed to avoid one another by staying at opposite ends of the shuttle, immersing themselves in work, and alternating their sleep schedules. They interacted only when necessary to share results from their respective tasks. Katy also had to periodically scan NuRikPo, in addition to herself, to track the spread of the micro-robotic infestation within their bodies.

That spread was progressing exactly as she had feared. The concentrations of metallic 'cells' were travelling from the two sapients' extremities, to their spines, and then upward to their central nervous systems. Small colonies of the little machines also were forming in their glands: the adrenal glands, ovaries, and thyroid in Katy Olu and their equivalents in NuRikPo, when adjusting for Zig anatomy and gender differences. The latter discoveries required some particularly unpleasant personal contact and discussions.

The micro-robots were hitting all bodily regulatory systems, including autonomous nervous functions, and were probably also setting up shop in the two sapients' brainstems and limbic structures. Emotional control was the most likely explanation. Not much of their cortical areas had been infested yet.

The pattern was both reassuring and puzzling. Direct control of an intelligent organism would be simpler by manipulating memory access, sensory content, motor functions, or overall executive functioning. If the machines wanted to rewrite bodies and minds, they could make far more overt changes. A limited time frame might be restricting gross modifications. Perhaps the robots would move on to more complex projects eventually. Or perhaps the system building within their bodies was learning: drawing a map before it remodeled the terrain. Such a scheme *would* ensure finer control and a more functional, believable automaton, not to mention more precise data about the original organism. If nothing else, such data would allow the next generation of micro-robots to more quickly convert new organisms of the same type.

At least they were not being remolded physically in the image of the ship's structure... or of its absent creators. Those ideas were among Katy's first paranoid hypotheses. Being made into a puppet by an internal control system was awful enough, but at least she would still *look* like herself. Perhaps she would still think like herself... with a few improvements.

Wait, what?

Such odd thoughts were the first warning signs that her mind was being tampered with. As the third day passed, Katy found herself increasingly experiencing stray thoughts and feelings at odds with her prior attitudes. Her fear of the micro-robots was decreasing. Her explorations continued, but flavored more with fascination than with revulsion. The ship outside seemed less like a hateful, foreign, hostile environment and more like an interesting new place to explore. The man-shaped construct outside their shuttle door no longer seemed like a threatening guardian, but a welcoming friend. Her sense of urgency declined. Sometimes it took an effort of will to go back to work, researching the systems being manipulated within her and trying to anticipate and counter the influences exerted.

NuRikPo, when asked, admitted to similar emotional changes. For him, however, the change was less from dislike to neutrality and more from irritation to positive engagement. He had viewed their entrapment within the unnamed ship, the subsequent jeopardy from the invading nanotechnology, and the necessity of researching counter-measures as unwelcome distractions from their original study of the ship's overall technologies. Certainly, they were learning quite a lot by necessity, but they were cut off from the rest of the ship. They were narrowly focused on one element while missing the wider context of the entire system. Such limitations grated on both NuRikPo's senses of duty and scientific curiosity.

He had been annoyed two days ago. Now he was "starting to appreciate the skillful design of a brilliantly integrated system". The invasion of his own body seemed like a courtesy, a demonstration of the subtle power of miniaturized technology. While he still yearned to explore the ship as a whole, his feelings were less about exploitation and more about appreciation. He could tolerate starting his investigations at the smallest scale and working his way outward.

It took longer for the two forcible collaborators to recognize the subtler changes in their emotional makeup. When they did, they were more offended than they had been by the changes in their outlook toward the ship. They were growing less hostile toward one another. Katy originally assumed that she no longer minded NuRikPo's awful chemical odor because her olfactory systems were overloaded. His misshapen, eye-bulging, narrow-lipped face had become too familiar to be properly repulsive. Even so, why was she no longer cringing at his terrible, dry jokes? His nervous tics and taps, which were grating noises before, now seemed like comfortable background rhythms.

Katy did *not* voice these observations to NuRikPo. For one reason, it would be humiliating to admit. Worse, he might admit to similar changes in feeling. She could deal with being artificially forced to not hate the obnoxious Zig. Having him abandon his own complaints about her for the same reasons – and not because he finally understood how bizarrely wrong those complaints were – would be disturbing. If he actually admitted to *enjoying her company* she might be forced to put a scalpel through his glittering eyeballs. That would really slow down his research. For such reasons, Katy kept her socio-emotional alterations to herself.

It was bad enough that she could *tell* NuRikPo was being affected. His insults slowed down and stopped. He was nearly courteous during their scheduled interactions and did not immediately turn away when finished with her. He almost lingered to make small talk, which cut off awkwardly when she glared at him, half-heartedly, in response. When she thought she saw the curmudgeonly engineer *smile* in her direction, Katy decided that the bugs must have invaded her visual cortex and were making her hallucinate. That possibility was more comfortable.

Unfortunately, her rational mind vetoed this idea. For one thing, major cortical modifications, so quickly, would have given her other hallucinations. Probably would have given her headaches, too. No, she was being subjected to alterations of lower brain regions. Oddly pro-social alterations, it seemed. Maybe the puppeteer machines would have them fight to the death later. For the short term, the changes seemed to produce pleasant and pacifistic ends.

Hopefully, remaining calm and avoiding antagonism would keep their rewiring to a minimum. At least, Katy told herself that as an excuse to avoid deliberately ruffling NuRikPo's feathers. She had to stifle a giggle at an image of the staid copper-skinned sapient plumed like a parrot, feathers askew.

Wow, she was getting deranged, fast. They could make a fortune selling the crawlers as a psychoactive drug. People would pay good money to bend their own minds so much.

That was, assuming that they could figure out and take control of the command structures for the system. There had to be some emergent programming built into the mechanisms themselves – possibly in the DNA-equivalent NuRikPo had discovered – or else the bugs were remotely coordinated using the radio generator and receiver elements Katy found on some of the units she dissected. Possibly both.

Such structures were the reason 'nano-' was the wrong prefix for the technology. Only some of the devices were less than one micro-meter in size. Most were larger. The devices were like bacteria: as large and complex as organic cells, with nanite-scale subordinate 'organelles', reproductive nuclei, and multiple intrinsic functions and behaviors.

Both Katy and NuRikPo became impressed with the machines, despite themselves. Or at least, despite their normal selves. With the influence of the machines also in play, they could not help being enchanted by their invaders. Katy saw the devices as clever mimicry of the structures biology accomplished

through eons of selective winnowing. NuRikPo saw them as the products of genius engineers; an entire culture of such engineers, like his own. Their creators
certainly possessed a valuable and unique technology.

In one of their conversations, Katy and 'Po agreed that the sapients responsible for the unnamed ship would have a good chance of acceptance into the
Collective. That was, provided the Collective did not find it necessary to destroy
the ship and its micro-technology for its own safety.

The thought upset them both deeply. As the first distinctly unpleasant feeling either researcher experienced throughout their third day aboard, the disturbance stood out sharply. Why did they suddenly care so much about what befell
the unnamed ship? The incongruity was enough to shake the two out of their
musings. They struggled anew against the increasingly obvious yet increasingly
powerful pressure on their psyches.

Katy had been right; the cells were an immune system. The ship was pro-
tecting itself. Instead of attacking them physically, the ship infiltrated their motivational systems. They were being encouraged to appreciate the ship. In time,
they might love it. The thought of harm to the unnamed ship was already
distressing. How long before they would fight on its behalf? Kill its enemies?
Sacrifice themselves for its survival?

Katy stoked her grim thoughts with anger. She struggled to maintain her
fury. Her body had been entered and changed without permission. Her emotions were being manipulated. She held out hope that such changes were not
permanent and that her mind would return to its former patterns after the micro-robots were disabled.

Such inner resistance was difficult. It seemed that the harder Katy fought
to rebel, the more strongly the little censors clamped down on her emotions.
Belatedly, she realized that she was making it easier for the bugs to find what
they wanted: her emotional triggers. Katy reversed course later in the day, attempting to calmly, rationally lay out the case for resistance within her mind. Her
motivations for working on a cure had to come from reason, not desire, or else
they were vulnerable to mechanical control through her biology. Her so-called

'higher' functions were not yet under the same assault.

Eventually, Katy decided to sleep. Her researches were running more and more slowly with less and less result. Part of that decline was due to fatigue. Part was due to mental resistance. But a certain part was due to the limits of her expertise.

She had identified the activity of the micro-robots, their course of attack, and their likely end goal. She had given her observations to NuRikPo, even including an analysis of the various construct types from the perspective of biological analogy. There wasn't much more she could do. Unless further observation yielded some unexpected insight, she estimated that her practical contributions were coming to an end. She might as well sleep and slow the progress of the infection.

When she awoke, she found NuRikPo sitting at the shuttle's control panel, head nodded forward. Two days ago, in a similar situation, she would have been furious with the engineer for violating their scheduled sleep rotation, contemptuous of him for working himself to exhaustion, and put off by the idea of having to wake him. She probably would have screamed something nasty at him from a distance.

Instead, she decided to walk over, quietly, and check on the drowsing Zig. She found him not asleep but staring distantly at the console's display. The screen was showing iterations of several simulations. These simulations showed the various forms of micro-robots replicating, interacting with biological cells and one another, and eventually being broken down and rebuilt by other robot types. Each simulation attempted to find weak points in the 'life cycle', where the machines could be dismantled or blocked from their activity by a counter-machine. This output would form the functional basis for construction of their counteragent: a cure for the micro-tech plague.

NuRikPo looked dazed, his large eyes staring transfixed at the animations. Katy laid a hand gently on his shoulder and shook him with care. He blinked and turned to look at the Human woman, raising one hand from the keyboard to lay it over her hand.

"They're just so… perfect," he mumbled, turning his head slightly to address Katy, but still keeping the screens in view.

"Perfect little monsters," Katy retorted, though without much feeling. It felt like a practiced complaint, delivered out of habit, not spite. Hatred was a reflex function for her, but now she stopped at the initial twitch of vitriol.

NuRikPo's reaction was predictable. "No, not at all. We're more monstrous: so irregular, so violent. Our systems are predicated on so much waste. We waste resources; we require mass suicides of cells to keep functioning. These constructs waste nothing. Destruction of units is carefully planned as a feature rather than a convenient default. All of the resulting materials are then reabsorbed and reused by the colony. There is no excretion… no waste product at all."

"No wonder you're in love. It's like a Zig's dream," Katy laughed lightly at her own jibe. How had such words once been the expression of her loathing? She knew so much about NuRikPo. The depth of her insults betrayed the depth of her attention to him. She had held his life in her hands once; she had been elbows deep in his body. How could she *not* feel a connection between them? She moved closer, her head next to his as they watched the simulations together. She turned to her companion's gleaming, red-gold cheek and leaned closer still…

"AAAAAAAugh!"

The two sapients were both startled by the abrupt, loud exclamation from Katy's throat. They leapt backwards from one another. NuRikPo nearly fell off the shuttle's anchored piloting chair. Katy had to catch herself on a strap to avoid falling into the engineer's workbench.

"What was that?" NuRikPo wailed as he pulled himself back upright, "Some bizarre primate joke? A sonic assault?"

"That was me almost *kissing* you, you shiny chunk of excrement! Either wake up and get back to work or take an actual nap and *then* get back to work, because I will *kill us both* if this continues much longer."

Katy was actually enjoying the sensation of nausea crawling through her throat. It felt honest and more real than the induced affection she had experienced moments before. Not surprisingly, her revulsion was already fading. Then, she felt a violent rage at being manipulated so thoroughly, but that emotion was also squashed fast. Her adrenaline cut off soon afterward.

The shift in limbic states was obvious if you knew what to expect. There were tell-tales to such blatant adjustments, particularly the lag while the bugs struggled to swap over her sympathetic and parasympathetic system responses. Adrenaline was easy to adjust, though. It would take the robots a while longer to edit out the feelings of revulsion sparked by almost coming into contact with Zig skin.

They're full of poison, you stupid fleas, Katy verbalized internally. She doubted that the machines could pick up complex linguistic thought, but why not try? Perhaps the emotive content of her derision would translate. Let them feel the depth of her resentment. Her will could be bent, but she could not be entirely broken. Some things were just too foul to allow.

NuRikPo's reaction further fueled her resolve. He looked hurt. At least, his expression was close enough to Human offense to suggest that interpretation. His eyelids drooped at the edges. He was frowning deeply, a disturbing enough variation by itself. His shoulders slumped.

"I see." *Dammit*, he couldn't even muster nonchalance or at least a decent scandalized attitude. He sounded sad and rejected.

"I admit I am tired, but I *have* been working, Katy." His tone sounded like an appeal rather than a reproach. "The counteragents are in synthesis."

Katy's head whipped rapidly between NuRikPo and his workspace. Indeed, his transmutation module was connected to several other devices, which were in turn linked to the shuttle's central computer. Blinking lights and readouts indicated the ongoing process of synthesis. Entire factories each barely a centimeter across had been erected within a sealed fabrication chamber, which was feeding factory each raw materials as they excreted armies of finished micro-robots. *Their* micro-robots, their soldiers against the invading forces.

"What? They're ready? Why didn't you wake me up sooner?" Even as she spoke the words, Katy knew the answer. The reason for NuRikPo's hesitation was obvious. Her own eagerness to be rid of the foreign bodies began to erode even as she spoke.

NuRikPo answered her anyway: "I started watching them… and thinking: If I don't design them correctly, our antibodies could escape beyond our bodies. They might hurt the ship, by attacking its cells. After that, I realized that we would already be hurting the units within us if we used this antigen. We would be destroying creations of unique beauty. Such a waste. They are not hurting us. If anything, they are making us better. I feel happier and healthier than I have in years. You do, too. Admit it. You haven't loved anything or anyone, in a long time. Now, you love…"

"I love *me*, you dope, the me that exists without any help." Katy was flailing against a web still being woven. Her objections fed the very strands that tangled her in ever-growing resistance. Still she struggled, trying to fight the demands to let go of her rejection.

"I hate *you*. I hate having to work with you, heal you, or even listen about other people talk about you. I hate the *Scape Grace*. I hate being stuck in that box of filthy, loud, violent idiots. I hate *this* ship. I hate its little crawly bits and its big disgusting bits."

"Listen to you," NuRikPo chided, "speaking the truth at last, with only one word mispronounced." He smiled… he actually smiled, a peaceful, beaming expression of joy. "Just try saying it the right way. You *love*…"

Katy struggled to withdraw her concussion pistol. NuRikPo stepped forward, raising his arms.

At first, she just wanted to warn him away. She would *not* be embraced. As she produced the weapon, his expression shifted to alarm, and he leapt forward, apparently to disarm her. Perhaps he was concerned she would follow through on her threats to kill herself.

The Zig academic was clumsy compared to Katy. He was her inferior in both physique and training. She slipped away from him easily, though there was little room in the shuttle to escape for long. She was not trying to shoot him, though, nor was she planning to hurt herself. Instead, she opened the chamber of the weapon. She withdrew the dart and showed it to NuRikPo, trying to pantomime 'safe' and 'empty'. She opened the dart, showing its empty cylinder.

Her ruse was successful. NuRikPo relaxed for a necessary moment. Katy closed, aimed, and fired the empty pistol, exploding its pressurized charge into the side of the plexiglass enclosure holding the manufactured counter-agents. The chamber's top popped open and flew back with a loud smack of plastic on plastic. NuRikPo looked further confused and stunned.

He began to say, "I see…. Yes, we should destroy them. But that's not the best way. Let me…" He moved toward the controls of the synthesizer.

Katy preempted him again, dipping the empty injection dart across the surface holding their micro-robots. A fine grey powder, like graphite dust, filled its cylindrical chamber. NuRikPo again reversed course to intercept her as Katy snapped the dart closed and loaded it into the pistol. She struggled to keep her feelings neutral, her thoughts empty, and her hands steady as she clicked the weapon shut.

NuRikPo held out his hands in a beseeching gesture. "Katy, please. I know what you're thinking. But please, listen to what you're *feeling*. You know this is wrong. You don't want to kill them."

"Sure, I do. And if you screwed up making these things, I won't mind killing *you*."

Katy raised the pistol and fired at NuRikPo's chest. The dart chuffed out with sufficient force to launch it across the small gap, push its needle tip through the Zig's bodysuit and tough skin, and inject its contents into his bloodstream. He staggered back, looking confused.

"Why?" he asked, blinking rapidly in his distress.

"Because I can hold out a little while longer. We need you able to make more antibodies. Also, I wouldn't know how to destroy your synthesizer. You could destroy it, if I left you infected. So you're the test subject. If it works, we win. If it kills you, poetic justice. If it just fails either way, we'll laugh idiotically about it later in bed."

"In bed?" NuRikPo had the decency to look confused. Then he frowned. "With you? What?" He sounded almost scandalized.

"Oh, good, it works fast. When you're ready, shoot me. I don't mind if you enjoy it." The paradox of her last sentence felt like a guilty pleasure. Katy was both pleased by the thought of being freed from the manipulative internal machines and saddened by the thought of their destruction. She wanted to please NuRikPo, but appreciated that she would soon enjoy offending him again.

NuRikPo continued to stare dumbly as she handed him the pistol.

Katy finished her directions: "Just get to work. I'll watch you for any bad signs: seizures or hemorrhaging or such. Hopefully, I didn't give you an embolism. If I try to get away or interfere with your work, shoot me with the blue darts; they're tranquilizers, safe for Humans. And hurry up; I'm already feeling the urge to apologize to you."

"I don't understand. If we were both being influenced so strongly, how is it you can resist while I could not?"

"The same way I realized what the machines were doing to us. The power of hate."

19

Returning to their normal antagonism was a painful relief for Katy Olu and NuRikPo. The decontamination process was excruciating and exhausting. While the hastily fabricated micro-robot destroyers quickly disrupted the functional effectiveness of their alien counterparts, their campaign to hunt down and execute every single foreigner took time and caused pain.

Unlike the original invaders, their predators were designed to work quickly and carelessly. In order to stay ahead of their prey, the constructs were permitted some collateral cellular damage. They moved directly to the sites of worst concentration, ripped apart as many foreign constructs as they could catch, then raced after any fleeing survivors seeking refuge in distant bodily interstices. Their hasty travel tore apart any interposing organic cells, creating small ruptures in various tissues. The microscopic soldiers also wielded weapons less selective than the tools used by the more subtle alien infiltrators. They had been given license to incinerate the occasional innocent cell if a fugitive robot attempted to use it for cover.

The first effect of this internal holocaust was agony, from a nervous system suddenly thrown out of balance. The interfering microtech had been rewiring Katy and NuRikPo's emotional reflexes, using individual artificial cells as bridges and blockages between real nerve cells. As the counter-agents crushed and zapped those neural stand-ins, they triggered protesting aches and twitches all throughout their hosts' bodies. The sudden absence of these connective links also produced odd numbness, tingling, and surges of emotion and sensation of various types.

Katy could trace the progress of the war within her by the location and character of the side effects she experienced. She quietly stretched out on a folding cot, under a thin blanket, during the battles for her amygdala and hypothalamus... the alternating explosions of discomfort and pleasure were stimulating some very personal areas.

NuRikPo had been more extensively remodeled. He barely had enough time to finish fabrication of Katy's inoculation before he began wincing and twitching. As she feared, he experienced a series of minor seizures as the first engagements began within his major nerve structures. As these attacks faded, they were followed by severe weakness and emotional swings.

At the observed rate of degeneration, they would need at least a day to sleep off the initial sickness caused by overloads in their nervous system. Regaining their natural hormonal and neurotransmitter balances would take longer, perhaps a week or more. Katy would need to requisition herself and 'Po some psychoactive meds from the ship's stores. As it was, she already felt traumatized by the narrowly averted romantic interlude between herself and the temporarily receptive Zig. Her preferred form of therapy, sexual intercourse, would not be helpful to relieve that particular mental hobgoblin. Hell, she might have flashbacks of him while *in* bed. The culture responsible for the alien ship and its microtech had a *lot* to answer for.

Before they could move on from exterminating the little robots to murdering their creators, the two sapients needed to recover. After that, they needed to set up internal protections against a second wave of intruders. The invasive constructs had not so far shown an ability to adapt to changing environments, but that was no reassurance that they could not learn. The ship might itself be able to produce a variety of micro-robots for different purposes. The next attack might be more intentionally fatal, particularly after its victims figured out how to disable the first wave of mind-control bugs.

Katy suffered less drastic torment than NuRikPo, but still felt like she had contracted a full-body infection. Every joint ached. Even after the major fusillades died down, the outrage of her disrupted body manifested as inflammation. They would both need anti-carcinomic treatments to avoid tumor development from all the cellular damage.

Still, the process was less drastic than the other alternative they considered: full-body electrocution. Sure, that would have disabled the attackers, but also might have given the hosts cardiac arrhythmia, major seizures, nerve damage, or memory loss. Whoever received the treatment first might be left incapable of administering it safely to the other patient.

Actually, once they understood the effects of the micro-robots better, Katy realized that any cure – other than antibodies – might become ineffective after one use. First, they didn't know what adaptive capability the micro-machines held; given time, they might reconfigure to become immune to any specific purgative. Second, a deeply infected victim might refuse to be treated, even going so far as to flee or fight back. The afflicted would also consider their condition a blessing to be spread. Only an unavoidable, internal prophylactic would guarantee immunity.

Even NuRikPo understood the insidious nature of the fascinating technology. A victim would not entirely lose their volition or ability. Only their resistance to the commands of the micro-tech would be modified. They would love and obey the ship it originated from… and the creators of that ship. Otherwise, slaves would retain their original memories, skills, and a portion of their original personality. They would be less obvious automatons than a fully rewritten organism or a facsimile android. They would also be much more useful. Was the ship trying to replace its original crew with biddable new sapients? Or were its aims more grandiose: luring in sapients to become carriers for the spread of its influence?

The significance of the 'greeter' construct outside their shuttle door became more clear. If it did indeed mimic the Ningyo, then it might have met them in person. If the Ningyo had come aboard, they could be infested. The Ningyo might have been less susceptible to attack, compared to humanoids… but their *suits* were easy targets, judging from NuRikPo's greater vulnerability. The suits could have been disabled and their biological components held captive for as long as it took the micro-robots to puzzle out an interface.

That scenario would explain why the Ningyo were stopping and recruiting ships – particularly pirate ships – for the unnamed vessel. They were snaring it new prey, to be transformed into new carriers. Katy had a horrible vision of the *Scape Grace* being transformed into an obedient, orderly assembly of brain-washed drones. Not that she cared much about the fate of the individual crew, but that ship was her home, the repository of all her belongings, and her ride between galaxies. She needed those reeking apes – Human and Mauraug both – to keep working on *her* behalf.

They had to leave this ship. They had to bring the cure back to *Scape Grace* and reverse whatever damage had already been done. There was no way that the morons still aboard would be capable of developing their own counter-agent. Katy had to admit that without NuRikPo, she would never have managed it. Alone, he probably would have failed as well. Only the fusion of their specialties produced a workable model capable of navigating a living body, identifying its targets, and selectively destroying just those undesirables.

It was nice to have understudies capable of filling in in their absence – Luuboh bash'Gaulig in her case, the Georges for NuRikPo – but those pale shadows would never identify the threat in time, much less know what to do against it. No, *Scape Grace* was doomed unless they could get back.

The major problem with escaping was the obvious problem: where was the exit? The ship had sealed up their point of entry, not only closing but also removing the portal entirely. If the material of the ship's hull was sufficient to maintain pressure and temperature against vacuum, not to mention reflect inter-stellar radiation and debris, then it would be difficult to breach.

The weaponry built into their shuttle might burn or blast a hole, but either method had its problems. An explosion of sufficient force would damage them also in the enclosed space; there was nowhere to move the shuttle far enough away from the walls to avoid that risk. An energy weapon of sufficient magni-tude carried the same hazard. A lower-powered beam could possibly carve their way out more slowly… but then they had to be concerned about the self-repair properties of the unique ship. Could they cut fast enough to outrace the hull material sealing itself back up? Could they get enough of a lead to open a hole large enough for the shuttle? Could they manage that basic feat, *plus* deal with sudden depressurization, suction, waste heat… and any unexpected defenses the ship might muster?

There were too many unknowns to act immediately. Or rather, to act as soon as they felt capable of action. Katy and NuRikPo slept for most of the day following their inoculation. They hardly had the strength to curse at one another, much less hold a conversation. Three meals and thirty hours passed before they could confer to evaluate their situation.

Katy shared her thoughts and was relieved to find NuRikPo in agreement. He added that, like the micro-robot antibody system, the other systems of the ship had to have their weaknesses. Rather than worry about a brute force solution to break their way out, they would be better served by resuming their study of the ship's anatomy. Ideally, they would learn something about the methods powering the various construct cell types and maintaining coordination between them.

"For example, do they communicate through a central controller? Do they form a central control structure among themselves? Or do they have a truly decentralized structure and act only based on local interactions with adjacent cells? I suspect that some combination of these possibilities is at work," NuRikPo theorized.

One of his first projects upon regaining his faculties was to search for signals. Not external signals from the *Scape Grace* – an automated program already was working on that problem over the last four days – but signals internal to the ship itself. NuRikPo identified some type of very short wave radio communication emanating from just outside the shuttle, but the signals were fragmentary and encoded in an unfamiliar manner. The latter property was unsurprising; there was no reason a truly foreign intelligence would employ the same coding structures used by Zig or any other Collective culture. Even after decoding, the underlying messages would be unintelligible without reference to a numerical or linguistic system or both.

What was odd was that the signals were individually short and weak and originated from multiple points simultaneously, in 'choruses' of signals with varying intensity, frequency, and duration, *and* differing ranges of each property for each signal individually. Rather than modulating one strong carrier wave, the system seemed to modulate the entire composite of multiple waves. Possibly, the component cells of the ship talked in an all-to-all manner, each receptive to only one or a small range of signal types. Or, groups of cells talked to groups of cells. The possibilities could permutate over a wide solution space.

"Much as I hate to say it, we could really use that wirehead right now," Katy groused. She was referring to Gleamer. "More specifically, we could use one of his programs to work on analysis."

"While speaking the native language might be useful, I'm afraid we'll need to wage war before we can consider diplomacy." The two of them sat across the shuttle cabin from one another, NuRikPo slumped askew in the control chair and Katy hunched over the side of the folding cot.

Katy fixed the Zig with a condescending look, brows raised as her chin tilted down. "If we could figure out their 'language' we might be able to interfere with their control structure. We might get access to their programming. I love the thought that we might override *this* system the way it tried to override ours. I suppose we don't have the time or resources right now, but when we get back, we might want Gleamer to look over our recordings and see if this ship's AI can be hacked."

"Ah, you want to manipulate it. My apologies, I should have anticipated that thought from you."

"Stick it between your spicules, you selenium-sucking stickbug."

"A pity your linguistic ability ground to a halt before you reached maturity. Fortunately, your victims respond well enough to suggestive grunts and gestures."

"Victims? Even if you're referring to my *marks*, I'd like to see you try to manage the same. You'd be dead in seconds, even if your target was a blind Zig widow."

"I admit I lack your *advantages*. Still, as our unwanted guests have demonstrated, there are means of persuasion that do not involve prostitution."

"Hey, penetrate or be penetrated, you still have to know what you're doing. They're effective, I'm effective, you're effective. I don't tell you how to tighten a bolt, you can do me the same courtesy."

"If it will get us off the current topic, then yes, I will agree to avoid insulting your *abilities*."

"Even your tone of voice carries insults. You could read technical instructions and sound condescending."

"Well, then pardon me my tone and I will pardon your behavior."

"*My* behavior? I don't need your *KetkeRakeh* pardon, *TimoTi*-RikPoNu!"

Katy was gratified to see her retort hit home. If she hit the inflections right, she had basically informed NuRikPo that he was acting out of character for his caste, assuming the privileges reserved for a Gold Caste spiritual leader. It was a devastating criticism if delivered by another Zig, a censure with no exact Human counterpart. The closest was something like the cliché: "Who died and made you God?"

NuRikPo certainly looked shocked, his reflective eyes opened wide and his fingers splayed as if to catch himself from falling forward. Then his eyes shut tight and his mouth drew taut, while his hands wrapped around his shoulders. He shuddered and rocked forward. Katy became briefly concerned that she might have overloaded his overburdened emotional balance somehow. The last thing she wanted – or needed – was for the engineer to have a mental breakdown.

When she saw drops of glittering moisture at the corner of his eyes, she was terrified that the Zig was crying. Then she finally reached across cultural differences and recognized the behavior. NuRikPo was laughing. He finally opened his mouth and a clicking, twittering noise poured from his throat as he continued to shake.

"What? I meant it, asshole. You have no right…"

"No," NuRikPo gasped, "You were close…" He struggled to stop shaking and draw breath to respond. "…but I think you meant to say *KettiRakeh*, 'inappropriate for one's caste', not 'inappropriate for one's family'. It sounded like you were telling me to stop acting like your father. Otherwise, I'm impressed by your grasp of *KetiNepaTi*." He was gradually managing to regain his composure, relaxing his mouth but still blinking furiously.

Katy rolled her eyes, "Close enough. I'm sure my father would sound like you if he were here. What I do is none of his business, either. Maybe we can act like professionals here and save the personal comments for… actually, never."

"Fair enough," NuRikPo agreed, nodding in intentional imitation of Human gesture. "I'm gratified that you even learned enough to attempt that phrase. Sometimes I wonder if Humans understand anything about Zig culture beyond our technology." He attempted to stand, but was forced to brace himself on the chair and console to stay upright.

"Huh, I thought you made it intentionally complicated so that outsiders would stay confused. I learned enough to push buttons… you know, like I do."

"It's actually *simplified* from several centuries ago, into more workable forms. I'd say Human culture is equally confusing. I have difficulty seeing you, captain Lerner, my assistants, and that appropriately-named Iron Simon as members of the same species. You personally look like Gold Caste and work like Copper; the captain leads like Gold Caste but looks like Iron. The other three at least match their appearance to their duties. Then I compare you to that Macauley person…" NuRikPo made an obvious flinch of revulsion.

"I don't know what you non-Humans have against him. I like his style," Katy teased, stretching herself and preparing to test her own legs.

"No surprise. He seems your intellectual type, if not physical. But surely you can recognize why he disturbs saner sapients."

"I can like whoever I like, *Dad*."

"Please, can we get back to work now? Professional, remember?"

"Agreed."

After a quick meal heavily spiked with electrolytes and nutrients helpful for regrowth of their damaged tissues, Katy and NuRikPo began packing for their expedition outside of the shuttle. They agreed that they needed to investigate the structure of the unnamed ship more thoroughly. As a proximate goal, they needed to identify its limitations and weaknesses to find points for exploitation. They needed to escape. At a minimum, they needed to transmit a message to *Scape Grace*. Somewhere in between was their idea of expelling a beacon containing a sample of the counter-agent. Perhaps with a sample for reference, their understudies could manage to bridge the gap between their comprehension and their superiors'.

The distal goal for the two investigators remained the same as their original assignment: explore the unnamed ship, document its technologies, and collect whatever they could for use or resale to the highest bidder. It appeared that this goal was a holistic endeavor. Either they would comprehend the unique design and structures of this ship, in total, or else its separate parts were worse than useless... they might be actively dangerous to export.

20

After some heated discussion, Katy Olu and NuRikPo finally compromised: they would exit the shuttle armed, but with weapons holstered. Katy wanted to emerge ready to fire at the first sign of threat; NuRikPo argued that they should leave their firearms behind. He believed that their standard weaponry would have little effect if the ship actually intended them harm. Worse, brandishing weapons might be interpreted as a hostile action, leading to a self-defense response. He argued that, for all they knew, the incursion of micro-robots into their bodies might have been the immune response they originally took it for: a reaction to damage.

Katy disagreed, pointing out that the invasion of their bodies went far beyond simple defenses. The system was tailored to take control of biological organisms. That much was obvious and beyond dispute. Once the ship realized that its first attack had failed, it might well escalate to more overt measures or attempt to destroy them as a threat to its plans. She wanted to be ready for a physical attack.

Ultimately, Katy had to agree that their guns could do little more than annoy their host. Still, she was reluctant to leave any tool behind and demanded that they keep the weapons at hand.

So it was that they emerged from the shuttle's door aiming scanners, not side arms. Katy was recording a three-dimensional spatial map of their surroundings using both light and sound reflection, with an active program tracking their movement and comparing successive scans. The application would act both as a motion detector and as a warning in case the ship changed the layout of its internal spaces. In the event that a doorway disappeared behind them, the system would help them identify the relative location of their shuttle. While they might not be able to blast a path into space, they might be able to at least cut their way back to the shuttle if the ship tried to separate them.

NuRikPo continued to monitor electromagnetic traffic both within and without the ship. The latter was still cut off, but just in case something broke through, he would be ready. His augmented compad maintained a link to the shuttle's systems, allowing him to control the boat remotely, if necessary. He had a wireless camera and microphone button pinned to his collar and was simultaneously recording video and audio of their surroundings. Programs within his 'pad would try to match what they observed to known patterns, prompting hypotheses about the likely functions of objects in case the two explorers missed an idea.

An AI or even a sub-AI would have made their work much simpler and more effective, but of course NuRikPo wouldn't consider such an idea, and Katy's AI was safely locked away in her quarters. Old Griot, her family's AI for the last century, was too valuable to risk elsewhere in the ship, let alone bringing on a hazardous mission like this one. After Katy was expelled from Antananarivo Medical University on Terra, Griot became her sole teacher, continuing her education in medicine. He was a wellspring of miscellaneous knowledge and good advice, having served generation after generation of Olus. Griot did not judge, not even after her decision to leave home, leave Terra, and even leave the Terran sphere of planets. He guided her across multiple worlds, doing his part to keep her safe from the consequences of one bad decision after another.

She still wasn't sure if joining the pirate crew was a good or a bad decision. Evgeny Lerner had drawn her onto the *Scape Grace*. At the time, the rugged, gruff captain seemed like a useful ally and a means of escape from her current entanglements. As the medic and moll of a criminal syndicate leader, Katy met Evgeny when the pirates arrived to talk business with her boss/boyfriend/captor. They were immediately attracted to one another. Suggestive talk turned into definitive action when negotiations over the price of goods went sour. Katy gave the pirates an opening to double-cross the gangsters, *then* managed to convince Evgeny that the betrayal of her former lover in no way suggested any likelihood of turning on him, her new paramour. She had been a prisoner, exploited for both brains and body. If Evgeny treated her well, she would use her talents in his service, not to his downfall.

Their collaboration actually turned out to be of mutual benefit. For the first time, Katy was able to keep a significant share of the profits her work earned. The job was so good that even when she lost the fringe benefit of sleeping with the captain, she decided to stay aboard anyway. Evgeny turned out to be a bit boring anyway, very routine and repressed. Who would have thought a pirate captain could be dull?

Unfortunately, when the captain's protection ended, Katy began to reap the results of the crew's resentment of her privileged status. The worst was a humiliating wrestling match with the Mauraug first mate, Soloth. Katy had suggested that the genderless gorilla watch its step or else it might wake up from cybernetic maintenance *actually* neutered. In response, Soloth dislocated Katy's shoulders – both of them simultaneously – and folded her head back to touch her feet.

That day was when Katy first made friends with Luuboh bash'Gaulig. She trained the uniquely obliging Mauraug out of self-interest. She needed *someone* to reset her joints properly and help out while her torn muscles healed.

NuRikPo was a constant thorn. The Zig had not been impressed while Katy had the captain's ear (and other parts), but wasn't any nastier after she lost her queendom. 'Po seemed equally distant and hostile whether she stayed quietly in the medical room, mingled with the beefcake among the combat crew, or went off-ship on assignment to work a contact. Their spheres only intersected when 'Po was badly hurt or Katy needed her equipment repaired, and those necessary contacts were unpleasant for both.

Perhaps the real reason for their antagonism was that they had no *reason* to reconcile. They could generally avoid one another, and when they couldn't, they could still relish their mutual distaste without it impeding their work or transitioning into violence.

Katy had reason to hate Soloth, but kept the expression of that feeling under control for her own safety. She hadn't even needed a personal reason to hate Soloth. She disliked most Mauraug, foremost for the same reasons most Humans did: historical precedent. The two simian species had been at odds ever since they met and the first Mauraug took a shit on its Human counterpart.

That wasn't a metaphor; it literally defecated upon the Human representative. Ever since, the theocratic, militaristic, uptight Mauraug Dominion had been trying to take a metaphorical crap on the Terran sphere. Even Mauraug *not* part of the Dominion were dangerous: raiders and rogue colonists and other criminals. The fact that almost half of the *Scape Grace* crew was Mauraug did little to improve Katy's view of their species. How the captain could put up with the preachy, bitchy apes was beyond her understanding. Wasn't his home blown up by Mauraug, after all? It didn't matter which faction was fighting which other one, they were all violent zealots.

For similar reasons, Katy kept matters civil with the Vislin, Tklth. They had a simple agreement: each would do their respective jobs and not kill one another. The moment that changed, one of them would die. Soloth might enjoy administering pain, but Tklth was a professional murderer. Katy could respect that. She kept her medical care as painless as possible for the twitchy lizard and kept her pistol close and loaded with tranquilizers while she worked.

Right then, her concussion pistol was loaded with two types of ammo: hypodermic darts loaded with their counter-agent machines – in case the ship tried another microtechnology assault – and explosive rounds that might provide enough punch to rip a door-valve open or knock back a smaller, mobile construct.

The 'greeter' outside was one such construct, though the only one they had seen. Katy and NuRikPo did not expect to see many more such ambulatory entities. The ship's composite nature meant that it could use its own mass to create 'crew' at need, but there was probably an energy cost for doing so, and the ship could likely control its own systems internally without the need for an external manipulator. Thus, separate bodies would have specific uses, like providing a face to talk to… or pursuing and restraining other mobile organisms.

The creature itself was right outside their door. It presented the first and most obvious threat. While the fact that it had not attacked the shuttle was reassuring, its constant presence and attempts to draw their attention were disturbing. Now, as NuRikPo opened the door and began to exit, it stood back two meters and watched them closely.

NuRikPo took an experimental step forward and diagonally away, toward the red-lit exit doorway. The entity turned its head slightly to track him, monochrome 'eyes' rotating as well. Its mouth, containing facsimiles of teeth and tongue, flexed and articulated words.

"Why kill?"

NuRikPo stopped, already staring at the metallic grey entity. He blinked, and the other being mimicked the reflex. Turning to Katy, he asked, "What does it mean? For that matter, why can it speak now?"

Katy shrugged in response. "Maybe it has records from the Ningyo. Maybe it just didn't have a reason to bother before. Maybe with its cells crawling around in our brains, it recorded and transmitted enough data to start a translation. Maybe all of the above."

Frowning and turning back to the entity, the Zig asked, "Kill... what? Why *did* we kill... or why *should* one kill?"

"Why kill... parts?"

"It's not discussing philosophy, 'Po. It's asking why we disabled its component cells. Let me talk; it's something I'm good at, *remember?*" Katy hoped that NuRikPo could read her intent better than a novice speaker. She meant: *I'm good at deception.* NuRikPo nodded in response, either understanding or just handing off responsibility.

Katy turned back to the figure, assuming her best innocent expression. "We were afraid. You did not warn us. Your... parts... entered our bodies. We thought you would hurt us. We protected ourselves."

The figure turned to face Katy and responded, "Not attack. I share. I hear. You… angry. I make you happy. We join." It punctuated its speech with an appropriate gesture, hands clasping together.

Katy answered with a gesture of her own, hands pushing forward, palms open. "Whoa. 'Joining' takes two. You *ask* first. We are not easily persuaded."

Surprising her, the being interrupted, asking, "Persuaded?"

"Damn… uh, convinced? Made to agree?"

"Agree. We must agree. You fear. You resist. Do not. Accept. Agree. Be joined."

"Show us. Who are you? What are you? Why should we join? Help us understand. If we know more, we will agree."

"Yes. Agree. I show. You understand. We join. Come." With this apparent agreement, the construct turned and walked away, toward the exit. It paused at the ovoid opening and turned around, evidently waiting on Katy and NuRikPo to follow.

"Well, like it says, come on," Katy tilted her head toward the passage and stepped forward as well.

"You're right, you *are* good at that," NuRikPo grudgingly observed as he fell into line behind Katy. His voice dropped to a lower volume as he added, "It's doing what you want because you told it what it wanted to hear, a tactic apparently effective on many forms of mind."

Katy turned back to him as they neared the construct, giving him a wide-eyed stare of exasperation. Her lips pursed as she hissed, "Ssh."

The engineer was slow to register her objection, continuing: "Which makes me wonder, why have you never tried these skills on *me*? Even false courtesy…"

Katy interrupted his complaint with her *sotto voce* reply: "Because I never wanted anything from you."

The entity either did not hear or else did not grasp the nuances of their conversation. It continued forward, leading them deeper into the hallway, a claustrophobic tube with a lopsided ovoid cross-section, wider at the base and narrowing toward the top. The red lighting emanated from strips of clustered globules, each glowing weakly but summing to provide greater illumination. Other than these protrusions and a few regularly spaced centimeter-sized holes, the hallway was composed of the same regular hexagonally tiled substance as the shuttle bay walls.

As they walked, NuRikPo sidled closer to Katy and continued, "Never? Why not? Do you think I have no value as an ally?"

Katy muttered between clenched teeth, "Can we discuss this some other time? Kind of inappropriate right now. Focus on learning what we can while it's friendly."

Finally, the possible hazards of their conversation dawned on the Zig, and he fell silent, watching their guide closely for any signs of suspicion. It continued to appear oblivious.

They emerged from the far end of the passage after a walk of at least one hundred meters. The exit opened onto a chamber like the inside of a rounded trapezoidal solid, again wider at its base and rising to a narrower domed rectangle at its peak. More of the light clusters protruded from that roof, rendering the space almost bright enough for comfortable sight. Its contents were unremarkable: extrusions from the floor resembled abstract seats and platforms. One section of the wall was a smooth, darker, rounded film, like a plastic or glass panel set into the surrounding composite material.

NuRikPo crossed to the panel and passed his recorder over its surface. He turned to the entity and asked, "Is this a display screen? An interface? May I touch it?"

"A display. Yes. It shows images. No interface. I… am… interface."

That explanation made a certain amount of sense to both investigators. Once, some Terran ships were actually integrated with AI 'crew' and could be operated by voice commands from the Human partners of those AIs. Manual controls would still exist, however. Further, no sane designer would make an entire ship the body of a single, all-powerful AI… not even before the Terrans joined the Collective and certainly not afterward. The creators of *this* ship apparently placed much greater trust in their artificial intelligences, if they gave their ships singular minds and let each mind operate its ship directly. Creating such a ship was just too close to unleashing a giant, spacefaring sapient for the comfort of any small, dependent, sapient passenger.

Speaking of which… Katy decided to ask a question that had been troubling her since the captain sent them off on this ill-planned errand.

"What should we call you? Do you have a name?"

"I am… Traveler… for Mission… of Meeting… and Joining… Second Model."

"That is not a name; that is a title. A description. It says what you do."

"What is name?"

"What others use to identify you. A label. I am Katy, Katy Olu."

"What is 'Katy'?"

"My name. It doesn't mean anything other than *me*."

"Names do not have meaning?"

NuRikPo broke in to observe, "Actually, names typically do start with meanings and some names attain meanings later. My name means: Po, unique identifier, of genealogical descent Nu, of training program Rik. I lack the fourth syllable designating honorific or title because I never earned or inherited one."

Katy looked back at him, nonplussed. "That's nice. What I really wanted was something to call our host rather than, 'the unnamed ship'." Turning back to the construct, she interpreted, "Should we call you Traveler? Second? Your name is very long."

"What about 'Emissary'? Still a title, but it sums up the description well," NuRikPo suggested.

The construct confirmed, "I accept Emissary."

"I thought I was handling the talking?" Katy groused at NuRikPo.

The Zig popped his lips in amusement. "Well, at the moment, Emissary and I have more to talk about." He indeed took over the conversation, directing a question toward the newly named entity: "Emissary, please display the view of outside space?"

The construct looked toward the display screen and it immediately darkened, then lit up with a familiar image. Her two crew members saw the rear exhaust of *Scape Grace*, engines alight with nuclear incandescence. A distinct rippling distortion signified the bending of physical law around both ships, which permitted their acceleration to violate the normal limits of matter and energy.

"Our ship is moving… but not away from us," NuRikPo mused. "Are we moving also?"

"Yes," Emissary replied, "I follow. We find fuel, find others, join others. Mission. Success."

"Then go home?" Katy interjected.

"Make home," Emissary corrected her, "Home with others. Home here. All join. Family. All happy." It opened its arms to symbolically embrace them, the displayed *Scape Grace*, and perhaps the wider, surrounding star system. "All join, happy, family. Build Third Model for next mission."

Katy lost her diplomatic demeanor for a moment, responding with a phrase matching NuRikPo's feelings perfectly: "Oh, shit."

21

After a clumsy explanation for Katy's expletive, she and NuRikPo continued to accompany the extruded avatar of Emissary through the remainder of its anatomy. Their wonder at the art and technology of the foreign ship was tempered by their new understanding of its mindset and capabilities.

Its goals seemed simple: explore new systems, meet new neighbors, and render them friendly by any means necessary. Its design also seemed simple on the surface. There were no specific controls, few displays, and only a few pre-designated work spaces. The ship created open rooms at need, just as it was now creating passages between areas to suit its guests. Otherwise, it contained all of the functional elements of any starship: engines, sensory receptors, environmental controls, manipulation tools (including weaponry), and control systems to interface across those subsystems.

Underneath the basic functional description, however, was a substrate of startling complexity. Only portions of the engine and the central 'skeletal' structure of the ship were cast as a continuous, solid frame. Everything else – from the furnishings, the display screens, the sensors, the environmental systems, the weapons, and the thousands of smaller components that made up those organs – was composed of individually formed and replaceable cells, or structures built by those cells. Emissary could quickly repair most damage, not only hull breaches. The ship could lose a stabilizer, an oxygen extractor, or a cannon muzzle and have a new one ready for use within minutes.

The ship's mind was similarly complex. As best as the investigators could decipher from its answers to their inquiries, Emissary's program was the net result of a nervous matrix distributed across multiple regions of the ship, incorporating the functions of billions of cellular units. It maintained several 'brains', clusters of cells capable of retaining and rebuilding its core program and personality even if a significant portion of its structure were destroyed.

The cells themselves were effectively decentralized, following through on their routine functions without a central processor's orders. Yet their composite 'organs' were receptive to conscious control from the overall entity-mind. The interplay between remotely distributed elements – as contrasted with adjacent elements – explained the volleys of radio signals NuRikPo continued to detect as they explored the ship. When messages could not be transmitted between systems through electrical or chemical signals, nor via short-range cellular messengers, then specialized cells employed radio communication on behalf of their neighbors.

Katy was once again impressed despite herself. Nature required billions of years to produce systems that elaborate, working out the problems of simultaneous design limitations through trial and error, refereed by the constant demands of survival and replication. This structure had been directly designed by other sapients, presumably over a much shorter time-span. Emissary confirmed this idea, stating that its predecessor, First Model, was assembled in a vast orbital laboratory. Only one such ship needed to be built manually. The ships were granted reproductive capabilities, deduced from Emissary's claim to have been created by First Model directly and its plan to create a Third Model, itself.

The problem with all this sharing and learning was that Katy was coming to suspect that Emissary's motives might *also* be more complex than they first appeared. Certainly, what the ship already admitted about its goals was problematic enough, amounting to brainwashing, conquest, and colonization. Yet it presented these plans couched in seemingly innocent, pleasant language. It claimed to be offering help: peace, unity and prosperity. Katy could not yet decide if it was an alien enough mind to genuinely conflate bodily violation as 'helping', if it was having trouble with the translation of terms, or if it was just trying to coerce them with clumsy bluff and propaganda.

During their investigation of the ship, Emissary persistently attempted to convince them to "join" with it again. Any time they showed interest in a particular system or asked for details about a specific innovation, it would take their attention for admiration and suggest that they, too, could be a part of its wonderful self. Even so, Katy had to admit that it wasn't even the pushiest suitor she had ever dealt with. Plenty of entities wanted to put parts of their anatomy into hers. Leading a 'lover' along far enough to serve her purposes while still maintaining her bodily integrity was a familiar dance.

The revelation that they were on their way to a confrontation gave their explorations added urgency. Not only would a fight potentially pose a risk to Emissary and its passengers, the distraction of a battle might give Katy and NuRikPo their best chance for escape. If the foreign ship was successful in its plans to create a permanent home within Collective space, their knowledge might be vitally necessary to prevent 'joining' on a wider scale.

While the pirates of *Scape Grace* might be parasites and exploiters of their surrounding civilization, they needed that civilization to continue for their own support. The crew members each also had personal attachments to their native cultures, home worlds, favored associates and preferred ports of leave. As much as many crew members had alienated or been alienated by some part of the Collective, most could not honestly wish its disruption.

All too soon, Emissary's display screens began to show the irregular illuminated arc of a dwarf planetoid. The body's dimensions and color were familiar. NuRikPo was first to recognize the features of their former target, the Zig mining operation.

"I don't know why I'm surprised. We were in the neighborhood and got dragged along on this 'mission'," he groused, obviously grudging that their second chance at the mining base would still provide no opportunity for his personal enrichment.

"No," Emissary responded, its language skills and comprehension having improved steadily during their hours of interaction. "Not dragged. I chose you. You came here before. You know this place. I will help. Separately we fail. Together we succeed. Joining is best."

"We'll see," Katy taunted coyly.

She managed to mask her dismay at the revelation that Emissary and its Ningyo allies were already familiar with their attack on the Zig miners. Their abductors either tracked their escape or anticipated their path and laid a trap well calculated to draw *Scape Grace* in. Either this alien AI was a tactical genius, such genius arose from its partnership with the *Black Humor* and her Ningyo crew… or else the identity and behavior of *Scape Grace* was far better known than her crew suspected.

Notoriety was no asset to an interstellar pirate. "Striking fear into the hearts of their victims" was counterproductive. Anonymity and the ability to get close to a target without raising alarms was much more useful. Moving in and out of systems without notice or under the guise of an innocent salvager's registry… that stealth was necessary for their continued operation. If '*Grace's* description and nature were becoming widespread news, it was only a matter of time before she was spotted or tracked, captured or destroyed.

"Danger begins soon," Emissary warned them, beckoning with a curl of its construct's fingers and hand. "I must change, maybe fast. Dangerous for you. Go to shuttle. Stay safe. We join when danger ends."

It seemed that they would have to suspend their survey. As much as their explorations were incomplete – NuRikPo was particularly frustrated by their inability to take samples – the opportunity to return to their shuttle peacefully was too good to pass up. Emissary was right; they would be safest within the shielded, rigid hull of their own vessel. Even if the strange ship shifted and flowed around them, they would slosh around within it like a mollusk in the tides.

Emissary's construct escorted the two back to their shuttle door, parting with a sorrowful wave. As they boarded, Katy looked back to close and seal the hatch. She saw the construct melt and flow, its constituent units reabsorbed into the material of the deck. In the shuttle's outer lighting, it glittered like a collapsing pile of iron filings. It was a beautiful and wondrous form of life. Even without it twisting her feelings, Katy would have preferred its anatomy to that of most biological organisms she had studied, sentient or otherwise.

It was a shame it was such a threat, one which might need to be destroyed in self-defense.

The final two days of travel followed a remarkably parallel routine aboard the *Scape Grace*. The survey of Emissary by Katy and NuRikPo was echoed in several respects.

Their tour of Emissary was akin to a tour of *Scape Grace* undertaken by the Ningyo, Jolly and Punch. On the fourth day, the two Ningyo grew bored and asked to be shown around the ship. Originally, they insisted that captain Lerner be their guide. He managed to defer that service to Burnett and Zenaida Georges on the basis that the two engineers-in-training would be better able to answer questions about the ship's design and functions. To his relief, Jolly accepted this logic.

Evgeny's ulterior motive was to buy himself time on the bridge, unsupervised. He had managed to pass secret orders to Gleamer and Luuboh via their private communications relay, but feedback was limited by their opportunities to check messages unobserved.

Individually, Gleamer's research and Luuboh's examinations matched NuRikPo's and Katy's discoveries, respectively. Gleamer's analysis of the mysterious radio signals had originally outstripped NuRikPo's understanding of the patterns hidden in the electromagnetic 'choruses' used by the miniature robots to coordinate their activities. After a time, the frequency of the signals declined and Gleamer's lead shortened, due to the lack of novel raw data for his linguistic programs. Luuboh, by contrast, began and stayed far behind Katy's comprehension of the structure and functions of the micro-robots. Yet, it grasped the essential nature of the invaders well enough: their form, their abilities, their influence on a subject's mind via manipulation of its body, and their subtle danger as a result.

Luuboh had plenty of time to converse with Tklth while stuck in the medical room. Overtly, the Vislin was much more pleasant a companion than she had ever been before. She was not only no longer threatening, she was actually polite and even solicitous. Even so, the contrast between her former and present self was unnerving. Every pleasantry she spoke was a reminder about how easily one's personality could be warped by a few cellular modifications.

The worst parts were her pleas for release. She began by reassuring Luuboh that she was healthy, she was calm, she was healing, and she would cause him no harm if the magnetic shackles were removed. When he deflected or ignored these suggestions, she moved on to polite requests. After that came the persuasive arguments: she was harmed by immobility; the shackles were restricting her circulation; Luuboh was acting out of fear and not concern for its patient's well-being; she could help it with whatever work distracted it so; and so forth. Luuboh was afraid she would resort to pleading, begging, and eventually, threats.

During this time, Evgeny became the point of synthesis for Gleamer and Luuboh's separate discoveries. He worked out that Tklth's infestation was probably one of the two sources of communication Gleamer identified, with one or both of the Ningyo being the secondary origin. This idea was unpleasant, but reassuring for another reason: if no one else was 'broadcasting' in the same way, the encroachment of the micro-tech might not have extended beyond the Vislin. Luuboh was still suspect, but as long as the Mauraug continued working to expose the miniature invaders, Evgeny had to assume it was still on his side and not compromised.

Evgeny was certain that the Ningyo brought the micro-tech aboard, but still could not decide if they had done so intentionally or unwittingly. His suspicions about the odd coincidence of unique technology coupled with the discovery of a unique foreign ship began to approach the truth. As Luuboh added reports about Tklth's anomalous behavior, Evgeny became more and more convinced that the Ningyo were acting out of character. Not that Ningyo didn't normally act strangely, but that basic alienness could easily hide further alien influences. Jolly seemed abnormally pacifistic, shrugging off the death of its crew member with philosophical jargon. That might be normal behavior for its culture… or it might be manipulated behavior to suit the goals of the micro-robots' controller.

There were still several major pieces of knowledge Evgeny lacked, elements he and his remaining crew could not uncover in the limited time available for study. Evgeny took advantage of his time alone with Gleamer to pass on a compad filled with data from Luuboh's research, which he had picked up by feigning an injury to cover a trip to medical. Even so, Gleamer and his attendant programs could not work miracles with limited observations.

A similar relay was managed – out of sight and hearing of the ship's public systems – when Soloth stopped into Evgeny's private quarters. The two hastily compared notes on their tactical plans for the upcoming battle, including strategies for compromising *Harauch* and double-crossing both of their 'allied' ships. Most of their plans included the regrettable necessity of abandoning Katy Olu and NuRikPo, unless the entire operation went according to Jolly's optimistic plans and the two sides actually parted ways amicably. That scenario seemed increasingly unlikely the more Evgeny learned about the micro-tech loosed onboard. Neither side could safely allow the other to leave with the knowledge that they gained during their association.

For similar reasons, Evgeny and Soloth discussed the disposition of their combat crew, particularly the assignment of substitute officers. They would have to place specific persons where their individual abilities and tendencies would allow them to react appropriately as situations changed. Soloth would not have much opportunity to discuss counter-strike plans against the Ningyo with individual crew members. Anywhere it might talk to combat crew was under observation. The common lot could not be made privy to the secret 'dark areas' of the ship where they might safely hold private conversations.

After all, Evgeny thought to himself, *I don't even want to mention Bay 3e to Soloth. It was* supposed *to be my secret with Luuboh. If everybody knows about a secret asset, why bother?*

Eventually, all time for studies, clandestine maneuvers, and plotting came to an end. Just as Emissary cut off Katy and NuRikPo's investigations, their onrushing destination forced a change in activities upon *Scape Grace*.

First mate Soloth bash'Soloth executed its first layer of plans by dispatching crew to their assigned stations. It called Havish bash'Buurem up the bridge to assume Tklth's post at weapons. The Mauraug veteran arrived dressed in canvas knee pants, heavy boots, and an impact-armor chest plate printed with the insignia of its old military unit. Sol Metaxas, looking much better rested and groomed than he had at the crew briefing, went to engineering to serve as assistant to the promoted chief engineers, Zenaida and Burnett Georges. Soloth delegated the Mauraug 'leader', Kuugan bash'Ranpool, to 'assist' Luuboh bash'Gaulig in medical. In reality, they both understood that Kuugan would act as chaperone to both Tklth and Luuboh, blocking them from leaving the medical room in case they were compromised. For example, they might try to sabotage the *Scape Grace* or protect the Ningyo.

Soloth ordered the rest of the combat crew to hold themselves at readiness for either assault or defense duties, depending on how the attack against the Zig went. Whichever way the battle turned, Soloth wanted Macauley at the point of greatest danger: in the outermost, lower hold during the combat with the Zig fighters; at the forefront of an assault team sent into the breached Zig mining base; or leading a defense team pressed to keep boarders from taking out their key systems.

Every crew member, plus the intruding Ningyo, moved to stations as *Scape Grace* closed on the planetoid. *Harauch* and the 'unnamed' ship followed in formation. Evgeny joined Jolly, Punch, Gleamer, Soloth, and Havish on the bridge and found himself with nowhere to sit. He eventually decided to station himself between Soloth's navigation post and Gleamer's communication console, at the far forward edge of the bridge. He became a somewhat deliberate obstruction between Jolly (seated at Evgeny's command console) and the primary display screen. It was a petty nuisance, but at the moment, it was the most provocation Evgeny could afford.

The conflict to come would determine if he must obstruct the Ningyo still further. Evgeny was torn between hope for an opening created by the chaos of battle or a quick, clean, profitable resolution. He still wanted the Ningyo, Jolly and all his crew, to die slowly… but the likelihood of that happening without significant concurrent damage to his ship, his crew, and himself was low. If Jolly turned out good to its word and capable enough to pull off its plans successfully, then Evgeny would just have to accept profit in trade for his revenge.

Revenge and profit were just two possibilities. If years of criminal enterprise taught Evgeny Lerner anything, it was that the actual outcome of a mission rarely matched any ideal result. At best, you escaped alive, claiming something of value, with a minimum of your own assets burned. There were so many, many ways for a job to go wrong. In a complex, varied universe, a quick death was by no means the worst possible outcome.

22

The effectiveness of their attack plan was nearly compromised by Jolly's insistence on keeping *Scape Grace* within close range of the other two ships until the last possible moment. If the Zig were watching carefully, they could have already spotted the oncoming objects. Depending on the attentiveness of the miners' observations, they might perceive three separate ships or one large vessel. Either way, if they saw two associated ships split off and approach from lateral vectors, the lure of the familiar pirate ship might not draw the full force of the defenders.

Like that practical consideration, the Ningyo ignored certain aspects of Evgeny and Soloth's strategic planning, without explanation. He only hinted at "secret reasons" for his decisions.

As such, Evgeny should have been less surprised when Gleamer announced, "The foreign ship… it's getting all blurry."

"What's that?" Evgeny responded.

"My readings are getting scrambled. Its mass, volume, albedo, output signature… everything detectable is varying randomly across its respective spectrum."

Jolly intruded to explain, "Didn't I say our friend is quite mutable? It can be an anomaly instead of a familiar face. Is it a ship? Is it an asteroid? No, it's… well, it is a ship. Also, an artificial organism. And it's *tricksy*."

"Great," Evgeny retorted, "We'll need more than tricks. Are we ready to start the *strategy*?"

"What is a strategy but a whole lot of tricks played in the right order? But yes, sound the trumps and start the game. We shall bid high and claim the pot!" Jolly sounded perversely enthusiastic. Even Punch nodded in evident readiness.

Jolly plugged its suit into the command console, transmitting a signal to *Harauch* and the unnamed ship. As the latter vessel pulled away, Evgeny could see its hull rippling and shifting. The former falsified insignia was gone, wiped away in a shimmer of color as the foreign ship obscured its identity once again. It was not only reshaping its exterior. Sections of its internal structure were being reworked, judging from the new bulges and pits appearing in its profile. Evgeny hoped Katy and NuRikPo were cached somewhere safe within the malleable mass.

Even as it transformed, the engines of the strange ship flared to greater fury and it leapt away past sight. At that cue, *Scape Grace* also accelerated, aiming directly toward the planetoid ahead. *Harauch* fell behind, both due to its lower maximum speed and its lateral course, opposite the direction selected by the foreign ship.

Harauch would arrive after and to one side of *Scape Grace* after following a wide arc away. Its separate but converging course would hopefully add to the apparent threat posed by *Scape Grace*, drawing more of the Zig fighter craft into engagement. Once the battle was joined, the late-arriving *Harauch* would force the Zig to choose between dividing their force to deal with both threats separately or else swarming the *Scape Grace* exclusively, leaving themselves vulnerable if they were still engaged as *Harauch* closed.

Scape Grace was a known threat. She had reduced the fighter fleet by five craft before the battle turned against the pirates. Unless the Zig rebuilt those five plus another half-dozen more, the two pirate-salvagers together held a slight advantage.

All that advantage meant was that one or both ships *might* survive the battle. They would be badly damaged under most projections. The predicted outcome could be swayed far in either direction by strategy or simple fortune. Mischance or a tactical error could result in total destruction; only a stroke of luck or genius would get them through the fight intact.

It was not a fight captain Lerner would have chosen. In fact, he *had* rejected it before and was not responsible for choosing it a second time. Still, he could hardly abdicate responsibility for his ship's survival while still desiring – and intending to reclaim – authority over 'Grace. Thus, Evgeny gave his best input to the planning of a foolish endeavor. He would also lend his full expertise to its execution.

He issued his own orders: "Full speed ahead, Soloth. Let's smoke the bees out of the hive so that baby bear can get its honey."

Jolly tilted its head toward Evgeny, "That's not half bad. Clumsy... but at least the metaphor *sticks together*. Ha!" It raised one hand, palm open and fingers splayed, lowering it in a violent gesture toward Punch. The other Ningyo had already raised its hand at the elbow and reached upward in a matching gesture. Their two molded plastic palms smacked together with a sharp crack as they met in midair.

The movement and noise startled Havish, the Mauraug replacement gunner. It looked back at the two Ningyo in alarm, hands coming off the weapons console in preparation for defense. When the robotic figures settled back into position as if nothing important had happened, Havish began to relax.

Soloth grunted, "Ningyo," and that was explanation enough. Soloth increased their speed. *Scape Grace* hurtled forward on an apparent collision course with the planetoid ahead.

The opening moves of the assault played out exactly as Jolly intended. A squadron of crude fighter craft launched from the Zig encampment well before *Scape Grace* was close enough to singe with their weaponry. In the first clash between the pirates and miners, the Zig kept the existence of their fighters concealed until *Scape Grace* entered orbit and began to organize a landing. Struggling to recall her shuttle had delayed the pirate ship's escape. The delay gave the miners several minutes of free shots. Evgeny thought of the farce as the equivalent of getting caught with his pants down and around his ankles. This time, now that each party knew the other's assets, there was no point in secrecy.

The fighters spread out in a loose net, separated widely enough to anticipate and intercept any lateral movement by *Scape Grace*, but not divided so far as to lose the advantage of their numbers. No doubt the Zig pilots were assisted by mathematically precise computer simulations which took their capabilities into account and adjusted for the actions of their enemy. The *Scape Grace* had similar programs, plus the flexibility of Human-made sub-AI systems. The balance of technology once again returned the outcome of battle to the choices of fallible biological minds.

Soloth reported eleven fighters arrayed against them. Two appeared cruder than the rest; these might have been the products of hasty assembly by the miners or else hasty repairs on the damaged fighters they could salvage. Gleamer monitored their comm traffic and reported that the fighters were relaying signals back and forth with the main base on the planetoid beyond. The transmissions were encoded: not well enough to stymie the programmer for long, but long enough to make them inaccessible before the attack started. Gleamer recorded and started decoding everything anyway, on the chance that the information he gleaned might prove useful later.

Havish tracked the closest targets and reviewed its choices from among the array of destructive tools NuRikPo added to *Scape Grace's* arsenal. Energy beams, high intensity lasers, magnetically accelerated projectiles with or without payloads, and even miniature, suicidal drone ships were among its options. There was great variety but limited uses of each weapon. Obviously, once the physical ammunition was spent, they had no replacements. But even the energy weapons drew power from the *'Grace's* finite fusion engines.

That limitation was part of the trouble of fighting a many-on-one battle: there were only so many shots one could fire, at once or in total. Getting left without offense was bad enough, but it was possible to be left defenseless also. The best defense against physical attacks was to shoot them down with intercepting fire. Plus, if the guns were overused, power could drop so low that defensive fields would fail.

The first Zig volley employed their energy weapons, which had greater range but much weaker impact, *particularly* at longer ranges. *Scape Grace* demonstrated that her defensive fields had been adequately repaired by refracting the incoming radiation. As 'Grace drew closer, the pirate also demonstrated the disadvantage of a many-on-one scenario for the many: friendly fire. The fighters' attacks would have an increasing chance of striking an ally via ricochet off the lone enemy's fields. If the fighters tried to surround 'Grace, stray, missed shots could become a hazard, as well.

The Zig chose the tactically sound option of remaining effectively stationary between the approaching *Scape Grace* and its target, their mining base. They would allow the attacker to draw close, weakening its defenses as it neared and falling back steadily to maintain distance as long as possible. Only when backed up against the planetoid's gravity well would the fighters at the fringes begin to break off and seek vulnerabilities at *Scape Grace's* flanks.

Rather than fall into this pattern, *Scape Grace* veered to one side, intentionally in the same direction as *Harauch's* original tangent. This maneuver drew the fighters in that same direction as they struggled to maintain their screen. *Harauch* was on the returning arc of its course by that point. It appeared beyond *Scape Grace* and headed for the leading edge of the Zig formation.

By that time, *Scape Grace* was close enough to choose targets with her own guns. Havish fired a dozen shots, removing one and then a second fighter from the battle. They were small and maneuverable ships, but relatively slow and piloted by amateurs. Most of Havish's misses were near ones, as it led its targets expertly and capitalized on any piloting errors.

Then, the *Harauch* was within range, and the Zig were put to their decision. To Evgeny's relief, they chose to respect *Scape Grace's* threat when they split their remaining strength. Three fighters broke off to intercept *Harauch* in an equilateral formation. The remaining six closed upon *Scape Grace*, trying to pull in close enough to engage their physical weaponry and maximize the damage of their energy attacks.

"Reserves below fifty percent of full charge," reported Soloth, monitoring data relayed from the engineers Georges. "At this rate, we cannot withstand long enough to remove the remaining fighters."

"Alone, no," Jolly rebutted, "but *Harauch* will do its part and pick up where we slacken."

Indeed, its faith was justified, as the formerly innocuous-seeming *Harauch* released its own volley of fire and removed one of the three oncoming fighters. The remaining two split widely, approaching their target from opposite sides.

Scape Grace answered this point with a score of her own: Havish unleashed one of the drone ships from its anchoring. The miniature vessel carried suffi-cient fuel only for a single burst of trans-light drive, but that charge was sufficient to launch it through a much larger ship. In this case, one of the fighters suffered the fatal impact. Both ships shattered in an uncontrolled fusion reaction, releas-ing sufficient force to nudge two other fighters *and* the *Scape Grace* away.

"Watch your radius!" Soloth bellowed at Havish. The other Mauraug grunt-ed in acknowledgement, annoyed at its own error.

They would have to deal with the fighters at even closer range soon. If only one or two remained while the pirate ships still survived, those Zig might choose suicide runs in order to protect their comrades back at home. Havish would be hard-pressed to shoot down each ship before it smashed into *Scape Grace*. Even if it hit every target, the backwash from their deaths might still cripple or destroy their enemy. The likelihood of such heroics was unknown. If the pilots were Iron Caste volunteers, then they almost certainly would die in defense of their fellows.

Jolly interrupted the rising intensity of the battle with an announcement: "Our friend is in position."

Soloth confirmed, "Energy discharge from outside of the atmosphere, strik-ing the Zig base on the surface."

"Hopefully your friend doesn't melt down all the goods in the process," Evgeny sneered at Jolly.

Jolly asked innocently, "Don't you cook your meals?"

"Oh, yeah, distress calls from the base," Gleamer chimed in, "aaaand now they're quiet. Punched in the throat. Good job, no-name."

"Maybe with nothing to defend, those fighters won't be so willing to stand and die," Evgeny ventured hopefully.

All through this discussion, the fighters, *Scape Grace*, and *Harauch* had been dancing and firing, spears of light igniting and dispersing as they beat against one another's defenses. Havish was doing its utmost to connect solidly with its own shots, while Soloth tried to present a difficult target to the fighters. '*Grace* had greater power on both offense and defense, but was forced to absorb more attacks. The fighters would fall to a direct hit, but were more likely to avoid attacks entirely.

A few early projectile attacks were attempted on both sides, but the range was still too great to give these much effectiveness. Even *Scape Grace* could veer away from a slug thrown at a mere thousand kilometers per second. The Zig most likely did not have the resources to spare for guided projectiles. However, given their technical expertise, their shells could easily contain deadly payloads. One hit with a ferrovorous catalyst could quickly strip away portions of *Scape Grace's* hull and multiple vital systems. Without NuRikPo aboard to counter such catalytic agents, their doom would be assured.

Still, the fight was going in their favor. Evgeny began to think they could hold out long enough for the unnamed ship to finish subduing the mining base. Then, even if the Zig defenders felt like continuing the fight – to avenge their fallen co-workers – the three attackers could join together and wipe out any remaining resistance.

Evgeny's igniting optimism was quickly snuffed by reactions from Gleamer, Jolly, and Punch. The three reeled back as if hearing a painfully loud noise.

Gleamer explained his reaction: "Really big magnetic wave from the planet. Distinct rhythm. Magnetic acceleration launcher."

Jolly's response was more cryptic: "She's hit… it's killing her!"

Soloth belatedly confirmed, "Replay shows a magnetic acceleration lift of a mass from the planetoid's surface, near the base. It might have been an escape shuttle, except that its trajectory aimed it at the unnamed ship. It likely made impact."

Evgeny shrugged. "They got off a desperate last shot. That ship ought to be able to absorb a crash…and we didn't see any explosion. It's not blowing up."

Jolly swiveled sharply to look at the other captain. "It's a Zig weapon. It contained crystallizing catalysts. Our friend did absorb the impact but the payload is freezing up her… systems."

Looking back toward the view screen, Jolly fell quiet.

Soloth reported, "*Harauch* is pulling away."

Oh, good, Evgeny thought to himself, *they're giving up the alien as lost. Too bad, but at least we aren't too badly hurt by this idiot's…*

Soloth amended, "*Harauch* is moving toward the base and the unnamed ship, on an intersecting course. Zig fighters are remaining behind, on their way to us."

"Wait, what?" Evgeny shouted, turning from Soloth to Jolly. "They're leaving us here alone? We can't manage all of the remaining fighters alone, not without a serious chance of death."

Jolly ignored Evgeny this time, continuing to focus its attention on the signals passing to and from its connections to the other two ships.

It was Punch who replied, instead, in a bizarre, harsh falsetto, "We must remain and do our best. *Harauch* will protect our friend. The base remains a threat. She must be protected until she can heal."

Gleamer gave further insight: "Confirmed: the Zig planetside are arming a second maglift projectile. I have their comm code worked out. They're talking between the cannon site and the base. The launcher's range is enough to protect them from direct on-site landings."

"But not enough to threaten us if we pull back. Come on, Jolly, pull us back. You did your best. Don't waste your people just to protect that foreigner. Don't waste *my* people to buy time." Evgeny struggled between commanding and pleading tones.

Punch answered him again, "It is necessary. She cannot be left to die. The mission must succeed. Nothing else is acceptable."

Evgeny was done arguing. "No, *this* is not acceptable."

Scape Grace emphasized his tension by shuddering. Havish had winged one of the fighters, and flying debris carved from its structure bounced off the pirate ship's nose. The hull in that section was dented and a storage bay became slightly smaller. Fortunately, the tough outer material held and the hull remained unbreached.

"Thirty percent reserves," Soloth announced. "Seven fighters remain operational. They are regrouping. These are familiar conditions. Now would be a good time to withdraw, once again."

"Do it," Evgeny ordered, "Retreat. Full speed. They'll go back to protect their base."

Soloth tapped in commands once, then twice, then turned back to look at Evgeny and then Jolly. "No response. Command override… your codes."

Evgeny looked at the Ningyo as well. Jolly remained unresponsive, still frozen as it communed with whatever master guided its devotion. It had locked Evgeny out of his own ship. It was forcing them to stand their ground and die.

"That does it. Fuck you, and fuck your friend," Evgeny spat at the two Ningyo.

He then raised his face to the ceiling. As the flares and impacts of the re-joined battle surged around them, Evgeny Lerner started to sing.

"Waltzing Matilda, Waltzing Matilda…"

A youthful, feminine voice answered him from the speakers above: "You'll come a'Waltzing Matilda with me!"

<h1 style="text-align:center">23</h1>

The reactions to Evgeny's musical outburst were varied. Neither Jolly nor Havish gave any visible response: Jolly was apparently lost in its own mind, and Havish was too busy tracking Zig targets. What they thought of the anomaly or whether they had even noticed it went unknown.

Punch only stared mutely at Evgeny, evidently confused. Gleamer turned full circle in his seat but also gaped dumbly at the captain. Soloth was startled at first, but its expression soon darkened as it understood the meaning of Evgeny's serenade-turned-duet.

"Matilda, assume full override, all functions. Evade and fire at need, but get us out of this system. Full reverse." Evgeny barked his orders with nimble-tongued speed.

The girlish voice that had answered his song replied with slower, prim diction: "I may be very smart, but give me a moment. It takes some time to wake up, especially when you've been sleeping for a decade." The voice had a distinct, archaic accent, particularly with its flattened R's and elongated Ah's.

Despite Matilda's protests, she was clearly catching up quickly. Havish tapped repeatedly at a firing control that had ceased to react to its touch. Jolly shuddered and finally looked down to where Evgeny stood. Soon after Matilda's response, the view screens showed the results of her work: the image of the dwarf planetoid was beginning to shrink. The Zig fighters also swirled away and vanished to points in the distance.

Gleamer cocked his head, still receiving outputs from various processes even if he could not input new instructions. He put the pieces together with admirable speed. Turning to Evgeny, he howled, "You said your Brin was dead! I am *so* pissed at you right now… also really, really jealous. That was *awesome*."

Soloth only snarled in response to the Human sentiment.

Jolly's anger was more surprising. The Ningyo captain roared, "Bring us back! NOW! They are all under attack! We are dying… she is dying… your crew will die… undo this, Evgeny Lerner, and give me back control."

Its enforcer, Punch, wasted no words but drew two weapons: its electrified slapstick and the spare spatial fold generator taken from the deceased Comus. It pointed the generator at Evgeny, emphasizing its commander's demand.

Evgeny stood defiant. "Go ahead. This ship is *mine*. Better, it's *my* friend. Kill me, and she'll guarantee you die. Either way, we're not going back to that deathtrap. Your people are gone… accept that and count yourself lucky to have escaped."

"Kill the Mauraug," Jolly ordered Punch. It was no longer bantering. It seemed to have switched to a new personality, cold and empty, in place of its eponymous cheer. As Punch sighted on Soloth, Jolly unslung its own weapon.

No individual sapient could have tracked all of the actions that followed. Gleamer, operating on boosted reflexes, moved first… throwing himself flat on the deck.

Havish's honed responses gave it the second fastest reaction. It was already reaching beneath its chest armor for a hidden stiletto as soon as Jolly began to rant. When Punch turned its weapon on Soloth, Havish leapt forward and shoved the masked Ningyo backward. With one hand, the scarred Mauraug pushed the generator aside, swinging its muzzle toward Jolly. This parry stopped Punch from firing.

With its other hand, holding the thin, hardened stiletto, Havish stabbed Punch beneath its oversized abdomen, aiming for the flexible joint at its waist.

The stiletto punched through the outer membrane of that articulatory area and slid between its interlocking plates. The force of the Mauraug's blow was just enough to crack the casing of the Ningyo's inner compartment. A whistling jet of released pressure screamed from the gut wound.

Punch responded with unexpected coordination. Not only did it hold its fire with the one hand, it swung its other hand, holding the electric baton, in a solid strike against Havish's exposed neck. The Mauraug stumbled backward and slammed against the far wall of the bridge, stunned by current passing through its central nervous system.

Jolly and Soloth acted next. The Ningyo captain was already going to shoot Havish, but paused when it and Punch became interlocked. As soon as the two figures separated, Jolly had a clear shot again. It re-aimed and fired. Unlike the glancing shot on Tklth, this spatial disturbance was solidly centered on Havish bash'Buurem. A swirling globe of energy expanded to encompass the Mauraug, along with circular sections of the wall and floor. The sphere flashed with an eye-wrenching moiré pattern, relocating volumes of matter to new, randomly distributed positions. The remains of Havish spattered wetly into a newly-formed hole in the deck, along with several chopped slices of composited metal and plastic.

Soloth was already racing forward. It wasted no time in grief for the unlucky substitute gunner. The space fold generators had a brief recharge time, and Soloth did not intend to allow Jolly a second shot. Punch had not yet fired. If it recovered, Soloth was still its intended target. The surviving Mauraug intended to get close enough to Jolly to use the Ningyo as cover.

Only Evgeny did not move from his original position. Instead, he continued to give rapid-fire directions to his omnipresent AI. "Matilda, broadcast to all decks: Internal attack. Ningyo. Defense positions. Unleash hell."

Matilda understood that her Human's orders applied to her as well. She adapted to circumstances with admirable speed, even for an artificial intelligence. Correlating past recordings with present observations, she identified Jolly's direct physical link as a weak point. She sacrificed the bridge command console, increasing its power supply sharply in order to send current surging through the linked cables and into the Ningyo captain's body. This gambit produced a satisfactory result: Jolly jerked and smoked as its circuits were overloaded.

"Roger *that*," Matilda cooed aloud.

Punch was forced to abandon its attacks and instead rescue its commander. Dropping its baton, it grabbed Jolly's arm — careful not to allow the current to redirect through its own body — and pulled sharply, disengaging the cable link connecting Jolly and *Scape Grace*. The Ningyo captain slumped downward, falling out of the command chair and landing on its knees. Though dazed, Jolly was not dead. Punch, on the other hand, continued to bleed internal atmosphere in a noisy squeal. Once Jolly was safely disconnected, Punch used its free hand to plug the hole in its midsection.

All this action cost the Ningyo time to react to Soloth's approach. Afterward, no time was left. Seeing Jolly incapacitated, Soloth skirted the command chair, circling around to pounce upon Punch. One black, wide, leathery hand grabbed the white, slender, robotic hand holding the space fold generator. Soloth's other hand wrapped around the neck of Punch's suit. With a casual gesture, the mechanically strengthened Mauraug pulled, wrenching Punch's arm free in a spray of sparks. It spun the Ningyo around and repeated the procedure with its other arm. Punch kicked and struggled in vain. It was an insect caught by a very strong, very angry, very sadistic child. If it was fortunate, Soloth would be content to leave the suit's inhabitant alive within an immobilized torso.

Evgeny was fascinated, himself. Soloth was executing one of the torments he had fantasized upon the Ningyo, though not on the exact target he envisioned. A portion of the Mauraug's anger probably stemmed from Evgeny's deception and the revelation of his not-so-dead AI partner. This fact did not impair Evgeny's enjoyment of the fruits of that anger.

With the bridge crew variously dead, cowering, enthralled, or enraged, no one paid heed to Jolly's recovery. The electrocuted Ningyo stood unsteadily but managed to stay upright. It tried to raise its weapon but found its coordination impaired. Its arms and legs jerked sporadically, circuits partially fused and control systems erratic. Recognizing that it could no longer fight, Jolly chose to attempt flight. It had to leave immediately or not at all; Evgeny's warning to the crew meant that defenders were moving to protect important ship systems. They might soon be blocking exits, as well.

Jolly staggered toward the bridge door and managed to fire a small burst of spatial distortion at the hatch. The portal, though sealed by Matilda's override, ceased to be an obstacle as it shattered into disparate sections. Jolly threw it-self forward and out into the hallway, racing toward the descending ladder. Its movements became steadily smoother as its suit's sophisticated systems began to compensate for damage. The micro-units suffusing its body were also doing their best to repair both biology and machinery.

Seeing the Ningyo leader escaping, Evgeny was forced to turn away from the spectacle of Soloth removing Punch's remaining leg. There could be only one destination for the Ningyo captain, the one route of escape from *Scape Grace*. Jolly was going for its shuttle. After all that mess, captain Lerner was not about to let its perpetrator run free. He darted after Jolly. The Ningyo already had a lead the length of the bridge. Matilda might be able to slow it down, but the space fold generator would clear away any barriers she could create.

Chasing after the armed Ningyo was a stupid risk, but Evgeny was not thinking clearly. He wanted Jolly *dead* and his enemy was getting away. Worse, if it reached its shuttle, it might engage a spatial drive within the hold, blinking instantly out of reach while also crippling *Scape Grace*. There was, once again, no time for hesitation and no one else to take the necessary action.

It was only fitting that a captain rescue his ship or die trying.

Luuboh bash'Gaulig had little to contribute during the ship-to-ship fight-ing. It might be adequate in traditional combat, but had neither the training nor temperament to lend aid in a battle waged via remote technologies. Even so, it balked at being sequestered in the medical room. The space was tight and cut off from the information flow of the *Scape Grace*.

Luuboh wasn't even useful there for medical purposes. Most injuries sustained during a space battle would either be instantly fatal or else consist of bumps, bruises, or breaks that could be treated long after the shooting was done.

Regardless, Kuugan bash'Ranpool stood outside the door of medical, ready to 'help' should injuries be reported. Both Mauraug knew that Kuugan was really present to watch Luuboh and its patient, Tklth. Luuboh supposed that Soloth sent its own understudy to keep Luuboh on task, out from underfoot, and watched for any signs of instability. Luuboh did not realize that captain Lerner seconded that supervision, specifically on the chance that Luuboh itself was being compromised by the alien technology it was studying in such close proximity.

Luuboh was quite sure it remained free of infestation, but was not sure how much longer that security would last. Tklth's own body was thoroughly overtaken, providing more data than the tissue samples Luuboh originally tested. The micro-robots were reaching such concentration in her spine and brain that their activity registered on both magnetic and electrical scans.

Less subtly, the machines had begun rebuilding her damaged tissue. When Luuboh finally removed the cautery patches, it found a gridwork of fine silvery threads already in place at the wound sites. The scars left by the searing chemicals bulged outward, not with infection but with expanding, healthy tissue. Beneath a keloid seal reinforced with artificial netting, the microtech was slowly adding muscle, blood vessels, and approximate analogues of bone and nerve. The few samples Luuboh was able to extract and study suggested that the robots were building a new tail and leg. The result would be something neither wholly organic nor wholly cybernetic, but a novel fusion of substances. Whether this blended technology would yield results superior to true regeneration or pure cybernetics was debatable, but it was certainly a unique approach to the problem.

Tklth did not seem pained or even troubled by this process. She was cheerfully talkative before Kuugan arrived but seemed to understand that the new presence was not friendly. She stopped trying to argue for her release and fell into a meditative rest. That silence was the one benefit of being watched, Luuboh supposed. It gave the fatigued Mauraug a moment's peace.

The quiet lasted only a moment. A ship-wide announcement indicated the start of hostilities. Ideally, for those in medical, that announcement would be the only indicator that a battle was occurring. Any other sensations transmitted to the internally situated medical room would probably indicate damage to *Scape Grace's* structure. Any warning signals – fire, low atmosphere, or other environmental failures – were also undesirable updates. The arrival of patients would be the worst source of information.

An alert of another sort came from Tklth. Several minutes after the initial announcement, the Vislin shuddered sharply. Luuboh, who had been trying to stay distracted with recreational reading, looked up as its patient cried, "She is hurt!"

Luuboh's first thought was that Tklth was dreaming, reliving a memory, or else hallucinating from some effect of the micro-robots. Still, it responded, "Who is hurt? What do you mean?"

"Our friend, the one who gave me her gifts. She is dying and we cannot come to her aid." Tklth was becoming frantic, snapping her beak and pushing against the magnetic restraints of the medical bed.

"Do you mean the Ningyo? Comus?" Luuboh was still genuinely baffled; Jolly's suggestion that Comus might have been female provided its only guess at Tklth's meaning.

"The traveler, the emissary, the bearer of gifts." Tklth struggled to explain something she did not entirely understand herself. "Please let me go. I need to help her. I can return to my post. We are fighting her enemies while others go to help… I must do *something*."

Luuboh, not privy to the plan of battle, could not connect Tklth's explanation to the foreign ship. It also did not realize that Tklth was receiving messages relayed from one mass of micro-robots to another; only Evgeny had deduced that much from the combined reports of Luuboh and Gleamer.

What Luuboh *did* understand was that Tklth was being affected by the invasive technology clustered on its nervous system. Where that influence once rendered the formerly irritable reptilian peaceable, now it was goading her to agitated action.

A rattling noise from behind distracted Luuboh from its observations. One of its sample cases, the one provided with a nutrient bath that allowed the micro-robots to flourish, was vibrating slightly. The muscle tissue within had expanded grotesquely and was pulsating against the walls of the plastic dish. Whatever was triggering the units within Tklth was apparently also affecting the separate colony. Both sets originated from the Ningyo, Comus, but that host was dead. What was activating the cells, simultaneously?

Luuboh's lapse in attention gave Tklth time to act. With a coordinated movement, Tklth lifted her leg and both wrists and snapped open the bed's restraints. The electromagnets that previously held them closed were no longer functional, having lost their charge. As Luuboh would later deduce, specialized miniature constructs had slipped out of her body, infested the bed, and sabotaged it. These commandoes undertook a suicide mission, using their own bodies to link sections of circuitry and short out the magnets.

Even with only one leg, Tklth was a dangerous opponent. Luuboh backed away the few feet available, against the far wall of the medical room. To its relief, Tklth was not interested in attacking her physician, so long as it did not further restrain her. Instead, she levered herself to her foot and hopped to the exit.

When she opened the door, she found herself face-to-face with the expectant Kuugan bash'Ranpool. The Mauraug guard raised a plasma pistol and pointed it toward Tklth's midsection.

"No one leaves…," Kuugan began to warn her.

Tklth did not wait for the rest. She threw herself forward onto the armed Mauraug. Surprised, Kuugan fired and caught the onrushing Vislin in the flank. The wound would be painful and hazardous to future health, but would not be fatal if treated.

It certainly was not enough injury to stop Tklth's attack. The claws of one hand dug into Kuugan's forearm, trying to force it to release the weapon. At the same time, Tklth bit at the Mauraug's face. She received a nasty surprise when her beak met plastic and steel, rasping across Kuugan's prosthetic nose and upper jaw.

As they struggled, the two combatants fell to the floor. At that point, Luuboh might have come to Kuugan's aid and perhaps even balanced out the fight. However, its thoughts went first to escape: escape from the medical room, escape from the twin hazards of Tklth and Kuugan, and escape to the bridge. Its instinct was a mixture of base self-preservation and a nobler urge to communicate its observations to its superiors.

Whatever set off Tklth might be germane to the conflict facing the *Scape Grace*. Also, if *both* Kuugan and Luuboh were overcome, who could warn the crew about the danger posed by Tklth? More specifically, who would warn them about the dangers living within her flesh, whether or not she died?

So, instead of attacking Tklth, Luuboh leapt over her back — also clearing Kuugan's prone form — and loped down the central hallway toward the forward portion of the ship. Its intent was to reach the scaling ladder and climb up one level. From there, it could hurry to the bridge.

Luuboh was almost to the ladder when it heard an unfamiliar, female Human voice over the loudspeakers: "Internal attack. Ningyo. Defense positions. Unleash hell."

Was that the *she* of Tklth's ranting? If so, why was 'she' warning about an attack on the ship *by* the Ningyo? Luuboh tried to rearrange its thoughts logically as it ran. The message's phrasing sounded like orders to ship's crew to defend it against boarders. It didn't sound like anyone familiar. The voice was Human, but too young and too oddly accented to be one of the female combat crew.

Once again, Luuboh had been left out of the plots and plans. It had not been privy to the combat crew's private briefings, either. Still, Luuboh knew something the grunt crew didn't. The Ningyo were planning to infiltrate the ship... and its crew... all along. They seeded the ship with microscopic robots designed to reprogram biological sapients. Who knew which crew members were compromised? The *Scape Grace* could find itself at war between the enslaved and the free.

Luuboh at least knew *it* was clean. It had checked its own scans numerous times. Unlike Tklth, it was definitely not feeling peaceful. Cowardly, yes, but still quite angry and violent. Most importantly, it was still opposed to the Ningyo. Their intent in employing the micro-robots might have been to neutralize any opposition. At least whoever triggered that warning message was still fighting. Otherwise, Luuboh might be the ship's last bulwark against total capitulation.

Still, it would have to fight alone for a time. It would need weapons. It would also need a tactical position. It had some ideas where both could be found.

Luuboh neared the scaling ladder and was alarmed to hear the clicking of plastic on metal as something descended. The most likely source of that sound was one of the Ningyo using the ladder. They were coming in Luuboh's direction. Were they coming for Tklth? For Luuboh, who knew too much, who still resisted? The lone Mauraug was defenseless where it was.

It raced down the ladder to the third level and sprinted toward the shuttle deck, ducking into the adjacent storage bay. There were weapons there. Even better, the controls to the shuttle deck were close at hand. It could flush the shuttle into space. If the Ningyo threatened, they risked losing the means of return to their own ship. It was a weak bargaining point, but Luuboh hoped it would be enough nuisance to dissuade the occupiers from pressing their attack.

After all, the crippled, harmless Mauraug was not much threat by itself. The enemy could be persuaded to leave it alone, rather than lose their shuttle... hopefully?

24

Katy and NuRikPo's knowledge of the battle outside went from complete ignorance to sudden chaos. Despite the transformations occurring across the ship, the chamber where their shuttle rested was left unchanged. While *Scape Grace* and *Harauch* traded fire with the Zig defenders, the two sapients sat quietly isolated. They continued to wait in suspension even as Emissary closed on the Zig mining base. Emissary did not relay any updates on the progress of its assault. The firing of its weapons produced no effects in their section of the ship.

Only when the Zig base finally returned fire did any stimulus reach the two captives, and then two disturbing events arrived in close succession. The surrounding ship shuddered, strongly enough to shake the shuttle within. Then the composite substance of the walls rippled, not only detectable by energy reflectance but visible to the eye. Katy and NuRikPo looked at one another in alarm.

There was no time for discussion, as NuRikPo's attention was immediately drawn away by multiple signals. His long fingers skittered across the shuttle's interface panel, accessing and sorting the new inputs. Katy stepped forward to watch over his shoulder. With a glance at her and a wave of his hand, NuRikPo selected the most important of the signals and switched it to the main communication channel. The audio message was broadcast for both listeners in a flat, unadorned synthetic voice, but the identity of the 'speaker' was obvious from the message's content and phrasing.

"Katy and 'Po, do you read? Are you ok in there? Can you hear me yet? We saw you get hit."

Katy tuned to the signal and switched in a response using *Scape Grace's* pre-ferred frequencies and encryption. She replied, "Gleamer! We're ok for now, hearing you finally. We're working on getting out of here. This ship is bad news. What hit it?"

The response was surprisingly slow to return, stretching their nerves taut. Over sixty seconds later, Gleamer's proxy replied, "The Zig miners. Maglift shells with some kind of crystallizing catalyst… a molecular seed. The Ningyo are going berserk. They're insisting that we come to the rescue. Gene is standing them off. I think they're getting orders from your end. Wait, captain is saying we have to run… out of system… better get out and follow our vector. Might have to leave you there. Sorry…"

Gleamer's fragmentary signal reflected his scattered, racing thoughts. Final-ly, it cut off entirely. The carrier remained intact, but no further message was broadcast.

Katy called back, "Gleamer, get out how? Which vector? Don't leave us hanging here."

NuRikPo had been only partially attending the conversation. He was dis-tracted by a second array of abruptly active sensors. At the word 'crystallizing', he did look up and toward the audio output, as if trying to confirm the message with its speaker.

After Katy responded, he spoke up: "That explains the readings I'm getting. The short-wave signals generated by Emissary's coordination cells have been surging and then dropping at several locations. The cells are likely shouting warnings before they are disabled. If so, the wave of damage is forward of us and to starboard. At its current rate of progress, the cascade will reach our re-gion in about ninety seconds."

He added, "The vector Gleamer referenced is probably our prior exit path from this system, used when we fled the first time."

Katy prompted, "So, how do we get out of here before we're 'crystallized'? You Zig make some really nasty weapons, you know that?"

"I know." NuRikPo's acknowledgement carried a note of pride. "Weapons are supposed to be awful… and effective. First, we need to get out of physical contact with this ship. If our hull touches recently crystallized matter the catalyzing wave will spread throughout this shuttle. The effect is intentionally contagious."

His fingers twitched over the controls again. "Engaging lift. Hopefully we can hover in this space until the conversion reaches its conclusion."

He acted as he spoke, cycling up the drives that would normally propel the little craft within a planet's atmosphere and gravity. He was forced to adjust the strength and direction of these lifters several times as Emissary's own gravitational generators failed. The shuttle bounced jarringly off the 'ceiling' of the surrounding space.

"Watch it!" Katy griped, holding onto a hand rail for balance.

"I am, otherwise that would have been worse. We are in freefall. Compensating."

Their cameras showed the chamber walls veering close and then moving away as NuRikPo struggled to keep their floating shuttle from moving too far in any one direction. Small impacts indicated that his efforts were not entirely successful. Still, he was getting better at adjusting their angle and momentum, balancing against their residual motion until the shuttle was merely rotating and drifting slowly.

This motion made looking through the exterior cameras a nauseating experience. Still, they kept the view on and were rewarded for their perseverance with an advance warning of the encroaching threat. One section of the deck material rippled physically and changed color from uniform metallic charcoal to a paler, dusty grey. The Zig catalyst was forcing certain elements in the cells to attract and align, rendering the composite structures inert and brittle. With Emissary's unique construction, the effect was like petrifying flesh. Portions of the ship were dying as they crystallized.

Against a standard starship, the weapon might make a hull difficult to protect: vulnerable to further impacts and resistant to defensive energy fields. If not isolated, the effect would spread, knocking out electronic systems. However, careful hardening of key systems could protect a ship from such attack, by surrounding them with substances inert to crystallization.

The *best* defense against a catalyst was a counter-agent that would arrest the process. Ships blessed with a well-prepared engineering section – and preferably, a Zig engineer – might even be able to reverse most of the damage. Failing that, it was necessary to cut away and jettison the affected areas before the cascading effect spread too far.

Ironically, Emissary was *more* capable of the latter defense than any standard ship. It could have pinched off the afflicted area, amputating one mass of cells to protect the rest. Unfortunately for the foreign ship, it did not understand the nature of its threat and allowed the affliction to spread widely. Perhaps it resisted the idea of amputation as strongly as any biological organism.

Katy would later sympathize with the distress the artificial organism must have experienced as its 'body' froze solid. At that moment, though, she was in more fear for her own life. She could not spare any consideration for the entity that held them captive. Its impending death was their opportunity for escape.

"'Po! It can't heal now! Blast us out!"

NuRikPo's hands were already on the weapons controls as Katy spoke. Their thoughts followed the same track. He fired, and gouts of accelerated particles sprayed against and through the paralyzed section of Emissary's wall.

"First C-section I've done from inside. This baby's gotta go," Katy babbled, bouncing with adrenaline from mingled fear and urgency.

"Could you do more than just talk? Perhaps take over firing while I steer us out?" NuRikPo struggled to maintain his own calm.

"Oh, yeah, sure," Katy almost shouted as she bolted around NuRikPo's back and switched over top of him on the weapons controls. They brushed hands briefly; it was a testament to the seriousness of their situation that neither shuddered nor complained at the contact.

The sight of deep blackness and the suction of vacuum were welcome indicators of progress. Between the immobilization of the hull material and the destruction of that matter by the shuttle's weaponry, they were managing to open a widening gap straight outside. The pull of atmosphere rushing out nearly dragged them into collision with the crystallizing material, but NuRikPo managed to recover by thrusting steadily backward. With the shuttle almost pressed against the far wall of the surrounding chamber, Katy fired repeatedly at the edges of the growing hole. It needed to be wide enough to allow the shuttle to escape comfortably, without risking contact between hull and shuttle.

The visible, rippling wave of the crystallization effect now flowed in all directions, creeping across the floor and outer wall of the shuttle chamber. They were losing the remaining 'safe' areas, where NuRikPo might allow a brief bump of contact due to overcompensation.

That balancing act would not get any easier with time. Once the ship was entirely converted, it would also cease to resist the pull of the nearby planetoid. Being dragged rapidly into a gravity well would make steering even more difficult. Their chances of a safe escape were dropping steadily.

Katy shifted her firing pattern. Rather than gradually carving away at the edges of the original hole, she fired a series of shots in a circular pattern around a wide perimeter. NuRikPo looked at her handiwork curiously at first, then nodded in understanding. He backed the shuttle up as far as it could go, nestled against the final remaining unafflicted inner wall.

Then Katy launched their projectile weapon, a magnetic mortar. An alloyed steel slug chuffed out from the magnetic acceleration tube slung underneath their shuttle. The shell was filled with the finest explosive cocktail and fitted with a remote detonation trigger. Katy activated the charge acceptably near the center of the puncture pattern she had created.

The roar of detonation was audible even with their microphones inactive, through the thinning atmosphere and through their armored hull. The concussion wave itself was weakened by the lack of a medium. Plus, NuRikPo had already braced their back, so the blast could not throw them against the wall. The shuttle took less damage than would normally occur when firing its mortar in a confined space.

The explosion's effect on Emissary's brittle, perforated hull was much more potent. It did exactly what Katy had hoped. Distressed material shattered away from the point of impact, opening a gaping wound far larger than necessary for their shuttle's diameter. Without further prompting, NuRikPo reversed thrust and shot them through the hole and out into open space.

The planetoid sped by beneath them as the shuttle accelerated, breaking free from the pull of that significant mass. Behind them, Emissary spun slowly, no longer able to move away from the target it once menaced.

"I wonder if the miners had that weapon ready when we were here the last time?" Katy mused. She was no longer firing but stayed near the weapons controls in case they met resistance on their way out of the system.

NuRikPo answered as he steered them away: "Perhaps so, or perhaps they constructed it in reaction to our attack. If the former, being driven off by their outer defenses possibly saved *Scape Grace* from the same fate as Emissary."

Those outer defenses, the flock of crude fighter craft that bested *Scape Grace* twice, now pursued the *Harauch*. No longer needing to focus on either the departed *Scape Grace* or the crippled Emissary, the little ships circled the remaining 'Mauraug' pirate. Good sense would suggest that *Harauch*, too, should run. It had removed two of the remaining seven fighters, but showed signs of damage in return. Attrition would eventually prove fatal for any outnumbered ship, and *Harauch* was reaching the tipping point. Still, it remained, stubbornly trying to reach the dying alien ship.

As the pathetic scene dwindled away behind them, their shuttle's instruments registered another launch from the planetoid's surface. *Harauch* flashed with an impact. It had shielded the other ship with its own mass, accepting a direct hit meant for Emissary. It was a meaningless sacrifice. Now, both ships would certainly die.

At least, both ships would certainly die *if* the Zig miners had the good sense to incinerate them in space. The miners hopefully would not risk either wreck crash-landing on the planetoid. The problem was worse than any damage from impact alone. The miners wouldn't know about the danger from Emissary's unique structure, but they'd be on guard against any aftereffects of their catalytic weapon.

If any remaining active catalyst came into contact with the world's surface, it would start working rapidly on the metal-rich crust, destroying valuable ore before its effect was expended. Clearing out that mess would cost more than the remaining ore would be worth. The miners would be bankrupted, even if they weren't first killed by the catalyst disabling their environmental equipment. Hopefully, the miners would not take any further risks and would reduce both ships to carbonized dust.

But there was another, equally reasonable scenario: The Zig might plan to deliver a counter-agent to one or both ships, neutralizing and partially reversing the crystallization process. They would assume the occupants of both ships to be dead. The disabled ships then could be towed into a safe orbit and salvaged for valuable materials.

Based on what Katy Olu and NuRikPo had observed, Emissary's unique structure might not actually be 'dead', either in part or in whole. Crystallization might only deactivate the cells, rendering them inert but not permanently disabled. Separately, Emissary might have realized what was happening to its body and protected some portion of itself by creating a buffered area, a cyst of unharmed cells, just large enough to rebuild from. There were a few other ways that cells from the alien ship could have avoided total death. In any of those cases, deactivating the crystallizing agent might revitalize the ship.

Afterward, any Zig who came aboard were at risk of infestation by micro-tech. They would soon want to help Emissary, feed it, protect it, rebuild it... The Mission might continue with only a short interruption.

"We really should warn somebody," Katy spoke aloud as they fled the system, searching for a track from *Scape Grace*. "That ship is dangerous."

NuRikPo nodded, but countered, "First, we need to warn our own people. We might need to rescue them. Based on what we know, the Ningyo are likely under Emissary's influence. Who knows if they were able to spread its microbes to others? Then again, we have to hope *Scape Grace* rescues *us* first. This shuttle won't get us very far. If they left us behind…"

He didn't need to finish the thought. Fortunately, its unpleasant implications were pushed aside by communications from *Scape Grace's* channel. An unfamiliar, female Human voice spoke: a very real-sounding voice, rather than the earlier synthetic reading of Gleamer's recoded thoughts.

"Dr. Olu, NuRikPo, please follow to coordinates 5-point-69, 4-point-33, 55-point-30. I am stopping to let you catch up. Are you hurt in any way?"

"Hmmmm… no, no serious physical damage, to us or the shuttle. Thank you… '*Grace?*'" NuRikPo replied carefully.

"You're welcome, but my name is Matilda. So glad to hear you're unharmed. Hurry up… you're needed for repairs, both of you." The speaker sounded young, pleasant, and carefully thoughtful. She definitely did not sound like anyone Katy or NuRikPo could remember meeting aboard *Scape Grace*.

Oh, well, one more mystery to resolve, among many. Hopefully, *Scape Grace* could hold together a few minutes longer, so that they could dock and get to work on whatever crises demanded their attention most urgently.

25

Normally, a captain would have an advantage navigating on his own ship, particularly a captain with ten years' experience pursuing a newcomer with only six days aboard. Evgeny ought to be catching up easily, despite Jolly's lead. His quarry was also unsteady from recent electrocution.

Unfortunately, the Ningyo had several offsetting advantages. First, its powerful native spatial perception and memory maximized its limited experience of the ship. It had also taken advantage of opportunities to study the ship's layout via her own logs. Most importantly, theirs was not an extended chase. From bridge to shuttle bay was typically a three-minute journey. At their breakneck pace, the pair covered that distance in under one minute. Whatever differential advantage remained to captain Lerner did not draw him much nearer in that time.

He might even have fallen further behind if not for Matilda's aid. Jolly was forced to pause twice, briefly, to deal with doors shut in its path. In each case, it did not bother to try the controls – it was quite aware that the ship's systems were under the control of a hostile AI – but instead used its spatial fold generator to clear the way. The weapon doubled as a powerful if imprecise tool, reducing even the strongest materials to scrap. The first interposing door had sealed off the fore section of the third deck down, the route to the shuttle deck itself. The second door was the inner airlock door blocking Jolly's access to its shuttle.

Evgeny turned a corner to see the airlock door crashing down in pieces as the spatial fold effect dissipated. Jolly was positioned halfway between the door and Evgeny's point of arrival. Beyond the gleaming white figure, through the three-meter-diameter hole it had created, Evgeny could see… nothing.

The shuttle bay was empty.

Jolly whirled around, aiming the projecting end of its weapon at Evgeny. It had just fired, so the threat was only symbolic during the seconds the device would require for recharge. Evgeny raced forward, intending to close the distance between them before that deadline was up.

Thinking even more quickly, Jolly reversed its direction of fire, pointing toward the outer airlock door. It both aimed and moved backward, retreating from the grim-faced Human.

Jolly commented, "Blowing your holds to spite my face, captain? Or did your Brin decide to trap me? I only wanted to leave, to salvage what I could of the ruined mission, now that this ship is useless to us."

From the overhead speakers came Matilda's voice, conveying offense: "I didn't do it. Well, I did permit it, I confess. But the idea wasn't mine."

Evgeny was surprised. He might well have had Matilda eject the Ningyo shuttle from the ship, *if* he possessed both the presence of mind to conceive that maneuver and the time to issue the order. He had enjoyed neither. Matilda was brilliant and even clever, but she was not devious. Her experience with treachery was intentionally limited. It made sense that someone else suggested the act and she recognized the idea's value.

"Give it up, Jolly," Evgeny thundered in his best command voice. "There's nowhere to go. Drop the weapon and we'll settle for leaving you marooned with a nutrient dispenser."

"This deal is getting worse all the time. I have no reason to trust you. You've broken your word already. I'd rather take what's behind door number two. Leave me alone here. I hold your hull hostage. I will leave only to board *Black Humor*. If you advance, we both go playing among the stars."

"You won't kill yourself. You might shoot me, but you value life too highly to waste your own." Evgeny was just guessing, but hoped that saying the words aloud might convince Jolly that they were true. He took several slow steps forward.

"I might give my life to end *yours*. *You* do not value life. You left her to die, her and all our fellows. You have no understanding of what is important. To remove such an evil mind, a threat to all your future victims, that would be worth my death."

Jolly's words stung until Evgeny remembered it reducing Havish bash'Buurem to a pile of shredded meat just a few minutes before. It had also been willing to trade his entire crew's lives for the survival of one *artificial* life. And what about the Zig miners that died defending their claim? Evgeny Lerner might be a murderous villain, but he wasn't the only one present.

He charged, closing with Jolly while the Ningyo was still ranting.

Evgeny was surprised to find the space fold generator already pointed back in his direction. During its protest, Jolly found the focus to choose its target. It pressed the triggering button on the device's grip. Evgeny felt the first unsettling sensations of being caught within multiple spatial distortion fields at once.

He would later have the unique privilege of processing and reflecting upon that perceptual experience. Few sapients exposed to intersecting spatial fold areas would ever have the same opportunity. It required that one be within the target area at the beginning of the effect but outside of it very quickly afterward. Otherwise, one's nervous system was no longer able to process anything, as distances of several centimeters between nerves absolutely prevented any transmission of impulses.

In this case, the target area for spatial folding rapidly moved away from Evgeny. This motion was due to the motion of the generator creating the fields... because its holder was moving... due to the suction of vacuum... due to the outer airlock door having opened.

The ejection sequence had been triggered. This time, the emergency version was selected. *Scape Grace's* safety measure for dealing with unwanted guests included an override of basic airlock safety features.

There were no warning lights or sounds. The door did not cycle gradually and then open gracefully once pressure was equalized. Instead, the door slid open with a motor-grinding screech and a crash of metal on metal. Jolly, both hands on its weapon and closest to the door, was unable to resist the sudden pull. It went flying through the breached inner door, out through the opened outer door, and was flung, spinning, into empty space.

Evgeny very nearly suffered the same fate. He was buffeted by escaping atmosphere and thrown toward the bottleneck formed by the hole in the inner airlock door. At the same time, a nearby storage room door opened and a black-and-white body launched from that space.

Luuboh, too, was caught and thrown by the outrush of air, but it had prepared. A length of braided carbon rope anchored it to a magnetic clamp affixed to the storage room floor. It spread its furred body wide and flew fast toward Evgeny, snagging the tumbling Human by his ankle. At the end of the tether, the rope snapped taut and the two bodies jerked like fish on a line. Though stunted by Mauraug standards, Luuboh was sufficiently strong to maintain its grip.

Shortly afterward, Matilda was able to override and reverse the airlock purge. The outer door clanged shut and both occupants of the shuttle deck dropped to the floor. Contused and winded, both Human and Mauraug gasped and writhed... also much like landed fish.

After a few seconds, Evgeny was able to pull in a deep breath. He sat up painfully and shook his head to clear it. Luuboh knuckled itself to its feet shortly thereafter. The Mauraug custodian put out its hand and helped Evgeny to his feet. The captain inhaled and exhaled cautiously a few more times before speaking.

"Matilda, just one more thing. Could you please target that piece of shiny trash we just vented?"

"Easily, Evgeny. Tracking it now."

"Fire."

"Deep space is now a bit cleaner."

They spent the following hour reassembling the scattered sapients of *Scape Grace*. Evgeny and Luuboh hastened back to the medical room, where they found Kuugan bash'Ranpool standing guard over a battered and trussed Tklth. The Mauraug was nursing wounds of its own. It had taken time to patch the worst of the punctures inflicted by Tklth's beak and claws.

When Luuboh reappeared, Kuugan looked relieved. It had been concerned it would have to hunt down its other ward. Evgeny explained in indisputable tones that Luuboh was no longer suspect, seeing as how it killed the Ningyo commander. The look of shock on Kuugan's somewhat immobile face was Evgeny's first repayment to Luuboh for saving his life and possibly his ship.

After leaving Kuugan the continued responsibility of watching Tklth, Evgeny and Luuboh returned to the bridge. On the way, they caught up one another on the major events of their last few minutes. Luuboh confessed to suggesting that Matilda purge the Ningyo shuttle. Evgeny both forgave and applauded it for the idea.

As they talked, Matilda interjected, notifying Evgeny that NuRikPo and Katy Olu were alive, reasonably well, in their shuttle, freed, and hurrying to rejoin the *Scape Grace*. It came as welcome news, although the AI's phrasing suggested that their reunion would not be entirely joyful.

Shortly afterward, Evgeny and Luuboh arrived at the gaping hole where the bridge hatch once stood. With strange guilty twinges, Evgeny asked the Mauraug to fulfill his usual duties: clearing away the remains of Havish bash'Buurem and Punch. Unfortunately, Luuboh was the only one currently present with knowledge of effective biological cleanup procedures. The dwarfed Mauraug agreed with no hint of reluctance. It even seemed pleased to be of assistance.

Gleamer observed Evgeny's return with jittery impatience. Once he finished speaking with Luuboh, Evgeny was bombarded with questions:

"We got a great view from here. Did you know Luuboh was waiting down there? Did you plan to space the shuttle *and* the Ningyo? Is there still any active microtech on the ship? I'm not getting any readings anymore. Oh, and how the hell did you hide a Brin from me all this time?"

Evgeny stared wearily at the younger, fresher, and unwounded Human. He would have to answer a few questions but didn't plan on answering that many, that fast. Some questions he would leave unanswered forever, if he could.

To forestall Gleamer's curiosity, he replied only, "I didn't hide Matilda, she hid herself. She's always been a part of *Scape Grace*. You never noticed her because you were used to her as background code As to what just happened, we'll reconstruct that later. For now, we have work to do, *all* of us. Matilda, return controls to normal. You're relieved of duty. Well done, my dear."

"Thank you, Evgeny," Matilda cooed.

Gleamer snapped back to his console as he regained access to his usual systems, just as Evgeny intended. Given the opportunity to research his own answers, the programmer preferred to return to his digital world rather than drag information out of Evgeny in analog time.

It would not be so easy to placate Soloth bash'Soloth. His first mate also looked back to its controls at navigation, verifying that it could again steer *Scape Grace*. Afterward, Soloth's deep black eyes looked back into Evgeny's shallower grey ones, meeting his gaze with an intensity it rarely showed toward its Dominator.

"I want the AI *out* of ship's systems, entirely," Soloth demanded, with unnecessary volume for the confined space.

Evgeny considered fighting the battle. After all, Matilda had shown her value against the Ningyo. If she was active from the beginning, their occupiers might have been overcome much sooner. Her presence, more than any private codes or secret cameras, enforced Evgeny's position as owner and master of *Scape Grace*.

Underneath those rationales was a more fundamental cultural feeling: like most Humans, Evgeny deeply appreciated his Brin. He trusted her. He already felt safer with her active. He wanted her to have an active role in his life again. He resented any insult to her or limitation on her freedom.

Still, it was obvious he would have to make a choice between Matilda and Soloth. The Mauraug's demeanor made that dilemma clear. If Evgeny pressed the point, the *best* outcome he could hope for would be his first mate's resignation and departure from the ship. The worst possibilities included a challenge for dominance, a physical confrontation, or both together.

Evgeny decided to surrender the battle in the interests of peace. He stared back at Soloth in a way Humans were usually advised *not* to stare at Mauraug.

He answered, "Fine. I'll move her to my compad as soon as I can get to my quarters. In the meantime, like I said, we have more immediate concerns."

Soloth grimaced, retorting, "Living under the whim of a false soul *is* an immediate concern. I trust your word, though. You only deceived by omission… but now you have answered and must be true." It nodded as if confirming an oath and turned to look at the remains of Havish bash'Buurem. "You are correct, though, that some matters require more timely responses."

"Right," Evgeny agreed, relieved to follow the change in topic. "Quick briefing, if Gleamer didn't get to it already: the Ningyo brought some kind of nanotech…"

"…microtech…," Gleamer interjected without turning away from his console.

"…microtech onboard, inside their suits. It interacts with biological systems. It got into Tklth pretty badly and bent her mind. That's what Luuboh was looking into for me. It seemed to make her pacifistic… up until the Ningyo were threatened. Then, she went berserk as usual. The rest of us might have picked up a few of the bugs, so stay on your guard for any strange thoughts or feelings. We'll have Katy and 'Po look into it when they get aboard. In the meantime, I'm keeping the crew where they are to reduce the spread."

"Except for Luuboh," Soloth observed.

"Except for Luuboh, who had been exposed almost as long as Tklth, who knows the signs to watch for, who has checked itself out already, who knows the proper containment procedures, *and* has already shown that it had no problem with scrapping said Ningyo," Evgeny rattled off with surprising heat.

"By your judgment," Soloth replied, making the phrase sound like both acceptance and accusation.

Evgeny decided to leave it at that. He had intended to share more with his first mate, but Soloth's grudges grated on him too much at the moment. Let it wait and wonder what else he was omitting. If some detail was necessary for the Mauraug to do its job, Evgeny would pass that datum on.

The three sat in sullen silence until Luuboh returned, sealed into a fresh new clean suit and armed with two more body bags. It worked quickly both for its own sake and for the sensitivities of the other sapients present. It gathered up Havish's remains; Luuboh would incinerate them later with its best effort at appropriate funeral rites for the disgraced Dominion soldier.

Punch's separated limbs were placed with its torso in the second body bag. The biological Ningyo was already sealed – with the exception of the fatal leak – into its own customized plastic casket. The loss of its arms ensured that the containment breach opened by Havish's stiletto did release all of the pressurized atmosphere within Punch's suit. The Ningyo died of suffocation before its body exploded.

With a sudden realization, Evgeny spoke up as Luuboh set aside the filled bags: "Drop off that Ningyo suit in engineering along with its weapon. I owe 'Po something for hazard pay. If you didn't space the other one along with the Ningyo shuttle, you can stack that bag alongside the first."

"I did put the first dead Ningyo in storage," Luuboh admitted, "In case I or doctor Olu needed more samples for study, later."

"Well, that tech, along with their suits and guns, is ours now. A poor trade for one crew mate dead, one crippled, and several wounded… not to mention *'Grace'* getting a few new holes in her."

Luuboh looked up as it prepared the biosolvent sprays that would clear the remaining gore from the bridge's decking. "Actually, captain, if we leave the micro-robots active in Tklth, they might repair her leg and tail entirely. They have already begun regenerating the tissue destroyed by cautery of her wounds."

Evgeny shook his head, torn between reactions. "*If* we have a choice, I'd rather not take any chances. We don't know what those things might be doing to her mind. I'm already afraid she's useless as crew now. From your description, she's somewhere between a saint and a psychotic. If that doesn't go away when… if… those robots are disabled, then we may have to put her down. The old Ticklish would have preferred it that way."

His words were cruel. They were also true. Any of the crew that knew Tklth would agree that the proud, prickly Vislin would rather be dead than artificially gentled. Her fury was both her shame and her pride. Having it either deleted, or worse, bent to serve an alien purpose, would disgust her.

Her survival depended on the return and the skill of her absent 'pack' mates.

With Matilda's guidance, the ship's shuttle was brought back home. NuRik-Po squealed in horror as soon as the outer airlock door opened and the ravaged inner passage became visible. He paced in unconcealed agitation as they waited for the door to close and the entire hallway to be repressurized.

Katy groused at him, "You think this looks bad? Now you know how I'm going to feel when I start running physical workups on the crew. We both have *thousands* of holes in our internal structure. Luuboh says the same robot creepers have been running around *Scape Grace* for the last week. You'd better set your people to mass production of those counter-agents."

"We were right, then? The Ningyo were infested and carried Emissary's cells within them."

"Like stacking dolls of evil robotic biological mimicry."

"If I didn't already have a headache…"

"…I'd give you one, right."

After this seemingly eternal torment, stuck together for several long minutes, the two were finally released from the shuttle. They parted directions, yet continued to follow parallel courses despite being physically separated.

The two first raced toward their respective centers of power within the ship: NuRikPo to resume his tenure in engineering and Katy to relieve Luuboh of any remaining pretenses of medical practice. They each ejected the combat crew member assigned to their domains: NuRikPo dismissed Sol Metaxas with a relatively gentle rebuff for daring to attempt recalibration on *his cannons*, while Katy threatened Kuugan bash'Ranpool with a depilatory bath if it didn't get its hairy posterior out of her doorway. Then they went to work.

From the more comfortable distance of several decks apart, Katy and NuRikPo could collaborate professionally without the distress of personal presence. They compared notes as NuRikPo produced more sophisticated and numerous counter-agents. Some, he intended for patrol within the ship's systems, in contrast to the previous strain created for use within biological environments. Katy accepted deliveries of the latter agents and began calling crew to medical for their inoculations. Captain Lerner chimed in to make it clear that these invitations were *not* optional; "report or die" was his exact phrasing.

Burnett Georges brought down the batches of micro-robots. Katy couldn't be sure if NuRikPo's choice of courier had any underlying meaning. Burnett was the only Human male aboard *Scape Grace* that Katy had not yet taken to bed. In fact, she had tried, once, and was firmly rebuffed. Just as Zenaida declined the captain's invitation, her cousin was not interested in Katy's.

Was 'Po's selection a taunt, a reminder of their bizarre argument aboard Emissary? Or was it a peace gesture, either as an offering for her to claim or an acknowledgement that she was not wholly depraved? More likely, the oh-so-sensitive Zig was still dull as a sphere regarding social interaction and meant absolutely nothing by sending Burnett to her.

It must be nice to be so oblivious, Katy thought, *just focus on your work and let all that emotional mess pass you by.*

She sent Burnett back without even making a half-hearted pass.

At captain Lerner's orders, Katy tested the first new batch of counter-agent on Tklth. They would find out if the gunner could be salvaged, not to mention whether such an extreme case of infestation could be reversed without long-term damage.

Katy was already certain that she and NuRikPo would heal, physically at least. The miniature robots were surprisingly gentle toward nerve cells and even repaired much of the damage done to their hosts' muscle tissue and blood vessels as the cells infiltrated. Compared to the widespread destruction or alteration hostile nanotech could potentially achieve, Emissary's cells were subtle and careful of their surroundings. By contrast, the counter-agent was rather crude and harsh, causing far more cellular collateral damage.

Katy could not dismiss a certain lingering respect for the alien life-form, even while cautiously monitoring her own thoughts for rationality. Emissary's acts might have been abhorrent and unethical, but its… her?… methods were sophisticated and her intent seemingly pure.

She and NuRikPo had been made more peaceful and loving, just like Tklth. It made sense that some of that love was oriented on Emissary; after all, what was an immune system for but to protect its generating organism? But that peace and love turned to rage when the progenitor was threatened. It was fundamentally false bliss, just mechanical and chemical manipulation.

After all, *real* happiness came from… fuck it. Katy Olu had no idea what real happiness came from. She just knew that she hadn't found it yet. Mechanical and chemical manipulation might be the only 'real' answer.

Tklth could struggle with the problem just like the rest of them. Katy stuck a needle between the multicolored scales of her patient and injected an extra-large dose of the cure for peace.

26

All its parts gathered up, the *Scape Grace* scrambled away, retreating a second time into deep space. Her navigators chose a different trajectory this time, aimed in the opposite direction out from the system of the Zig miners. Once again, repairs filled the time between destinations, but this time, more than the physical structure of the ship needed repairing.

Her crew had suffered damage as well, and only part of that harm was physical. On the macro level, several crew members were injured. Kuugan bash'Ranpool and Tklth had done one another significant harm during their struggle. Evgeny Lerner and Luuboh bash'Gaulig were bruised from their battering in the shuttle bay. Tklth, of course, had two appendages missing. Her leg and tail would remain missing; doctor Olu deemed the salvaged scraps of Vislin tissue useless for reattachment, not least because of their contamination with Ningyo bodily fluids. Tklth was fitted with temporary prosthetics which granted her mobility, if not comfort or strength. True cybernetic modifications would have to wait on other priorities.

The crew also experienced a process of repair within each of their bodies, as each sapient endured the purgative patrol of injected counter-robots. Over the following days, jokes about the "glitter-shits" made the rounds of ship-wide comedy. The dismantled invaders and deactivated hunters had to exit the body *somewhere*, after all. Better to excrete them, than to leave debris to clog vessels and ducts or to be poisoned as the various compounds broke down.

Here again, Tklth was the worst off. From her example, Katy Olu learned that the invasive effects of the micro-robots were not entirely reversible. To the relief of most, Tklth did regain her natural Vislin reflexes, including both frenzy and nighttime hibernation. Those responses had not been removed, only blocked. Yet, Tklth confessed that she no longer felt at the mercy of her frenzies; an edge had been ground off her anger. She suspected that if she *did* enter full battle frenzy in the future, it might not be as potent, but it might also be more controllable. Perhaps, for the first time, she *could* retreat when a situation suggested that as the safer alternative.

Katy understood what the twitchy lizard meant. She, too, felt calmer and less driven by her personal demons. A week ago, she would have felt deeply befouled by the necessity of exploring the Vislin's endocrine system. Instead, she was only mildly repulsed.

In layman's terms, their brains had been rewired. In neurological terms, the paths laid down manually by the chained micro-robots modified the connections between biological nerves. Maybe that was accidental; if left alone, the cells would have done a better job of producing the intended behaviors on command. Maybe not; perhaps the long-term function of the mind-altering units was to shape an organism that would be friendly and pliable on its own, without the need for further influence.

Intentional or not, such changes were the inevitable results of altering the physical and chemical environment of neurons. Such restructuring was especially likely when the motivational structures of the brain were being tweaked.

Katy supposed they should be grateful that the results were not paradoxical, like psychoactive withdrawal effects. She and Tklth could have reacted to the removal of the micro-robots with their flaws *exaggerated*, not muted.

The changes were a non-voluntary violation. For all that, the technology that accomplished such changes would be extremely valuable for certain desirable applications. Behavioral modification was still an incomplete science. With a few modifications, a benevolent programmer using the micro-robotic cells might selectively reduce or suppress psychosis, neurosis, trauma, anxiety or depression in a patient. The technology would revolutionize behavioral medicine.

The problem was, an unscrupulous programmer could *increase* all of those torments in a victim. Worse, the same tools could obviously be used for mental control. All the fear and loathing directed toward psionics would be more validly applied toward the potential use of micro-tech to bend minds.

The mitigating factor for both applications was the volume of robots necessary. Both Luuboh and Gleamer saw the clues to this property. Just a few micro-robots were individually stupid. They would follow their internal programs but accomplish little more than moving into position and possibly tweaking the odd nerve signal. That minor adjustment was all most of the *Scape Grace* crew experienced.

But amass enough total robots, of enough different types, and they became an exponentially complex distributed system, collaborating directly within one local area or indirectly across a distance via extremely low frequency radio communication. The masses within Katy Olu and NuRikPo were enough to influence their emotional drives, but only with the guiding influence of Emissary's critical mass close by. The larger gathering within Tklth had learned how to modify and rebuild Vislin tissues. Between Tklth and the Ningyo, the horde of robots within the *Scape Grace* had begun talking back and forth, sharing plans, thoughts, and other data.

So what, said the AI Devil's advocate? So, it took a big dose of micro-robots to reprogram a nervous system. Why was that a problem, other than the higher materials cost?

The problem, answered Katy Olu, was that you needed an even *bigger* mass than could fit into a biological body. The micro-robots alone weren't enough.

Emissary contained a multitude of other artificial cellular types beside the mobile invasive units that managed biological interactivity. Asking what part of the alien ship gave her her identity was like asking which lobe or ganglion or neuron gave a biological sentient its 'self'. Suffice it to say that all the scattered parts of Emissary showed allegiance toward one another. They were similar enough entities to recognize one another, even when divided across types, across hosts, or across space. Katy had taken enough literature courses to consider and then cringe at the metaphor: Emissary was her own Collective of artificial life.

And for all her admiration of Emissary's bio-technology and the singularity of her existence, Katy concluded that the foreign ship was an enemy. In interaction with intelligent, biological life, she became a parasite. They could not use or sell the cellular units that came directly from the ship, for fear that the technology might redevelop a mass intelligence no longer under its creators' control. Whether it recognized its origins from Emissary or became a new, separate composite being, it would still pose a danger.

Katy could not even be sure that a reverse engineered, separately synthesized version of the same micro-tech would not lead to the same outcome. She wondered if the distant sapients that created the First Traveler for the Mission of Meeting and Joining had lost control of their technology.

Under one scenario, those creators could have lost even their autonomous thought, as they were remolded into the servants of their promiscuous creation. Was the ship uncrewed because her crew was dead? Because she never had crew to begin with, having only inherited the form of a 'star ship' from her predecessor? Was that shape only a convenient disguise? Were all of her creators' species safely left behind at home, abandoned as their creation explored space in their name alone?

Katy and NuRikPo shared these thoughts back and forth and came to similar conclusions. They agreed to record the details of the alien technology, but not to attempt its sale, either as a finished product or as schematic data. They reported their joint compact to captain Lerner, expecting some resistance.

They met none. After reviewing their respective reports and collaborative conclusions, Evgeny agreed that they would be fools to risk allowing such technology to infest Collective systems further.

The Collective was not the pirates' friend, but it *was* their prey. Its star systems were their hunting grounds. Allowing a plague to spread within that territory was not in their interests. Aside from that dispassionate analysis, individual crew also had sympathies toward their respective species and cultures. The picture Katy painted, of entire cultures lulled into passivity by mental parasitism, would repulse any sapient that valued its native kind. Humans, Mauraug, Zig, or Vislin, turned into peaceful 'lovers' instead of explorers, conquerors, inventors, or hunters? Surely a horrible thought.

An assertion of normalcy was the final sort of cleanup required aboard the *Scape Grace*: a spiritual cleansing, an emotional sorting, a mental wiping-up. For some, their remedy was a return to routine.

Luuboh went back to the galley. The combat crew shared meals in mess, brawling and joking and gossiping among one another. Sometimes, they shared their revels with the occasional senior member who joined them. Katy Olu and NuRikPo went back to ignoring one another. The Georges disappeared back into engineering, emerging only to replace the missing walls and doors demolished by Jolly's exit from the ship. Gleamer returned to whatever his private projects were.

For Evgeny and Soloth, restoration required the forging of new understandings. Evgeny demonstrably moved Matilda to his personal compad, imposing the same isolation upon the Brin that she would have endured within Collective jurisdiction. Soloth declared itself satisfied that no trace of the AI remained within *Scape Grace's* computers.

Without Matilda's oversight, Evgeny saw no point in keeping his private escape pod a secret from his first mate… although the two of them did keep the bolt hole their mutual secret from the rest of the crew.

Evgeny did *not* share the secret of Bay 3e with Soloth. After all, deceptions of omission were apparently forgivable, and a leader had to keep *some* advantages in reserve.

In return, Soloth agreed to stay aboard *Scape Grace* and keep doing what it did best. It helped in its own way with the process of stabilizing the ship's society. No one was allowed to slacken in their duties; the bizarre intrusions they had suffered were not excuses.

Soloth did offer the uncharacteristically generous gift of a detailed briefing to the general crew. It explained the nature of their most recent venture, not glossing over the choices and mistakes made by the officers of *Scape Grace*. It *did* perhaps cast those choices in a more positive light than was supported by reality, but the point was to make sense of the matter, not to give the crew excuses to doubt their leaders. Thus, it gave the semblance of a cohesive story – one which fit the unavoidable evidence of events – while omitting the chaotic chance of the actual actions taken. In this light, Soloth's presentation was less for education and more for propaganda. Its tale was better than simply denying the crew any explanation at all, but not *quite* an honest retelling.

Within this narrative, Soloth spun events so that *Scape Grace* came out ahead. Simply surviving an insane encounter was not enough credit for captain Lerner or his crew. They could not directly benefit from anything learned aboard the alien ship. So, what profit had they reaped? Soloth gave several good answers.

First, they had collected two Ningyo environmental suits, one mostly intact. Second, there were the weapons: an electric baton, a projectile thrower, and two spatial fold generators.

Beyond the utility of these tools, their true value was in the technology they represented. The spatial fold tech was a serious coup. Given enough time and insight, NuRikPo could reverse-engineer the devices and produce his own. It might even be possible to refit *Scape Grace* with a spatial fold drive. It was un-likely that the captain would approve such a risky project or even its preliminary tests, but the potential was valuable enough. As always, the devices themselves or knowledge about their tech would fetch a decent payday on the black market.

The suits were also useful for investigation: Gleamer and NuRikPo would soon learn how to sabotage the Ningyo protective systems, both for outright offense and for more insidious control of suit functions. Some non-Ningyo within the Collective might already possess such knowledge, but it was officially unknown in public. Buyers might welcome intel that gave them an advantage against the robotic dolls. Gleamer was already discussing the possibility of re-pairing and animating one of the suits to create a Ningyo impersonator. It was too bad that Jolly was incinerated; they might have used it personally as a puppet if and when *Black Humor* tracked them down.

That was the real reason behind their interest in Ningyo countermeasures. If *Black Humor* followed up Jolly's last orders, the ship would not rest until it found and destroyed *Scape Grace*. Fighting the Ningyo command ship would be an insurmountable challenge without a few tricks prepared.

Soloth did not share this particular detail with the crew. No reason to create a panic that might send the vermin scurrying off ship at their next port of call.

Scape Grace traveled as it healed. After fourteen days' wandering, the pirate ship managed to locate an unguarded star system and latch onto the gravity well of a blue subdwarf. With a double dose of relief – both at returning from the deeps and at the continued functionality of *'Grace's* idled hyperdrive – Evgeny set a course for a reliable port.

They would visit the Great Family world of Spore, where Collective law was still heavily diluted. The captain and Katy Olu knew solid contacts there who could broker their new acquisitions and translate those funds into supplies for *Scape Grace's* restocking, refueling, and refitting.

Those solid contacts had apparently become a bit porous. Shortly after returning to normal space, Evgeny shot a message to his customs liason on Spore, a bureaucrat of negotiable flexibility. They arranged the arrival of *'Saving Grace'* to the Spore system and her docking space at Layafflr City. Their registry was entirely legitimate, using a borrowed name and codes.

The treacherous bastard must have turned around and sold them out to the Ningyo for a better price. That was the problem with having powerful enemies; they could pay higher bribes than you.

As the *Scape Grace* closed inward on her target system, a vast sphere of empty space ahead of her shimmered in a sickeningly familiar pattern. An oversized, bulbous, shining white vessel appeared moments later. Soloth was forced to maneuver sharply to avoid collision, while Gleamer's head snapped up in reaction to another stimulus.

"We have a hail… *Black Humor* asking for Jolly." Gleamer's speech slowed and fell in pitch as sickening realization hit the comms officer.

The confrontation had come far too soon. Not only was *'Grace* barely recovered from her last two fights, her technicians had just begun to devise their countermeasures. They were not ready for a battle, not with a foe this capable. If the crew was clever and fortunate, they might be able to run in an unexpected direction to escape *Black Humor*… but that meant another span of aimless travel until they could redirect to a new port. That strategy could only last so long, until their fuel ran low or the *Black Humor* intercepted their escape vector. The Ningyo ship only needed to catch them once.

"Put them on," Evgeny responded in equally fatalistic tones, "Might as well hear their threats while we work on our options." The thought sounded uncomfortably familiar. The last time he tried to negotiate with Ningyo, he ended up infested with miniature robots and nearly thrown into vacuum. Maybe this time, he would just die in a nice, neat explosion.

"*Black Humor*, this is *Saving Grace*." Evgeny decided to play the Ningyo game a bit. They seemed to like having their jokes thrown back at them. Using the ship's pseudonym might be read as a protestation of innocence.

"What up, *'Grace?'* the voice from *Black Humor* responded. It transmitted no video. It seemed the acting Ningyo captain was not suited up or else did not feel the need to be seen.

Evgeny continued, "Jolly is no longer aboard. Your commander violated our agreement. It led us into an unnecessary conflict with a Zig mining operation, then left the ship, along with its shuttle, when the battle went against us."

It was almost the truth. That the Ningyo commander and its shuttle departed separately was an unhelpful detail.

"That is some seriously harsh shade you're throwin', brah. Got any vids to back up your dis?" The voice seemed slurred and had a strange cadence, as if the speaker were impaired.

Evgeny looked at Gleamer for translation. The programmer provided one: "It said those are strong accusations. Do we have any proof?"

They did indeed. Unfortunately, the unadulterated proof cast both the Ningyo *and* the pirates in poor lighting. The other problem was: could they trust the Ningyo aboard *Black Humor* to objectively review whatever evidence was provided? If Jolly had been acting independently, due to Emissary's influence, then resisting the commander's orders and thwarting its purpose might not be viewed poorly.

There were two potential problems there. *Black Humor* might not care, because the entire ship might be compromised already. Admitting what they knew and what they had done might prompt the other ship to capture or destroy *Scape Grace*. Granted, reflexive violence was not Emissary's tendency, but she did seem willing to strike out at a threat in self-defense. Trying to hold and suborn the population of a hostile ship seemed more likely in this case.

Actually, if *Black Humor* was infested, that was the likely outcome whether or not Evgeny provided any evidence backing up his accusations against Jolly. The controlled Ningyo would not let them leave either way.

If, instead, Emissary's influence was limited to just Jolly and a few other Ningyo – including Comus and Punch – providing *Black Humor* with their information might save the other ship – and possibly the Collective – from a comparable fate. The problem was that the Ningyo might either not believe them, thinking the evidence an elaborate hoax, or else might believe them and destroy *Scape Grace* anyway. That reaction might come from fear and an urge to purge the infection. Alternately, the Ningyo might destroy them to hide the evidence of *Black Humor's* complicity with the alien ship.

Evgeny decided that since *Black Humor's* standing orders were to destroy them, anyway, he might as well attempt to give warning. It was a better chance than standing defiant and trying to outmaneuver the superior ship.

"Yes, we have 'vids'. We will transmit shortly," Evgeny responded, then slashed the air to signal Gleamer to cut the outgoing channel.

When Gleamer nodded acknowledgement and muted the line, Evgeny directed him: "Give them anything non-technical on the micro-robots and the alien ship: your notes, Luuboh's, Katy's, 'Po's. Video from public channels, anything except the part where we blasted their leader out of the airlock. External records of the attack on the Zig base."

"Even the part where Tklth and Havish popped their other two boarders?" Gleamer was already assembling and editing the relevant files as he asked.

"Yes, since the way they died tells part of the story. We can't produce them anyway. They might believe Jolly went out on the shuttle if it was alone, but not that all three fled together. We also don't have any footage of the other two fleeing in that direction."

"Pretty sneaky, Gene. Okay, I think I have a packet ready. Sending to their channel… receipt acknowledged."

After that transaction came a long, nervous wait. Evgeny called down to Tklth's quarters, requesting that she report to the bridge. Shooting back would probably be futile against the Ningyo command ship, but an extra set of claws and trained reflexes at the controls might be helpful if they had to bolt. *Black Humor* hung silent and still where it had appeared, a white circle on their viewers and a space-bending mass on gravitic sensors. Its verdict hung similarly large, suspended in time.

"This would be a good time to run," Soloth observed, broad hands hovering over the navigation controls for emphasis.

"I don't think there *is* any best time to run in this situation," Evgeny rebutted, scratching his scalp. "If we avoided them, we'd look guilty, and they'd come after us anyway. We're trying to cheat on the prisoner's dilemma by confessing *and* protesting innocence. At the least, if they only want to arrest us on Collective criminal charges, they might be less likely to invest time chasing us than for personal reasons."

They fell quiet again for another dozen anxious minutes. Finally, Gleamer perked up.

"Response coming in, putting on speakers," he announced, without asking permission.

"Duuuuuuuuuuuuuude," the voice projected from the Ningyo ship drawled, "That is some heinous hoodoo. Mad props for getting wise to those creepos. We had some similar spatially transmitted disease over herrr. Didn't notice the crabs until some of our away team started wiggin'... looks like about the time the mother ship got iced. Ha ha, iced. We passed out shots and got clean, too."

Evgeny stared a hole in the back of Gleamer's head until his Ningyo-to-Standard translator noticed the silence. "Oh, yeah. Um, they agree that the micro-tech was very bad and congratulate us on recognizing the threat. They suffered from the same problem. It wasn't noticeable until the alien ship was hurt, at which time their affected crew... the ones that visited Emissary, I assume... reacted badly. They investigated and effected a similar cure to ours."

"Oh." Getting the news at a time delay robbed some of the relief Evgeny might have felt. "So... you understand? Why we had to fight back and leave the *Harauch* behind?"

"Oh, yeah, dude. Totally *kapeesh*. You're gangsta and all, but that's a bad scene for even a capital G. If you hadn't monkey wrenched that queen bee's takeover, we might all be goose-stepfording across the Universe in a few years. Speaking of, we'd better bounce back that way and nuke the site from orbit. It's the only way to be sure."

Gleamer rephrased without prompting this time, "They understand. We might be violent criminals but we escaped a situation that would be dangerous even for professionals. If we hadn't interfered with the alien ship's plans, its influence might have spread throughout the region quickly. They will be returning to the Zig base to finish destroying any traces of Emissary."

Evgeny tried to respond casually: "Well, don't let us keep you. Thank you for understanding our position. I'm glad to see that we can appreciate one another even without the encouragement of outside influences."

"Don't hear me wrong, brah. We wrap up there, we're totally reporting your ass. See ya again, we'll cap ya without blinkin'. This is your only *grassy ass* and *low see in tow* combo. Plus, we can't waste the time to tangle right now. We just had to make sure you were clean before rollin' on. Peace out, E. L. Capitán."

Gleamer started his translation: "Don't mistake its meaning. Once they're done at the mining base, they will report on our activities. If they see us again…"

He was interrupted by a final transmission from the *Black Humor*, "Oh, there's just one more thing… sir… if you would be so kind… load up a tube with our two dead homies and their gats? We'll make sure they get a proper send-off. Wouldn't want to trouble ya with the arrangements."

Evgeny groaned. It had been too much to ask that they would escape *and* profit. Of course, the Ningyo would want their tech returned. Hopefully, NuRikPo had gathered enough data on the equipment to reconstruct their functions, but the Zig engineer was busy with other projects as well. It would have been helpful to keep the originals to check his work against. It *also* would have been nice to sell those items when the engineer was done. Those profits were apparently the price of their reprieve.

"Understood, *Black Humor*. We'll have your people launched momentarily. Stand by."

Gleamer again broke external communications. Evgeny toggled engineering from his own console and signaled NuRikPo.

"Po, bad news. The Ningyo caught up to us. They're going to let us go in order to clean up their captain's mess in person, but they want their tech back. Get whatever you can now, put back any pieces they might miss, and package their suits and the space fold generators into a cylinder for transfer."

"Too good to last," NuRikPo mourned, "I have scans, but they're of limited utility. We couldn't disassemble those generators safely without a high-energy containment facility… which would cover a volume half the size of this ship. Honestly, how the Collective tolerates such repressive policies on research and development, I'll never understand…"

The feed faded out as NuRikPo hurried away to prepare for the loss of his samples.

Evgeny turned to Soloth for an executive conference. "I don't trust the Ningyo to let us dock safely. If they knew we were coming, Spore is likely a trap. We'll come back later to kill whoever sold us out. Find us another port within range, ideally somewhere with even weaker Collective allegiances."

"Agreed," Soloth confirmed. "Anchor seems most ideal in terms of distance and the resources we need."

"Ugh, I'm tired of that place… but you're probably right. It's getting to be the popular stop for unpopular people lately. Set the course and get ready."

The last order was not simple preparedness; Evgeny had something specific in mind. His familiar senior crew caught his meaning. Soloth tightened its lips and breathed deep in its throat, the Mauraug equivalent of an evil grin and laugh. Even Gleamer nodded and grinned in appreciation of the nastiness their captain had in mind.

A ringing step and signal at the bridge hatch indicated Tklth's arrival. Its delay indicated both difficulty adapting to the prosthetic leg and, very likely, arousal from sleep by Evgeny's call. Her arrival to the bridge made Evgeny's plans even better. She would enjoy a bit of cruel humor at the Ningyo's expense.

Finally, NuRikPo called in and confirmed the package ready and loaded. Evgeny gave the order to launch.

"Advise the *Black Humor* that their property is on its way," he directed Gleamer.

Then Evgeny counted down sixty seconds, gauging the time between the transmission of that notice and the engagement of the other ship's maneuvering drives. As soon as he saw the pale orb start to grow in their view, he gave his second order.

"Target the star and engage hyperdrive."

Their visual display blanked out as the churning, dissociative feeling of hyperspace entry washed over the crew of *Scape Grace*. Normally, the captain would give his crew fair warning in order to avoid the ill effects of unprepared jumping. Normally, they would also move further away from other nearby masses, in order to avoid navigational errors. In the case of a nearby ship, one should also be further away than they were from *Black Humor*, in order to avoid rudely striking the other ship with the backwash of abused reality.

For most sapients caught in such backwash, the result would be an instant of nausea and vertigo. For the Ningyo, with their inherent sensitivity to spatial alignment and consequent intolerance of hyperspace travel, the effect would be like being momentarily turned inside out. Evgeny could only hope the experience was terribly painful and traumatic.

Not *too* painful, though, or long-lasting. They still needed the Ningyo to deal with the aftermath of their captain's blunder. His slap was just a sucker punch in passing, a reminder that *Scape Grace* might be small but she was still dangerous. Her crew was a capable, durable, unpredictable, and unethical lot… and they were *specifically* forearmed against Ningyo opponents.

These thoughts comforted captain Evgeny Lerner as he suffered through the throes of hyperspace transit. Maybe the *Black Humor* would come back for him in revenge. Maybe it wouldn't. If it did, he had time to get ready.

Hell, maybe he'd claim a shiny white capitol ship as a prize before he retired.

www.ingramcontent.com/pod-product-compliance
Lightning Source LLC
Chambersburg PA
CBHW070439120726
47910CB00003B/852